the hollow
chocolate bunnies
of the apocalypse

the hollow chocolate bunnies of the apocalypse

Robert Rankin

GOLLANCZ
London

The right of Robert Rankin to be identified as the author of this work
has been asserted by him in accordance with the
Copyright, Designs and Patents Act 1988.

First published in Great Britain in 2002 by

Gollancz
An imprint of the Orion Publishing Group
Orion House, 5 Upper St Martin's Lane, London WC2H 9EA

A CIP catalogue record for this book is available
from the British Library

ISBN 0 575 07313 6 (cased)
ISBN 0 575 07515 5 (trade paperback)

Typeset at The Spartan Press, Lymington, Hants
Printed in Great Britain by Clays Ltd, St Ives plc

This book is dedicated
to the memory
of Jon Jo

1

'Once upon a time,' said the big fat farmer, 'it was all fields around here.'

The traveller glanced all around and about. 'It's still all fields,' said he.

'And there you have it.' The farmer grinned, exposing golden teeth. 'Nothing ever changes in these parts. Nothing. Nor will it ever. And so much the better for that, says I. Though so much the worse, say others. It all depends on your point of view. But isn't this ever the way?'

'I suppose that it is.' The traveller nodded politely. He was hot and he was weary. He had wandered many miles this day. His feet were sore and he was hungry. He took off his blue felt cap and mopped it over his brow.

'The colour's coming out of your cap,' the farmer chuckled. 'Your forehead's gone all blue.'

'Which, you must agree, is different,' said the traveller. 'And admits, at the very least, to the possibility of change in these parts.'

'On the contrary.' The farmer dug about in his voluminous patchworked smock, brought forth something chewable and thrust it into his mouth for a chew. 'To me it admits something else entirely. To me, it admits that you, a ruddy-faced lad—'

'Tanned,' said the lad. 'Tanned from travel.'

'All right, tanned, then. That you, a tanned lad, of, what would it be, some sixteen summers?'

'Thirteen,' said the travelling lad. 'I'm tall for my age. Thirteen I am, which is lucky for some.'

'All right then yet again. That you, a tanned lad, thirteen years and lucky for some, scrawny-limbed and—'

'Spare,' said the tall, tanned lad. 'Spare of frame and wiry of limb and—'

'Dafter than a box of hair,' said the farmer. 'That you are a gormster and a dullard, with a most inferior cap, who understands little of the world and will surely come to grief in a time not too far distant.'

'Oh,' said the lad. 'Indeed?'

'Indeed.' The farmer spat with practised ease across the field of flowering crad. 'Nothing ever changes in these parts and there's a truth for you to be going along with.'

'And going along I mean to be.' The lad wrung sweat from his most inferior cap and replaced it upon his tanned and heated head. 'Just as soon as you have furnished me with answers to questions I must ask. You see, I have wandered from the road. I followed a sign that said shortcut, and now I find myself here.'

'It happens,' said the farmer. 'More often than you might suppose.'

'As *rarely* as that?' said the lad, who was never one prone to extravagant speculation.

'At the very least, but mostly a whole lot more.'

The travelling lad whistled.

'Please don't whistle,' said the farmer. 'It aggravates my Gout.'

'I am perplexed,' said the whistler. 'How can whistling aggravate Gout?'

'Gout is the name of my goat,' the farmer explained. 'I have a pig called Palsy and a cat called Canker. Once I owned a dog by the name of Novinger's syndrome, but his howling upset my wife, so I sold him to a tinker.'

'Oh,' said the lad once more.

'Yes, oh. And whistling aggravates my goat. As does poking him in the ear with a pointy stick. Which, in all truth, would aggravate me. And I'm not easily upset.'

'Righty oh.' The lad shifted from one weary foot to the

other, and his stomach growled hungrily. 'But regarding these questions that I must ask.'

'Are they questions of an agricultural nature?' the farmer enquired.

'Not specifically.' The lad shook his heated head.

'That's a pity,' said the farmer. 'Because my knowledge on the subject is profound. I trust it's not a question regarding clockwork motors. Because, for all the life that's in me, I cannot make head nor toe of those infernal machines.' The farmer made a sacred sign above his treble chin.

'It's not clockwork motors.' The lad made exasperated sighing sounds. 'I was lately apprenticed in that trade and I know everything I need to know regarding them.'

'Cheese, then?' said the farmer. 'I know much about cheese.'

'Directions only.' The lad blew droplets of bluely-tinted sweat from the tip of his upturned nose. 'All I wish for are directions. How do I get to the city from here?'

'*The city?*' The farmer almost choked upon his chewable. 'Why would a lad such as yourself be wanting to be going to the city?'

'I mean to seek my fortune there,' the lad replied, with candour. 'I am done with toiling in a factory. I will seek my fortune in the city.'

'Fortune?' coughed the farmer. 'In the city? Hah and hah again.'

'And why "hah", you farmer?' asked the lad.

'Because, my tanned and wiry boy, you'll find no fortune there. Only doom awaits you in that direction. Turn back now, say I. Return to the mother who weeps for you.'

'I have no mother,' said the lad. 'I am an orphan boy.'

'A little lost waif; my heart cries bloody tears.' The farmer mimed the wiping of such tears from the region of his heart.

'Let not your heart weep for me.' The lad straightened his narrow shoulders and thrust out his chest – what little he had of a chest. 'I know how to handle myself.'

'Turn back,' advised the farmer. 'Return the way you came.'

The lad sighed deeply. 'And what is so bad about the city, then?' he asked.

'Where to start?' The farmer puffed out his cheeks. 'And where to end? So many evil things I've heard.'

'And have you ever been to the city yourself?'

'*Me?*' The farmer placed his hands upon his over-ample belly and gave vent to raucous sounds of mirth.

'And why now the raucous sounds of mirth?'

'Because what do I look like to you, my poor lost laddo?'

'You look like a big fat farmer, as it happens.'

'And what would a big fat farmer be doing in the city?'

'Trading produce, perhaps? This crad that flowers all around and about us in these fields that never change.'

The farmer scratched his big fat head. 'And why would I want to trade my crad?'

'For money. To buy things.'

'What sort of things?'

'Food, perhaps?'

The farmer gave his big fat head a slow and definite shaking. 'You are indeed a mooncalf,' said he. 'I am provided here with all the food that I need.'

'Other things then. Consumer durables, perhaps.'

'What?'

'Consumer durables. I am not entirely sure what they are. But I am informed that the city holds them in abundance. And I mean to acquire as many as I possibly can.'

The farmer shook his head once more, and there was a certain sadness in the shaking.

'Clothes then,' said the lad. 'Everyone needs new clothes at one time or another.'

'And do I look naked to you?'

The lad now shook *his* head, spraying the fully clothed farmer with sweat. The farmer was certainly clothed – although his clothing was strange. His ample smock was a patchwork, as if of a multitude of smaller clothes all stitched together.

'My wife and I have all we need, my sorry orphan boy,' said the farmer. 'Only disappointment and despair come from wanting more than you need.'

'I've no doubt that there's wisdom in your words,' said the lad. 'But as I have nothing at all, anything more will represent an improvement.'

'Then return the way you came. Weave clockwork motors if you must. Hard work, well achieved, is sometimes rewarded.'

'No,' said the lad. 'It's the city for me. My mind is set on this. But listen, if you have never visited the city, why not accompany me? Your gloomy opinion of it might be modified by experience.'

'I think not. The city is for city folk. There are those who toil there and are miserable and those who prosper and are happy. The toilers exceed the prosperers by many thousands to one. So much I have been told, and what I've been told is sufficient to inform my opinion.'

'Perhaps I will return one day and alter this opinion.'

'Be assured by me that you will do no such thing. Many have travelled this way before you, seeking wealth in the city. None have ever returned wealthy. In fact, none have ever returned at all.'

'Perhaps they became wealthy and so felt no need to return.'

'Your conversation tires me,' said the farmer. 'And as I can see that you are adamant in your convictions and eager to be on your way, I suggest that we speak no more. I have discharged my responsibilities. My job is done.'

'Responsibilities?' asked the lad. 'Job?'

'My responsibility and my job is to stand in this field of flowering crad and discourage young lads such as you from travelling towards the city. Such was my father's job, and his father's before him.'

'Why?' asked the lad.

'Because that's the way we do business in these parts. Nothing ever changes around here. If you travel on towards the city, you will surely meet your doom. And when you do, you will blame me for it.'

'Why should I?' asked the lad.

'Because I know that you will come to grief. I know it. And if you were in my position and knew that travellers, should they travel in a certain direction, would come to grief, would you not advise them against it?'

'Of course I would,' said the lad. 'But—'

'But me no buts. I have advised you. I have warned you of an inevitable consequence. What more can I do?'

'You could be a little more specific,' said the lad, 'regarding the manner of this imminent and inevitable doom that lies ahead for me.'

'That I cannot do.'

The traveller shrugged. 'So which way *is it* to the city?' he asked.

'The city lies five miles to the south.' The farmer pointed. 'Cross yonder stile and follow the path. The path leads eventually to the outskirts of the city, but—'

'But *me* no buts,' said the lad. 'Thank you and farewell.'

The lad stepped carefully across the field of flowering crad, swung his long and agile legs over the stile and proceeded southwards down the path. Sparrows sang in the hedgerows, trees raised their leafy arms towards the sky of blue and the sun continued its shining down.

'A strange old breed are farmers,' said the lad to no one other than himself. 'And many folk hold to the conviction that the rustic mind, attuned as it is to natural lore, possesses a raw wisdom which is denied to the over-civilised city dweller, whose sophisticated intellect is—'

But he said no more as he tripped upon something and then plunged forward and down.

And then down some more.

★

Presently he awoke from unconsciousness to find that he was lying at the bottom of a pit. Rubbing at his head and peering blearily about, he became aware of a movement someways above. Looking up, he espied the face of the farmer.

'Thank goodness,' said the lad. 'Please help me. I appear to have fallen into a hole.'

'You have fallen into *my* hole,' said the farmer, 'the hole that a distant ancestor of mine dug to receive the bodies of the foolhardy boys who failed to heed his advice.'

'Oh,' said the lad, rubbing some more at his head and blinking his bleary eyes.

'A hole maintained by and through generations, and now by myself. Although it would appear that I must furnish its bottom with a few more sharpened spikes; you have missed those that there are, by the looks of you.'

'Oh,' said the lad once more.

'Nothing ever changes around here,' said the farmer. 'My forebears feasted upon the flesh of foolish boys, and so do I. It's a family tradition. Their meat fills my belly and their clothing covers my person. I would hardly be so big and fat and well-dressed if I subsisted upon crad alone, now, would I?'

'I suppose not,' said the lad, dismally.

'I gave you warnings,' said the farmer. 'I gave you opportunity to avoid travelling to your inevitable doom. But did you listen?'

'Perhaps if you *had* been more specific,' the lad suggested. 'I took your warnings to mean that the city spelled my doom.'

'You didn't listen carefully enough,' said the farmer. 'But doom is doom, no matter how you spell it. Unless, of course, you spell it differently from doom. But then it would be another word entirely, I suppose.'

'I suppose it would,' the lad agreed, in the tone of one who now knew exactly how doom was spelled. 'But I have no one to blame but myself.'

'Well said.' The farmer grinned. 'And so, as the spikes have failed to do their job, I must do it with this rock.' The farmer displayed the rock in question. It was round and of a goodly size. 'Perhaps you'd care to close your eyes whilst I drop it onto your head?'

'Not so fast, please.' The lad tested his limbs for broken bones, but found himself intact, if all-over bruised. 'How do you mean to haul my body from this pit?'

'I have grappling hooks,' said the farmer, 'fashioned for the purpose.'

'Hot work on such a day,' said the lad. 'Hard work, but honest toil justly rewarded, I suppose.'

'In that you are correct.'

'But *very* hard work, nonetheless.'

'And me with a bad back,' said the farmer. 'But what must be done, must be done.'

'Would it not make your job easier if you were to help me from the hole? Then I might walk with you to your farmhouse, where you could brain me at your leisure?'

'Well, certainly it would,' said the farmer.

'Thus also sparing you all the effort of dragging my body.'

'You are most cooperative,' said the farmer. 'But there's no dragging involved. I have my horse and cart with me.'

'Then let me climb aboard the cart. It's the least I can do.'

'I appreciate that,' said the farmer.

'It's only fair,' said the lad. 'You *did* warn me, and I failed to heed your warning.'

The farmer leaned over and extended his hand. 'Up you come, then,' said he.

The lad took the farmer's hand and scrambled from the hole.

'There now,' said the farmer. 'Onto the cart if you please, and let's get this braining business out of the way.'

The lad glanced over at the farmer's cart. And then he smiled back towards the farmer. 'I think not,' he said. 'Your purse, if you will.'

'Excuse me?' said the farmer. 'My purse?'

'I will have your purse. Kindly hand it over.'

'I fail to understand you,' said the farmer.

'I demand compensation,' said the lad, dusting himself down. 'For injuries incurred through falling into your hole. I am severely bruised and more than a little shaken. I'll take whatever money you have upon your person and we'll speak no more of this regrettable incident.'

'Climb onto the cart,' said the farmer. 'I will brain you immediately. Think not of fleeing; I am an accurate hurler of rocks.'

'Be that as it may,' said the lad, 'I will have your purse and then be off to the city.'

'This is ludicrous. Idiot boy.' The farmer raised his rock.

The lad produced a pistol from his sleeve.

'What is this?' the farmer asked.

'A weapon,' said the lad. 'A clockwork weapon. I built it myself for use in such eventualities as this. Its spring projects a sharpened metal missile at an alarming speed. Far faster than one might hurl a rock.'

'Bluff and bluster,' growled the farmer, swinging back his rockholding hand, preparatory to a hurl.

The lad raised his clockwork pistol and shot off the farmer's left ear. Which came as a shock to them both, though possibly more to the farmer.

'Waaaaaaaaah!' shrieked the man, dropping his unhurled rock onto his foot, which added broken toes to his woeful account.

'Your purse,' said the lad, waving his gun in a now most shaky hand.

'Waaaaaaaah! I am wounded!' The farmer took to hopping and clutching at his maimed head.

'The next shot will pass directly through your heart.'

'No,' croaked the farmer, 'no no no.'

'The world will be a better place without you in it.' The lad steadied his pistol with both hands. 'You are a monster.'

'And you are an iconoclast,' moaned the farmer, still hopping. 'With no respect for tradition.'

'Such is indeed the truth. Now hand me your purse. You are losing a great deal of blood. It would be well for you to return to your farmhouse and have your wife dress your wounds.'

'Damn you,' said the farmer, adding profanities to these words.

'Your purse, *now*!'

The farmer grudgingly produced his purse. It was a weighty purse, full as it was with the gold of a foolish boy who had passed that way earlier in the day and failed to heed the farmer's advice. This foolish boy presently hung in joints in the farmer's smoking house.

'On second thoughts,' said the lad, 'I think it would be for the best if you went down into the hole.'

'What?' cried the farmer. '*What?*'

'The path is narrow,' said the lad. 'Your horse might stumble into that hole, if it doesn't have something to place its hoof upon.'

'What?' the farmer cried again.

'I mean to borrow your horse; I have walked enough for one day.'

'This is outrageous. Preposterous.'

'Best to get it over with as quickly as possible. Before you bleed to death.'

'But the hole.' The farmer ceased his hopping and stared down into the hole. 'The spikes. I am not so scrawny as you.'

'Spare,' said the lad. 'Wiry.'

'I will puncture myself.'

'That's a chance we'll have to take. The hole, or die where you stand.'

'But the spikes . . .'

'Perhaps fate will smile upon you.'

'Fate wears a somewhat glum face at present.'

'Really? Yet I would swear that it grins in my direction.'

'You . . .' The farmer spoke further profanity.

'The hole, and now.' The lad cocked his clockwork pistol.

The farmer, groaning and moaning, lowered himself into the hole.

The lad tucked his weapon back into his sleeve, stepped over to the farmer's horse and detached it from the cart. Then he leapt onto the horse's back and prepared to gallop away. 'I've never ridden a horse before,' he called down to the farmer, 'so this should be something of an adventure.'

'I hope you are thrown and break your neck,' called the farmer.

'What was that?'

'Nothing. May good luck attend you.'

'Thank you very much. And what is the name of this mount, farmer?'

'Anthrax,' called the farmer. 'But he'll not answer to your commands. Quite the reverse, in fact.'

'I'm sure Anthrax and I will get along fine.' The lad held Anthrax by his reins. 'And so we say farewell, master farmer. Our acquaintance has been brief, but it has been instructive. We have both learned something, so let us not part upon bad terms.'

'I am stuck fast.' The farmer huffed and puffed and moaned and groaned. 'I might well die in this hole.'

'If no one comes looking for you, then in a day or two you'll be slim enough to climb out. Or perhaps loss of blood will facilitate a more immediate shrinkage and you'll be home in time for tea.'

'You filthy . . .'

'Quite enough,' called the lad. 'Your conversation tires me. I will now take my leave for the city. One day I will return this way with great wealth. Though not along this particular path.'

'One thing before you go.' The farmer raised his voice.

'And what thing is this?'

'Tell me only your name.'

'My name?' said the lad. 'My name is Jack.'

'That is good,' called the farmer. 'A man may not truly lay a curse upon another man without first knowing his name. I curse you, Jack. May you never know wealth. May all that you wish for be denied you.'

'A spiteful sentiment,' said Jack. 'And so farewell.' Jack dug his heels into Anthrax and Anthrax sprang forward.

The farmer, unable to duck his head, was heavily hooved upon.

2

Anthrax the horse jogged merrily along. There was a definite spring in his four-legged step. Freed from his death-cart constraints, he appeared a very happy horse indeed.

Jack, although pleased to be no longer walking, did not altogether share the horse's joy. Precariously perched, and lacking for equestrian skills, he clung to the horse's reins and counselled the beast to slow down a bit.

Which it didn't.

The path meandered, as paths often do, around grassy knolls and down through dingly dells. All was rural charm and niceness, all of which was lost upon Jack. He was rather peeved, was Jack. Peeved and altogether unsettled. He was peeved about falling into the farmer's hole. That had been a foolish thing to do. He should have listened more carefully to the farmer's warnings. To the phrasing of them. Jack's failure to interpret the farmer's words correctly had come close to costing him his life. That was very peeving indeed.

Regarding the altogether unsettledness, this was a twofold business. All that blood which had flowed from the farmer's maimed head: that was unsettling enough, but the fact that Jack had not actually meant to shoot the farmer's ear off in the first place was doubly unsettling. This had called into question the accuracy of Jack's clockwork pistol. He had meant to shoot the farmer in the knee. There would have to be a lot of work done upon that pistol if it was to prove any use at all as an accurate means of defence.

Anthrax kicked his back legs in the air, all but unseating Jack.

'Calm yourself,' cried the lad. 'No need to go mad, take it easy, please.'

The horse did a skip or two and settled into a trot.

'Slow down, please.'

The horse did not slow down.

The meandering path met up with a rugged track and Jack caught a glimpse of a signpost. It read TO THE CITY in fine big capitals.

'Jolly good show,' said Jack. 'Please slow down a bit, *please.*'

The horse began to canter.

'No!' Jack flung himself forward and clasped his arms about Anthrax's neck.

'Slow down!' he shouted into the horse's left ear. 'Slow down or I'll sell you for cat meat when we reach the city.'

The horse began to gallop.

'No!' shouted Jack, now altogether ruffled. 'Slow down! Slow down! No!'

If there is a faster thing than galloping that horses can do, this horse began to do it now.

Jack closed his eyes tightly and steeled himself for the inevitable concussion and imminent doom that awaited him.

Anthrax thundered forward, his hooves raising sparks on the rugged track, his ears laid back and a fair old froth a-forming round his mouth. The horse appeared possessed.

Eyes tight shut and mouth shouting, 'Slow down please,' Jack was borne along at the speed which is commonly known as breakneck.

The horse would not obey his commands. Quite the reverse, in fact.

And then Jack opened his eyes and a very broad smile appeared on his face. 'Faster!' he shouted. 'Yes boy, yes, faster! Faster! Faster!'

The horse slowed down to a gallop.

'Faster!' shouted Jack. 'Come on!'

The horse slowed down to a canter.

'Faster!'

A trot.

'Faster!'

A jog.

'Faster!'

The horse, all sweaty and breathless, slowed down to a gentle stroll.

'And faster.'

Anthrax came to a halt.

Jack released his grip from the horse's streaming neck and slid himself down onto the ground. He patted the horse on an area known as a flank, then stroked its foaming muzzle parts.

'I should have known,' said Jack, taking deep breaths to steady himself. 'I'm sorry, boy. It was all my fault, wasn't it?'

The horse made a kind of grumbling sound, as if it understood.

'The damnable farmer trained you, didn't he, boy? He trained you to go faster if you were told to go slower and likeways round. In case anyone stole you. I remembered what he said: "He'll not answer to your commands. Quite the reverse in fact." And I'm sure that when you had eventually unseated your rider and tired yourself out, you'd have wandered home of your own accord. It seems that I have much to learn of the ways of the world. I will be very much on my guard from now on.'

Jack led Anthrax on along the rugged track. Presently they came upon a horse trough and both drank from it. Suitably refreshed, Jack climbed back onto the horse.

'Stop,' said he, and the horse set off at a gentle pace.

The rugged track led now up a sizeable hill and Anthrax took to plodding. Jack sighed deeply, but, feeling for the animal which, he surmised, hadn't exactly lived a life of bliss so far, climbed down once more and plodded beside it.

The track led up and up. The sizeable hill seemed little less big than a small mountain. Jack huffed and puffed, and Anthrax did likewise.

'Good lad,' said Jack. 'We're almost there, I think.'

And almost there they were.

And then they were altogether there.

And Jack, still huffing and puffing, with blue sweat striping his face, hands upon knees and heart going bumpty-bumpty-bump, raised his squinting eyes to view what vista lay beyond.

And then he opened both his eyes and his mouth, very wide indeed.

For beyond, across a plain of grey and stunted furze, lay THE CITY.

Writ big in letters. Large and capital.

'Whoa,' went Jack, taking stock of whatever he could. 'Now that is a very BIG CITY.'

And as cities go, and in these parts, but for this one, they didn't, it was indeed a *very* BIG CITY.

And a very dirty city too, from what Jack could see of it. A great dark sooty blot upon the landscape was this city. A monstrous smut-coloured carbuncle.

Anthrax the horse made a very doubtful face. Which is quite a feat for an equine. Jack cast a glance at this very doubtful face. 'I know what you mean,' he said. 'It doesn't look too welcoming, does it?'

The horse shook its head.

'You're a very wise horse,' said Jack. 'And I apologise for that earlier remark of mine about having you converted into cat meat. If you get me in one piece to the city, I'll see that you're well cared for. But,' and he stared once more towards the distant conurbation, 'that is one ugly-looking eyesore of a city. Perhaps your previous owner was right in all he said. But we must remain optimistic. Shall we proceed?'

The horse shook its head.

'You would rather return to haul corpses?'

The horse shook its head once more.

Jack now shook his own. 'I'm talking to a horse,' he said to himself. 'The events of today have unhinged my mind.'

The sun, Jack noticed, was now very low in the heavens.

The blue of the sky had deepened and the day was drawing towards night.

'We'd best get a move on,' Jack told Anthrax. 'I need to fill my belly and find myself lodgings for the night.' He shinned once more onto the horse's back, told it to stop, and set off.

The rugged track wound down the biggish hill/smallish mountain and presently joined a paved and city-bound road. This pushed onwards through the grey and stunted furze. Onwards and onwards and onwards. Ahead, the city loomed, its outlying districts becoming more clearly defined. Jack was not impressed by what he saw. The road reached peasant huts, crude and weathered. Strange and pale little faces peeped out at him through glassless windows. Jack dug in his heels. 'Slower,' he told Anthrax, 'slower, boy.'

Anthrax got a trot on.

Beyond the peasant huts lay what Jack correctly assumed to be the industrial district: grim, grey factories with chimneys coughing smoke. The air was rank, and Jack took to covering his nose.

'Not very nice around here.' Jack patted Anthrax's neck. 'This is the kind of place I left behind, factories like this. But let us not be downhearted. I'm sure we can find a pleasant hostelry in a nicer part of the city.'

The sun was beginning to set.

At length, but a length too long for Jack's liking, the industrial district lay astern, or the equine equivalent thereof. Now the buildings showed traces of colour: a hint of yellow here and a dash of orange there. A trifle dusted over, but a definite improvement.

The style of architecture was new to Jack, and therefore looked exotic. The buildings were constructed from huge square bricks, each embossed with a letter of the alphabet. But these had not been laid in order to spell out words, but apparently at random.

Suddenly something rushed past Jack and his mount, causing Anthrax to panic. Jack shouted 'Faster!' very loudly indeed and Anthrax jerked to a halt. Jack viewed the rapidly diminishing rusher: some kind of mechanical vehicle.

'Car,' said Jack. 'Nothing to be afraid of. I worked upon cars at the factory. Went like the wind, though, didn't it, boy? I'll be having one of those myself some day soon.'

Anthrax shook his head about.

'Oh yes I will,' said Jack. 'Stop then, boy. We have to find a hostelry soon or I'll fall off your back from hunger.'

The sun was all but gone now, but light shone all around, from bright lanterns held aloft by iron columns that rose at either side of the road at intervals of fifty paces. These lit buildings that showed brighter colours now, reds and greens and blues, all in alphabet brick.

The colours raised Jack's spirits. 'Almost there,' he told Anthrax. 'A warm stable and a manger of hay will shortly be yours.'

Anthrax, all but exhausted, plodded onward.

'Listen,' said Jack. 'It's been a difficult day for the both of us. But you've got me here. I'll see you all right. You're a good horse. Hey, hey, what's that I see ahead?'

What Jack saw ahead was this: a long, low building painted all in a hectic yellow. A sign, wrought from neon, flashed on and off, as such signs are wont to do. Words were spelled out by this sign. The words were *Nadine's Diner*.

'There,' cried Jack. 'An eatery.'

If horses can sigh, then Anthrax did. And as they reached Nadine's Diner, Jack clambered down, secured Anthrax's reins to a post which may or may not have been there for the purpose, promised the horse food and drink, as soon as he had taken some for himself, squared up his narrow, sagging shoulders and put his hand to the restaurant door.

The door was an all-glass affair, somewhat cracked and patched, but none the less serviceable. Jack pushed upon it and entered the establishment.

It wasn't exactly a home from home.

Unoccupied tables and chairs were arranged to no particular pattern. Music of an indeterminate nature drifted from somewhere or other. A bar counter, running the length of the long, low room, was attended by a single fellow, dressed in the manner of a chef. He viewed Jack's arrival with a blank expression – but a blank expression mostly shadowed, for several bulbs had gone above the bar and he obviously hadn't got around to replacing them.

Jack steered his weary feet across a carpet that was much of a muchness as carpets went, but hardly much of anything as they might go. He squared up his shoulders somewhat more, squinted towards the dimly lit chef and hailed this fellow thusly:

'Good evening to you, chef,' hailed Jack.

'Eh?' replied the other in ready response.

'A good evening,' said Jack. And, glancing around the deserted restaurant, 'Business is quiet this evening.'

'Is it?' The chef cast his shadowed gaze over Jack. 'You're blue,' he observed. 'Why so this facial blueness? Is it some new whim of fashion from the House of *Oh Boy!* that I am hitherto unacquainted with? Should I be ordering myself a pot of paint?'

'Inferior cap,' said Jack, taking off his inferior cap and wiping his face with it.

'That's made matters worse,' said the chef.

'Might I see a menu?' Jack asked.

The barlord scratched his forehead, then wiped his scratching hand upon his apron. 'Is that a trick question?' he asked. 'Because I can't be having with trick questions. Chap came in here a couple of weeks ago and said to me, "Do you know that your outhouse is on fire?" and I said to him, "Is that a trick question?" and he said to me, "No it isn't." And I was pleased about that, see, because I can't be having with trick questions. But damn me, if I didn't take a crate of empties outside about an hour later to find that my outhouse had been burned to the ground. What do you make of a thing like that, eh?'

Jack shrugged.

'And well may you shrug,' said the chef. 'So your question is not a trick question?'

'No,' said Jack, 'it's not.'

'That's fine then,' said the chef. 'How may I help you, sir?'

'I'd like something to eat, if I may,' said Jack. 'And a stable for my horse and directions to where I might find a room for the night.'

'God's Big Box,' said the barlord. 'It's want want want with you, isn't it? Were you breast-fed as a baby?'

'I really can't remember,' said Jack.

'Nor me.' The chef shook his head, which appeared to creak as he shook it. 'But then, I never was a baby. It's funny the things that slip your mind, though, isn't it?'

Jack nodded politely. 'I'm dying from hunger,' he said. 'Please feed me.'

'About half past seven,' said the chef.

'Excuse me?' said Jack.

'Oh, sorry,' said the chef. 'I've got a woodworm in my ear. It crawled in there last Tuesday. I've tried to entice it out with cheese, but it seems to be happy where it is.'

'Food,' said Jack, pointing to his mouth. 'I've gold, I can pay well.'

'Boody fries, you need.' The barlord smacked his lips noisily together. 'Mambo-munchies, over-and-unders, a big pot of jumbly and an aftersnack of smudge cake. And if you'll take the advice of a professional who knows these things, add a pint of Keener's grog to wash the whole lot down with.'

'All this fare is new to me,' said Jack. 'But a double helping of each, if you please.'

'I *do* please,' said the chef. 'But the oven's broken down again, so you can't have any of those. Not even the grog. If I had my time over again, I would never have bought this crummy concession. I'd have trained to become a gourmet chef for some big swell on Knob Hill. Or I could have gone in with my brother; he has a specialist restaurant over on the East Side. Serves up smoked haunch of foolish boy, supplied by some local farmer who breeds them, I suppose.'

Jack took a very deep breath which, when exhaled, became a very deep and heartfelt sigh. He brought forth his pistol and levelled it at the chef. 'If you do not feed me at once,' he said, 'I will be forced to shoot you dead and feast upon *your* carcass.'

'That's something I'd like to see.' The chef gave his nose a significant tap, the significance of which was lost upon Jack. But the sound of this tap drew Jack's attention. It was not the sound of flesh being tapped upon flesh. Jack stared hard at the shadowy chef and, for the first time, truly took in what there was of him to be seen. There was something altogether strange about this fellow. Something unworldly. Jack looked at the chef's hand. It was a false hand. A hand carved from wood. Jack looked now, but furtively, towards the face of the chef. That nose was also of wood. A wooden nose. Upon . . . Jack's furtive glance became a lingering, fearful stare . . .

. . . upon . . . a wooden face!

The chef's entire head, so it appeared, was made of wood.

Jack blinked his eyes. That wasn't possible. He was surely hallucinating from lack of food. A man might have a false hand, but not a false head.

'Bread,' said Jack. 'Cheese, whatever you have. Hurry now, hunger befuddles my brain, as the nesting *woodworm* . . .' he paused, then continued, 'does yours.'

'As you please.' The chef shrugged, ducked down behind the bar counter and re-emerged with a plate of sandwiches held in both hands.

Both hands were wooden.

The hands worried Jack, but he viewed the food with relish.

'I regret that I don't have any relish,' said the chef, placing the plate upon the bar counter and clapping his wooden hands together. 'I've been expecting a delivery. For some months now.'

'I'll take them as they come.' Jack reached out a hand to take up a sandwich, but then paused. 'What are they?' he asked.

'Sandwiches,' said the chef.

'I mean, what's in them?'

'Ham. It's a pig derivative.'

Jack tucked his pistol back into his sleeve, snatched up a sandwich and thrust it into his mouth. 'Bliss,' he said with his mouth full.

'It's rude to talk with your mouth full,' said the chef. 'A mug of porter to wash them down?'

'Yes please.' Jack munched away as the chef drew a mug of porter. Jack watched him as he went about his business. There had to be some logical explanation. Folk could not have wooden heads. Perhaps it was some kind of mask. Perhaps the chef had been hideously disfigured in a catering accident and so now wore a wooden mask. An animated wooden mask. Jack shrugged. It was as good an explanation as any. And anyway, it was none of his business.

Eating was currently his business.

'We don't get many blue-faced youths in these parts,' the chef observed as he drew the mug of porter. 'Your accent is strange to me. Which part of the city are you from?'

Jack munched on and shook his head. 'I'm not from the city,' he said. 'I'm from the south.'

'I've never travelled south.' The chef presented Jack with his beverage. 'But they tell me that the lands of the south are peopled with foolish boys who travel north to seek their fortunes in the city. Would there be any truth in this?'

Jack raised an eyebrow and continued with his munching.

'Between you and me,' said the chef, 'I do not hold travel in high esteem. Folk should stay put, in my opinion. It's a wise man that knows where he is. And if he knows where he is, he should stay there, don't you agree?'

Jack nodded. 'No,' he said.

'Was that a trick answer?'

'Probably.'

'So you want a room for the night?'

Jack nodded once more. 'And a stable and fodder for my horse.'

'You won't need that,' said the chef.

'I will.' Jack pushed another sandwich into his mouth, chewed it up and swallowed it down. 'He can't stand out there all night.'

'Well, obviously not.' The chef adjusted his apron, which didn't really need adjusting, but he adjusted it anyway. It was a chef thing. 'But that's neither here nor there, is it?' said the chef, when he had done with his adjustments.

Jack took up the mug of porter and drank deeply of it. He was underage and shouldn't really have been drinking alcohol. But as the chef hadn't made a fuss about it, then Jack felt that neither would he. 'Why is it neither here, nor there?' he asked, without particular interest.

'Because someone just stole your horse.'

'What?' Jack turned to look out of the window.

The post was still there, but Anthrax wasn't.

'Oh no,' cried Jack. 'Someone has stolen my horse.' And leaving the balance of his porter untested, he rushed from Nadine's Diner.

Outside, he stared up and down the lamp-lit street. The only trace of Anthrax was a pile of steaming manure. Jack shouted out the horse's name, and listened in hope of an answering whinny.

To his great delight, one came to his ears.

'Good boy,' said Jack. 'This way, I think,' and he dashed around the corner of the diner and into a darkened alleyway.

'Anthrax,' called Jack, 'where are you, boy?'

And ahead Jack saw him, by the light of a distant lamp, being led along by something that looked far from human. Something squat and strange. 'Stop!' shouted Jack. 'Come back with my horse, you . . . whatever you are.'

And then Jack was aware of a movement behind him.

And then something hit him hard upon the head.

And then things went very black for Jack.

3

The moon, shining down upon the city, shone down also upon Jack, shone down upon the body of Jack, that was lying strewn in an alleyway. The moon didn't care too much about Jack. But then, the moon didn't care too much about anything. Caring wasn't in the moon's remit. The moon was just the moon, and on nights when there wasn't any cloud about, it just shone down, upon anything and everything really, it didn't matter what to the moon. The moon had seen most things before, and would surely see them again. And as for all the things that the moon hadn't seen, well, it would see them too, eventually. On nights when there wasn't any cloud about.

Not that it would care too much when it did.

It was a moon thing, not caring.

The moon couldn't help the way it was.

Jack lay, face down, in the bedraggled fashion of one who has been roughly struck down, rather than gently arranged. One who has been dragged and flung. As indeed Jack had.

He'd lain for several hours in this untidy and uncared-for state, and would probably have lain so for several hours more, had not something prodded and poked him back into consciousness.

This something was persistent in its prodding and poking. It prodded and poked until it had achieved its desired effect.

Jack awoke with a start, or a jolt, if you prefer, or a shock, if you prefer that. Jack had no particular preference. So Jack awoke with a start and a jolt and a shock. Jack awoke to find a big round face staring right up close and at him.

Jack cowered back and the big round face, governed by the laws of perspective, became a small round face. And in accordance with other laws regarding relative proportion, remained that way. Jack blinked his eyes and stared at the face. It was the face of a bear. A teddy bear. A knackered-looking teddy bear, with mismatched button eyes and a kind of overall raggedness that did not make it altogether appealing to behold.

The bear was wearing a grubby old trenchcoat.

'Bear.' Jack made limp-wristed pointings. 'Toy bear. What?'

'What?' asked the toy bear. 'What?'

'I'm dreaming.' Jack smacked himself in the face. 'Ouch!' he continued. 'Oh and . . .'

'You're new to these parts, aren't you?' said the bear. He had that growly voice that one associates with toy bears. Probably due to the growly thing that they have in their stomachs, which makes that growly noise when you tip them forward. 'I'm Eddie, by the way. I'm the bear of Winkie.'

'The who?'

'The bear of Winkie. I'm Bill Winkie's bear. And I'm not just any old bear. I'm an Anders Imperial. Cinnamon-coloured mohair plush, with wood wool stuffing throughout. Black felt paw pads, vertically stitched nose. An Anders Imperial. You can tell by the special button in my left ear.' Eddie pointed to this special button and Jack peered at it.

The button looked very much like a beer bottle top.

It *was* a beer bottle top.

'And what is your name?' asked the bear.

'I'm Jack,' Jack found himself saying. He was now talking to a teddy bear. (Granted, he had recently chatted to a horse. But at least the horse had behaved like a horse and had failed to chat back to him.) 'How?' Jack rubbed some more at his head. 'How is it done?'

'How is *what* done?' asked the bear.

'How are you doing that talking? Who's working you?'

'Working *me*? No one's working *me*. I work for myself.'

Jack eased himself into a sitting position. He patted at his person, then he groaned.

'Stuffing coming out?' Eddie cocked his head to one side.

'Stuffing? No.' Jack patted some more about his person. 'I've been robbed. I had a purse full of gold coins. And my boots. Someone's stolen my boots.'

'Don't knock it,' said Eddie. 'At least you're still alive. Listen, I've got to sit down, my legs are drunk.'

'Eh?' said Jack. 'What?'

'My legs,' said the bear. 'They're really drunk. If I sit down, then just my bum will be drunk and that won't be so bad.'

'I've lost it,' said Jack. 'Knocked unconscious twice in a single day. My brain is gone. I've lost it. I've gone mad.'

'I'm sorry to hear that.' The bear sat down. 'But it will probably help you to fit in. Most folk in the city are a bit, or more so, mad.'

'I'm talking to a toy bear.' Jack threw up his hands. His clockwork gun fell out of his sleeve. 'Oh, at least I still have this,' he said. 'Perhaps I should simply shoot myself now and get it all over with. I came to the city to seek my fortune and within hours of arrival I'm mad.'

'You came *to* the city? You're a stranger to the city?'

'This has not been a good day for me.'

'Tell me about it,' said the bear.

'Well,' said Jack. 'It all began when—'

'No,' said the bear. 'It was a rhetorical comment. I don't want you to tell me about it. I was concurring. Today hasn't exactly been an armchair full of comfy cushions for yours truly.'

'Who's yours truly?'

'I am, you gormster.'

'Don't start with me,' said Jack, slipping his pistol back into his sleeve and feeling gingerly at the bump on the back of his head. 'I've got brain damage. I can see talking toy bears.'

'Where?' asked Eddie, peering all around.

'You,' said Jack. 'I can see you.'

'You need a drink,' said the bear. 'And I need another upending.'

'Upending? I don't understand.'

'Well, I don't know what you're stuffed with. Meat, isn't it?'

Jack made a baffled face.

'Well, I'm stuffed with sawdust and when I drink, the alcohol seeps down through my sawdust guts and into my feet. I'd have to drink a real lot to fill up all the way to my head and I never have that kind of money. So I get the barman to upend me. Stand me on my head. Then the alcohol goes directly to my head and stays there. Trouble is, it's hard to balance on your head on a barstool at the best of times. You've no chance at all when you're drunk. So I fall off the stool and the barman throws me out. It's all so unfair. But that's life for you, in an eggshell.'

'It's a nutshell, isn't it?'

'Well, you'd know, you're the loony.'

'I'm not well.'

The bear scrambled nearer to Jack and peered very closely at him. 'You don't look too well,' said he. 'Your face is all blue. Is that something catching, do you think? Not that I'll catch it. Moth is all I catch. That's one reason that I drink so much, to ward off the moth.'

'It's not fair.' Jack buried his face in his hands and began to weep.

'Oh, come on.' Eddie Bear shifted over on his drunken bottom and patted Jack's arm with a paw. 'Things really could be worse. You'll be okay. I can direct you to the hospital, if you think you need your head bandaged. Or I'll stagger with you, if you want. Or you can carry me upside down and I'll sing you drunken songs. I know some really rude ones. They're all about pigs and penguins.'

'I had a cap somewhere,' said Jack, wiping his eyes and peering about in search of it.

'Was it blue?' asked the bear.

Jack nodded.

'Well, it isn't quite so blue now. I was sick on it. Mostly sawdust, of course, but evil-smelling; I had a curry earlier.'

'This really isn't happening.'

'I think you'll find that it is. Do you want to come back to my place? You could sleep there.'

Jack climbed painfully to his feet. He gazed down at the toy bear. 'You really are real, aren't you?' he said.

'As real as,' said Eddie.

'As real as *what*?' said Jack.

'Wish I knew,' said Eddie. 'But I can't do corroborative nouns. None of us are perfect, are we? I can get started. As big as, as foul as, as obscene as. But I can't get any further. But that's life for you again. As unfair as . . . Listen, wouldn't you rather go to a bar and have a drink? My bum's beginning to sober up. I seep at the seams. I've got leaks as big as . . . But we all have our problems, don't we?'

Jack agreed. 'I'm very confused,' he said. 'But I don't want to go to hospital. I don't like hospitals. And I'm really too young to go into bars.'

'You're quite big enough; let's have a beer. It won't lessen your confusion, though. In fact, it will probably increase it. But in a nice way and that's as good as, isn't it?'

'I should try and get my purse back. And my horse.'

'You had a *horse*?'

'A horse called Anthrax; he was stolen.'

'Then he's probably cat meat by now. Or being minced up to make burgers for that Nadine's Diner around the corner.'

'That's terrible,' said Jack. 'Poor Anthrax.'

'This isn't a very nice neighbourhood, Jack.'

'So what are *you* doing in it?'

'I'm on a case,' said Eddie Bear. 'I'm a private detective. Hence the trenchcoat.' Eddie did a bit of a twirl, then flopped back onto his drunken bum.

Jack shook his head, which pained him considerably. 'I am mad,' he said. 'This is all mad.'

'Come and have a beer,' said Eddie. 'I'll pay. And kindly carry me, if you will. My legs are still as drunk as, if you know what I mean, and I'm sure that you do.'

It was still a bright and moonlit night and as Jack, with Eddie underneath his arm and guided by the bear's directions, lurched painfully in his stockinged feet along this street and that and around one corner and the next, he was, all in all, amazed by the all and all that he saw.

'This is a very strange city,' said Jack.

'It's not strange to me,' said Eddie. 'How so is it strange to you?'

'Well,' said Jack, 'from a distance, as I approached the city, it all looked grey and dour. And it *was*, on the outskirts. But the deeper I go, the more colourful it becomes. And it's night now.'

'You'll no doubt find it positively garish in the daytime.' Eddie wriggled about.

'Careful,' said Jack, 'I'll drop you.'

'You're squeezing me in all the wrong places. You'll push me out of shape.'

'Sorry,' said Jack. 'But tell me this. Are you a magic bear?'

'A magic bear? What is a magic bear?'

'I'm thinking perhaps a toy bear brought to animation through witchcraft or something like that. Not that I've ever believed in witchcraft. Although I did once meet with a wise woman who could make ducks dance.'

'Did they dance upon a biscuit tin?'

'Now I come to think of it, yes. How did *you* know?'

'It's an old showman's trick,' said Eddie. 'Involves a lighted candle inside the biscuit tin.'

'Urgh,' said Jack. 'That's most unpleasant.'

'Works well, though. Look, we're here.'

'Where's here?'

'Tinto's Bar,' said Eddie. 'This is where I normally do my drinking, when I'm not on a case and getting thrown out of other bars. Put me down please, Jack.'

Jack put Eddie down and viewed the exterior of Tinto's Bar.

The exterior of Tinto's Bar was colourful, to say the very least.

'Ghastly, isn't it?' said Eddie. 'I've suggested he repaint the place. But does he listen? No, he just throws me out. That's the trouble with being a teddy. Well, one of the troubles. People throw you about. They take liberties with your person. It's not nice, I can tell you.'

'I quite like the colours,' said Jack.

'They're mostly brown,' said Eddie. 'Those that aren't blue. They clash, in my opinion.'

Jack stared at the bar's exterior. 'There aren't any browns or blues,' he said.

'There are from where I'm looking. But then from where I'm looking, all the world is either brown or blue. It depends which eye I'm looking through. I've only the two, you see, and one's brown and one's blue. Not that I don't have others. I've a drawer full. But I can't fit them. No opposing thumbs, you see.' Eddie waved his paws about.

Jack looked down. 'What?' he said.

'Pardon is more polite,' said Eddie. 'But it's the curse of the teddy bear. Paws rather than hands. They don't even amount to proper paws, really. Proper paws are like stubby fingers. Mine are just sewn sections; nothing moves. You have no idea how lucky you are. Fingers and opposable thumbs. Bliss. What would I give, eh? That would be as wonderful as.'

Jack pushed open the door and he and Eddie entered Tinto's Bar.

It wasn't too colourful inside. In fact, it was all rather monochrome, or whatever the black and white equivalent of monochrome is. Black and white, probably.

The floor was a chequerboard pattern. The ceiling was likewise. But there was something altogether wrong about that ceiling. It was far too near to the floor. Jack had to duck his head. There were tables and chairs, around and about, arranged in pleasing compositions. But as Jack viewed these, he could clearly see that their dimensions were wrong. The tables and chairs were much too small, built, it appeared, for children. And upon the chairs and seated at the tables, engaged in noisy discussion sat . . .

Jack stopped in mid head-duck and stared.

Sat . . .

Jack opened his mouth.

Sat . . .

Jack backed towards the door he had come in by.

Sat . . .

'Toys!' shouted Jack, and he fled.

It was another alleyway, and Jack was sitting down in it.

'You're really going to have to pull yourself together,' Eddie told him.

'Toys?' Jack made an idiotic face.

'So?' said Eddie.

'Toys. In the bar. I saw them. They were drinking and talking.'

'That's what they do. What *we* do. What's the big deal?'

'Am I dead?' asked Jack. 'Is that it? I'm dead, aren't I?'

Eddie shook his head. 'You're a bit messed up. But you're not dead. You're as alive as.'

'And so they were real?'

'As real as. This is a very weird conversation, and becoming somewhat repetitive. You're a very strange lad, Jack.'

'*I'm* strange? How dare you? I was in that bar. I saw toys. *Live* toys. Dolls and bears like you and clockwork soldiers and wooden things and they were alive. I saw them.'

'Well, what did you expect to see, insects? You're in Toy City and Toy City is where toys live, isn't it?'

'Toy City,' said Jack. 'I can't believe it.'

'Listen,' said Eddie. 'You're a nice lad and everything. But you really must pull yourself together. You're in Toy City, which is where toys live. Which is where toys *have* always lived and *will* always live. It's hardly Utopia, but we get by somehow. Nothing ever changes around here. Or shouldn't anyway, which is why I'm on the case I'm on. But this is where you are.'

'This can't be happening. I must have gone mad.'

'Yeah, well,' said Eddie. 'Perhaps you are mad. It's a shame. A real shame. Perhaps it would be better if we just went our separate ways. I wondered, I suppose. But perhaps I was wrong. I think I'll say goodbye.'

'Wondered?' said Jack. 'What did you wonder?'

'If, perhaps, you'd be the one. To help. It was only a thought. A drunken thought, probably. Forget it.'

'How can I forget it? I don't know what it was.'

'I need a partner,' said Eddie the Bear. 'I'm in a bit of a fix and I need a partner. I thought perhaps . . . But it doesn't matter. Go home, Jack. Go back to wherever you came from. This isn't the place for you to be. You don't under-stand about here. Sleep in this alley tonight, then go home, that's my advice to you.'

'I'm sorry,' said Jack. 'But I'm really confused. Real toys? Live toys? Living in a city?'

'You came to Toy City and you didn't expect to meet toys?'

'I didn't know it was *Toy* City. All I knew was it was *the* City. Where things happened. Nothing much ever hap-pened in the town where I lived. So I came here to seek my fortune.'

'Interesting concept,' said Eddie. 'I've never heard of anyone doing that before. But then, this is the first time that I've actually met anyone who came from outside the City.'

'Because no one ever reaches here,' said Jack.

'Why? Do they get lost?'

'No, eaten, mostly.'

Eddie shrugged. 'Well, I wouldn't know about that. All I know is what I am. I live in Toy City. Things are as they are.'

'But toys can't live. They can't be alive.'

'And why not?'
'Because they can't.'
'But why?'
'Because I say that they can't.'
Eddie Bear looked up at Jack.
And Jack looked down at Eddie.
Eddie Bear began to laugh.
And then, too, so did Jack.
'Shall we go and have that beer?' asked Eddie.
'Yes,' said Jack. 'Let's do that.'

4

Tinto's Bar looked no better to Jack on second viewing.

The interior was still the black and white equivalent of monochrome and the chairs and tables were still arranged in pleasing compositions. But the scale of everything was still all wrong and Jack had to duck his head once more, and keep it ducked. And all those *toys* were still there. And all those toys still worried Jack.

The lad steadied himself against the nearest wall. There was no longer any doubt in his mind regarding the reality of this. It *was* real. That it couldn't be real did not enter into it. He was here and all these toys were . . .

'Drunk!' Jack looked down at Eddie. 'All these toys are drunk.'

Eddie looked up at Jack. And Eddie shrugged. 'It's late,' he said. 'They've been in here all evening. Don't folk get drunk where you come from?'

'People do,' said Jack. 'But not . . .'

'Don't start all that again. Buy me a drink.'

'I don't have any money. I was robbed.'

'You've some coins in your trouser pocket. I felt them when you were unconscious.'

'What?'

'I was trying to bring you round.'

'You were going through my pockets?'

'Not me,' said Eddie. 'No can do. No opposing thumbs.'

Jack patted at his trousers.

'Other side,' said Eddie.

'Oh yeah,' said Jack, digging deeply into a pocket and winkling out a number of coins. 'That's a bit of luck.'

'Stick with me, kidder,' said Eddie. 'I'll bring you lots of luck.'

Jack gazed down at the shabby-looking bear and nodded his ducked head in a manner that lacked conviction.

'To the bar,' said Eddie, leading the way. 'Let's both get as drunk as.'

Jack followed on, keeping his head down and making furtive sideways glances as he did so. There were toys to all sides of him, and just a little below. They were chatting away in a rowdy fashion, banging their glasses on the tables and generally carrying on as folk carry on anywhere when they are well in their cups.

There were dolls and there were gollys, teddies and toy soldiers, and fluffy-faced animals of indeterminate species. And they all had that look of 'favourite toys' which have been loved to the point of near-destruction.

Jack watched Eddie climb onto a bar stool. How could he move about like that? He was all filled up with sawdust; he'd said so himself. He had no bones, no muscles, no sinews. How could it be possible?

Jack shrugged and sighed and sat himself down on a bar stool next to Eddie. It was a very low bar stool, beside a very low bar counter, and Jack found himself with his knees up high.

'Can't we go somewhere else?' he whispered to Eddie. 'This stool's too low for me. I look a complete gormster.'

'No you don't.' The bear grinned, a big face-splitter. 'You look as handsome as. Get the beers in.'

Jack sighed again. 'Where's the barman?' he asked.

'Howdy doody, what'll it be, sir?' The barman sprang up from beneath the bar counter, causing Jack to fall back in alarm.

'Control yourself,' said Eddie as Jack stared, all agog. 'It's only Tinto, the barman.'

Tinto was clearly mechanical, powered by a clockwork

motor. He was formed from tin and glossily painted, though much of the gloss was now gone. His head was an oversized sphere, with a smiling face painted on the front. His body was a thing-a-me-oid★ painted with a dicky-bow and tuxedo. The arms were flat, though painted with sleeves and shirt cuffs. The fingers of the hands were fully articulated.

Jack glanced at Eddie, who was staring covetously at those fingers.

'Howdy doody, what'll it be, sir?' said Tinto once again. The painted lips didn't move. The voice came from a tiny grille in the painted chest.

'I . . .' went Jack, 'I . . .'

'Beer,' said Eddie.

'Coming right up,' said Tinto. 'And anything for the complete gormster?'

'He'll have a beer too,' said Eddie. 'And he's my friend and he's paying.'

'No offence meant,' said Tinto.

'None taken,' said Eddie.

'There was too,' said Jack.

'No there wasn't,' said Eddie. 'Just relax and drink beer.'

'I.D.,' said Tinto.

'What?' said Eddie.

'I.D. for the gormster. He looks underage to me. Underaged and oversized.'

'*Underage?*' Jack's jaw dropped. '*Oversized?*' His face made a frown.

'I run a respectable bar,' said Tinto. 'Top notch clientele, as you can readily observe. I can't have blue-faced, stocking-footed ragamuffins coming in here and losing me my licence. You'll have to show me your I.D. or . . . I . . . will . . . have . . .' Tinto's voice became slower and slower and finally stopped altogether.

'What's happened to it?' Jack asked.

★ A cylinder with a hemisphere joined to each end of it.

'*Him!*' said Eddie.

'Him,' said Jack.

'Run down,' said Eddie. 'He needs rewinding. 'I gener-ally take advantage if this happens when I'm alone with him in the bar. Nip around and help myself to a free beer.'

'Do it now then,' said Jack.

'There're too many folk here now. But he loses his short-term memory when he's rewound, so just back me up.'

Jack shrugged. 'Fair enough.'

'Nellie,' called Eddie, 'Nellie, a winding needed here.'

A dainty doll with a huge wasps' nest of yellow hair hastened along behind the bar counter, turned Tinto around and began to vigorously crank the key in his back.

'See his name there, on his back?' said Eddie, leaning over the bar counter and pointing it out to Jack.

Jack perused the barman's back. 'It doesn't say Tinto,' he said, 'it says Tintoy. The "Y" has worn off.'

'You're right,' said Eddie. 'But don't mention it to Tinto. He thinks it makes him special.'

Jack opened his mouth to speak, but didn't.

'Thank you, my dear,' said Tinto, his head turning a semicircle. 'Almost ran right down there. Now, what was I doing?' His body revolved to catch up with his head.

'You were pulling two beers for us,' said Eddie.

'Was I?' asked Tinto.

'You were,' agreed Jack. 'You'd just scrutinised my I.D. and commented on the fact that I looked young for my age.'

'Did I?' said Tinto.

'You did,' said Eddie. 'And we'd just paid for the beers.'

'You had?' said Tinto.

'We had,' said Jack. 'Eddie did. With a gold piece. But we haven't had the beers yet and Eddie hasn't had his change.'

'So sorry,' said Tinto. 'I'll get right to it.' And he moved off along the bar to pull a brace of beers.

'A gold piece?' whispered Eddie. 'That's pushing it a bit.'

Jack shrugged. 'I was only backing you up. You can

always tell him it was a mistake if you want and say you gave him the right money.'

'Oh no,' whispered Eddie. 'A gold piece is fine. I must remember that in future.'

Tinto returned and presented Eddie and Jack with their beers and Eddie with a great deal of change. 'Cheers,' said Eddie, taking his glass carefully between his paws and pouring beer messily into his face.

'Cheers,' said Jack, doing likewise, though without the mess. The glass was tiny. Jack drained it with a single gulp and ordered another.

'So, Eddie,' said Tinto, doing the business for Jack, who paid with the change from his trouser pocket. 'Any word from Bill?'

'No,' said Eddie, manoeuvring his glass back onto the bar counter. 'He's been gone for a week now. But I'm sure he'll be back very soon.'

'Who's Bill?' Jack asked as Tinto passed him a new beer.

'My partner,' said Eddie.

Tinto laughed, a sound like small stones being shaken about in an empty tin can.

'All right, my *owner*,' said Eddie. 'Bill Winkie, the famous detective. I'm Bill's bear; I told you in the alleyway, Jack.'

'Bill Winkie?' Jack took a gulp and placed his latest empty glass on the counter. 'Bill Winkie, Private Eye?'

'The same,' said Eddie.

'I've read the books,' said Jack.

'I never get a mention,' said Eddie.

'No, you don't, but that's not the point.'

'It is to me. Without me he'd never solve a single case. I'm the brains behind that man.'

'That's really *not* the point,' said Jack. 'The point is that Bill Winkie is a fictional detective. He's not a real person.'

'He seems pretty real to me.' Eddie took up his glass once more and poured beer into his face. 'From the brim of his snap-brimmed Fedora to the toes of his smelly old socks.'

'You're telling me that Bill Winkie is real?'

'As real as.'

'Hm,' went Jack. 'It follows.'

'Eddie's not kidding you around,' said Tinto. 'He really does solve most of Bill's cases. He's a natural, a born detective.'

'Cheers,' said Eddie. 'I appreciate that.'

'Credit where credit's due,' said Tinto. 'But you'll only get that credit here. And I don't even give credit. This is a cash-only establishment.'

'What he means,' said Eddie, 'is that toys have no status. This may be Toy City, but toys have to know their place. Step out of line and you turn up missing.'

'I don't really understand,' said Jack.

'The status quo,' said Eddie. 'I'm a teddy. I'm supposed to do teddy things. Eat porridge, picnic in the woods, be cuddly, stuff like that.' Eddie made a face and spat sawdust.

'And you're not keen?' said Jack.

'I'm a bear with brains. I have ambitions.'

'About the brains,' said Jack. 'I have been wondering about those.'

'Oh yeah?' Eddie patted at his head with a paw. 'You've been wondering how a head full of sawdust can actually think?'

'It had crossed my mind, yes.'

'And so how does your brain think?'

'It's a brain, that's what it does.'

'It's a piece of meat,' said Eddie. 'And how does a piece of meat think? You tell me!'

'Well . . .' said Jack.

'You don't know,' said Eddie. 'Nobody knows. Except perhaps for Mr Anders. He knows almost everything.'

'And who is Mr Anders?'

'The kindly, loveable white-haired old Toymaker. He birthed me and everyone else in this bar, with the exception of you.'

'So why don't you speak to him about this status quo business? Tell him you want your recognition?'

'Er, no,' said Eddie. 'The Toymaker made me to be a teddy and do teddy things. The fact that I don't care to do them is my business. So I'll just keep my business to myself.'

'Or turn up missing?'

'I don't want to think about it.'

'So don't. Let's drink. Do you want me to turn you upside down yet?'

'No, not yet, but thanks anyway. You're all right, Jack. I like you.'

'I like you too, Eddie, cheers.' Jack raised his glass, but it was empty.

Eddie raised his, but it was empty too. Eddie fumbled with his paws and dropped his glass, shattering it upon the floor.

'Sorry,' said Eddie. 'It happens. A lot.'

'You haven't mentioned to the Toymaker that you would really like a pair of . . .' Jack stopped himself short. Of course Eddie hadn't. He could hardly ask the Toymaker to fit him with a pair of hands. That would not be maintaining the status quo.

'Sorry,' said Jack.

'Forget it,' said Eddie. 'Buy me a beer. It's your round.'

'You have a lot of change on the counter there.'

'Yes but that's *my* change and it's *your* round.'

'Fair enough,' said Jack. 'Although it isn't my round.' Jack purchased a brace of beers with the last of his money and the two took to drinking once more.

'Tell me,' said Eddie, 'about where you come from. I've never met anyone who wasn't brought up in this city.'

'It isn't much,' said Jack. 'It's just a small township, supported by a factory. They make clockwork stuff there. I used to build . . .' Jack drew Eddie closer.

'What?' asked Eddie.

'Clockwork barmen,' said Jack. 'Like Tinto. They said, "Howdy doody friend, what'll it be?" But that's all they said. They didn't talk like Tinto.'

'So you know all about clockwork?'

'You've seen my clockwork pistol. I designed and built it myself. It's not quite as accurate as it's supposed to be, though.'

'But you do know all about clockwork?'

'Pretty much all. But working in the factory nearly did for me. We were like slaves in there. I hated it. The sun used to beat down on us through the glass roof. And when the sun was at its highest, there was this bit of glass in the roof that was convex, like a lens, see, and at midday the sun would come through that and really burn me badly. I'll never forget it as long as I live. I had to get away. So I ran. I'd heard that there was wealth to be had in the city, so I came here to seek my fortune.'

'Pooh,' said Eddie. 'Sounds like you had a pretty rough time. You did the right thing running away.'

'I didn't have a lot of choice really. There was some unpleasantness; I don't want to go into that now.'

'That's okay with me. Your own business is your own business. So you've come here seeking work?'

'In a manner of speaking.'

'I could offer you work.'

'You?'

'Me,' said Eddie. 'I need a partner, I told you.'

'But you're Bill's bear.'

'And he's not here and while he's gone, I need a partner. I can do the thinking. But I can't do the hand working and I can't do the questioning and the driving around and . . .'

'The driving around?' said Jack.

'Bill left without his car and . . .'

'Car,' said Jack. 'What kind of car?'

'You know all about cars then, do you?'

'If they're clockwork cars. And what other kind of cars are there?'

'None that I know of.'

'I know all about them. I've helped build them.'

'But you've never actually driven one?'

'Well, one. But there was some unpleasantness, which I don't want to talk about either.'

'Well, Bill has one and it's standing in the garage. But I need a partner to do all the stuff that he could do and I can't.'

'Because of the status quo?'

'Exactly. If we solve the case, there'll be gold in it for you.'

'*If* we solve it?'

'*When I* solve it. Which I will.'

'So I get to drive you around and play the part of Bill Winkie, is that what you're suggesting?'

'In essence, yes.'

'Then I'm up for it,' said Jack. 'I'll do it.'

'Brilliant,' said Eddie. 'Then we're partners. Put it there,' and he stuck out his paw.

Jack took it between his hands and shook it.

'Partners,' he said.

'That's as brilliant as,' said Eddie, withdrawing his paw and employing it, with its fellow, to take up his glass once again.

'To partners and success,' he said.

'I'll join you in that,' said Jack. 'Cheers.'

'Cheers.' The two drank once again, drained their glasses and ordered further beers.

'So,' said Jack, 'tell me about the case that *you* are going to solve.'

'It's a pretty big number,' said Eddie. 'Prominent member of society brutally slain.'

'That's a job for the police, surely?'

'Surely,' said Eddie. 'And I'm sure they're doing their best to track down the murderer.'

'I detect a certain *tone* in your voice,' said Jack. 'One that suggests to me that you're not altogether convinced that the police will—'

'Exactly,' said Eddie. 'You're most astute. Bill received a cash-up-front advance from an anonymous source to take on the case. It was a great deal of cash. Enough to retire on, really. Bill has a lot of debts. He gambles a great deal and runs up big bar bills. And cleaning bills; he's very fastidious. Likes a clean trenchcoat, does Bill.'

'Er, just one question,' said Jack. 'Before Bill . . . er . . . went away, did he pay off his debts?'

'Not that I know of,' said Eddie. 'I'm sure he will when he comes back, though.'

'And he left, taking the big cash advance with him?'

Eddie nodded.

'Ah,' said Jack.

'Ah?' said Eddie.

'Nothing,' said Jack. 'You're pretty fond of Bill, aren't you?'

'I'm Bill's bear. I have been since he was a child.'

'So you trust him?'

'Of course, why do you ask me that?'

'Oh, no reason really.' Jack applied himself to his beer. 'So you'd like the case solved for him before he gets back from his holiday, or whatever?'

'That's it,' said Eddie. 'There's the promise of much more money, when the case gets solved.'

'And you think that you can trust this anonymous bene-factor to pay up when the case is solved?'

'Why wouldn't I?' asked Eddie.

'You're a very trusting little bear.'

'Don't patronise me,' said Eddie.

'Sorry,' said Jack. 'Did Bill leave you any money?'

Eddie shook his head. 'And the rent on the office is overdue. I'd like to get this case solved pretty quickly.'

'All right,' said Jack. 'I'll help you out. I'll be your hands and do all the stuff you want. Especially the car driving. I'm up for it.' Jack patted Eddie on the head.

'Jack,' said Eddie.

'Eddie?' said Jack.

'Pat me on the head like that again and I'll butt you right in the balls.'

'Sorry,' said Jack, withdrawing his patting hand.

'I know what you're thinking,' said Eddie. 'You're

thinking that Bill has absconded with the advance money, leaving the silly little bear to deal with the case. That's what you're thinking, isn't it?'

'Of course not,' said Jack.

'Then you *are* a complete gormster,' said Eddie. 'Because that's what's happened.'

'Oh,' said Jack. 'Then you . . .'

'Of course I know. But I don't care. Solving the case is all that matters to me. Applying the sawdust in my head to finding the solution. Proving to myself that I can do it, even if I never get the credit. Can you understand that, Jack?'

'Not really.' Jack shook his head.

'Then it's too subtle for you. But it's what I do and who I am. You'll get paid, you'll do well out of this, if you join me.'

'I *will* join you,' said Jack. 'I've said I will. And we've shaken hand and paw and we're partners.'

'Good,' said Eddie. 'But just as long as we understand each other. I have the measure of you, Jack. But you'll never have the measure of me.'

'If you say so.'

'I do. Drink up, and I'll buy you another.'

'I'm beginning to feel rather drunk,' said Jack. 'And on such small glasses of beer too.'

'The youth of today has no staying power.'

'I'll survive,' said Jack. 'I might throw up a bit later, but I'll survive.'

'I'll throw up with you; let's drink.' Eddie ordered more beer. 'We'll make a great team,' he told Jack.

'I'm sure we will.' Jack raised his glass and drank, spilling much of what little beer there was down his chin.

'We have so much in common,' said Eddie, doing likewise.

'This case.' Jack replaced his glass upon the bar, with some small degree of difficulty. 'This prominent member of society who got murdered, tell me about him.'

'Fat sod,' said Eddie. 'Big fat sod. Someone boiled him.'

'Boiled him?'

'Alive in his swimming pool. Heated the water to boiling point and pushed him in, or something like.'

'Fiendish,' said Jack.

'That's my opinion,' said Eddie. 'And I think there's some kind of cover-up. The papers are even suggesting that it was suicide.'

'Suicide? In a boiling swimming pool?'

'The papers are putting it about that he tried to commit suicide once before.'

'And did he?'

'Not in my opinion. He fell.'

'Fell?'

'Off a high wall. Broke half the bones in his body. There was a regiment of soldiers passing at the time, but they couldn't resuscitate him. Paramedics patched him up, though. They were conveniently close.'

'Come again?' said Jack.

'It was big news at the time. There was a song written about it. He was nothing before that song, but he got rich from the royalties. Because he wrote it himself.'

'Eh?' said Jack.

'Scam,' said Eddie. 'The whole thing was a set-up.'

'I'm lost,' said Jack. 'I have no idea what you're talking about.'

'But I bet you know the murder victim.'

'How could I? I'm new to this city.'

'You'll have heard of him. You'll even have sung about him falling off that wall.'

'I don't think that's very likely,' said Jack.

'Oh, I think you'll find that it is,' said Eddie. 'His name was Humpty Dumpty.'

5

Jack awoke to find himself in strange surroundings. As this was now becoming a regular habit, rather than a novelty, he merely groaned and blinked, rolled onto his belly and eased himself up on his knees.

He was in an office, a definite improvement on the death pit or the alleyway, but hardly the five star accommodation he'd been hoping for when first he entered the city. The words 'how did I get here?' came almost to his lips, but he withheld them. He had vague recollections of the latter part of his night out with Eddie. It had involved much beer, and later, much vomiting. Then there had been much staggering along streets, much climbing of stairs and then much floor and much oblivion.

Jack stretched himself, fretted at the clicking of his joints, ran gentle fingers over his pulsating forehead and said 'never again' in a whispery kind of a voice.

Underage drinking. Jack shook his head and regretted the doing thereof. Where *was* the pleasure in underage drinking? Jack tried to recall the pleasure.

It wasn't easy.

'Still,' whispered Jack, 'you have to keep at it. Overcome the miseries of the vomiting and the whirling pit. Pay your dues and work towards the real rewards of big-time adult drinking. Something to look forward to.'

Jack's knees buckled under him.

For now he needed a quiet sit-down.

Jack gave his surroundings a bleary perusal and took in what he could of them. An office, that was for certain. And yes, he recalled, the office of the now legendary Bill Winkie, *fictional* detective. Jack sniffed at the office. It didn't smell too good: musty and fusty and tainted by the smoke of many cigarettes.

But, for all of its overloaded atmospherics, here was an office that owned to a certain 'lack'.

There was a hatstand that lacked a hat to stand on it and a water cooler that lacked anything to cool. The filing cabinet lacked a bottom drawer and the desk, lacking a leg, was being supported at that corner by a large alphabet house brick (lacking a corner).

Jack eased himself carefully around the desk and settled down onto the chair that stood behind it. The chair lacked comfort. Jack turned gently around on it to face a window that lacked a pane of glass. He turned back, took in a ceiling fan that lacked a blade and a carpet that lacked a pattern.

Jack turned once more towards the window and raised his eyes, which pained him no little bit.

A Venetian blind, no doubt lacking a slat or two, was fastened in the up position. But, strung to the cord at ceiling height and dangling by the neck, was Eddie Bear.

'Oh no!' cried Jack, leaping from the chair and shinning onto the desk.

The desk that lacked a leg had a top that lacked support. It gave with a hideous crack and Jack fell through it.

He was only slightly dazed this time and his eyes soon reopened to find a big round face looming at him once again.

'What did you do *that* for?' asked Eddie. 'The guvnor will be very upset when he returns to see what you've done to his antique desk.'

'You were trying to hang yourself.' Jack beat away bits of desk, getting splinters in his fingers. 'I was saving you.'

'Ah,' said Eddie, de-looming his face. 'Ah no. I was sobering up. I hang myself in the upright position, then rely on natural seepage, through the feet. Stone cold sober again. Doesn't work for you meat-heads though, does it?'

'You might at least say sorry.'

'Why? I didn't break the desk.'

'Oh, never mind.' Jack climbed once more to his feet. 'I have *such* a hangover,' he said. And, looking up once more, 'How did you manage to climb up that cord in the first place?'

'Practice,' said Eddie. 'You need a drink.'

'No, I need breakfast. And the toilet.'

'The joys of the human digestive system. You should have a drink, though. Bill's hangover cure. His own special concoction. There's some in the desk drawer. Well, what's left of it.'

Jack rootled about in the desk drawers and finally un-earthed a sinister-looking green bottle.

'That's the kiddie,' said Eddie. 'You have a swig of that.'

Sighing and muttering by turn, Jack uncorked the bottle, sniffed at the contents, made a face of displeasure, then took a swig.

He looked at Eddie and Eddie looked at him.

'It takes a minute or two,' said the bear. 'I'd sit back down, if I were you.'

Jack sat back down. 'Would you say that I had a good time last night?' he asked.

'Certainly,' said the bear. 'You had a good time last night.'

'Did I? Really?'

'No,' said Eddie. 'Of course you didn't.'

'Then why did you say that I did?'

'Because you asked me to. What a strange young man you are.'

'I'm seriously thinking of going home.' Jack rubbed at his forehead. 'I don't think city life agrees with me.'

'It doesn't agree with most folk.' Eddie sat down at Jack's feet. 'But then, if you're poor, what kind of life does?'

'I came here to seek my fortune.'

'Then I hope you'll share some of it with me when you do. I ran up a bit of a bar tab at Tinto's last night. He wrote it down, in case he forgot about it.'

'Humpty Dumpty,' said Jack, and he groaned as he said it.

'Fat and dead.' Eddie plucked bits of fluff off himself. 'In that order.'

'No. Humpty Dumpty. That was why I got so drunk.'

'And there was me thinking that it was all the beer you consumed that was to blame.'

'He was the reason behind all the beer. A nursery rhyme character.'

'Ah,' said Eddie, once more. 'They don't like that term. They prefer "Preadolescent Poetic Personalities".'

'*They?* That's right, I remember. Miss Muffet, Georgie Porgie, Jack and Jill, the whole sick crew. They're all real people, according to you, and they all live here in the city.'

'They have to live somewhere.'

'Not if they don't exist.'

'Please don't start all that again, Jack. You went on and on about that last night. "They're not real." "Why not?" "Because I say so." Your conversation became extremely tedious. And very slurred.'

'Agh! Oooh! Ow! Urgh!'

'That's easy for you to say.'

'Aaaaaagh!' Jack clutched at his stomach and fell forward onto Eddie.

'Get off me.' Eddie flapped about. 'You'll have my seams bursting, get off.'

Jack got off. 'I'm sorry,' he said, 'but I feel . . .'

'How do you feel?'

'Actually,' Jack looked all around and about, 'actually, I feel excellent. In the very best of health.'

'Bill's lotion, works every time.'

'Lotion? Don't you rub lotion on?'

'Do you? Well, it's all the same, it worked, didn't it?'

'Yes, it did.' Jack took up Eddie and set him upon the ruins of the desk. 'I'd like some breakfast,' he said. 'And I still need the toilet.'

'Okey doke,' Eddie grinned. 'But we're still partners,

right? You'll help me solve the case? Be my hands, and whatnots?'

'Whatnots?'

'We'll not debase our conversation with cheap innuendo, will we, Jack?'

'Certainly not.' Jack had a big smile on. 'I'll give it a go. I'll help you solve your case, mad as it is. I keep my word. We shook hand and paw and we're partners.'

'Jolly good, now help me down, please.'

Jack helped Eddie down.

'I want to visit the crime scene,' said the bear. 'I haven't been able to thus far. The authorities won't give clearance to a teddy. But you'll be able to bluff us in, I feel confident of that.'

'I'm not sure that I do,' said Jack.

'Well I am, because I'll tell you what to say. Now, you did tell me that you could actually drive a car, didn't you?'

'In theory,' said Jack.

'Well, theory and practice are not too far removed. Come on, I'll show you Bill's car. But first we need to clean you up. Get all that blue dye off your face. You smell rank and you could do with a change of clothing and some shoes. I'll kit you out from Bill's wardrobe.'

'So I can play the part of Bill Winkie.'

'So you can *be* Bill Winkie. Men all look the same to toys. You'll be able to carry it off.'

Jack nodded thoughtfully. 'I'm up for it,' he said. 'But I want breakfast.'

'Do you have money to pay for breakfast?'

Jack patted his pockets and then shook his head.

'Perhaps there'll be something to eat at the crime scene,' said Eddie. 'A bit of boiled egg, or something.'

Now, there is a knack to driving a car. Any car. Even one that is powered by a clockwork motor. There is steering to be done and gears to be changed and this involves clutch-work, and, if reversing, looking into mirrors and judging distances. There are all manner of complications and knacks involved. And skills, there are definitely skills. In fact, the remove between theory and practice is a pretty large remove, when it comes to driving a car.

Let us take, for example, the deceptively simple matter of starting up a car. This is not something that should be attempted in a light-hearted and devil-may-care manner. It's not just a matter of turning a key and putting your foot down somewhere and *brrrrrming* the engine.

Well, it sort of is.

But then again, it isn't.

Jack considered that it probably was. And, it has to be said, when Eddie led him into Bill's garage and Jack switched on the light and beheld *the car*, Jack was heard to remark that it would be 'a-piece-of-the-proverbial' to 'burn that baby'.

'This phraseology is odd to my ears,' said Eddie. 'Does it mean that you are actually conversant with the whys and wherefores requisite to the *safe* locomotion of this vehicle?'

Jack rubbed his hands together and grinned broadly.

'That's not really an answer,' said Eddie.

'I know clockwork,' said Jack. 'I've worked on cars like this.'

'Yes, but driven them?'

'I'm sure I said yes to you last night.'

'You may have,' said Eddie. 'But we were both pretty out-of-it. I definitely recall you mentioning that there was some "unpleasantness" involved.'

'We'll have to wind it up first,' said Jack.

'This much I know.'

'Then we get in and I drive.'

'It all sounds so simple when you put it that way.'

'There's one thing,' said Jack. 'I don't have a driving licence. I'm too young to drive.'

'I don't think we should let a small detail like that stand in the way of the disaster that immediately awaits us as soon as you get behind the wheel, should we?'

'You're a most articulate little bear,' said Jack.

'Don't patronise me,' said Eddie. 'I warned you about that, didn't I?'

'You did,' said Jack. 'So should I wind?'

'Please wind,' said Eddie.

The car was an Anders Faircloud: pressed tin in the metallic blue of a butterfly's wing. It was long and low and highly finned at the tail, the way that every good car should be (apart from the short stumpy sports ones that go like poop off a scoop and generally come to grief on late night motorways with a celebrity (though rarely a Preadolescent Poetic Personality) in the driving seat). It had pressed tin wheels with breezy wide hubs and big rubber tyres. It was a blinder of an automobile and its all-over glory gave Jack a moment's pause for thought.

'Eddie,' said Jack.

'Jack?' said Eddie.

'Eddie,' said Jack. 'This is a superb automobile.'

'Bill's pride and joy,' said Eddie.

'So herein lies a mystery. Why would Bill Winkie not take his car when he went off to wherever he went off to?'

'What are you suggesting?' Eddie asked.

'Nothing,' said Jack. 'I was just wondering why he would have gone off and left his precious car behind.'

'I don't know,' said Eddie. 'Perhaps he didn't take the car because it is such a noticeable car. Perhaps he has gone off somewhere to be incognito. Perhaps he's working on the case, incognito. Is that enough perhapses for you?'

'Perhaps,' said Jack.

'Wind the car up,' said Eddie. 'Let's go to the crime scene.'

'Yes,' said Jack. 'Let's do that.'

Well, there *is* a knack to driving a car.

And Jack didn't have it.

No doubt he'd get it, given time, like he would getting drunk. But these things *do* take time, even the getting drunk

thing. He was okay on the winding-up part of the proce-
dure, though. There was no doubt about that.

'No!' howled Eddie as Jack backed out of the garage at
speed, before the garage door was actually raised.

'Stop!' screamed Eddie, as Jack performed a remarkable
handbrake turn in the middle of the traffic that moved (quite
swiftly) in the street beyond.

'We're all gonna die!' bellowed Eddie as Jack tore forward
on the wrong side of that street.

'I'm getting the knack of this,' said Jack, gronching the
gears and clinging to the steering wheel. 'These things take
time. I have the measure of it now.'

'No you don't!' Eddie ducked down in his seat. Even
lower than he already was.

'Piece of the proverbial.' Jack spun the steering wheel,
which at least took him onto the right side of the road. 'Does
this car have a music system fitted? One of those music bow
wheel-pin contraptions?'

'Forget the music.' Eddie covered his face.

'Easy-peasy.' Jack put his foot down somewhere. It was
the brake; the car did a bit of a spin; Jack took his foot off the
brake. 'What about *that*?' he said.

'You don't even know where we're going.'

'Do you?'

'Yes, the wrong way.'

'Well, why didn't you say so?' Jack spun the wheel again.
The Anders Faircloud moved from the on-going lane back
into the other-going lane, causing much distress amongst the
other-going-laners.

'Got it now,' said Jack. 'Out of the way, fellas!' And he
honked the horn.

'Well, you do know where the horn is.'

'Do you know what?'

'What?' said Eddie.

'I'll tell you what,' said Jack, 'this is great. Do you know
that? Great! I'm driving a car. Do you know how great this is
for me? This is . . .'

'Great?' said Eddie.

'As great as,' said Jack. 'As wonderful as, in fact. Marvellous. Incredible. I'm enjoying this *so* much.'

Jack took a sudden right turn, cutting across oncoming traffic and causing much sudden braking from it and much shunting of one car into another.

'And why did you do *that*?' Eddie asked from beneath the pressed tin dashboard.

'I don't know. Because I could, I suppose. Where would you like me to drive to?'

'I'd like you to stop. In fact I'd *love* you to stop.'

'Well, I'm not going to. So where would you like us to go?'

'Okay.' Eddie climbed out of his seat and peeped over the dashboard. 'Turn left at the next road and . . . Jack, do you feel all right?'

'I feel incredible,' said Jack, 'full of power, do you know what I mean?'

'It's the lotion.' Eddie covered his face as Jack put his foot down again. 'Bill's lotion, the stuff you were apparently supposed to rub on, rather than drink. I'd never actually seen him doing the actual rubbing in. I sleep late as a rule. I think it's pumped you up rather and . . . Oh my . . .'

Jack went 'Weeeeeeeeee,' and then he went 'Ooooooooooooh!' and then he went 'Oh!' and 'Damn.' And then he said, 'We've stopped.'

'The clockwork's run down,' said Eddie. 'You put it under – how shall we put this? – certain strain.'

'What a rush,' said Jack, sitting back in the driving seat. 'Did I love that? Or did I not? I loved it. I did. It was wonderful. It was . . .'

And then Jack passed from consciousness once more.

'I think this is going to be a very emotional sort of a relationship,' said Eddie, to no one other than himself. 'But let's look on the bright side. By sheer chance, or coincidence, or a force greater than ourselves, which guides our paths and moulds our destinies, we have stopped right outside Nursery Towers, the home of the late and lamented Humpty Dumpty.'

6

Humpty Dumpty.

Did he fall, or was he pushed, or was it that he jumped?

Or was it, in fact, none of the above?

There has always been controversy surrounding Humpty Dumpty's famous plunge from the wall. Historical details are sketchy at best. Eyewitness accounts conflict. And even the exact location of the original wall remains uncertain.★

Conspiracy theories abound. One hinges on the matter of Humpty's real identity. According to some, he was a failed Toy City TV stuntman called Terry Horsey, who reinvented himself by taking on the exotic, foreign-sounding name of Humpty Dumpty and performing a real-life stunt, without the aid of a crash mat.

This theory has been dubbed the 'Did He Fall (on purpose)? Theory'.

It does not, however, stand up to close scrutiny, as extensive searches through the Toy City TV archives have failed to turn up a single piece of footage, from any TV show, that involved a thirty-seven-stone stunt man.

The 'Was He Pushed? Theory' stands upon even shakier

★ In a famous lawsuit, two rival farmers, each claiming that the original wall stood upon their property, and each receiving a hearty annual turnover from tourists who paid to view it, sued each other. Humpty Dumpty refused to substantiate either claim and the case was thrown out of court. It is interesting to note that since his death in the swimming pool, several supposed 'Stones from the True Wall' have been put up for auction. Although of doubtful provenance, these have commanded high prices from collectors of relics.

ground (ha ha). It incorporates a number of co-related sub-theories, listed below:

Sub-theory 1: He was pushed by: (a) a jealous lover; (b) a miffed business associate; (c) a rival, either in love, or in business; or (d) an assassin hired by any of the above.

But he survived the fall.

Sub-theory 2: He did *not* survive the fall. In this theory, he actually died and was replaced by a lookalike.

Sub-theory 3: He *did* survive the fall, but was replaced by a lookalike anyway and went into seclusion somewhere.

Exactly where, and indeed *why*, is not explained.

The 'Did He Jump? Theory', currently enjoying a renaissance in Toy City's popular press, puts forward the failed suicide hypothesis. It hints at depression brought on by Humpty's obvious eating disorder and draws support from an interview he once gave on *The Tuffet*, a popular Toy City TV chat show hosted by the ever-youthful Miss Muffet, on which Humpty spoke at length about his weight problem.

Critics of this particular theory state that Humpty's appearance on the show was nothing more than a cynical marketing exercise to promote his latest book, *The H Plan Diet*.

Yet another theory has it that there was more than one Humpty Dumpty, but no wall involved: one Humpty fell from the side of a grassy knoll and another from the window of a book depository.

This is known as 'The Particularly Stupid Theory'.

Here endeth the theories.

For now.

There was a lot of manipulation involved. And that's not easy when you don't have opposing thumbs. Or even fingers. All you have to work with are paws, and crude paws to boot. (Or to paw.) Eddie dug around in the glove compartment. When he'd finally wormed out the hypodermic, it was the Devil-bear's own job for him to grip it and aim it and actually inject its contents into Jack.

The result was somewhat immediate.

'Are we there?' asked Jack, opening his eyes.

'We're here,' said Eddie, tossing the hypo out of the car and grinning painfully. 'Nice driving.'

'Piece of cake. So what now?'

'Okay. Well, we have to get in there. There might be a policeman on guard, so we . . . *whisper, whisper, whisper.*'

'We'll *what*?'

'You'll . . . *whisper, whisper, whisper.*'

'Why are you doing all this *whisper, whisper, whispering*?'

Eddie sighed. 'Did you understand any of it?' he asked.

'Yes, all,' said Jack.

'Then do it.'

'Fair enough.'

Nursery Towers was big. Which is to say, *big*. It was a major complex on the lower western slope of Knob Hill. Only the very rich lived here. Nursery Towers rose up and up and spread all around and about.

'There's money here,' said Jack, peering up. 'Big money.'

'Please try and keep your mind on the job.'

Jack swung open the driver's door and removed himself from the vehicle; Eddie followed him. 'Don't forget your fedora,' said Eddie.

Jack retrieved the hat from the rear seat, stuck it onto his head and closed the car door. Then he did much adjusting of his trenchcoat, straightening the belt and turning up the collar. 'How do I look?' he asked Eddie. 'Pretty darn smart, eh?'

Eddie sighed and nodded. 'What is it about trenchcoats,' he asked, 'that bring out the vanity in a man?'

'Search me.' Jack did shoulder-swaggerings and turned down the brim of his hat. 'But do I look the business, or what?'

'As handsome as. Now, you do remember everything I whispered to you?'

'Of course. I'm Bill Winkie, private eye and—'

'Save it 'til it's needed; follow me.'

'Ah no,' said Jack. 'I'm the detective, you're the detective's bear, *you* follow *me*.'

'Sweet as,' said Eddie, scowling as he said it. 'So which way do we go?'

'Right up the front steps and in through the big front door.'

'Wrong,' said the bear. 'Around the back and in by the tradesmen's entrance.'

'Oh, come on now.'

'Just do it the way I told you, please.'

'Well, as you ask so nicely. Then let's go.'

And so they went.

The tradesmen's entrance was in an alleyway. This was litter-strewn and unappealing. Jack turned up his nose.

'Knock at the door,' said Eddie, 'and do your stuff. Make me proud of you, eh?'

'Leave it to Bill,' said Jack, a-knocking at the door.

There was a bit of a wait. And then a bit more. Then there was a longer wait and then a longer one still.

'I don't much care for this waiting,' said Jack.

'It's second nature to me,' said Eddie. 'When I'm not getting drunk, or being thrown around, I'm generally waiting for something or other.'

They waited some more and then Jack knocked again.

This time there was no wait at all; the tradesmen's entrance door croaked open.

Jack was taken somewhat aback. 'It croaked,' he whispered to Eddie, 'rather than creaked. Why did it do that?'

'Who's on the knock at this fine tower block?' asked a very strange voice indeed.

Jack looked in and then Jack stepped back. Smartly, and right onto Eddie.

'Ow!' howled Eddie. 'Get off me.'

'Big frog!' howled Jack, getting off Eddie.

'Yes?' said the big frog. 'Bright as fizziness. What is the nature of your business?'

Jack chewed upon his upper lip. The big frog was a very big frog indeed, easily equal to himself in height, standing erect upon its long rear legs and all decked out in a rather spiffing tailcoat and wing-collared shirt, replete with a dashing spotty bow-tie. The big frog appeared to be made out of rubber.

'I am the concierge,' said the big frog. 'And you are a gormster, I perceive. Hurry up and take your leave.'

'Winkie,' said Jack. 'Bill Winkie, private eye. Here upon the business of Mr Anders.'

'Mr Anders, maker of toys, greatly beloved of girls and boys?'

'Do you know of another Mr Anders?'

The big frog licked his lips with an over-long flycatcher of a tongue. 'Naturally I know several,' it said, taking in a deep breath. 'Panders Anders, the pale poom runner, right royal rascal and son of a gunner. Ackabar Anders, the starlight meanderer, profligate poltroon, feckless philanderer. And of course, Anthony Anders the third, tall as a trouser and beaked as a bird.'

'What is all this?' Jack muttered in Eddie's direction. 'He speaks in rhyme.'

'Rhymey Frog,' said Eddie. 'Haven't you ever met a rhymey frog before?'

Jack shook his head. The rhymey frog prepared to slam shut the door.

'Ah, no,' said Jack, putting his foot in it. 'Very important business. Mr Anders, and all that. Kindly let us in.'

'Us?' said the frog. 'There's only one of you I see. Or do you wear a crown and use the royal "We"?'

'There's me and my bear,' said Jack, waving a hand towards Eddie.

'Hi,' said Eddie, waggling a paw. 'Pleased to meet you, I am sure.'

'I shall need from you a letter of introduction. To admit your entrance without any further interruption.'

'That didn't scan too well, did it?' said Jack.

'It's all in the enunciation,' replied the frog in a haughty tone. 'But to the crude, uncultured ear, even champagne sounds like beer.'

'My apologies,' said Jack. 'Now please let us in or I will be forced to shoot you dead.'

'No,' said Eddie. 'That's not what we agreed.'

'Yes, but—'

'Show him the money,' said Eddie.

'Money?' the frog said. 'Coin of gold? It's often used to bribe, I'm told.'

'Then you were told correctly.' Jack held out the few meagre coins that Eddie had given to him. The rhymey frog blinked bulbous and disdainful eyes at them.

'I know it's not much,' said Jack. 'But consider it a token down-payment. I have come to collect certain sums owing to Mr Anders. I am to collect them from the penthouse apartment of the late Humpty Dumpty. I am instructed by Mr Anders to furnish you with a percentage of these certain sums, to accommodate you for any inconvenience caused.'

'Well remembered,' whispered Eddie.

'Well . . .' said the frog, thoughtfully.

'Or I could come back later,' said Jack. 'Perhaps when you've gone off shift and the night porter is on.'

'Welcome, friend,' said the frog, swinging wide the door and snatching the coins from Jack's outstretched hand.

The big frog took the stairs in leaps and bounds. Jack and Eddie took the lift.

'Rhymey frog!' said Jack. 'What is *that* all about?'

'Have you never heard of energetic engineering?' Eddie asked.

'Are you sure you've got that right?' Jack asked.

'Of course. Well, possibly. Well, probably. It's something to do with very busy work being done in toy factories.'

'There's a great deal of that; I can vouch for it,' said Jack, having a fiddle with the lift buttons.

'Please don't touch those,' said Eddie.

'But it's the first time I've ever travelled in a posh lift like this. Can we stop at all the floors?'

'No,' said Eddie. 'But, as I was saying, energetic engineering. Busy busy busy. It's been known to drive men mad. And mad men make mistakes. Rhymey frogs, fluffy trains, grumpy clocks, frank chickens.'

'Don't they just get scrapped?'

'Not when they amuse Mr Anders.'

'I'd like to meet this Mr Anders.' The lift came to a standstill. 'We're here,' said Jack.

'No we're not. You pressed one of the buttons. I told you not to. Press the penthouse one. Let's see if we can beat that frog.'

They didn't beat that frog. He was waiting at the penthouse door, a bunch of shiny keys in his froggy fingers. He looked a little puffed, though. But then, frogs often do.

'The policemen stuck all this tape across the door,' said the frog. 'They said they'd come back some time soon, to stick on a whole lot more.'

Jack ran his finger along the strip of brightly coloured tape and licked his fingertip. 'Yellow berry,' he said. 'Very tasty.'

'Doing that's illegal,' said the frog.

'It is,' agreed Eddie. 'Yellow berry? Are you sure?'

Jack broke off a strip of the strip and stuck it into his mouth.

'Illegal,' said the frog once more.

'You're not rhyming that with anything,' said Jack, making lip-smacking sounds.

'That's probably because he lives in mortal dread of the police,' said Eddie. 'Them dishing out such vicious on-the-spot punishments to offenders and everything.'

'Quite so,' said Jack, hastily wiping his mouth. 'So, shall we go inside? Attend to the financial business of the important Mr Anders? Kindly open up the door, Mr Froggie.'

Mr Froggie handed Jack the keys. 'I'd rather you did it,' he said. 'I'd prefer not to touch the tape.'

Jack glanced at Eddie.

Eddie shrugged. 'We're here now,' he said. 'Might as well do it.'

Jack pulled away the yellow-berry-flavoured tape. 'Which key?' he asked the frog.

'Any one of them will do; they're all the same and none are new.'

'That's not very secure, is it?'

'No one who's not official ever gets past me. I'm as vigilant as it's frog-manly possible to be.'

'You can't argue with that,' Eddie said. 'Open up the door, Bill.'

'I'm in charge here.' The door to the late Humpty's apartment was a richly panelled silkwood affair, decorated with all manner of carved reliefs – mostly, it appeared, of fat folk falling from walls. Jack eyed the door appreciatively. This was a proper door. A proper rich person's door. The kind of door that he'd have for himself as soon as he'd made his fortune.

Jack turned a key and opened up the door. 'You wait here,' he told the frog as he and Eddie slipped into Humpty's penthouse. 'We won't be long.'

'Perhaps I ought to come inside,' said the frog. 'It's best that I, in there, should be. In the interests of security.'

Jack slammed the door upon him.

'Well, we're in,' said Eddie. 'Although it could have been easier.'

'I thought I did very well. I'm new to this detective game. Remember it was *me* who got us in. Not you.'

'I seem to recall that you were all for shooting the frog.'

'I was bluffing.'

'Right,' said Eddie. 'To work.'

'Right,' said Jack. 'I'll have a look around. See if I can find some clues.'

'No,' said Eddie, 'you just sit down quietly and don't touch anything. *I'll* search for clues.'

'Yes, but—'

'Jack,' said Eddie, '*I'm* the detective. You're my partner. *Junior* partner.'

Jack shrugged. 'Please yourself then.'

Humpty Dumpty's penthouse was opulent. It was palatial, it was magniloquent. It was eggy.

There were egg motifs on the richly woven carpets and the elegant silk wallpaper and on the fabrics of the furniture and even on the switches for the lights. Jack tinkered with one of these and lit up a gorgeous chandelier that hung overhead. It was festooned with hundreds of crystal eggs. Jack shook his head and whistled.

So this was what being rich was all about, was it? Then he'd have some of this. But not exactly like this. There was something all-too-much about this. It was the scale, Jack thought, thoughtfully. Where Tinto's bar had been too small for him, everything here was much too big.

Jack sat himself down on a great golden chariot of a chair in the vestibule and stretched his hands to either side of him. He couldn't even reach to the chair's arms. This Humpty had evidently been a fellow of considerable substance. Positively gargantuan.

Jack watched Eddie as he went to work. The bear paced up and down, cocking his head to this side and the other, backing up, throwing himself forward onto his stomach, wriggling about.

'How are you doing?' called Jack.

'Would you mind opening the doors to the pool area for me?' said Eddie.

Jack hastened to oblige. It took considerable effort to heave back the enormous doors, but when this was done, it proved well worthwhile.

Jack found himself in the pool area. The pool itself was egg-shaped, which came as no surprise to Jack. It was mosaic-tiled all around and about and many of these tiles were elliptical.

The entire pool area was sheltered by a great stained-glass dome of cathedralesque proportions. Jack gawped up at it in wonder. There were no egg motifs to be found up there; rather, the whole was a profusion of multi-coloured flowers, wrought in thousands of delicate panes of glass. The sunlight, dancing through these many-hued panes, cast wistful patterns over the pool area and Jack was entranced. He had never seen anything quite so beautiful in all of his life.

The apex of the dome was an enormous stained-glass sunflower, its golden petals radiating out from a clear glass centre. Jack gave another whistle. He'd definitely have one of these roofs when he'd made his fortune.

Jack pushed back the brim of his fedora. The roof was stunningly beautiful. But there was something . . . something that jarred with him. Something that didn't seem entirely right. That appeared to be out of place. But what was it? Jack shrugged. What did he, Jack, know about stained-glass roofs? Nothing, was the answer to that. The roof was beautiful and that was all there was to it.

The beauty of the roof above, however, was somewhat marred by that which lay directly below it. Specifically, in the pool, or more specifically still, on the surface of the pool's water: a very nasty crusty-looking scum.

'So how *are* you doing?' Jack asked the ursine detective.

Eddie shook his tatty head. 'It's tricky,' he said. 'So many policemen's feet have trampled all around and about the place. But there's no evidence of a struggle. Humpty was bathing in the pool. The murderer took him by surprise.'

Jack peered down at the pool with its nasty crusty scum. 'Boiled him?' he asked. 'How?'

'Not sure yet,' said Eddie. 'My first thoughts were that the murderer simply turned up the pool's heating system. But that would have taken time and Humpty would have climbed out when the water got too hot.'

'Perhaps Humpty was drugged or asleep in the pool.'

'That's not how it was done. I'll tell you how it was done as soon as I've figured it out.'

'Hm,' said Jack, putting a thumb and forefinger to his chin and giving it a squeeze.

Eddie paced around the pool, did some more head cocking, some more backing away and then some more throwing himself down onto his stomach and wriggling about. Then he stood up and began to frantically beat at his head.

'What *are* you doing?' Jack asked.

'Rearranging my brain cells,' said Eddie. 'Vigorous beating peps them up no end.'

'Your head's full of sawdust.'

'I know my own business best.'

'I'll leave you to it then.' Jack sat down on a poolside lounger. It was a most substantial poolside lounger, capable of accommodating, at the very least, a fat family. Possibly two. No, that would be silly, *one* fat family. And no more than that.

Jack swung to and fro on the lounger and looked all around and about. Around and about and up and down, then up again once more.

Eddie was down on his belly once again, leaning over the pool.

'What are you doing now?' Jack asked.

'Come and give me a hand, if you will.'

Jack swung out of the lounger.

'Take my legs,' said Eddie. 'Lower me down. But *don't* drop me in the water.'

'Okay. What have you seen?' Jack lowered Eddie over the edge.

'Eleven, twelve, thirteen,' said Eddie. 'Interesting. Pull me up, please.' Jack pulled Eddie up.

'See it?' said Eddie, pointing with a paw. 'The scum on the side of the pool. The pool water's lower than it should be. The scum has left traces, like beer does on the inside of a glass as you drink from it. There're thirteen separate lines going down. And it's thirteen days since Humpty was boiled. What do you make of that?'

'The pool water has dropped a little each day. Perhaps there's a leak.'

'The water would drain away steadily if there was a leak; there wouldn't be any lines.'

Jack shrugged. 'Evaporation,' he said. 'It's warm enough in here.'

'Not *that* warm. The stained-glass roof keeps direct sun-light out, as you can see.'

Jack looked up again. The roof looked the same as it had done before: stunningly beautiful, but not entirely *right*.

'Get me that rubber ring,' said Eddie. 'I want to get an overview from the middle of the pool.'

'You're going to float about in that scummy water?'

'*On*, not *in*.'

Jack brought over the rubber ring, put it into the pool and lifted Eddie onto it. 'Push me out,' said Eddie. Jack pushed him out.

'It's something very clever,' said Eddie, 'whatever it is.'

'Eddie,' said Jack, 'what was the exact time of death? Does anybody know?'

'Midday,' said Eddie. 'Mr Froggie was doing his rounds; he heard the scream.'

'Midday,' said Jack, thoughtfully. 'What's the time now, do you think?'

'I don't have a watch. Around that time, I suppose.'

'Eddie,' cried Jack, 'get out of the pool.'

'What?' said Eddie.

'Get out of the pool, quickly.'

'Look,' said Eddie, 'I'm the detective and although I appreciate you trying to help – no, strike that, actually I don't. I think that the best thing you could do is—'

'Bong!' went a clock, somewhere in the late Humpty's apartment.

'Eddie, get out of the pool. Row or something.'

'I'm not putting a paw in that scum.'

'Get out of the pool.'

BONG.

'What are you going on about?'

BONG.

'Eddie, quickly.'

'What?'

BONG.

'Hurry.'

'What?'

BONG

'Waaaaaaaaaaah!' Jack dived into the pool.

BONG.

'Have you gone completely insane?' called Eddie.

Jack struck out with a will.

BONG.

Jack floundered in the scummy water and grabbed the rubber ring.

BONG.

Jack floundered further and grabbed Eddie.

BONG.

Jack snatched Eddie from the ring.

BONG.

Jack swam fiercely and dragged Eddie to the edge of the pool.

BONG.

Jack hauled himself and Eddie out of the horrible water.

BONG.

A shaft of light swept down through the central portion of the stained-glass window. Through the eye of the great sunflower. Through the huge, clear lens. The magnified concentrated sunlight struck the water, causing an all-but-instantaneous effect. The water boiled and frothed. Viciously. Brutally. In a deadly, all-consuming maelstrom.

'Stone me,' said Eddie, from the safety of the poolside.

Jack spat Humpty scum, but didn't have much to say.

★

'Clever,' said Eddie, squeezing himself and oozing scum water from his seams. 'I did say clever. And *that was* clever. Clever and fiendish.'

The two were now in Humpty's kitchen; Jack was swathed in towels. Eddie ceased his squeezings and struggled to pour hot black coffee. 'I'd have been a goner there,' he said. 'I'd have cooked. I don't know what the effects would have been, but I'd bet I wouldn't have been Eddie Bear any more. Horrible thought. Thanks for saving me, Jack. You're as brave as.'

'No problems,' said Jack. 'Although I don't feel altogether too well. I think I swallowed some Dumpty.'

'It's been repeatedly boiled. It should be free of any contamination.'

'That doesn't make me feel a whole lot better.' Jack sipped at the coffee. 'And look at my trenchcoat and my fedora, ruined.'

'I'll see to it that you get brand-new ones, made to measure. Somehow. You saved my life. How did you work it out?'

'The stained-glass roof just didn't look right. I didn't see what it was at first. Then I realised that the centre of the sunflower at the very top of the dome was clear glass, and convex. A huge lens. And *sun* flower. And midday sun. It all sort of fell into place. I told you how I worked in the factory and the sun used to beat in through the glass roof and there was this one bit like a convex lens and how it used to burn me at midday.'

'I remember,' said Eddie. 'We'll make a detective out of you yet. So old Humpty was taking his regular midday dip and . . . whoosh.'

'What I don't get,' said Jack, 'is why the murderer didn't return and remove the lens?'

'Why should he bother? The job was done.'

'Because it's evidence. The police could surely trace the maker of the lens. *We* could, couldn't we? Do you want me to climb up there and get it down?'

'And how do you propose to do that? We're twenty-three storeys up and I can't see how you'd get to it from the inside. That dome is huge.'

'We'll leave it then,' said Jack.

'This is no ordinary murderer we're dealing with,' said Eddie. 'Mind you, it's the bunny that intrigues me the most.'

'Bunny?' said Jack. 'What bunny?'

'This bunny,' said Eddie. 'This bunny here. Eddie fumbled open the door of Humpty's fridge. It was a fridge of considerable dimensions. 'Mr Dumpty was a notable gourmand. That fat boy knew how to eat, believe me. Yet his fridge is completely empty, but for this. A single hollow chocolate bunny.'

Eddie took the dear little fellow up in his paws and gave it a shake. 'What do you make of that then, Jack?'

'Let's eat it,' said Jack. 'I'm starving.'

'I think it's probably evidence.'

'Let's eat it anyway. We can remember what it looked like.'

There came now a sudden beating at the apartment door. This beating was accompanied by shouts. These shouts were the shouts of policemen. 'Open up,' shouted these shouts. 'This is the police.'

'Oh dear,' said Eddie. 'I think Mr Froggie has done us wrong.'

'You talk to the policemen,' said Jack. 'I'm in a towel.'

'I think we should run, Jack. We're not supposed to be here. Gather up your wet clothes.'

'Yes, but.' Jack gathered up his wet clothes and his sodden fedora.

'Put on your wet clothes and hurry.'

'Yes, but.'

'Believe me, Jack, you really don't want to get involved with policemen.'

'All right,' said Jack, trying to struggle into his soggy trousers.

'Hurry,' counselled Eddie.
Policemen put their shoulders to the door.
And Jack took frantically to hurrying.

7

It is a fact well known to those who know it well that we can only truly know what we personally experience. Above and beyond that, it's all just guesswork and conjecture.

Of course, there are those who will take issue with this evident profundity. They will say, 'Ah, but what do we *really understand* by *truly know* and *personally experience*?' But to these issue takers we must say, 'Get a life and get a girlfriend.'

We really *can* only truly know what we personally experience. And when we experience something entirely new, something that we have never experienced before, it can come as something of a shock. And it can be hard at first to fully comprehend.

Jack, for instance, had never before heard a really big, expensive silkwood apartment door being smashed from its hinges. And so the sounds of its smashing were alien to his ears.

The fraboius grametting of the lock against its keep was positively malagrous in its percundity. The greebing and snattering was starkly blark.

And as for the spondabulous carapany that the broken door made as it struck the vestibule floor . . .

. . . the word phnargacious is hardly sufficient.

Rapantaderely phnargacious would be more accurate.

And as to what happened after this, it is probably all for the best that Jack neither heard nor saw any of it.

Laughing policemen bounced into the late Humpty's vestibule. They fairly bounced, and they 'ho ho ho'd' as they did so.

They were all jolly-jolly and all-over blue,
With big jolly bellies, a jollysome crew.
Their faces were jolly,
Their eyes jolly too.
And they wouldn't think twice,
About jolly-well knocking seven bells of blimey out of
you if you so much as looked at them in a funny way.
Because for all their jollity, they were a right bunch of
brutal, merciless, bullying . . .

And so on.

Which at least was how the rhymey frog would have put
it. But the rhymey frog did not accompany these jolly
laughing policemen into the apartment. Instead, they were
joined by a short and portly jolly red-faced being, composed,
it appeared, of perished rubber. He answered to the name of
Chief Inspector Wellington Bellis. But only to his superiors.

Mostly he answered only when called 'sir'.

For all his jolly red-facedness, Chief Inspector Bellis was
having a rough day. It is the nature of Chief Inspectors, no
matter where they are to be found, nor indeed upon which
day of the week they are found, to be having a rough day.

Chief Inspectors are *always* having a rough day.

It's a 'Chief Inspector thing'.

Chief Inspector Bellis was having a particularly rough day
on this particular day. Earlier, he had been called into the
presence of his superior, The Chief of All Police, the one
being that Bellis called 'sir', and torn off a strip (a strip of arm
on this occasion), upbraided (with the use of real braid) and
berated (which involved a genuine bee, a wooden rat, but
happily no ed).

The Chief of All Police wanted results. He wanted to
know why Bellis had not yet tracked down the murderer of
Humpty Dumpty. Although the Toy City press were selling
the populace the story that Humpty had committed suicide,
the police knew that it was Murder Most Foul, and
questions were being asked in very high places as to why
Bellis had not yet tracked down the murderer.

The Chief of All Police had handed Bellis a secret memo and Bellis had raised his perished eyebrows and dropped his perished jaw onto his perished chest. The memo contained most terrible news. And then the telephone had rung.

The Chief of All Police had handed the receiver to Bellis. 'There's a rhymey frog on the line,' he had said. 'Deal with it.'

And so here was Bellis, now having a *really* rough day, here to deal with it.

Bellis stood in the ruptured doorway puffing out his perished cheeks and making fists with his podgy, perished hands.

'Why?' he shouted. 'Why? Why? Why?'

'Ho ho ho and why what, sir?'

'Why, officer,' asked Bellis, 'did you break down the crubbin' door? I ordered you to wait until the rhymey frog went and got his spare set of keys.'

The laughing policeman made a troubled, though no less jolly-looking face. 'I . . . er . . . ha ha ha, was using my initiative, sir.'

Bellis scowled and shook his fists. 'Well, now we're in, I suppose. Go and arrest the malfeasant.'

'The *what*, sir?' the officer chuckled.

'The criminal, the intruder, the unlawful trespasser.'

'Which one of these do you want arrested first, sir?'

'Do you have a name?' asked Bellis, glaring upward daggers.

'Officer Chortle, sir. I'm a Special Constable. I've got my name printed on my back, see?'

The officer turned to display the name that made him special. Bellis kicked him hard in the backside. 'Go and arrest. It's what you do, isn't it? It's what you're for?'

'To uphold the law, using reasonable force when necessary, which, as you know, is always necessary, sir.' Officer Chortle saluted with his truncheon, bringing down a shower of crystal eggs from the chandelier.

'Then get to it. Bring me the offender. All of you, get to it!'

Police officers to the right and left of Bellis hastened to oblige.

'And don't break anything else.'

The police officers went about their business, leaving Bellis all alone in the vestibule, to listen to expensive things being broken by officers of the law.

Bellis recognised these sounds. These sounds weren't alien to his perished ears. He'd heard such sounds, and similar, many times before. The Chief Inspector sighed and shook his head and then delved into a perished pocket and brought out the secret memo. He read it once more and once more shook his head. This was bad, very bad. The day, already a rough day, looked like getting altogether rougher.

At length, and at breadth, the officers returned, downcast.

'Gone,' said Officer Chortle, with laughter in his voice. 'They've all gone, even the dressmaker.'

'Trespasser!' Bellis threw up his hands and made fists with them once more.

'You've dropped your piece of paper,' said Officer Chortle.

'Shut up!'

'Oh dear.' The rhymey frog peered in at the devastation. 'If you please, I've brought my keys.'

'Somewhat late,' said Bellis. 'The bird has flown.'

'Bird, too?' said Officer Chortle, a giggle escaping his lips.

'Shut up. Go downstairs and wait by the wagon. All of you. Now!'

The officers took their leave, laughing merrily as they did so and all but marching over the rhymey frog.

'Gone,' said Bellis. 'Escaped. Do you have any thoughts on this?'

The rhymey frog opened his big wide mouth and prepared to express his thoughts in an epic forty-verser.

'No,' said Bellis, raising once more the hands he had temporarily lowered. 'I do not wish to hear them. Speak to me only of the trespasser. And speak to me in prose, or I'll run you in and lock you up and have Officer Chortle do things to you that you'll never wish to recite. And he'll laugh all the time as he does them. Which always makes it that little more frightening, in my opinion. What do you think?'

The knees of the rhymey frog began to knock together. 'Tricky,' he said. 'Tricky, dicky.'

'Careful,' cautioned Bellis.

'It was a man.' The rhymey frog took to rolling his eyes. 'And men all look the same to me.'

'A *man* was here?' Bellis raised his eyebrows high.

'Your face all cracks when you do that,' said the frog. 'Mr Anders could fix that for you. With a stick and a brush and a small pot of glue.'

'I have no wish to bother Mr Anders,' said Bellis. 'Tell me about the man who was here. Anything. Anything at all.'

'He had a bear with him,' said the frog. 'A rotten old bear with mismatched eyes. And a big fat belly about this size.' The frog mimed the dimension. The Chief Inspector glared anew.

'No more rhyming! And I don't want to hear about some stupid teddy bear. A major crime has been committed here. One of the city's most notable elder citizens has been murdered.'

'The papers say it was suicide,' said the frog.

'You heard the scream!' shouted the Chief Inspector. '*You* reported the crime.'

'Oh yes,' said the rhymey frog. 'So I did. That was very public-spirited of me, wasn't it?'

Chief Inspector Bellis rocked upon his perished rubber heels. 'The trespasser was probably the murderer,' he said, 'because murderers always return to the scene of the crime.'

'Why?' asked the rhymey frog.

'Because it's a tradition, or an old charter, or something. Never mind why, they just do.'

The rhymey frog now began to tremble all over.

'Yes,' said Bellis. 'Exactly, he could have done for you too. I will have to ask you to accompany me to the station, where Officer Chortle will beat a statement out of you.'

'Oh no.' The rhymey frog was now all-a-quake.

'Then make it easy on yourself. Give me a detailed description of the man.'

'I don't know. I just don't know. All men look the same to me. I'm sorry.'

'All right,' said Bellis, 'never mind. Go off about your business.'

The rhymey frog looked all around and about. 'I'll get a dustpan and a brush, some paper and a quill. I'll list all the broken things and then I can send you the bill.'

There was a moment of silence. It was brief.

'I think I'll just go and have my lunch instead,' said the frog. And he turned to hop away.

And then he paused and then he turned back to Bellis. 'There is one thing,' he said. 'I don't know if it will be of any help.'

'Go on,' said Bellis.

'The murderer told me his name,' said the rhymey frog. 'His name is Bill Winkie.'

'There you go,' said Eddie Bear. 'They've all gone now. They've made a terrible mess, but they've gone.'

Jack stared around at the mess and then he stared down at Eddie. Jack's face was blue once more, but this time it had nothing to do with inferior headwear.

'F . . . f . . . fridge,' stammered Jack. 'W . . . why did w . . . we have to hide in the f . . . f . . . fridge?'

'Because it was the best place to hide,' said Eddie. 'The police neglected to look in it the first time they were here. It seemed a pretty safe bet to me that they wouldn't look in it this time either.'

'I'll die.' Jack shook from the frosted hairs on his head to the trembly toes on his feet. 'I'm f . . . f . . . frozen. You're not even s . . . s . . . shaking.'

'I'm a bear,' said Eddie, brightly. 'We bears don't feel the cold. Not even when we're as sodden as. If you know what I mean, and I'm sure that you do.'

Jack gathered his trenchcoat around himself. It was even colder than he was. 'I'm going home,' he managed to say. 'I've had enough of city life.'

'Don't be a quitter.' Eddie gave Jack's shaking leg an encouraging pat.

'I'm dying.'

'You'll thaw out. Hobble back to the pool area. It's nice and warm out there.'

Eddie led the way and Jack did the hobbling.

At length, and at quite some length it was, Jack was finally all thawed out, and pretty much dried out too. Throughout this lengthy process of thawing and drying, Jack maintained a brooding silence.

Eddie, being not a bear to cherish a silence, spent the period smiling encouragingly and doing cute little teddy-bearish things. Not that Eddie was capable of doing cute little teddy-bearish things with any degree of genuine commitment.

'So then,' said Eddie, when the time seemed right, 'shall we be off about our business?'

'You can,' said Jack. 'I'm leaving.'

'Oh no,' said Eddie. 'Don't say that. We're partners, Jack. You agreed. We shook on it and everything.'

'Maybe we did. But being with you is a dangerous business.'

'Yes, but danger is exciting. And you wanted some excitement in your life. Didn't you?'

Jack shrugged. The shoulders of his trenchcoat rose to his ears and then stayed there.

'Look at me,' said Jack. 'I'm a wreck. I'm starving and I'm cold and I'm broke, my fedora's ruined and my trenchcoat's all gone crisp.'

'It's a dry-clean-only,' said Eddie.

'A raincoat that's dry-clean only?'

'Bill Winkie would never have gone out in the rain wearing his trenchcoat.'

Jack shook his head.

'But it does look good on you. You're a born detective. Come on, perk up. I'll buy you lunch.'

'You don't have any money.'

'I've a penny or two.' Eddie patted at the pockets of his trenchcoat. Eddie's trenchcoat looked as good as new. He grinned painfully. 'I can wangle us some lunch at a chum of mine's. Stick with me, kidder. We'll succeed and you'll get all the fortune you came seeking.'

Jack shook his head dismally. 'You'll be better off without me,' he said. 'I'm nothing but bad luck. It's because I'm cursed. A farmer I met on the way to the city cursed me. He said, "I curse you Jack. May you never know wealth. May all that you wish for be denied you."'

'What a horrid man,' said Eddie. 'Why did he curse you like that?'

Jack shrugged again and this time his trenchcoat returned to his shoulders. 'Bad grace, I suppose. Just because I shot off his ear and made him jump into a pit full of spikes.'

'There's no pleasing some people,' said Eddie. 'But we're a team, you and me. And listen, Jack, I need you. I can't solve this case without you. Please don't run away. We did shake and you did give me your word.'

Jack managed one more shrug. 'All right,' he said. 'I did give you my word. I will stay until you've solved the case. But then I'm moving on. There will be another city somewhere. Perhaps I'll find my fortune there.'

'Another city?' Eddie made a thoughtful face. 'I wonder if there *is* another city.'

'Bound to be,' said Jack.

'Well, perhaps. But I find such thoughts as fearsome as. I'll stick with what I know. And what I know is *this* city.'

'Feed me in this city,' said Jack. 'Feed me now.'

'Right,' said Eddie. 'Let's go. Oh, and we'll take that

hollow chocolate bunny with us. That's a clue if ever there was one. It might have fingerprints or something.'

'Ah,' said Jack, and he made a certain face.

'Ah?' said Eddie. 'And what is the meaning of that certain face you're making?'

'About the bunny.'

'What about the bunny?'

'I ate it,' said Jack. 'While we were in the fridge. I was so hungry. And there were all these alien sounds. These malagrous gramettings and really spondabulous carapany.'

'You *ate* the evidence?' said Eddie. 'Well, that's a new one.'

'I'm sorry, but I was starving.'

A sudden high-pitched shriek caused Jack and Eddie to turn their heads. In the doorway to the pool area stood the rhymey frog, dustpan in one hand, brush in the other.

The rhymey frog shrieked once again, cried 'Eeek it's the murderer!', dropped his dustpan and his brush and hopped away at speed.

Jack looked at Eddie.

And Eddie looked at Jack.

'What did he mean by *that*?' asked Jack.

'Ah,' said Eddie. 'You didn't hear everything that went on while we were hiding in the fridge, did you?'

'No,' said Jack. 'Only the alien sounds. I wolfed down the bunny and stuck my hands over my ears after that. Why did the frog just call me a murderer?'

'Well . . .' Eddie made a certain face of his own. 'I think it better if I explain that to you over lunch.'

Eddie followed the direction taken by the frog.

'Hold on,' cried Jack. 'Tell me what's going on.'

'It's no big deal. Let's do lunch.'

'It *is* a big deal. Come back.'

'I'll tell you on the way, then.' Eddie reached the vestibule.

'Tell me now,' said Jack, scooping Eddie up and holding him out at arm's length.

'Don't do that to me.' Eddie struggled. 'It's undignified; let me down.'

'Tell me what's going on. Tell me now.' Jack shook Eddie all about.

'No.' Eddie struggled some more. 'Put me down.'

'I won't put you down until you've told me.'

'Hold on, Jack, what's that?' Eddie pointed.

'Don't try to distract me. Answer my question.'

'No, there's something there on the floor. It wasn't there when we came in.'

'It's a broken door,' said Jack, shaking Eddie ever more violently.

'No, the paper. Help. Stop. Let me down.'

Jack let Eddie down.

'There,' said Eddie, wobbling on his paws. 'Pick that up, Jack. What is that?'

'It's just a piece of paper.' Jack picked it up and handed it to Eddie. 'Now tell me why the frog called me a murderer.'

'In a minute. Oh dear me!' Eddie let the piece of paper fall from his paws.

'What does it say?' Jack asked. 'What does it say on the paper?'

'It says,' said Eddie, and he paused, 'that Little Boy Blue has been murdered.'

8

Jack, who was feeling somewhat down, perked somewhat up when he was once more behind the wheel of Bill's splendid automobile. But as he swung this wheel around, the pendulum of his mood swung with it. 'About this business of the frog calling me a murderer.' Jack brrrmed the clockwork engine.

'Forget all that.' Eddie, standing on the passenger seat, pointed through the windscreen. 'I think he was just a bit upset about the door getting broken and the apartment getting ransacked and everything. Don't let it upset you, Jack. Cast it from your mind. It's as irrelevant as. Turn right, please.'

'Hm,' went Jack. 'Then what about this second murder?' Jack turned right rather sharply, causing a clockwork cyclist to spill from his clockwork cycle.

'Careful,' said Eddie. 'Please be careful. We don't want to draw any more attention to ourselves.'

'Any *more* attention?'

'Just drive, Jack. First on the left here.'

Jack took the first on the left on the two left wheels of the car.

'But what *about* this second murder?' Jack asked once more when the car was back on four wheels and spinning merrily along. 'Tell me this, Eddie. Humpty Dumpty and Little Boy Blue. They were – how shall I put this?'

'Meatheads?' Eddie suggested.

'Men,' said Jack. 'They were men, rather than toys.'

'The old rich,' said Eddie, covering his face with his paws as toy pedestrians scattered before the on-rushing motorcar.

'You won't find many of your race here in Toy City. But those you will find are generally rich.'

'On the fortunes they made from royalties on their nursery rhymes.'

'Like I told you, yes. Look out!'

'Look out at *what*?' There was a clattering of tinplate against tinplate and something colourful mangled under the wheels. 'What *was* that?' Jack asked Eddie.

'Only a clockwork clown,' said the bear. 'He's a bit mashed-up, but I think he'll be all right. I've never cared much for clowns myself. How about you, Jack?'

'I don't like them,' said Jack, and drove on.

Shortly, however, the clockwork motor ran down and Jack was forced to get out and rewind the car.

Then Jack drove on some more.

'So what *about* this second murder?' Jack asked once again. 'Do you have any theories?'

'We haven't visited the crime scene yet. We'll get some lunch first and see about fixing you up with a disguise.'

'Disguise?' Jack asked. 'Why do I need a disguise?'

'Trust me,' said Eddie. 'You *do* need a disguise.'

At Eddie's bidding, Jack brought Bill's car to a wheel-shrieking halt, which raised an impressive shower of sparks that Eddie wasn't impressed by.

'You've worn out the tyres,' he told Jack.

'Sorry,' said Jack. 'So where are we?'

'At my chum Wibbly's.'

'And Wibbly runs a restaurant?' Jack peered out through the windscreen. They were not in the swankiest part of town. The buildings, although constructed in the vernacular Alphabet brick that typified the architecture of Toy City, had that faded, tired look to them, which told Jack that this wasn't one of the better neighbourhoods.

Jack made disdainful sniffings with his nose. 'Not a gourmet restaurant then? Do you not have any posh, rich friends, Eddie?'

The bear did not dignify this with a reply.

'Sorry,' said Jack, once again. 'So what does your chum Wibbly do?'

'Well.' Eddie pushed open the passenger door. 'He used to be a professional wobbler, but since the accident, he doesn't do much of anything.'

Jack climbed from the car and leaned upon the bonnet. 'But he does have food in his fridge?'

'Fridge?' Eddie rolled his button eyes, which really had to be seen to be believed. 'Just follow me, Jack. And when you meet Wibbly, try not to look shocked by his appearance.'

'This sounds promising,' said Jack, and he followed Eddie.

Wibbly inhabited a basement flat, but of course it wasn't referred to as a basement flat. No one who actually lives in a basement flat ever refers to it as a basement flat. It's just not done. People who live in basement flats refer to their flats as *garden* flats. So Wibbly lived in a *garden* flat. Though without a garden. Or indeed, any windows.

Which made it a cellar, really.

The cellar steps had been boarded over to form a steep wooden ramp. Jack struggled down this, attempting to maintain his balance. Eddie gave up the unequal struggle and simply tumbled to the bottom.

Jack helped Eddie up. 'It doesn't smell too good down here. Somewhat ripe, shall we say.'

'Just be polite,' said Eddie. 'Wibbly is my friend. And please try not to look shocked when you see him.'

'Trust *me*,' said Jack. 'Would *I* let you down?'

'Knock at the knocker.'

'You're nearest,' said Jack.

The door was low, the knocker was low. Eddie knocked at the knocker.

Knock knock knock, went Eddie Bear. 'Just smile and be polite,' he said to Jack.

'Just trust me. I won't let you down.'

From beyond the door came creaking sounds, and sounds

that were, for the most part, new to Jack. He recognised the basic creakings, but the subtle nuances of the scranchings and the endulating shugs had him cocking his head upon one side.

'Don't do that,' said Eddie. 'It makes you look like a complete gormster.'

'Sorry,' said Jack, and he straightened his neck.

'And be polite.'

'I will. I promise.'

The door eased open a crack and a beady eye peeped out.

'Wibbly,' said Eddie Bear.

'Eddie Bear,' said Wibbly.

Wibbly swung wide the door.

'Aaaagh!' screamed Jack. 'It's a monster.'

Jack was counselled to stay out of sight whilst Eddie engaged in sensitive negotiations through the letterbox. Much emphasis was put on the fact that Jack was a bumpkin from out of town, all but bereft of intelligence and given to sudden unexpected outbursts. But he was a harmless, simple soul, whom Eddie had taken under his wing.

Out of sight, Jack stewed over this. But the thought of stew made him ever more hungry. And so he suffered in silence.

Presently Wibbly, brought almost to the point of tears by Eddie's pleas for mercy on behalf of the poor simpleton, allowed the two of them in.

Eddie made Jack promise once more to be polite.

Jack made Eddie go first.

The 'sub-level' apartment – apparently Wibbly preferred this term to 'cellar' – was 'economically furnished'. Which is to say that there wasn't much furniture at all.

There weren't any chairs, but then, why would there have been? Wibbly couldn't sit down.

Wibbly was one of those wibbly wobbly toys with legless, convex bottom portions, filled up with lead shot that could be endlessly battered backwards and forwards, only to roll upright again and again and again.

Until they finally broke.

It wasn't easy to break them, as they were made of stern and durable stuff. But a child has a lot of time on its hands. And a determined child can break anything, even an anvil, if he or she is determined enough.

Wibbly still wobbled and wouldn't fall down.

But he lacked for a lot of his head.

He possessed a degree of face, located on the left-hand side. But much of his head was merely void. He had a dangling eye and a row of exposed teeth. He was not a thing of joy to gaze upon.

'Wibbly, this is Jack,' said Eddie. 'Say hello to Wibbly, Jack.'

Jack made the face of a simpleton and did that thing with his hands that people do when impersonating simpletons, that thing which is no longer considered politically correct, but which people still do anyway, because it makes other people laugh. Particularly when the doer and the viewers have all had a few drinks.

'What a complete gormster,' said Wibbly. 'Looks like he's been taking a swim in that dry-clean-only trenchcoat. Why did you bring him here, Eddie?'

Jack looked on in morbid fascination as the exposed teeth rose and fell and half a tongue waggled between them. How could this thing speak? How could it move? It was all but hollow. Jack shook his head. There was some big secret here, in this strange city. Some *big* secret.

Mr Anders, the kindly, loveable white-haired old toy-maker, had to be the brains behind it all. He had to be the one who held the Big Secret. Jack wondered whether Mr Anders might be looking for an apprentice. Working for him and learning the Big Secret would be infinitely preferable to knocking about in dark cellars, conversing with fractured wobbly men and having to impersonate a dullard.

Infinitely preferable!

'He's Bill's cousin,' said Eddie, smiling towards Jack. 'I'm looking after him while Bill's on his holidays.'

'Holidays?' said Wibbly, revolving on his axis, which afforded Jack a view of his all–but–hollow head. 'The word on the street is—'

'I don't care what the word on the street is.' Eddie tried to fold his arms, but, as ever, failed. 'Bill will be back. But until he is, I'm dealing with his case. And Jack here is helping me.'

'Just what this city needs, another Jack.' Wibbly wobbled (but he didn't fall down).

'What of this?' asked Jack.

'The city does suffer from a surfeit of Jacks,' Eddie explained. 'There's a Jack B. Nimble, and Jack of Jack and Jill, and Jack Spratt.'

'And Little Jack Horner,' said Wibbly.

'And Big Jack Black,' said Eddie.

'Who's Big Jack Black?' asked Jack.

'Another Preadolescent Poetic Personality.' Eddie sat down on Wibbly's floor.

'Well, I've never heard of him.'

'Of course you haven't. Because he never got famous. He's one of the sorry few meatheads whose nursery rhymes never caught on.'

Jack did sniffings. 'So why did Big Jack Black's rhyme never catch on?' he asked.

Wibbly chuckled loudly. The sound echoed up from his hollow belly and, had there been windows, would surely have rattled them. 'Recite it, Eddie,' he said to the bear. 'You can remember it, can't you?'

'I think so,' said Eddie. 'It goes like this:
'Big Jack Black
'Lived in a sack,
'Lived in a sack did he.
'He dined upon cripples,
'And little boys' nipples,
'Served upon toast for his tea.'

' 'Nuff said, I think,' said Wibbly.

Jack shook his head once more and his stomach grumbled loudly.

'Nice grumbling.' Wibbly offered Jack half a smile, for it was all he possessed. 'Your belly's as empty as my own. I generally have a bucket or two of lead shot at this time of day. Perhaps you'd care to join me?'

'I don't think that would agree with my digestion,' said Jack.

'He's fussy. For a loon,' said Wibbly.

'Don't wind the lad up, Wibbly,' said Eddie. 'Give him some bread and milk or something.'

'Anything edible will do,' said Jack.

Wibbly had some bread, which was not altogether hard, if you left the crusts. And some milk that wasn't altogether evil-smelling, if you didn't smell it too closely. And even some cradberry jam that wasn't altogether unspeakable, if you didn't speak about it and took the trouble to scrape the fur off the top.

Jack, who had now reached the point where he was prepared to eat almost anything, ate almost everything. With relish.

But without relish, as there wasn't any relish.

Eddie ate what was left of the jam. Including the furry bits. 'I don't know what it is about jam,' he said, wiping a paw over his now jammy face. 'I can't stand honey, but I do love jam.'

'Nonconformist,' said Wibbly, ladling lead shot in through the hole in his head. 'So what have you really come for, Eddie? It wasn't just for a free lunch.'

'Well, it *was*.' Eddie had his paw now stuck in the jam pot. 'But it was also for a bit of information and a small favour or two.'

'That's what friends are for,' said Wibbly.

Eddie smiled. And struggled.

'To ponce off,' said Wibbly.

'Oh, come on, Wibbly.' Eddie now fought to free his paw. 'Remember that it was Bill who found you this place and built you the ramp down the stairs and . . .'

'Yes, all right,' said Wibbly. 'And I look after his dodgy gear and everything.'

'You store certain sensitive items.' Eddie rolled around on the floor, fighting with the jam pot. Jack, who could bear no more of it, eased out Eddie's paw and helped him back to his feet.

'Thanks,' said Eddie. 'Friendship, see.'

'Dullards don't count,' said Wibbly. 'Dullards will befriend anyone who feeds them. But go on, what do you want?'

'A disguise for the dullard.'

'What?' said Jack. 'This disguise business again. I like the trenchcoat and the fedora.'

'You're going under cover. You need a disguise.'

'I don't want a disguise.'

'He doesn't want a disguise,' said Wibbly.

'Thank you,' said Jack.

'He wants a smack,' said Wibbly. 'Shall I give him one? I used to be red-hot at head-butts. But, you know how it is.'

'I *don't* want a disguise,' said Jack once again.

'He *does* want a disguise,' said Eddie. 'From Bill's trunk.'

'He'd look good as a clown,' said Wibbly with another hollow chuckle.

'I thought, a whore,' said Eddie.

'*What?*' said Jack.

'Only joking,' said Eddie. 'Actually, I thought you'd look best as a gentleman.'

'A gentleman?' Jack preened at his trenchcoat lapels. 'I like the sound of that. Will I have a dandy cane and an eyeglass and everything?'

'The dullard is truly a dullard,' said Wibbly, chuckling once again.

'I said, a gentleman,' said Eddie, 'not a fop, although—' He winked at Wibbly. Wibbly winked back with his dangling eye. It wasn't a pretty sight.

'Okay,' said the wobbly one. 'I'll get him kitted out from the trunk. What else did you want, Eddie?'

Eddie looked up at Jack. 'It's a personal matter,' he said. 'We can discuss it whilst Jack is changing.'

'Follow me then, Jack,' said Wibbly. And he led Jack from the room, his convex bottom making sounds upon the floor that Jack now recognised.

Wibbly returned presently to the company of Eddie, who spoke to him in hushed and urgent tones.

Presently still, Jack returned to the company of Wibbly and Eddie, was soundly mocked and laughed at for his choice of costume and was then led from the room once more by Wibbly.

Presently presently still, Wibbly returned to the company of Eddie, in the company of Jack, who now cut something of a dash. Not to say a sprint. Or even a full-pelt run.

'Natty,' said Eddie. 'As natty as. Give us a twirl then, Jack.'

'Pretty smooth, eh?' said he.

Jack looked more than pretty smooth. Jack looked truly magnificent. He wore the costume of a dandy: a pale pink frock-coat, with quilted lapels and ruffled cuffs; a cloth-of-gold waistcoat with bright jewelled buttons; white silk stockings, fastened at the knees, beneath red velvet pantaloons. Buckled shoes and a natty cravat completed this pretty-as-a-picture.

'He'll certainly be noticed,' said Wibbly.

'That's the intention,' said Eddie.

'Oh,' said Jack. 'Is it? I thought the disguise was for undercover work.'

'I'll explain everything to you on the way.'

'I wish you luck,' said Wibbly. 'Shall I look after the trenchcoat and fedora and whatnots?'

'We'll take them with us,' said Jack.

'We will,' said Eddie. 'Thanks for everything, my friend.'

Wibbly smiled and wobbled.

But he still didn't fall down.

★

'I didn't like him at all,' said Jack, back at the wheel of the car. 'He's a very scary individual.'

'I think he's very level-headed, considering he only has half a head to be level with. I wonder how well you'd get on with only half a head.'

'I'd be dead,' said Jack. 'And better off that way.'

'Just drive the car, Jack.'

'To the crime scene?'

'I'll point the way, and promise me you'll drive carefully this time.'

'I promise you,' said Jack, putting his buckle-shoed foot down hard.

9

For those who are unacquainted with the career of Little Boy Blue subsequent to his period of employment as a somnambulant shepherd, a period notable only for his inactivity, exemplified by his famous haystack slumberings, which permitted his untended sheep to carouse in the meadows whilst his cows laid pats amongst the corn; a brief history follows.

According to his best-selling autobiography, *I May be Blue, but I'm Always in the Black*, his rags-to-riches rise was an overnight affair, with his self-penned rhyme going straight into the charts at Number One, toppling Mary Mary, who had held the position for fourteen consecutive weeks.

This is not altogether true, firstly because Mary Mary did not achieve her own fame until several years later, and secondly because Boy Blue did *not* write his own lyrics.

They were the work of a professional rhymester by the name of Wheatley Porterman, whose distinctive lyrical style can be discerned in several other 'self-penned' classics of the genre, *Georgie Porgie, pudding and pie* and *There was an old woman who lived in a shoe* (the house version), to name but two.

Wheatley Porterman's gift was for identifying social problems, which he set in verse that touched the public's imagination, in the case of Boy Blue, the scandal of child labour in rural areas which drove underage shepherds to exhaustion.

With *Georgie Porgie*, it was sexual harassment in the play-ground, by teachers against schoolgirls, Porgie being an overweight geography teacher whose notorious behaviour had previously gone unreported, due to his connections in high places.

Regarding *There was an old woman who lived in a shoe*, Wheatley's finger was once more unerringly upon the button of the public conscience. Whether there actually *was* an old woman who lived in a shoe and had so many children that she didn't know what to do remains in some doubt. Wheatley asserted that she was allegorical: a cipher, or symbol, for the hideous overcrowding in certain inner city areas.

A consultation with the curator of *The Hall of Nearly All the Records* discloses that the rhyme is registered as the 'exclusive property of Old Woman Inc.', the chairman and sole shareholder in Old Woman Inc. being one W. Porterman, Esq.

But be this all as it may (and well may it all be too), Little Boy Blue, either in partnership with Wheatley, or under contract to him, claimed to have written the rhyme himself. And a world which didn't care much either way, but appreciated celebrity for the sake of celebrity alone, took his claims at face value.

Within weeks of sleeping rough beneath haystacks and smelling strongly of sheep dung, the Boy had made it to the big time. His trademark shepherd's smock, now blue silk, with pearls upon the cuffs, was adopted as *the* fashion look of the year (blue, as ever, being the new black, when some other colour isn't having its turn).

His establishment of an exclusive haute couture fashion house, *Oh Boy!*, was inevitable. In less time, it seemed, than it took to shake a crook at a scurrying lamb, Boy Blue found himself lionised by the cream of Toy City Society. Facsimiles of his famous portrait, *The Blue Boy*, still hang in many homes.

And in Toy City, blue is still the new black.

All of the foregoing Eddie passed on to Jack as Jack passed through the streets of Toy City – rather more speedily than Eddie cared for.

'Fashion House, eh?' said Jack, swerving, to Eddie's relief, around a number of teddies who were crossing the road. 'The fashion in my town was for grey overalls. That's all the workers ever wore. And as all the townsfolk were workers, that's all anyone ever wore.'

'You weren't wearing grey overalls when I met you,' Eddie observed.

Jack laughed. 'I traded them in at a farm I passed by, in exchange for a new set of clothes, although the cap was somewhat inferior. The farmer was convinced that grey overalls must be the very height of town fashion, seeing as all the town dwellers he'd ever met wore them.'

'This wasn't the same farmer whose ear you shot off?'

'That was an accident. But no, that wasn't him.'

'Hey, look,' said Eddie. 'Up ahead. Stop the car here, Jack.'

Jack looked up ahead and then he stopped the car. Up ahead was blocked by a heavy police presence. A cordon stretched across the road. Laughing policemen held back a crowd of on-looking toys, a crowd that *cooed* and *my-oh-my*'d and peered up at the façade of *Oh Boy!*.

'Policemen?' Jack asked. 'They look very jolly.'

'Don't be fooled by that,' said Eddie. 'They won't bother you, if you do *exactly* as I tell you.' And Eddie went on to explain to Jack exactly what he was to do.

And Jack, having listened, smiled broadly. 'And I will actually get away with doing *that*?' he asked.

'You certainly will,' said Eddie. 'And the more you do it, the more you'll get away with it.'

'Right then,' said Jack. 'And what will you be doing, while I'm doing what I'll be doing?'

'I'll be doing my job,' said Eddie. 'Examining the crime scene for clues.'

'Okay, then. Let's get on with it.'

The façade of *Oh Boy!* was something in itself. It was a triumph. A triumph of bad taste.

Why it is that bad taste always triumphs over good is one

of those things that scholars love to debate, when they don't have anything better to do, such as getting a life and a girlfriend.

Is there actually such a thing as 'good taste'? they debate. Or 'Is it all not merely subjective?'

Well, of course there is such a thing as good taste! Some things actually *are* better than other things, and some people are capable of making the distinction.

But . . .

Bad taste will always ultimately triumph over good taste, because bad taste has more financial backing. There is far more profit to be made from selling cheap and nasty products, at a big mark-up, than selling quality items at a small mark-up. And you can always produce far more cheap and nasty items far more quickly than you can produce quality items. Far more.

And, as every successful dictator knows, it's far easier to convince a thousand people en masse of a bad idea, than it is to convince a single individual. It's a herd thing.

Or a flock thing.

Flocks are controlled by a single shepherd.

Like Little Boy Blue, for instance.

Peering over the low heads of the toy folk and the higher heads of the policemen, Jack stared up at the façade of *Oh Boy!*. It was a regular eyesore: big and brash and in-your-face gaudy, smothered in flashing neon that brought up the outline of a leaping lamb here and a snorting shepherd there, in less-than-modest many-times-life-size which simply screamed 'Success!'

'Very tasteful,' said Jack.

'It's as foul as,' said Eddie. 'You've no taste, Jack.'

'Oh yes I have,' said Jack. 'My taste is for wealth. And if this is the taste of the wealthy, it's tasteful enough for me.'

'Curiously, I can't argue with that,' said Eddie. 'Go on then, Jack, do your stuff.'

'Okey dokey.' Jack raised his chin, puffed out his chest, straightened the ruffles on his cuffs, dusted down his quilted lapels and then swaggered forward, shouting, 'Make way, peasants,' in a loud and haughty tone.

Toy folk turned and stared. Those who had faces capable of expression glared somewhat too. But they cowered back and cleared a path before the tall and well-dressed swaggering shouter.

'That's it, out of my way.' Jack swaggered onwards, with Eddie following behind.

Policemen loomed, big and blue and jolly, but clearly now to Jack no laughing matter at all. There was something all too menacing about the way they curled their smiling rubber lips towards the shouting swaggerer and fingered their over-large truncheons.

Jack swallowed back the lump which had suddenly risen in his throat. 'Stand aside there,' he told them. 'I am a patron of this establishment. Step aside lively, oafs. Go on now.'

Officer Chortle, for as chance would have it, it was he, stared at Jack eye to eye. 'What do *you* want?' he asked, in the tone known as surly. Though naturally he smiled as he asked it.

'You dare to question *me*?' Jack made the face of one appalled. 'I'll report you to your superior. What is your name?'

'Name?' went the officer, scratching his head with his truncheon.

'Name,' said Jack, in an even haughtier tone.

'Chortle,' said Chortle. 'Special Constable. My name is on my back. That's how special I am.'

'Move your stupid rubber arse,' said Jack.

Eddie grinned behind Jack's back. How dearly *he* would have liked to have said *that* to a policeman.

The Special Constable stood aside. His jolly face contorted into a hideous scowl.

Jack swaggered up the steps and through the great open doorway and into *Oh Boy!*.

Now, if it was tasteless on the outside, what would you *really* expect within? Jack did whistlings from between his teeth. 'This is *really* swank,' he said to Eddie. The bear peered all around and about.

'It's certainly something,' he said.

The Grand Salon of *Oh Boy!* was a monument to just how far you could truly go if you had more money than taste. The furnishings were of gold and gilt, with settees that dripped tassels and fringes. A central fountain was composed of countless naked pink marble cherubs which sprinkled scented water from their privy parts. The similarly pink marble floor was strewn with pinkly-dyed sheepskin rugs, their stuffed heads showing emerald eyes. The walls were hung with numerous oil paintings of the Blue Boy himself, posed in the most surprising positions.

There were many policemen around and about. Some were coming and others were going. Most, however, were just standing around, laughing, but looking rather lost. Some were touching things that they shouldn't. A voice called out loudly to one of these: 'Don't touch that, you cretin.' It was the voice of Chief Inspector Wellington Bellis. Eddie recognised this voice.

Eddie ducked behind Jack. 'That's Bellis,' said Eddie. 'He's the Chief Inspector. Keep him talking for as long as you can, while I give the crime scene a once-over. I'll meet you back at the car.'

'Right,' said Jack. 'I say, *you*! Yes, you there with the perished head. Who are you?'

Bellis glanced bitterly in Jack's direction. 'And who are *you*?' he said.

'And that's quite enough of *that*.' Jack made his way towards Bellis. 'I've already had to upbraid one of your dullard constables for his impertinence. I'm a patron of this establishment. A personal friend of Boy Blue. What is going on here?'

'Oh, my apologies, *sir*.' There was a certain tone in that *sir*, a tone that wasn't lost upon Jack. 'There has been an incident.'

'Incident?' said Jack.

'Homicide,' said Bellis. 'I regret to tell you that Boy Blue is dead.'

'Dead? *Dead?*' Jack put his hands to his face, which made the expression of horror. 'Boy Blue, my dearest friend? How did this happen?'

'Perhaps you'd care to view the body?' There was now a different tone in the Chief Inspector's voice. A tone of malice, perhaps.

'Well,' said Jack, feigning immoderate distress, 'I don't know, I mean, well, is it messy?'

'I wouldn't exactly describe it as messy.' Bellis glanced down and Jack followed the direction of Bellis's glancing. A silken sheet covered a huddled something. The body of Boy Blue, Jack supposed. 'Go on, have a peep,' said Bellis.

'My dearest friend.' Jack made snivelling sounds. 'I mean, I don't know. If such a terrible thing has happened, such a shock, I don't know. I should, perhaps, pay my respects. Oh, I really don't know.'

'Have a little look,' said Bellis, a big wide smile upon his rubber face. 'Pay your last respects.'

'Well,' said Jack. 'Perhaps just a little look.'

'Officer,' said Bellis to one of the officers who was touching things that he shouldn't. 'Kindly lift the sheet and show the nice gentleman the deceased.'

'Yes sir, chief.' The officer smirked, stooped and whipped away the sheet with a flourish.

Jack stared down and his eyes grew wide and his mouth fell hugely open. And then Jack crossed his legs and he said, 'Ouch.'

'Ouch would be about right,' agreed Bellis. 'You might recognise the murder weapon. It's his crook. His original crook, from the days when he was a humble shepherd. It was kept in the showcase by the door. It would appear that he was bending over, tying his shoelace. We think someone took the crook, then ran at him, using the bottom end as a spear. It entered his own bottom end, and left via his mouth. Much in the manner that one might spit a pig for a barbecue.'

Jack nodded his head and chewed upon his lower lip. The manner of the murder was, to say the least, grotesque. The problem with it was – and Jack, for all he could do, was now finding this a *real* problem – the problem with it was that, in the darkest way possible, it was also very funny indeed.

Jack looked over at Bellis.

The moulded smile upon Bellis's face was spreading up towards his ears.

'Right up the old farting box,' said Bellis, restraining a titter.

'How dare you!' said Jack. 'This is no laughing matter. My dear friend. My . . .' Jack chewed harder upon his lip and told himself that this wasn't funny. It *wasn't*. This was a dead man here. It wasn't funny!

'Sorry,' said Bellis. He let free a giggle, then controlled himself once more. 'Cover him up again, officer.'

The officer, still smirking, stooped once more and re-covered the corpse.

'Terrible business,' said Bellis, with as much solemnity as he could muster up.

'Terrible business,' Jack agreed.

'Terrible business,' said Eddie, when Jack returned to the car to find him waiting there. 'Most unprofessional.'

'But I was rude,' said Jack, settling himself back behind the driving wheel. 'You said that I should be as rude and obnoxious as possible. Act like a rich man, you said. Behave badly.'

'I mean about the laughing,' said Eddie. ' "Terrible business" you said to Bellis and then the two of you collapsed in laughter.'

'It was nerves,' said Jack.

'It wasn't. You thought it was funny.'

'I'm sorry,' said Jack. 'But it was.'

'You wouldn't have thought it so funny if it had happened to you.'

'Well, obviously not. Other people's misfortunes are far funnier than your own.'

'It's *not* funny,' said Eddie, shaking his head as he said it. 'Well, perhaps it is, a little. But that's not the point. It's another murder and that *isn't* funny.'

'Well, it's really nothing to do with us. We're supposed to be investigating the murder of Humpty Dumpty. That's what Bill got the money for.'

'You don't think that perhaps these two murders might be in some way connected?'

Jack shrugged. 'How should I know? This is the big city. How many murders do you get here in a week?'

'On average?' said Eddie. 'None.'

'None?' said Jack.

'None,' said Eddie. 'Humpty's murder was the first ever murder of a meathead. Which is why, in my opinion, the newspapers are covering it up, spreading the suicide rumour to avoid panicking the population. Certainly toys are forever getting into fights and pulling each other to pieces. But that doesn't count as murder and doesn't merit a police investigation. This is men who are being killed, Jack. The old rich. This is serious stuff.'

'So you're thinking . . . What are you thinking?'

'I'm thinking,' said Eddie, 'that it's the same murderer. I'm thinking that Toy City has a serial killer on the loose.'

10

'What is a *serial* killer?' Jack asked.

'It's a term that I've just made up,' said Eddie. 'It means a killer who murders more than one person. Serially. One after the other.'

Jack whistled and diddled with things on the dashboard. 'It's possible, I suppose,' said he. 'But what about evidence? Did you find any clues?'

'Plenty,' said Eddie, making a very pleased face. 'Firstly, the killer did not run at Boy Blue, using his crook like a spear. The crook was fired from some contrivance across the street. One of the panes of glass in the front door was shattered. The crook was removed from the showcase and fired at Boy Blue when he was bending over.'

'Tying his shoelace,' said Jack.

'Did you see any laces on his shoes?'

'I didn't look.'

'I did,' said Eddie. 'I peeped. He was wearing slip-ons. Boy Blue bent down to examine this.'

Eddie displayed a bundle on his lap. 'And before you ask me what it is, I'll show you. I was able to liberate it before some big clod of a policeman stood upon it. Have a look at this, Jack.'

Eddie unwrapped the bundle and Jack stared down.

'Bunny,' said Jack. 'It's another hollow chocolate bunny.'

'Just don't eat this one,' said Eddie. 'It's evidence.'

'Of your serial killer?'

'It could hardly be a coincidence, could it?'

Jack made free with another whistle. 'So where do we go from here?' he asked. 'Back to Bill's office?'

'Ah, no.' Eddie shook his head. 'I don't think we'll go back there for a while. As this is the only clue we've got, I think we'll follow it up. Do you fancy a visit to the chocolate factory?'

'Do they give away free samples?' Jack asked. 'Because I'm really quite hungry again.'

'Rewind the car and drive,' said Eddie. 'I'll show you which way to go.'

Jack was beginning to gain some sense of direction. The major streets of the great metropolis were slowly beginning to familiarise themselves. It wasn't all such a mystery any more. Well, a lot of it was. But some wasn't.

'I recognise this bit,' said Jack. 'There's Tinto's bar, and right along there is Bill's office.'

'Straight on,' said Eddie, 'up Knob Hill.'

The hill road wound upwards, as hill roads will do, unless you're coming down them, of course.

Jack drove past Nursery Towers. 'What's that dark-looking house at the very top of the hill?' he asked.

'That's where Mr Anders lives.'

'The kindly loveable white-haired old toymaker. I'd like to visit him; do you think we could stop off and say hello?'

'Not without an appointment,' said Eddie. 'And you're on your own when you do it.'

At Eddie's instruction, Jack turned off the hill road and was very soon outside the gates of the chocolate factory.

If *Oh Boy!* had been tasteless, the chocolate factory was style personified. It was an elegant building, composed of yellow brick, all sweeping curves and fluted arabesques. It rose like an anthem, in praise of life's finer things.

'Ugly-looking dump,' said Jack.

Eddie shook his head.

'Do you want me to be rude and obnoxious again?'

'I wouldn't want to put you to the effort.'

'It's no effort, I assure you.'

'Just follow me,' said Eddie.

★

Now it is a fact, well known to those who know it well, that detective work is rarely straightforward, because finding things out is rarely straightforward. Getting information from folk, when folk do not wish to part with information, can be difficult. *Is* difficult. And on the rare occasions when folk are eager to part with information, it often turns out that this information is inaccurate. Which can lead to all kinds of confusion.

But if, at the end of the day, and such like, the information you have managed to acquire, in the course of your detective work, leads to an arrest, then you've got a result. And if the suspect is convicted, then you've got an even bigger result.

And if the suspect is a murder suspect and gets sent off to the electric chair, then you've got an even bigger bigger result.

And if it turns out later that the murder suspect was in fact innocent, and was sent off to the electric chair because the information you acquired was inaccurate, well, tomorrow's another day, isn't it? You can try and get it right the next time.

The chocolate factory had big gates at the front. There was a gatekeeper in a tiny box beside these gates, keeping them, as it were.

Jack sniffed the air. It smelled sweet. It smelled of chocolate. Eddie addressed the gatekeeper. 'This is, er, Lord Dork,' said Eddie, indicating Jack. 'He is a connoisseur of chocolate and I've brought him here on a special visit.'

'Then you've come to the right place,' said the gatekeeper. 'Because I'm a special gatekeeper. I'm the head gatekeeper. Because, although, as you can see, I'm only a head, I'm also the gatekeeper. Which makes me the head gatekeeper. Which makes me very special, don't you agree?'

Eddie nodded and peeped in at the special head gatekeeper. He was indeed nothing but a head. A little round wooden head. 'So, can we come in?' Eddie asked.

'No,' said the gatekeeper. 'We're closed to all visitors.'

'But this is Lord Dork. *The* Lord Dork.'

'One Lord Dork is much the same to me as another,' said the gatekeeper.

'So you're not inclined to grant us entry?'

'Even if I were, I couldn't. Look at me, I may be a special head, but I'm only a head. How could I possibly open the gate?'

'Who generally opens the gates, then?' Eddie asked.

'Search me,' said the gatekeeper. 'I've been here for years, in rain and snow and fog and fug; I've yet to see those gates open up at all.'

'But don't the workers go in and out?'

'There aren't any workers,' said the gatekeeper.

'I smell chocolate,' said Jack. 'Someone is making chocolate.'

'If I had shoulders, I'd shrug them,' said the gatekeeper. 'And if I had legs, I'd probably walk. It's not much fun at times being me, I can tell you.'

'I could pull your head out of the box and we could drop it off somewhere,' said Eddie, helpfully.

'No thanks, I like it here. It's not much of a job, but it's all I have. I'll make do. Goodbye.'

'We have to get inside,' said Eddie. 'It's very important. It's about this.' Eddie held up his bundle and showed the chocolate bunny to the gatekeeper.

'What is that?' the gatekeeper asked.

'It's a hollow chocolate bunny.'

'Oh,' said the gatekeeper. 'So that's what chocolate looks like. I'd always imagined it to be pink.'

'Pink?' said Jack. 'You've never seen chocolate?'

'I have now,' said the gatekeeper. 'And I'm very disappointed. It's not nice having all your illusions shattered. Please go away, you've quite spoiled my day.'

Eddie made an exasperated face.

'We're getting nowhere,' said Jack. 'Shall we just climb over the gates?'

'You can't do that,' said the gatekeeper. 'It's not allowed.'

'Really? And so what are you going to do about it?'

'I'll sulk,' said the gatekeeper. 'I sulked the last time and I'll sulk this time too.'

'Last time?' Eddie asked. 'What last time?'

'The last time someone got past the gates. They didn't even speak to me; they just leapt over. I really sulked, I can tell you. I don't know whether it helped or not. But what else could I do?'

Jack shook his head.

'Perhaps you should have raised the alarm,' Eddie suggested.

'I'm not employed to do that,' said the gatekeeper. 'I'm employed to stop people going through the gates without my authorisation.'

'And how do you do that?'

The gatekeeper laughed. 'It's a fine joke, isn't it?' he said. 'I never have to. The gates are always locked.'

Jack scratched at his head. 'Yes, but—'

Eddie stopped him. 'So you're only employed to stop people going *through* the gates? Not *over* them?' he asked the gatekeeper.

'My contract only says *through them*.'

Jack shook his head once more.

'This person who leapt over the gates,' Eddie said. 'What did they look like?'

'Looked like a meathead,' said the gatekeeper. 'And all meatheads look the same to me.'

'There's nothing specific that you can recall?' Eddie asked.

'They had a sack,' said the gatekeeper. 'I remember that. It was an empty sack when they jumped over, but it looked weighty and full later, when they jumped back again.'

'Significant,' said Eddie. 'Is there anything else you can remember?'

'I remember a sparrow that once built its nest in that tree over there.'

'About the meathead who climbed in and out?'

'No, she just looked like a meathead.'

'*She?*' said Eddie.

'It was a female meathead,' said the gatekeeper. 'They have those things that stick out in the front.'

'Tits?' Jack asked.

'Feathers,' said the gatekeeper.

'We're talking about the meathead, not the sparrow,' said Eddie.

'Me too,' said the gatekeeper. 'She had big feathers, sticking out of the front of her bonnet.'

Back in the car, Eddie said, 'Well, it was a struggle, but we got there eventually.'

'I didn't get any chocolate,' said Jack. 'And I'm still hungry.'

'But we got information. Someone leapt over the gates of the chocolate factory and stole a sack full of somethings.'

'Bunnies, you're thinking?'

'Let us assume so. And it was a woman.'

'It might have been a man in a feathered hat.'

'Does that seem likely to you?'

Jack shrugged. 'The unlikely is commonplace in this city,' he said.

'It's a woman,' said Eddie. 'We're looking for a woman. Perhaps it was a love triangle. She was the scorned lover of both Humpty and Boy Blue. Or something.'

'So what is the significance of the bunnies?'

'Some love thing. I don't know. Men give chocolates to women.'

'You're clutching at straws,' said Jack. 'I don't believe it was a woman. Did a woman climb onto Humpty's roof and put in that lens? Did a woman fire that crook from across the street? Did a woman leap over those gates? Did you see how high those gates were?'

'We're looking for a woman.'

'We're not.'

★

Jack drove the car back down Knob Hill and, at Eddie's instruction, towards Tinto's bar. He didn't look in the driving mirror as he drove along, but then Jack rarely, if ever, looked into the driving mirror.

Which was a shame as it happened, because if Jack *had* looked into the driving mirror, he might well have noticed the car that was following him.

It was a long and low expensive-looking car and it was being driven by a woman.

A woman who wore a feathered bonnet.

11

The sun was drifting down towards the horizon as Jack steered Bill's car along one of the more colourful streets of Toy City. Eddie had suggested that they take the pretty way back to Tinto's bar.

This street was a shopping area for toys. There were brightly lit bazaars, shaded by decorative awnings. Produce in baskets, tubs and crates spilled onto the pavements.

Jack slowed the car and kerb-crawled along, peering out and marvelling at the wares and wonders, and at those who shopped and strode and moved: toys, and more toys.

Jack's thoughts were all his own and his thoughts were about thoughts. How could all these creations, these things wrought from tin and wood and padded fabric, *think*? How could they move and talk? It was ludicrous, impossible, and yet it was so. Jack thought back to the gatekeeper at the chocolate factory.

'A head,' said Jack, with a shake of his own. 'A talking head in a box. Now I ask you, how does that work?'

'Most inefficiently,' said Eddie. 'The way he just let people leap over the gates. Outrageous. I'd have sacked that head if it had been working for me. I'd have told that head to hop it.' Eddie tittered foolishly.

'You know exactly what I mean.'

'I do,' said the bear. 'But must you keep going on about it? You admit that you don't even know how your own brain works.'

'But at least I *have* a brain. Your chum Wibbly had

108

nothing at all in what he had left of his head. It can't work, none of it can.'

'But it does. Your own eyes attest to the fact. Don't let it get you down, Jack. If you ever meet up with the toymaker, you can ask him all about it.'

'And do you think he'll tell me?'

Eddie shrugged. 'I doubt it. But at least you will have asked.'

'Mad,' said Jack. 'It's all quite mad.' And he lapsed into a sullen silence.

Eddie leaned back in the passenger seat and tried once more without success to fold his arms. Thoughts moved about amongst the sawdust in his head; how they did and what they were was anybody's guess.

At a length that was shorter rather than long, he had done with thinking, and also with Jack's silence.

'Jack,' said Eddie, all bright and breezy, 'Jack, are you a virgin?'

'*What?*' went Jack, and the car swerved onto the pavement, scattering shoppers, who shook their fists and shouted words of abuse.

'A virgin?' said Eddie. 'Careful where you're swerving.'

'What kind of question is *that*?'

'An easy one to answer, I would have thought.'

'Well, I'm not answering it.' Jack regained control of the car.

'So you *are*,' said Eddie. 'It's nothing to be ashamed of; you're still a young lad.'

'I'm old enough,' said Jack.

'But you haven't done it yet?'

'Eddie, change the subject, please. We're supposed to be on a case. Two murders. Concentrate on the murders.'

'I am,' said Eddie. 'Take a left here.'

Jack took a left there.

'So you've never been in a doll's house,' said Eddie.

'A doll's house?' said Jack.

'A doll's house, a bordello, a knocking shop.'

Jack rammed his foot down hard upon the brake, dislodging Eddie from his seat and causing him to fall in some confusion to the floor.

'Oooh ouch,' went Eddie. 'Steady on. Help me up. I'm all in a mess down here.'

Jack helped Eddie up and positioned him back on the seat. 'Talk about something else,' he said. 'Talk about the case.'

'But it's pertinent to the case. I know a place where we might get some information regarding the suspect. Tarts wear feathered hats, don't they?'

Jack nodded in the manner of one who had some knowledge of these matters.

'Yes, well, they do,' said Eddie. 'And tarts are to be found in bawdy houses. And I know of only one bawdy house in this city. And I know of it most intimately.'

Jack shook his head once more. 'And you are a patron of this establishment?' he asked.

'A regular patron, as it happens.'

Jack stared down at Eddie. He stared down hard and he stared down in particular towards a certain area of Eddie Bear's anatomy. 'But you're a teddy bear,' he said. 'You haven't got a w—'

'I *have*, you know,' said Eddie. 'It's just that I keep it tucked away when it's not in use.'

'I don't believe you,' said Jack. 'Teddies don't have—'

'You want me to show it to you?'

Actually Jack did. 'No, I certainly don't,' said he.

'Bears are noted for their sexual prowess.' Eddie puffed out his plump little chest.

'I think you'll find that's rabbits,' said Jack. 'But I really must insist that you change the subject. This is becoming most distasteful.'

'It's nature,' said Eddie. 'It's as natural as.'

'Nothing in this city is *natural*. But tell me about this bawdy house.'

'Ah,' said Eddie. 'Now you're interested.'

'Only if it's pertinent to the case.'

'Yeah, right.'

'Eddie,' said Jack. 'This murderer, this serial killer of yours. He—'

'She,' said Eddie.

'He, or *she*. They won't stop at two, will they? They'll go on killing?'

Eddie made with the very grave noddings. 'It's more than probable,' he said.

'Then don't you think that we should, perhaps, be trying to work out who's likely to be murdered next? Then we could warn them. And lie in wait for the murderer, or something.'

'You're getting the hang of this detective game, Jack. Drive on; we'll go to the bawdy house.'

Jack threw up his hands and then Jack drove on.

The streets became less colourful and soon Jack was driving along grim and narrow roads that were positively grey.

'It's horrible here,' he said. 'This is a really horrible district. What a foul place. What a really foul place.'

'I was brought up here,' said Eddie.

'Well, I'm sure it has its good points.'

'It doesn't,' said Eddie. 'Park here.'

'Are we there?' Jack asked.

'Of course we're not. But no one ever parks their car *outside* a bawdy house. They park a couple of streets away and approach on foot. Normally wearing some kind of disguise.'

'I'm wearing a disguise,' said Jack.

'You certainly are, Jack. Oh, and don't forget to lock the car. Then there'll be the vague chance that it will still be here when we get back.'

Jack and Eddie left the car and Jack locked up the doors.

'Follow me,' said Eddie.

And Jack did so.

A little ways behind, and altogether unobserved, another car drew silently to a halt. It was long and low and expensive-looking. The driver's door of this car opened and a lady's leg appeared. It was a long and slender leg, tightly sheathed in black rubber. At the end of this leg was a dainty foot, shod with a wonderful shoe. Its highly raised heel was a delicate chromium spiral. Its toe was a dagger of steel.

The exterior of the bawdy house was nothing to speak of.

The interior, however, was quite another matter. It was one of those grand salon jobbies, but this was where any similarity between it and the house of *Oh Boy!* ended.

The ceiling was a gentle dome, richly figured with plaster reliefs of amorous cupids and garlanded satyrs. The walls were made gay with pastoral paintings of frolicsome centaurs and dainty Arcadians. These were engaged in the most intimate pursuits, but had been wrought with such charm and whimsy as might bring an appreciative smile to the face of the most worthy cleric.

Pale silkwood caryatids rose between these paintings. They had been lovingly carved and bore delicate features and robes, which seemed all but diaphanous. They held, in their outstretched hands, crystal candelabra which lit the salon to a nicety.

The furnishings were rich, but of a richness which is restrained, tutored, composed. The colours of the fabrics were of the subtlest shades: dainty pinks and tender violets. Billowy cushions were cast here and there, creating an atmosphere of comfort and informality. And all around and about were elegant vases from which the most gorgeous blooms breathed their precious fragrances.

'Oh my,' said Jack as his feet all but sank into a carpet woven with a thousand blushing roses. 'Oh my, oh my.'

'You approve?' asked Eddie.

'Well, I think it's incredible.' And it was incredible. It was overwhelming in its beauty. Jack was overwhelmed. And he was nervous too. For after all, he *was* a virgin. And wonderful and marvellous as this place was, it *was* a bawdy house. An actual bawdy house. Where there would be actual women who had actual sex on a professional basis. Which was actually somewhat daunting.

Actually.

'You wait until you see the bedrooms,' said Eddie, rubbing his paws together.

'Eddie,' said Jack. 'Just one thing. We are here on business, aren't we?'

'Of course,' said Eddie.

'Because if there's one thing I do know about ladies who work in bawdy houses, it is that you have to pay them. With real money. And we don't have any money.'

'Do I spy an expression of relief on your face?' Eddie asked.

'You do *not*,' said Jack. 'I'm just saying, that's all.'

'I have an account here.' Eddie grinned from ear to furry ear.

Jack didn't grin, but now another thought entered his head. 'Eddie?' said Jack.

'Jack?' said Eddie.

'Eddie, when you, you know, *do it.*'

'Yes,' said Eddie. It was a low, deep, growly kind of yes.

'Do you do it with a dolly?'

Eddie's button eyes virtually popped from his head. 'A dolly?' he said in the voice of outrage. 'A *dolly*? Do I look like some kind of pervert who'd do it inter-species? I do it with another bear! Female, of course. Dolly! That's gross!'

'I'm sorry,' said Jack. 'Oh look, who's this?'

'It's Mother,' said Eddie.

'Your mother? But . . .'

'Mother Goose,' said Eddie. 'Or Madame Goose, as she prefers to be called.'

Madame Goose was indeed a goose, and a very large goose was she. Jack could see that she wasn't a clockwork goose, rather, some great soft toy of a thing, fully feathered and most convincing. She was a profusion of petticoats and a gathering of gingham, with glittering rings on the tips of her wings. And she walked with a quack and a waddle and a quack and a flurry of eiderdown (which hopefully didn't infringe any copyrights).

She came a–waddling across the rose-pelted carpet, the light from the crystal candelabra twinkling on her gorgeous gingham.

'Eddie,' said Madame Goose, bending low and pecking kisses at the bear's cheek. 'It's been too long. Have you come to settle your account?'

'I've come to introduce a close friend of mine,' said Eddie. 'This is Lord Schmuck.'

Jack narrowed his eyes at Eddie.

Madame Goose curtseyed low, her petticoats spreading over the carpet like the petals of some exotic bloom, or a pink gingham jellyfish, dropped from a height. Or something else entirely.

'Always a pleasure to meet with members of the aristocracy,' she said. 'You'll find that we can satisfy your every wish here.'

'Verily,' said Jack, once more adopting the haughty foppish tone that he'd previously employed upon the policemen. 'Well, naturally I am used to the very best of everything. So I trust that the damsels on offer are more well-favoured than yourself in the looks department. You fat old turkey.'

Madame Goose fell back in horror, flapping her ring-tipped wings all about.

Eddie head–butted Jack in that certain area of his anatomy.

'Gurgh!' went Jack, doubling over in pain.

'Don't be rude in here, you schmuck,' counselled Eddie at Jack's now lowered ear. 'These are my friends. Apologise at once.'

'I'm sorry, Madame.' Jack clutched at himself in an unbecoming manner and took to the drawing of deep breaths. 'I'll get you for that, Eddie,' he whispered from between his gritted teeth.

'Please pardon Lord Schmuck,' said Eddie, stepping

briskly beyond Jack's kicking range. 'His manners aren't up to much. But his heart and his wallet are in the right places.'

'Quite so,' said the Madame, smoothing down her ruffled feathers and curtseying once more.

'Any chance of a morsel of food?' Jack asked. 'And a glass of wine, please.'

'Seat yourself, gents,' said Madame Goose. 'I will bring you something at once.'

'You sit down, Jack,' said Eddie. 'I'll accompany Madame to the kitchen. Have a few words, if you know what I mean.' Eddie tapped at his nose with his paw.

'Don't be long,' said Jack, lowering himself with care onto an overstuffed settee.

'I'll be back as soon as.' Eddie followed Madame from the salon.

Jack sat awkwardly, nursing himself. He sighed and he made a sorry face. He felt most uncomfortable here. The opulence, the colours and the fragrances were indeed pleasing, but he wasn't pleased. This was, after all, a whorehouse. A high-class whorehouse, perhaps, but nevertheless, a whorehouse. Its wealth was founded upon degradation: money earned by women who sold their bodies to men. Jack glowered at the rosy carpet.

He had never considered himself to be a lad with high moral values. He was basically honest, but above and beyond that, he'd never given the subject of morality a lot of thought.

'I think I'll go and wait outside,' said Jack to himself.

'Oh no, don't go.'

Jack looked up. The face of a beautiful girl smiled down upon him. Her mouth was wide and smiling, displaying a row of perfect teeth. Her head was a bouquet of golden curls, the colour of sun-ripened corncobs. Her eyes were dark and large, brown and glossy as burnt sugar, fringed by gorgeous lashes. And there was a troubled sadness in those eyes.

Jack stared into those eyes.

'I'm Jill,' said the beautiful girl.

'Oh,' said Jack, 'I'm pleased to meet you.' And he rose to shake her hand.

Jill curtseyed low and Jack could see right down her cleavage. Jill had a beautiful body. It went in and out in all the right places, and just by the right amounts too. Jack estimated that she could be little more than his own age – although with teenage girls it's often very hard to tell. 'I'm, er, Lord, er.' Jack took a deep breath. 'My name is Jack,' he said.

'Jack and Jill,' Jill giggled prettily. 'What about that?' she asked.

Jack managed a lopsided grin. 'What about that,' he said.

'Madame sent me out to entertain you. None of the other girls have arrived yet. We don't really open until later in the evening. But I am here, if you'll have me; just tell me what you wish for.'

'Oh,' said Jack. 'Well, nothing like *that* at the moment, thank you. I'm just waiting. For a friend.'

'I can be your friend. I can be anything you want me to be.'

'Please sit down,' said Jack.

Jill sat down and Jack sat down beside her.

She reached out a hand to clasp his own, but Jack returned it politely.

'Don't you like me?' Jill asked.

'I don't know you,' said Jack. 'But you look very nice. Very pretty.'

'Thank you very much. You're very handsome.' Jill's eyes took in the jewelled buttons on Jack's waistcoat. 'And I love your clothes.'

'They're not mine. I only borrowed them.'

'I rent mine from Madame,' said Jill.

'Do you mind me asking you something?' Jack lowered his eyes. 'I mean, you're very young, aren't you? To be working in a place like this?'

'I have to eat,' said Jill, her fingers toying with one of Jack's jewelled buttons. 'But let's not talk about me. Let's talk about you. Would you like to come upstairs with me now?'

'I'd love to,' said Jack, easing himself away. 'But it's not right.'

Jill looked somewhat sternly at Jack and when she spoke, there was fire in her voice. 'What are you saying?' she asked. 'That there's something wrong with the way I make a living? I'm good at what I do and what I do is not illegal. Are you some God-botherer, come to convert me from my wicked ways or something?'

'No,' said Jack. 'Slow down. No offence meant. It's just—'

'You're a virgin, aren't you?' said Jill.

'I'm *not*,' said Jack rising to leave. 'I have to go.'

'Please don't,' said Jill. 'I'm begging you, please don't.'

'Begging?'

'If you walk out, I'll be in trouble with Madame.'

'I wouldn't want that,' said Jack, sitting down again.

'Thank you,' said Jill. And her fingers stroked at his buttons once more.

'But tell me, and I don't mean to offend you, isn't there some job other than this that you'd rather be doing?'

Jill cast him a look that was filled with contempt. 'I'd quite like to be a princess,' she said. 'Do you know any princes who are looking for a tart to marry?'

'Please be calm.' Jack raised calming hands. 'The reason I'm asking is that I ran away from the factory where I worked. Because I hated it. I came to the city to seek my fortune.'

'You came *to* the city.' Jill laughed. 'You thought you'd seek your fortune *here*? You are clearly a gormster. No offence meant.'

'None taken,' said Jack, as if none *was* taken.

'But you came *to* the city.' Jill shook her golden curls. 'I've never heard of anyone coming *to* the city before. I've heard that beyond the bounds of the city are desolate realms peopled by cannibals.'

'You're not altogether wrong there.' The image of a now-one-eared farmer filled Jack's head. 'And perhaps I'll never find my fortune. Perhaps I am well and truly cursed.'

'I know that I am.' Jill's voice was scarcely a whisper.

'What did you say?' Jack asked.

'Nothing,' said Jill. She placed a hand upon his. This time Jack didn't remove it.

'You said you were cursed,' said Jack.

'No, I didn't. So, do you want to come upstairs with me?'

Jack smiled wanly. 'I don't have any money, I'm afraid.'

'You can open an account.'

'I don't know,' said Jack.

'If you do come upstairs,' said Jill, 'I can promise that you won't be disappointed. And if you are a virgin, then you'll lose your virginity in a manner that you'll remember all your life.'

'Well,' said Jack.

'And if you don't come upstairs,' said Jill, 'then Madame will beat me and possibly throw me out on the street. And you wouldn't want that, now, would you?'

Jack shook his head.

'Come on then,' said Jill.

Outside, clockwork cars purred on the streets and the denizens of the great metropolis went on doing whatever they were doing. Five miles to the north, a foolish boy fell into a farmer's pit. The sun sank beneath the horizon and night came upon Toy City.

And on a white bed, in a white room, with white curtains, Jack lost his virginity. Which was quite some going, considering his tender years.

And when his virginity was lost, elegantly lost, he lay, all spent, his head upon a silken cushion, staring at the ceiling. Jill, in Jack's arms, tousled his hair.

'How was that for you?' she asked.

'Wonderful,' said Jack. 'Quite wonderful.'

'I'm pleased.'

Jack sighed and smiled. 'I love you,' he said. 'Will you marry me?'

'Certainly,' said Jill, 'as soon as you become a prince. In the meantime, I'll make out your bill.'

When Jack left the white room, he moved upon feet that scarcely touched the floor. He fairly soared. He felt marvellous. He felt that he had now become a man.

Just wait 'til Eddie hears about *this*, he thought. And, I wonder how you go about actually becoming a prince, he thought also.

As this had now become his goal in life.

Down the stairs Jack wafted. Light as thistledown and dishevelled as a nettle bed. He had lipstick all over his face and the jewelled buttons on his waistcoat were missing.

'Eddie.' Jack reached the bottom of the stairs. 'Eddie, where are you?'

All was silent and Jack breathed in all there was. The subtle perfumes seemed almost more subtle. But now Jack felt a twinge of guilt. Had what he'd just done been wrong? Immoral? Corrupt? Well, yes it had, but.

But.

Jack pressed all such thoughts aside. What had just happened had been wonderful, beautiful. And something that was wonderful and beautiful couldn't be wrong, could it? And Jill acted as if she'd been enjoying it too. And if she'd enjoyed it too, then it definitely wasn't wrong.

It was right.

'Yes,' said Jack. 'It was. Eddie, where are you?'

All was as silent as before.

Rather too silent, really.

Jack crossed the salon and pressed his hand against the door that led to the kitchen. He was very hungry now. And very thirsty too. A snack was in order. A celebratory snack, all washed down with a glass of bubbly wine.

Which could go on Eddie's account.

Jack pushed the door open.

'Eddie,' he called once more, 'where are you? Come on.'

Beyond the doorway was a hallway and beyond this hallway, yet another door. Which is often the case with hallways, especially those that lead from one room to another. Jack pranced down this hallway and knocked upon the door that it led to.

And as there was no answer to his knockings, he turned the handle and pushed the door open. It was the door to the kitchen. Jack peeped in.

The kitchen was a magnificent affair, the kind of kitchen that Great Houses had. And this was indeed a great house. There was a flagstoned floor, a huge central table, ovens and ranges and rows and rows of hanging pots and pans and skillets.

Jack was impressed by this kitchen. 'This kitchen,' said Jack, 'is what I call a kitchen. This is a magnificent kitchen. The kind of kitchen that Great Houses have. And this is indeed a great house. The only thing I don't like about this kitchen, the only thing that really spoils this kitchen for me, is *that*.'

And Jack stared at the thing that spoiled the kitchen and Jack felt just a little sick. Because on the huge central table lay Madame Goose. She lay as a goose stripped for cooking. Her legs were trussed and her neck had been wrung.

Mother Goose was dead.

'Jack,' said the voice of Jill, 'Jack, what are you doing in the kitchen?' And now Jill's hand was upon Jack's shoulder.

Jack turned and said, 'Go back. Don't come in here.'

'Why not?'

'Something's happened, something bad.'

'Show me, what?' Jill pushed past Jack. 'Oh no,' she said, and she screamed.

'Just go back,' said Jack. 'I'll deal with this.'

'Deal with *what*? She's dead, isn't she?'

'Pretty dead,' said Jack, approaching the body on the

table. His heels clacked upon the flagstone floor. Jack's feet were truly back upon the ground.

'This is terrible.' Jill wrung her hands; big tears welled in her eyes. 'Terrible, terrible.'

'I'm sorry,' said Jack, viewing the body. 'I'll get something to cover her body.'

'I'm not sorry about *her*,' said Jill. 'But if she's dead, then I'm out of a job, which is terrible.'

'Right,' said Jack, peering some more at the body. 'Whoever did this must be very strong. Hardly the work of a woman.'

'Woman?' said Jill.

'Eddie thinks . . .' Jack paused. 'Eddie,' he said. Then, '*Eddie!*' he shouted. 'Where are you, Eddie? Are you hiding somewhere?'

No reply gave comfort to Jack's ears.

'*Eddie!*' shouted Jack.

'Jack,' said Jill, 'I think you'd better look at this.'

'What?' Jack asked. And Jill pointed.

The kitchen door was open, but it was towards the doormat that Jill was pointing.

Jack followed the direction of this pointing, and then Jack said, 'Oh no.'

On the doormat lay something which filled Jack with horror.

That something was a large pile of sawdust.

12

'Eddie?' Jack went all weak at the knees. 'Eddie, is that you?'

A gentle breeze entered at the kitchen door and rippled Eddie's innards all about.

'Waaagh!' went Jack. 'Get a dustpan and brush! Gather him up in a bag!'

'Have you gone mad?' Jill asked.

'It's Eddie! My friend! This is dreadful!'

Jack was at the door now and he stared out into an alleyway beyond. 'I'll go after him,' he told Jill. 'I'll try to find the rest of him.'

'Jack, stop,' said Jill. 'It's a toy. Who cares about a toy?'

'I do,' said Jack. 'He's my friend.'

'You're a bit old for that kind of thing, aren't you?'

'He's my partner,' said Jack.

'Get real,' said Jill. 'It's a toy. Toys don't care for our kind and if you're smart, you won't care for theirs. You can always find yourself another toy bear, if that's the sort of weirdness you're in to.'

'What?'

'No wonder you were so useless in bed.'

'*What?*'

'Perhaps you'd have preferred it if I'd put a fur coat on.'

'Stop!' cried Jack. 'Stop now! Sweep Eddie's sawdust up and put it in a bag. Then call the police. I'm going after Eddie. I'll be back.'

'Oh yes, *sir*,' said Jill.

Jack cast her a very stern glance. 'Sweep him up and call the police,' he said.

Jack moved cautiously along the alleyway. There was always the chance that the murderer might still be lurking there, lying in wait. Ready to pounce.

Sprinkles of sawdust lay here and there amongst discarded refuse. Jack's sunken heart sank deeper. 'Eddie,' he called, throwing caution to the wind that was ruffling Eddie's sprinklings. 'Are you there? Anywhere? Eddie? Eddie!'

The alleyway led out to a street.

Further sprinklings of Eddie led to the pavement kerb.

Beyond this, on the road, were two black skid marks.

'Kidnapped,' said Jack. 'Or,' and he paused, 'or murdered.'

Jack returned with drooping shoulders to the kitchen.

Jill was sitting on the table, casually plucking feathers from a wing of the deceased Madame.

'Stop doing that,' said Jack. 'Did you call the police?'

'They're busy,' said Jill. 'Apparently Little Boy Blue has been murdered. How about that then? Another rich bag of rubbish done away with.'

'You don't really care about anybody, do you?' Jack asked.

'And why should I? Nobody cares about me.'

'I care,' said Jack.

'Of course you don't.' Jill dusted feathers from her delicate fingers. 'You only care about me because I'm the first girl you've ever had sex with.'

'That's not true,' said Jack.

'Then let's see how much you care about me when you get the bill.'

'I don't have time for this.' Jack peered all around and about the kitchen. 'My friend has been kidnapped and I have to find him. There must be some clues here. What would Eddie do?' Jack paced about in the manner that Eddie had at

Humpty Dumpty's apartment. And then Jack recalled that it was actually he, Jack, who had solved the riddle of how Humpty met his grisly end.

'I can do this,' said Jack. 'I *can* do this.'

'You're a detective then, are you?'

'Sort of,' said Jack. 'Sort of.'

'Oh, sort of, is it? And so what are your deductions, Mr sort-of-detective?'

'Give me a minute,' said Jack, peeping and peering around.

'Give me a break,' said Jill.

Jack made an exasperated face. 'You may not care about anybody or anything,' he said, 'but I do. Someone has injured and taken my friend. And murdered this goose here.'

'And so you're looking for clues?'

'I am,' said Jack.

'Then why are you looking in all the wrong places?'

Jack, who was now under the table, straightened up, striking his head. 'Ouch,' he said. 'And do you know the *right* places?'

'All the clues you need are staring you in the face. You're just not looking at them properly.'

Jack got to his feet once more and stood, rubbing at his head. 'What are you saying?' he asked.

Jill eased herself down from the table. 'Do you want me to explain it all to you?'

'As if you could,' said Jack.

'I could,' said Jill. 'I could tell you exactly what happened here and give you a description of the person who did it.'

'I'll bet,' said Jack, searching for clues in the breadbin.

'But if you don't want your little teddy bear back, then forget it.'

Jack replaced the lid of the breadbin and turned once more towards Jill. 'Go on then,' he said.

Jill shook her corncob-coloured head. 'Oh no,' she said. 'You owe me money. Quite a lot of money, as it happens. I charge double for virgins.'

'You'll get your money,' said Jack. 'In fact, if you can lead me to Eddie, I'll pay you double your double.'

'He must be losing a lot of sawdust,' said Jill, pointing towards the paper bag which sat beside her on the table, the paper bag which now contained the kitchen-sweepings of Eddie. 'He could be nothing more than a glove puppet soon.'

'Treble your double, then.'

'It's a deal.'

Jack sat himself down on the table. Then, finding himself far too near to the corpse, got up and stood by the stove. 'Go on then,' he said wearily, 'impress me.'

'Right,' said Jill. 'Well, when you went off down the alleyway, I had a few moments to give this kitchen a looking-over before I called the police and swept up the bits of your friend. These were my immediate impressions.'

Jack disguised a sigh as a yawn. Or possibly he didn't.

'Firstly,' said Jill, 'I examined the kitchen door after you went through it into the alley. No signs of forced entry, yet that door is always locked.'

'It was unlocked and open,' said Jack.

'Exactly,' said Jill. 'And the key is always in the lock on the inside, but it isn't now, it's in the outside of the lock. The killer entered through that door by pushing a piece of paper under it from the outside, then poking the key from the lock with a stick, or something. The key drops onto the paper and the paper is pulled under the door. It's very basic stuff. Everyone knows how to do that.'

'Of course,' said Jack. 'Everyone knows that.'

'You obviously didn't. Our killer is now inside, in an empty kitchen, but hears someone coming and so hides.'

'The killer hides?' said Jack. 'Where does the killer hide?'

'The killer hides in that cupboard,' said Jill, pointing to an open cupboard. 'It's the broom cupboard. The door, as you see, is open and the brooms have all been pushed to one side. That's not how I left them.'

'Okay,' said Jack. 'The killer hides in the cupboard; what then?'

'Madame Goose and your friend Eddie enter the kitchen from the hallway. They talk, Eddie helps himself to jam—' Jill pointed to an open jam pot, surrounded by messy paw marks. 'Whatever your friend says to Madame upsets her.'

'How can you tell *that*?' Jack asked.

'Because Madame took down her brandy bottle from that shelf and poured herself a drink. She doesn't drink before midnight unless she's upset about something.'

'Yes, all right,' said Jack. 'This is fair enough. Because you work here. You put the brooms in place, you know about the brandy. I couldn't be expected to figure that stuff out. It's not clever. It's obvious to *you*.'

'Fine,' said Jill. 'Then how about this? The killer burst out of the cupboard, struck down Madame Goose with a broom, picked up a kitchen knife and slit your partner's throat.'

'Whoa, stop,' said Jack.

'Broom,' said Jill, pointing. 'Knife on floor, sawdust on mat. And your killer is a woman, Jack.'

'What?'

'A woman. She's about five foot six in her exclusive high-heeled footwear and she wears pale pink lipstick. She smokes *Sweet Lady* brand cigarettes and favours *Dark Love* perfume.'

'What?' said Jack once more.

'There's the butt end of her cigarette in the broom cupboard. Her lipstick's on it and the mark of her high-heeled boot. I could smell her perfume in the air when I came into the kitchen. As to her height, she swung Madame Goose's body up and onto the table after she killed her, then she trussed her legs. A taller person would have tied them higher, further from the feet. *She* tied them as high as she could reach without climbing onto the table – there are no heel-marks on the table, I looked. She's about my height. She's *very* strong.'

'Oh,' said Jack.

'And she wears a feather bonnet. There's a feather stuck in the door jamb of the cupboard.'

'Oh,' said Jack, once again.

'Now, my guess is,' said Jill, 'and here it's only a guess, so correct me if I'm wrong, my guess is that if you are a sort-of-detective, you're working on a case. Probably two cases. The two *big* cases that are on the go at the moment: namely, Humpty Dumpty and Boy Blue. Now I'm guessing once again here, but what if these two were linked to a woman, possibly in some romantic fashion. Revenge crimes, per-haps. A wronged lover. A wronged lover in a feathered hat.'

Jack made groaning sounds.

'My feelings then,' said Jill, 'would be that the killer was on to you and your friend. Followed you both here. Over-heard what Eddie had to say to Madame Goose and what she in turn said to Eddie, then silenced the both of them. How do you think I'm doing?'

Jack made further groaning sounds.

'There's only one thing that mystifies me.'

'Go on then, what is it?'

'It's *that*,' said Jill and she pointed to the mantelpiece. 'What is *that* doing here?'

Jack looked up at the mantelpiece.

On it stood a hollow chocolate bunny.

Jack drove once more through the streets of Toy City. This time Jill sat beside him. On her lap was the paper bag. The paper bag made Jack very sad.

'I like this car very much,' said Jill. 'Is it yours?'

'It's borrowed,' said Jack. 'So where are we going?'

'We're going to find the killer. You want your friend back and I want my money. Such is the nature of our business arrangement. Why did you change your clothes? I don't think much of that trenchcoat.'

'My waistcoat lost its buttons,' said Jack. 'I can't imagine how that happened, can you?'

'Turn left here,' said Jill.

Jack turned left and then left again, and then Jack said '*Oh Boy!*'

'We're here,' said Jill.

'But why are we here?'

'Because it's the only connection we have. Feathered bonnets are this season's fashion amongst the wealthy. It's another "Bucolic Woodland" look. It's a Boy Blue thing. And the heel marks on the cigarette butt, "Boots by *Oh Boy!*".'

'The police have all gone,' said Jack. 'Do you want to go inside?'

'Obviously I do. I'd like to have a little look through Boy Blue's client list. Perhaps we can identify this mystery woman.'

'Let's hope so,' said Jack.

They entered by the rear door of the premises. It was a simple enough business, involving, as it did, Jack sliding a piece of paper under the door, winkling the key out from the inside of the lock with a stick, or something, then pulling the key on the paper under the door.

'As easy as,' said Jack.

Which made him sadder still.

The two slipped into the silent building.

'Let's find the office,' said Jill. 'There'll be a filing cabinet or something.'

Jack followed Jill. They passed through the grand salon, where soft light fell upon the pink marble floor, highlighting a taped contour shape where the body of Boy Blue had lain.

'How did he die?' Jill asked. 'You know, don't you?'

'It wasn't nice,' said Jack. 'Although, I must admit, it was rather funny.'

'Let's go upstairs,' said Jill.

'Where have I heard that before?'

Jill turned a scathing glance on Jack.

'Upstairs it is,' said Jack.

Upstairs they came upon Boy Blue's private office. The door was unlocked and they went inside. Moonlight cast pale shafts through tall windows, lighting upon expensive-looking items of furniture and a very grand desk indeed.

Jill began rooting about in the drawers of the desk.

Jack began touching things that he shouldn't.

'Don't touch those things,' said Jill.

'Don't tell me what to touch.' Jack touched something else, which fell and broke.

'Smench!' it went on the floor.

'Sounded expensive,' said Jill.

Jack joined her at the desk.

'Switch the desk light on,' said Jill.

'Do you think we should? Someone might see the light.'

'Not up here.'

Jack switched on the desk light. 'What have you found?' he asked.

Jill laid a large leather tome on the desktop and began to leaf through it. Vellum paper pages fell one upon another.

'The Spring and Catch Society,' said Jill. 'It's a secret organisation.'

'Then how do you know about it?'

'You'd be surprised the things men tell me.'

'No, I wouldn't,' said Jack.

'Well, it says here that Boy Blue was a member. And so are most of the old rich. These are rituals, see.'

'They don't make any sense.' Jack peered at the page. The words meant nothing to him.

'They're in code.'

'I don't think it's a clue. What about the client list?'

Jill pushed the tome aside and pulled another from the drawer. 'Accounts,' she said, 'let's have a look through this.' She began leafing once more through paper.

'Please get a move on,' said Jack.

'Be patient.'

A sudden sound came to Jack's ears. 'What was that sudden sound?' he asked.

'Nothing. Don't worry.'

'But I heard something. Oh.'

Another sudden sound, this time accompanied by a lot of sudden movement, caused Jack to leap back in shock.

There was now a lot of sudden light. Big and sudden and bright and all shining right at Jack.

'Take him, officers!' shouted a sudden voice.

And all of a suddenness, big, blue, jolly, laughing figures were all over Jack. And Jack was pinned to the floor.

From beneath much pressing weight Jack found himself staring fearfully into the perished rubber face of Chief Inspector Wellington Bellis.

'Gotcha,' said Chief Inspector Bellis. 'They always return to the scene of the crime. I knew I was right. I just had to wait this time.'

'Now hold on there.' Jack struggled without success.

'And you answer to the description of the suspect who broke into Humpty Dumpty's, earlier today. Bill Winkie, private eye, I arrest you for murder.'

'No, stop, this isn't right.'

'Take him to the station, officers,' said Bellis. 'And if he gives you any trouble, then . . .'

'No,' wailed Jack as laughing policemen dragged him to his feet. 'You've got the wrong man. Tell him, Jill. Tell him.'

But Jill was nowhere to be seen.

13

It is a fact, well known to those who know it well, that there is scarcely to be found anywhere a society which does not hold to some belief in a supreme being.

A God.

A Divine Creator.

Toy City is no exception.

In Toy City a number of different religions exist, each serving the spiritual needs of its particular followers. Four of the more interesting are The Church of Mechanology, The Daughters of the Unseeable Upness, Big Box Fella, He Come, and The Midnight Growlers.

Followers of *The Church of Mechanology* are to be found exclusively amongst members of Toy City's clockwork toy population: wind-up tin-plate barmen, firemen, taxi drivers and the like.

These hold to the belief that the universe is a vast clockwork mechanism, the planets revolving about the sun by means of extendible rotary arms and the sun in turn connected to the galaxy by an ingenious crankshaft system, the entirety powered by an enormous clockwork motor, constantly maintained, oiled, and kept wound by The Universal Engineer.

The Universal Engineer is pictured in religious icons as a large, jolly, red-faced fellow in greasy overalls and cap. He holds in one holy hand an oily rag and in the other, the Church's Sacred Writ, known as *The Manual*.

The Manual contains a series of laws and coda, but, as is

often the case with Holy books, these laws and coda are penned in a pidgin dialect of unknown origin, which leaves them open to varied interpretation. An example of its text is *Winding is not to facilitate in counter to the clockways direction for tuning the to.*

Followers of The Church of Mechanology consider themselves special and superior to all other varieties of toy, in that, being clockwork, they are *in tune* and *at one with* the Universe.

A number of sub-sects, breakaway factions and splinter groups exist within The Church, with names such as *The Cog-Wheel of Life, The Spring Almost Eternal* and *The Brotherhood of the Holy Oil.* These are End Times Cults, which subscribe to the belief that, as individual clockwork toys enjoy only a finite existence due to the ravages of rust, corrosion, spring breakage and fluff in the works, so too does the Universe.

Their prophets of doom foretell The Time of the Terrible Stillness, when the great mechanism that powers the Universe will grind to a halt, the planet will no longer turn upon its axis, the sun will no longer rise and even time itself will come to a standstill.

If asked what The Universal Engineer will be doing at this momentous moment, they will politely explain that He will be cranking up a new Universe elsewhere, powered by something even greater than clockwork.

If asked what this power could possibly be, they will like as not reply, 'And there you have it! What power *could* be greater than clockwork?'

The Daughters of the Unseeable Upness is a movement composed entirely of dolls – but only those dolls that have weighted eyes which automatically close when the doll's head is tilted backwards. Such city-dwelling dolls can never see the sky, as their eyes shut when they lean backwards to look upwards. These dolls therefore believe that the sky is a sacred place that must not be seen, and that all who do see it risk instant damnation.

As with clockwork toys, dolls enjoy only a limited existence before they eventually disintegrate, and as the onset of disintegration in dolls is inevitably marked by one of their eyes sticking open, followers of this religious persuasion invariably wear large, broad-brimmed, sanctified straw hats, or have their eyes glued in the half-shut position.

According to the followers of *Big Box Fella, He Come*, as everything new, especially a toy, always comes in a box, then so too did the universe.

The universe, they claim, is a construction kit, which God assembled with the aid of his little helpers. It is God's toy. One day, they claim, God will tire of his toy, disassemble it and, being a well-brought-up God, put it back in its box.

And that will be that for the universe.

This particular religious belief system is predominant amongst Jack-in-the-boxes. They consider themselves to be special and blessed because they are the only toys that actually remain within their original boxes, the toy nearest to perfection being the toy that has never been taken out of its box.

They believe that the universe is cubic, the shape of its original box, and so see themselves as microcosmic. The assembled universe consists of a number of boxes, one inside the other, the smallest of these containing the Jack himself. This exists within a larger cubic box, the city, which stands upon a cubic world, within a boxed solar system.

Mortals, they claim, cannot travel between the separate boxes: only Big Box Fella can do that – he and his nameless evil twin.

Big Box Fella is one of God's little helpers. He and his brother were given the task of assembling the city, which was part of the Universe Kit. It was God's intention that, once the city had been correctly constructed, Big Box Fella and his brother would tend to its upkeep and protect its also-to-be-assembled population (you have to remember that the universe is a very complicated construction kit).

However, things did not go quite as planned, because Big

Box Fella's brother refused to follow the instructions, thereby committing the first ever act of evil. He improvised, with the result that certain things were incorrectly assembled, other things had parts left out and a city that would otherwise have been perfect was anything but.

Big Box Fella cast his brother out of the city and attempted to put things right, but, out of spite, his brother had taken the instructions with him, and so the task was impossible.

Some followers of this cult think that Big Box Fella is still in the city, tirelessly working to correct all his brother's mistakes. Most, however, believe that he left the city and went in search of his evil twin, to retrieve the instructions, and that he will return one glorious day and make everything perfect.

This, they hope, will happen before God tires of his toy universe, takes it all to pieces and puts it back in its box.

The Midnight Growlers has been described as 'a robust and rumbustious cult, more a drinking club than a religion, characterised by rowdy behaviour, the swearing of mighty oaths, the imbibing of strong liquors in prodigious quantities and the performance of naughtiness, for the sake of naughtiness alone'.

For the greater part, the teddies of Toy City (The Midnight Growlers is a teddy bear cult) are law-abiding model citizens, who picnic and go walky-round-the-garden, behave with good grace and exhibit exemplary manners. That within this dutiful ursine population such a wayward faction as The Midnight Growlers should exist is a bit of a mystery.

An investigative reporter from the Toy City press sought to infiltrate this cult. He donned an elaborate teddy costume and managed to pass himself off as a bear, and spoke at length to the Grand High Muck-a-muck of the cult, who referred to himself as The Handsome One. The Handsome One explained many things to the reporter, but the reporter, who was finding it difficult to match The Handsome One drink for drink in the downtown bar where the meeting took place, became too drunk to remember most of them.

The reporter did manage to recall that there was a great deal of convivial camaraderie within the cult, and The Handsome One constantly told him that he was 'his bestest friend'.

The reporter was eventually unmasked, however, when he fell from the barstool, on which he was attempting to balance upon his head, and passed out on the floor.

In none of these religious movements, it is noteworthy to note, is the kindly loveable white-haired old toymaker worshipped as a God. Although he is feared and revered, those toys inclined towards religious belief consider him to be a doer of God's work, but not actually a God in his own right.

The Handsome One declared that he didn't have any particular views on the subject of God, but that as far as the toymaker was concerned, he was 'his bestest friend'.

Then he too fell off his barstool.

At this present moment, however, The Handsome One and Grand High Muck-a-muck of The Midnight Growlers Cult (indeed, if the truth be told, the *only* member of The Midnight Growlers Cult) was a most unhappy bear.

He lay downcast and best-friend-less upon the cold damp floor of a cold damp cell, and he dearly wanted a beer.

The coldness and dampness of his circumstances did not concern him too much, but other things concerned him greatly.

The nature of his being, being one.

And this is not to say the *cosmic* nature of his being.

It was the physical nature of his being that presently concerned him. And the nature of this being was, to say the very least, *desperate*.

Eddie Bear raised himself upon a feeble paw and gazed down at the state of himself. It was a state to inspire great pity.

Eddie was no longer a plump little bear. He was a scrawny bear, an emaciated bear, a bear deeply sunken in the stomach regions. A bear with only one serviceable leg.

This leg, the right, was a weedy-looking article, but was superior to its companion, which was nothing but an empty flap of furry fabric.

Eddie groaned, and it hurt when he did so. Eddie's throat had been viciously cut and his head was all but severed from his body.

Eddie surveyed the bleak landscape of himself. This was bad. This was very bad. Indeed this was very, very, very bad. Eddie was in trouble deep, and such trouble troubled him deeply. Eddie Bear was afraid.

'I am done for,' mumbled Eddie.

And it hurt very much as he mumbled it.

Eddie tried to recall what had happened to him, but this wasn't proving an easy thing to do. The contents of his head were slowly leaking out through the gash in his neck. Eddie settled carefully onto his back and tried to scrape some in again.

What could he remember?

Well . . .

He could remember the kitchen. And Madame Goose. And asking her what she knew about an agile woman in a feathered bonnet who was capable of leaping over the locked gates of the chocolate factory.

Now why had he been asking about that?

Eddie gave his head a thump.

Ah yes, the woman was the suspect. The serial killer.

What happened next?

Eddie gave his head another thump and it all came rushing painfully back.

That was what happened next.

Eddie recalled it in all its hideous detail:

The door of the broom cupboard opened and Eddie was the first to see her emerge. He was impressed by the way she moved. It was smooth, almost fluid. And you couldn't help but be impressed by the way she looked. She wore a feathered bonnet, but it wasn't so much a bonnet, more some kind of winged headpiece, which fitted tightly over her skull and covered the upper portion of her face: a mask with cut-away eyeholes and a slender beak that hid her nose. The mouth beneath was painted a pink that was as pink as. And this was set into a sinister smile. The teeth that showed within this smile were very white indeed.

Her body was, in itself, something to inspire awe. Eddie had never been an appreciator of the human form. All women looked pretty much the same to him (apart from the very fat ones. These made Eddie laugh, but he found them strangely compelling). This woman wasn't fat anywhere. She was slim as a whispered secret, and twice as dangerous, too.

Her body was sheathed in contour-hugging black rubber, held in place by many straps and buckles. Eddie had never seen an outfit quite like it before. It looked very chic and expensive, but it also had the down-to-business utility quality of a military uniform about it. It flattered in an impersonal manner.

She hadn't spoken a word. And this made her somehow more terrifying – because, if she inspired awe in Eddie, she also inspired terror.

She leapt right over the table and she wrung the neck of Madame Goose with the fingers of a single hand. And then she picked up a kitchen knife and cut Eddie's throat with it.

The rest was somewhat hazy.

Eddie vaguely recalled being hauled up by his left leg, dragged along an alleyway and flung into the boot of a car. Then there was a period of bumping darkness. Then a horrible light. Then dark corridors. Then here. The cold damp cell.

And oblivion.

And now he was awake again. And gravely injured.

And very scared indeed.

★

Jack wasn't so much scared as furious.

He had been wrongfully arrested. And he had been beaten about and thrown into the rear of a police van. And now he was being driven uptown at breakneck speed. And there was a big policeman sitting on his head.

'Get your fat arse off me,' cried Jack. 'You're in big trouble. You can't treat me like this.'

Officer Chortle, whose bottom it was, laughed loudly. 'We have you bang to rights, meaty-boy,' he said. 'We've all been waiting for this one.'

'What do you mean?' Jack asked.

'For the chance to bring one of your lot to justice.'

'I don't have a *lot*,' said Jack. 'I'm just me.'

'You're a man,' said Officer Chortle. 'And men think they're above the law. The law is for toy folk, not for men. But you've killed your own kind and we have you now.'

'I demand my rights,' Jack demanded. 'And I demand to see a solicitor.' Jack had read about solicitors in a Bill Winkie thriller. Suspects always demanded to see their solicitors. It was a tradition, or an old charter, or something.

It was a suspect thing.

'No solicitor for you,' said Officer Chortle, who read only weapons manuals. (Though mostly he just looked at the pictures.) 'You're going uptown and we'll lock you away until all the paperwork's done. Then I think we'll take you to pieces, to see what makes you run.'

'No!' Jack shouted. 'You can't do that to me.'

'Tell it to Bellis,' said the officer.

'Is he here?'

'No, he went on ahead. Probably to warm your cell for you. He left me to act on my own initiative. I love it when he does that. It means that I can hit things.'

'Listen,' said Jack, trying to think straight, 'can't we make some kind of a deal?'

'Are you trying to bribe an officer of the Law?'

'Frankly, yes,' said Jack.

'Go on then,' said the officer of the Law.

'All right,' said Jack. 'You hate meat-heads, don't you?'

'I do,' said Officer Chortle. 'We all do.'

'So you don't really care about them being killed.'

'Not at all,' said the officer.

'So the more that get killed, the happier you'll be.'

'That's true,' the officer agreed.

'So let me go and I promise to kill loads more of them. I'll kill them all, if you want. What could be fairer than that?'

'Well,' said Officer Chortle, 'if you put it that way,' and he raised his bum from Jack's head.

'Thanks,' said Jack.

'Had you fooled.' Officer Chortle sat down once more. 'That's all the confession we needed. You heard what he said, didn't you, men?'

'Yes we did,' said the officers, laughing fit to burst.

The police van sped onwards through the night-time streets of Toy City, the bell on its top ringing loudly. The ringing of this bell gave Jack a headache. The pressure of Officer Chortle's bottom didn't help to soothe the pain.

'You've got the wrong man, you know,' Jack ventured.

'You've said enough,' said Chortle. 'Be silent now, or I will be forced to plug your mouth.'

Jack maintained another of his sulking silences.

At length a new sound came to Jack's ears. It was louder than the ringing bell and it caused Officer Chortle to raise his bum once more.

'What is *that*?' he shouted above the sound, which had grown to an all but intolerable din. It was now accompanied by a considerable grinding vibration.

The driver of the police van shouted back at Officer Chortle. 'It's a fire engine,' he shouted. 'A Mark 5 Roaring Thunderer. The deluxe model. It's trying to push us off the road.'

'What?' shouted Officer Chortle. 'That's outrageous. Push it back.'

'But sir, it's a Roaring Thunderer. It's bigger than us. Much bigger.'

Officer Chortle glared out through the police van's rear window. The Roaring Thunderer *was* much bigger. Very much bigger indeed.

'Do something, driver,' he ordered. 'I'm in charge here. Take evasive action.'

The driver took evasive action. He swerved onto the pavement, scattering pedestrians, including several who had, by coincidence, been earlier scattered by Jack.

'He's coming after us,' shouted the driver. And the Roaring Thunderer was.

It really was a magnificent vehicle. Constructed of heavy gauge pressed steel and finished in glossy red and black, it had a nickel-plated ladder, with wheel-operated rotating turntable and elevation extension, powered by a crank handle, pressed steel wheels and a cab-mounted bell. It normally came complete with six tinplate firemen, two with hose-gripping hand attachments.

Had Jack been able to see it, he would have admired it. And he certainly would have wanted to drive it. The reflected streetlights glittered on its polished bits and bots. It was mechanised by two extremely powerful double-sprung synchronised clockwork motors which took five clockwork firemen to turn its enormous key.

The Roaring Thunderer careered along the kerb, striking down lampposts and tearing the overhanging awnings from the shops and bazaars. It struck the police van once again. The driver of the police van took to praying.

'You're not a mechanologist,' shouted Officer Chortle. 'You're a bendy policeman. Cut that out and drive faster.'

'The van won't go any faster. Oh no!'

The police van overturned. Over and over and over it overturned.

Within the van, the officers of the Law and their captive revolved in a blur of blue bouncing bellies and long lanky limbs. The rear doors burst open and Jack found himself airborne.

And then things went very black for Jack.

Very black indeed.

Eddie moved once more into the black. Unconsciousness was never anything other than black for Eddie, for teddy bears don't dream while they sleep. They exist in a state of non-being which is truly un-conscious.

How long Eddie remained in this particular period of blackness he was unable to say, because he didn't have a watch. He had tried to wear one in the past, but it always fell off, his stumpy little arm lacking a wrist. This particular period of blackness ended in an abrupt fashion when a bright light shone upon him.

Eddie peered up, shielding his eyes with a floppy paw.

A figure stared down upon Eddie.

Eddie flinched.

The figure said, 'Eddie, it's you.'

Eddie said, '*Jack?* My bestest friend? Is that you?'

'It's me,' said Jack. 'It's me.'

'And you've come to save me. Jack, this is wonderful, how—'

But Eddie's words were cut short as Jack was suddenly propelled forward at considerable speed. He landed heavily upon the bear, raising a cloud of sawdust and causing Eddie's button eyes to all but pop from his head.

Before he passed once more into blackness, Eddie was able to glimpse the force behind Jack's untoward propulsion.

Standing in the doorway of the cell was the woman in the winged headpiece.

She didn't speak a word. She just smiled.

And then she slammed the cell door shut upon both of them.

14

'Kidnapped.' Jack sat shivering in the coldness and dampness and in the mostly darkness of the horrid little cell. 'She kidnapped me. She hijacked a fire engine, drove the police van off the road, I fell out, she picked me up and threw me in the boot of a car and drove here. Where is here, by the way? Oh, Eddie, I'm so glad to see you.'

'Kidnapped?' Eddie whispered. 'Police van?'

'It's a long story,' said Jack, giving the bear's sunken belly a gentle pat. 'And it's far from over. Who is she, Eddie? She's really scary.'

Eddie tried to shake his head, but couldn't.

'I'm sorry I fell on you,' said Jack. 'And I can't see you too well in this mostly darkness. But from what I can see, you look in a terrible state. Is there anything I can do for you?'

'Get me out of here,' Eddie's voice was faint. 'Get me to the toymaker. Only he can save me.'

'Oh Eddie, I'm so sorry. Can't I stuff you with something? I could tear up your trenchcoat.'

'Won't work. Get me to the toymaker, Jack. Save me.'

'But how?'

'Use your clockwork pistol. Shoot the lock off.'

'Chief Inspector Bellis confiscated my pistol. He said it was evidence.' Jack rose and peeped out through the little grille in the cell door. 'Perhaps the key's in the lock,' he said. 'I know this really clever trick.'

'Everybody knows that trick.' Eddie made small moaning sounds. 'The key won't be in the lock.'

142

'There might be a loose flagstone with a secret passage under it. There often is in books.'

Eddie moaned a little more.

'Don't worry, Eddie, I'll get us out of here.' Jack knelt once more and cradled Eddie's wobbly head. 'You'll be all right,' he said. 'I'll get you to the toymaker. He'll have you as good as new. Better than new.'

Eddie's button eyes crossed.

'Stay awake, Eddie.' Jack stroked the bear's head. 'We're in this together. We're partners, aren't we? Partners don't let each other down. Partners stick together through thick and thin.'

Eddie said nothing.

'Come on, stay awake.' Jack shook Eddie's head, but gently. 'Don't you . . .' His words tailed off. 'Don't you . . .'

'Die?' whispered Eddie. 'Get me to the toymaker.'

'Right,' said Jack. And he leapt to his feet.

'Ow,' went Eddie as his head struck the floor.

'Sorry, sorry. But I'll get us out. I will.'

Jack looked all around and about. Around and about looked hopeless: a horrid little cell of coldness and dampness and mostly darkness. A sturdy cell door and not a hint of window. The floor was of concrete, with no hint of flagstone.

'Only one way out,' said Jack. 'I'll have to pick the lock.'

Eddie said nothing. The chances that Jack could actually pick a lock were so remote that they did not require commenting upon.

Jack peered into the keyhole. A wan light shone through it.

'Hm,' went Jack thoughtfully. 'That would be a big old lock, by the look of it.'

To save his energy, Eddie groaned inwardly.

'But,' said Jack, 'it's probably just your standard side-crank mortise lock, with a single-arc lever action and a drop-bolt sliding movement.'

'Uh?' went Eddie.

'Locks are only clockwork motors without the motors,' said Jack. 'And if I do know about anything, Eddie, I know about clockwork.'

'Mm,' went Eddie, in an encouraging manner.

'So,' said Jack. 'All I need is something to pick it with.' He rooted around in his pockets. 'Ah,' he went at length. It was a discouraging 'Ah'. The kind of an 'Ah' that a lad might make when he finds that he has nothing whatsoever in his pockets to pick a lock with.

'Eddie,' said Jack.

Eddie said nothing.

'Eddie, I don't suppose you have a piece of wire about your person?'

Eddie said nothing once more.

'It's only that if you did, I really *could* pick that lock. But I don't seem to have anything on me.'

Eddie raised a feeble paw.

Jack knelt down beside him. 'Sorry,' said Jack.

Eddie's mouth opened.

Jack leaned closer.

'Growler,' whispered Eddie.

'Well there's no need to be insulting. I'm doing my best.'

'My growler. Use my growler.'

'What?'

'There's wire in the diaphragm of my growler, use that.'

'What?' went Jack again.

'Put your hand down the hole in my throat. Pull out my growler; do it quickly, hurry.'

'But,' went Jack, 'are you sure it won't kill you or anything?'

'Just do it now, Jack. There's no time left.'

Jack made a pained expression. The idea of putting his hand through the hole in someone's throat and tearing out their voice box was most unappealing. But then, Eddie was only a toy.

Jack made a brave face. Eddie wasn't *only* a toy. Eddie was his friend. His bestest friend. And he had to save his friend.

Jack steeled himself and then, very gently, he did what had to be done.

Eddie sighed softly. His mouth moved, but no words came from it.

'We're out of here,' said Jack. 'Just trust me.'

Now as anyone who has ever tried to pick a lock will tell you, there's a definite knack to it: a bit like riding a bike, or holding a tiger by the tail, or dining with the devil with a very long fork. Or, if you are into sexual gymnastics, engaging in that position known as 'taking tea with the parson'.

Or doing algebra.

Or climbing a mountain.

Or knowing the secret of when to stop.

But the point of all this is, that some of us have the knack.

And some of us haven't.

And when it came to picking locks, Jack hadn't.

'There,' said Jack. 'That's got it.'

But it hadn't.

'There,' he said once more. '*That's* got it.'

And it had.

Which certainly proves something.

Jack eased open the cell door. No hideous groaning of hinges broke the silence.

What light that could fall through the cell doorway fell through, in and onto Eddie. It displayed, in gruesome detail, just how dire the little bear's condition now was.

'You'll be fine,' said Jack, although there was a lack of conviction in his tone. 'I'm going to have to fold you up a bit and stuff you into my big inside pocket. I'll stick you in head downwards, so you don't, you know, lose any more brains or anything.'

Jack did the business as delicately as he could.

He closed and buttoned his coat. Patting softly at the bulge that was Eddie, he whispered, 'You'll be okay, my friend.' And then, upon very light feet indeed, Jack tiptoed up the passageway.

It was a low and narrow passageway and all along its length there were other cell doors. Jack didn't stop to peep in at any, but he felt certain he could feel eyes peering at him through the nasty little grilles. Jack hastened his tiptoeing. This was not a nice place to be.

Up ahead was an iron staircase. Jack took the steps two at a time.

And then there was another passageway.

And then another.

And then one more.

And then another one more.

And then there was an iron staircase leading down.

And then another passageway.

And then Jack was back at the open cell door.

'Ah,' said Jack. 'Now there's a thing.'

Jack retraced his footsteps.

Now it would be tedious indeed to continue with this kind of stuff for too long, what with some of us knowing the secret of knowing when to stop. So let it just be said that after a great deal more passageway perambulation, Jack eventually came upon a door that led to a street. And, having picked its lock, opened it. And on that street, which was not one that Jack recognised, there stood an automobile.

It was long and low and expensive-looking. And Jack, who still had some lock-picking left in him, availed himself of this automobile and drove it away at some speed.

Jack drove and drove until the car ran down, rewound it and drove on some more. He eventually found himself in an area of the city that he recognised, and finally he drove up Knob Hill towards the house of the kindly loveable white-haired old toymaker.

It was a fine old house. A fine *dark* house: all turrets and spires and gables. Its leaded glass windows were deeply mullioned and its slated roofs pitched at queer angles.

There were buttresses fashioned with grinning gargoyles and all kinds of glorious architectural fiddly bits. These fussed around and about the house and offered the eye of the beholder much to dwell upon.

There were no fences or gates, only a bit of a gravel drive. Jack parked the car upon this, told Eddie, 'We're here,' and removed himself at speed to the toymaker's door.

The door was a singularly magnificent affair. It put Jack in mind of Humpty Dumpty's door. It was old-style grand.

At its centre was a large, carved smiley face with a huge brass ring through its nose. This ring was the knocker. Jack reached out towards it.

'Don't even think about touching that,' said the carved smiley face. 'You can't come in. Goodbye.'

Although little about Toy City now surprised Jack, the carved smiley face on the door caught him somewhat unawares.

'Oh,' said Jack. 'Oh.'

'Oh?' said the face. 'Is that all you have to say for yourself?'

'I have to see the toymaker,' said Jack.

'Say please then.'

'Please,' said Jack.

'No,' said the face. 'Go away.'

'I *have* to see the toymaker. It's urgent. It's a matter of life and death.'

'It always is,' said the face. 'No one ever comes just to pay a visit. Or bring presents. Oh no, they turn up here at all hours of the night saying "my arm's fallen off", or "my spring's coming loose", or "a rat's gnawed my foot", or . . .'

Jack reached out his hand.

'Don't touch my knocker,' said the face. 'I'll bite you.'

'I have a bear here that needs fixing.'

'There you go,' said the face. 'See what I mean? I knew it. I just knew it. Go away. Come back tomorrow.'

'Let me in now,' said Jack.

'And what happened to *please*?'

'Right,' said Jack. 'Stuff you.' And he pulled out the wire from Eddie's growler and prepared to pick yet another lock.

'What are you doing?' asked the face.

'Letting myself in,' said Jack.

'You can't do that. It's more than my job's worth to let you do that.'

'Do you have a brother by any chance?' Jack asked.

'Certainly do. He's the gatekeeper at the chocolate factory.'

'What a surprise,' said Jack. 'Well, I'm letting myself in.'

'But you can't *do* that.'

'And what are you going to do about it?'

The face made a thoughtful face. 'You've got me there,' it said. 'If you were in my position, what would you do?'

'Well,' said Jack. 'You discourage folk from entering, don't you?'

'I certainly do,' said the face. 'Lot of selfish timewasters. I keep 'em out. Stop them from bothering the toymaker.'

'And that's your job, is it?' Jack was growing frantic.

'Not as such,' said the face. 'I act on my own initiative.'

'So when was the last time you actually let anyone in?'

The face made an even more thoughtful face. 'Can't remember,' it said. 'Ages ago.'

'So no one ever gets to see the toymaker?'

'He's busy. He designs toys.'

'How do you know what he does?' Jack's fingers were now at the keyhole.

'I can see what you're doing,' said the face.

'So what are you going to do about it?'

The face made a thoughtful face, perhaps even *more* thoughtful than the previous one. Then suddenly it made an enlightened face. 'Raise the alarm,' it said.

'How?' Jack asked.

The face began to frantically knock its knocker.

'Inspired,' said Jack. 'You certainly are a credit to your profession.'

Knock Knock Knock Knock Knock went the knocker.

And at length the door opened.

Jack looked in.

And a very old face looked out at him.

It was a very old face, but it was a big one: a big face on a large head that was attached to a little body.

Now it is another fact, well known to those who know it well, that very famous people always have big faces. They have big faces and little bodies. Why this is, no one knows for sure – even those who know facts well don't know it. But it's true and there it is.

Jack said, 'Sir, are you the toymaker?'

'I am the kindly loveable white-haired old toymaker,' said the toymaker, and he indicated his hair and the kindliness of his features. And they *were* kindly. *Very* kindly.

'Then, sir, please, I need your help. My friend has been grievously injured.'

'I can only help toys,' said the toymaker.

'Intruder!' shrieked the wooden face. 'Call the police!'

'Be quiet, Peter,' said the toymaker.

'My friend is a toy,' said Jack. 'He's a bear.' Jack opened his coat.

The toymaker peered in. 'From what I can see, he looks a little under the weather,' said he. 'You'd best bring him in and I'll see what I can do.'

'Thank you, sir,' said Jack.

'And enough of that *sir* business. My name is Mr Anders. You can call me Anders.'

'That doesn't sound too polite.'

'It's my first name. I'm Anders Anders.'

'Oh,' said Jack.

The toymaker swung wide the door and, much to the disgust of the carved knocker face, ushered Jack inside.

It's strange how some homes are so much bigger on the inside than you would expect, isn't it?

So it came as a huge surprise to Jack to find just how really small the toymaker's house was inside.

Jack had to duck his head.

'It's a spatial ambiguity thing,' the toymaker explained as he led Jack towards his workroom. 'Something to do with the transperambulation of pseudo-cosmic antimatter. Easily explainable in terms of quantum physics, if you know what I mean.'

'Haven't a clue,' said Jack.

'Well, let's get your little friend onto the workbench and see what can be done for him.'

'Yes,' said Jack. 'Let's do that.'

The workroom was *exactly* as Jack might have expected it to look.

Tools of many persuasions were racked on every wall between shelves and shelves of gingham and lace and kapok and countless jars containing glass eyes that stared out blankly at Jack. Sewing machines and other machines jostled for space upon a workbench crowded with half-completed toys. Beneath this, rolls and rolls of fur fabric of every bear shade were piled upon one another in furry confusion. From the low ceiling hung dolls' arms and legs of all sizes and shapes.

A coal fire burned brightly in a tiny fireplace and beside this stood a comfy-looking chair.

'Onto the bench with him then,' said the toymaker.

Jack carefully eased Eddie from his pocket and laid him down on the workbench.

'Oh dear,' said the toymaker. 'This is a very sorry-looking bear. I think we'd be better just to bin him.'

'No!' said Jack. 'No, please, he's my friend. Save him if you can.'

'Your friend,' said the toymaker. 'He really *is* your friend?'

'He is,' said Jack. 'I care about him.'

'Nice,' said the toymaker. 'Very nice.' And he looked once more upon Eddie. 'Ah,' he said. 'I know this model. It's one of the old Anders Standards.'

'I was given to understand that he's an Anders Imperial,' said Jack. 'He has a "special tag" in his ear.'

Mr Anders viewed the "special tag". He raised a quizzical eyebrow and then he laughed. 'Toys will be toys,' he said. 'And this one, you say, is your friend?'

Jack nodded. 'My bestest friend,' he said.

'Nice,' said the toymaker once more. 'Everyone should have a bestest friend. And a bear is as good as any to have. But this little bear is all but gone. Perhaps I should empty out his head and give him a complete refill.'

'No, please don't do that. He's Eddie, let him still be Eddie.'

'You really *do* care, don't you?'

'Very much,' said Jack.

'I'll leave his head alone then and just re-stuff the rest of him.'

'He needs a new growler,' said Jack.

'He's lost his growler? What a careless little bear.' The toymaker shook his kindly white-haired old head. 'Well, you go and sit yourself down in that comfy-looking chair and I'll see what I can do to save your Eddie.'

'Thank you, sir.' Jack took himself over to the comfy-looking chair and sat down upon it.

'You can't sit here,' said the chair.

'Oh,' said Jack, leaping up.

'Quiet, you,' the toymaker told the chair. 'He's my guest. Sit down again, my boy.'

'Jack,' said Jack. 'My name is Jack.'

'There'll never be a shortage of Jacks in this city,' said the toymaker, and he set to work upon Eddie.

Jack sat down once more. The chair made a grumpy sound and did what it could to make itself uncomfortable.

Jack watched the toymaker at work.

So this was him: the man behind it all. The man who somehow brought toys to life. The man with the Big Secret. And here he was in his workshop, putting Eddie back together. And being so kindly and loveable and white-haired and everything.

And then it all hit Jack. All of a sudden. Like.

The toymaker didn't know, did he? He had no idea at all about what was going on out there in Toy City. He didn't know what a ghastly dystopia of a place it had become. He was all cosseted away here, guarded by the knocker on his front door.

'How are you doing?' Jack asked the toymaker.

'It will take a bit of time. Perhaps you'd better come back in the morning.'

Jack thought about this, but, no, he had nowhere to go. He was a wanted man. The police were after him. And the wild woman with the winged hat. She'd probably know by now that he'd escaped, *and* stolen her car.

'I'll stay here, if you don't mind,' said Jack.

'Then get yourself some sleep,' said the toymaker. 'That chair is very comfortable.'

'Thanks,' said Jack as the chair made rocky fists beneath his bum. 'I am rather tired, as it happens. And rather hungry too, as that happens also.'

'I'll wake you for breakfast then,' said the toymaker.

What a nice man, thought Jack and, even with rocky fists under his bum, was very soon fast asleep.

15

Jack did not enjoy a lot of restful slumbering. Jack spent the night assailed by terrible dreams. And they really *were* terrible, filled with murder and mayhem and him running and running, pursued by all manner of monstrous nasties. Jack tossed and turned and fretted and mumbled and finally awoke to find that he had been thoughtfully covered by a colourful quilt, but had the silly big face of a bear grinning down at him.

'Waaah!' went Jack, leaping up.

'Easy, chap.' The silly big face vanished as Eddie Bear fell to the floor.

'Eddie, it's you. You're fixed.'

'I'm as good as.' Eddie fairly beamed.

Jack looked down at Eddie. Eddie looked up at Jack.

'Eddie,' said Jack.

'Jack, chap?' said Eddie.

'Eddie,' said Jack. 'That isn't your voice.'

'New growler, chap,' said Eddie. 'Posh, ain't it?'

'Very posh,' said Jack. 'But I don't like the *chap* business.'

'Sorry, chap. I mean, sorry, Jack. And thank you. Thank you very much.'

'My pleasure,' said Jack. 'And oh, I smell breakfast.'

Jack and Eddie took their breakfast with the kindly loveable white-haired old toymaker. It was a banquet of a breakfast; a belly-busting beano; a guzzling gourmand's groaning-board blowout. It consisted, amongst other things, of creamed crad, honeyed ham, devilled dumplings and grilled greengages, not to mention the sautéed salmon, spiced spinach, parboiled pumpkin and peppered persimmon. Nor indeed, the caramelised carrots or the fricasséed frog.

And during the course of this eclectic and alliterative breakfast, Jack did his best to engage the toymaker in conversation.

'Sir,' said Jack, 'I'm so very grateful to you for saving my friend. If I had any money, then I'd gladly pay you. But if there is anything I can do for you, please tell me and I'll do it.'

'There isn't,' said the toymaker, munching on marinated mallard.

'Anything at all,' said Jack, toying with his tenderised tit.

'Nothing,' said the toymaker, skilfully spearing stuffed starfish with his filigreed fork.

'I'm very good with clockwork.' Jack diddled with a deep-fried dogfish. 'I was apprenticed.'

'Where?' the toymaker asked as he pursued a pickled pea around his plate.

Jack told him where.

The toymaker raised a snowy eyebrow. 'And you left there to come to the city?'

'It's a long story,' said Jack, 'but if there's anything I can do . . . if you need an apprentice or an assembler or—'

Eddie kicked Jack under the table.

'When I've finished the work I'm presently engaged in, of course.' Jack scooped up and swallowed a sliver of souffléd sugar beet.

'And what work is that?' asked the toymaker.

'I'm—'

Eddie kicked Jack again.

'Ouch,' said Jack and he glared at Eddie.

Eddie put his paw up to his mouth and made shushing sounds.

The toymaker looked from Jack to Eddie and then back at Jack once more.

'It's lowly work,' said Jack. 'Compared to what you do, it's absolutely nothing.'

'I don't consider what I do to be work.' The toy-maker pushed a portion of potted plums onto his plate. 'What I do is fun and games. Everything I do is fun and games. The fun for me is in the game. The game is in the fun.'

'Right,' said Jack, 'but, sir—'

'Call me Anders,' said the toymaker. 'Anders Anders is my name.'

'Mr Anders, then. Can I ask you a question?'

'I don't know,' said Anders Anders, '*can* you?'

'*May* I ask you a question?'

'You may.'

'Then please will you tell me, how is it done?'

'How is what done?'

'The toys, how do you bring them to life?'

'You can't ask *that*.' Eddie, whose face was full of flambéed flamingo, spat much of it all over Jack.

'Steady on,' said Jack, wiping himself.

'You can't ask Mr Anders *that*! Bad chap!'

'He can,' said Mr Anders. 'He can ask.'

'Then how *do* you do it?'

'I said you could ask. I didn't say that I would tell you.'

'And so you won't?'

Mr Anders shook his kindly loveable white-haired old head. 'No,' he said.

'Then please just tell me this,' said Jack. 'Is it magic?'

The toymaker shook his head once more. 'Not magic,' he said. 'Science. And that is all I will say. One day I may well take on an apprentice. And one day, perhaps, that apprentice will be you. But not today and not for a long time yet to come. So, for now, would you care for some more of this frazzled falafel?'

'Yes please,' said Jack.

'Me too,' said Eddie. 'And another of those bevelled brownies.'

When the breakfasting was finally done with and Jack and

Eddie, big-bellied both, bade the toymaker farewell, Jack offered his hand and the ancient fellow shook it.

'I'm very grateful, sir,' said Jack. 'I really truly am.'

'Anders,' said Anders Anders. 'Just call me Anders.'

'Thank you, Anders,' said Jack. 'I am deeply grateful.'

'That goes for me too, chap,' said Eddie. 'Chap, *sir*. Thank you, thank you, thank you.'

'Look after each other,' said the toymaker. 'And be good.'

The door closed upon them. 'And don't come back,' said the carved face of Peter upon it.

'Well,' said Jack. 'Wasn't he the nice one.'

'A regular gent,' said Eddie.

'You know I'm sure that if we'd asked him nicely, he'd have seen his way clear to fitting you out with opposable thumbs.'

'*Waaah!*' went Eddie.

'Waaah?' queried Jack.

'Waaah there,' Eddie pointed a paw with a non-opposable or any otherwise thumb. 'It's *her* car! *She's* here.'

'Calm down, Eddie,' said Jack. 'I stole the car.'

'Right,' said Eddie. 'Well done, chap.'

'Please stop it with the *chap* thing.'

'I can't help it. It's the new growler. It'll wear in, bear with me.'

Jack laughed.

'Why are you laughing?'

'You said bear with me. And you're a bear.'

'That is *very* sad,' said Eddie.

'You're the same old Eddie,' said Jack. 'Shall we go?'

'We shall,' said Eddie.

'And where to?'

'Back to the serial killer's hideout. We'll stake the place out and then plan how we can capture her.'

'Ah,' said Jack. 'Ah.'

★

Jack drove the car and Eddie sat trying to fold his arms and look huff-full.

'Never made a note of the address,' said Eddie. 'How unprofessional is *that*?'

'I was thinking of *you*. I just wanted to get you to the toymaker's.'

'Yeah, well.'

'How dare you "Yeah, well" me. I saved your life.'

'Yes, you did. And I'm very grateful. But we have to stop this thing.'

'You were right, though, Eddie. It's a woman.'

'I wasn't right,' said Eddie. 'Take a left here.'

Jack took a left. 'Why weren't you right?' he asked.

'Because she's *not* a woman.'

'*Not* a woman? You're saying she's some kind of toy?'

'She's not a toy,' said Eddie.

'Not a woman and not a toy? So what is she, Eddie?'

'I don't know,' said the bear. 'And that's what really worries me.'

'She's a woman,' said Jack. 'A very strange woman, I grant you, but she's a woman. I know what women look like and she looks like a woman.'

'But she doesn't smell like one,' said Eddie. 'Under the perfume, she doesn't smell like a woman. I've got a bear's nose.' Eddie tapped at that nose. 'My nose knows.'

'She's a woman,' said Jack.

'She's not,' said Eddie. 'Take a right.'

Jack took a right. 'Where are we going?' he asked.

'Back to Wibbly's,' said Eddie. 'I asked him to check out a few things for me. We'll see how he got on.'

Eventually they arrived at Wibbly's. Jack waited in the car while Eddie slid down Wibbly's ramp. Eddie returned and Eddie didn't look at all well. He flopped in the passenger seat and stared at the dashboard.

'What did he say?' Jack asked.

'He didn't say anything.'

'He didn't find out anything?'

'No, Jack,' Eddie looked up at Jack. 'He didn't say anything because he couldn't say anything. Wibbly is all over the floor. Someone smashed him all to pieces.'

'No,' said Jack.

'We have to stop her,' said Eddie. 'Whatever she is, we have to stop her. Madame Goose was bad enough, but Wibbly was a close friend. This time it's personal.'

Jack stared out through the windscreen. 'We've got her car,' he said. 'Can't we trace her through the car?'

A smile broke out upon Eddie's face. 'Good one, Jack, chap,' he said. 'Let's have a go at that.'

The showrooms of the Clockwork Car Company were in the very best part of the city, just five doors down from *Oh Boy!*.

The building itself was a magnificent affair and a description of its architectural splendours might well have filled several paragraphs, had anyone been in the mood to write them down. But if anyone had been in the mood, then that mood might well have been modified by the fact that the showrooms of the Clockwork Car Company were presently fiercely ablaze.

Jack leapt out of the car. Eddie leapt out with him. Clockwork fire-fighters were unrolling hoses. Crowds viewed the holocaust, oohing and ahhing. Jolly red-faced policemen held back these crowds, ha–ha–hahing as they did so. A crenellated column toppled and fell, striking the pavement with a devastating sprunch.

'She got here first,' said Jack. 'She's very thorough, isn't she?'

'Very,' said Eddie. 'Very thorough.'

Jack gawped up at the roaring flames.

'Eddie,' he said.

'Jack?' said Eddie.

'Eddie, if she's that thorough, then she knew we'd come here, didn't she?'

Eddie nodded.

'And would I be right in thinking that she probably wants to kill us now?'

Eddie nodded again.

'So doesn't it follow that she'd probably be here? Awaiting our arrival?'

'Back into the car,' said Eddie. 'Quick as you can, please, chap.'

And quick as they could, they were back in the car.

'Drive?' said Jack.

'Drive,' said Eddie. 'No, don't drive.'

'Don't?' said Jack.

'Don't,' said Eddie. 'That's exactly what she wants us to do.'

'It's exactly what *I* want us to do,' said Jack. 'And fast.'

'Exactly. So that's exactly what we mustn't do. If we make a run for it, she'll come after us. We must stay here amongst all these folk. She's less likely to attack us here.'

'A vanload of policemen didn't worry her too much last night,' said Jack.

'Well, unless you can come up with a better idea.'

'There's policemen here,' said Jack. 'And the police are after me. They think I'm the murderer.'

'Forget about the policemen,' Eddie said. 'Worry about her. We can't have her hunting us. That's not the way detectives do business. It's unprofessional. Bill Winkie would never have let that happen. We're going about this all the wrong way.'

'Well done,' said Jack.

'It just makes sense,' said Eddie.

'No I didn't mean that. I meant that you got seven whole sentences out without once calling me chap.'

'Let's go and watch the fire, *in the crowd*,' said Eddie. 'Chap!'

It's a sad-but-truism that there really is a great deal of pleasure to be had in watching a building burn. There shouldn't be, of course. A burning building is a terrible thing: the destruction of property, the potential for loss of life. There shouldn't be any pleasure at all in watching a thing like that. But there is. And every man knows that there is, not that many of them will own up to it.

It's a small boy thing, really. Small boys love fires. They love starting and nurturing fires, poking things into them, seeing how they burn. Small boys are supposed to grow out of such small boy things when they become big boys, of course. But they don't. The bigger the boy, the bigger the fire the bigger boy likes to get started.

And when bigger boys become men, they never lose their love of fire. They can always find something that needs burning in the backyard.

And when a man hears the ringing of those fire engine bells, the temptation to jump into the car and pursue the appliance is a tough one to resist.

And if a man just happens to be walking down the street and actually sees a building on fire . . . Well.

Jack stared up at the flames.

'What a tragedy,' he said.

'What a liar you are,' said Eddie. 'You're loving every moment.'

'No I'm not.'

'Then why were you jumping up and down and cheering?'

'Was I?' Jack asked.

'You were,' said Eddie. 'Bad, bad chap.'

'It's a small boy thing,' Jack explained. 'You wouldn't understand.'

'I certainly wouldn't,' said Eddie. 'I'm full of sawdust, remember?'

'Sorry,' said Jack. 'So what about your plan?'

'We hunted are going to become the hunters. Merge into the crowd with me, Jack, and keep your eyes open for her.'

It wasn't that easy for Jack to merge into the crowd. Most of the crowd were about Eddie's height.

'Perhaps you should crawl,' Eddie suggested.

'Oh, very dignified.'

'She might well have you in the sights of some long-range gun type of item. Of the variety capable of projecting a shepherd's crook across a street and right up Boy Blue's bottom.'

Jack dropped to his knees. 'After you,' he said.

Above them the inferno 'ferno'd on, watched by the crowd of toys who, for various personal reasons, didn't really enjoy the spectacle the way it should be enjoyed.

The clockwork fire-fighters had their hoses all unrolled now, but were decidedly hesitant about turning them on. Being clockwork, they greatly feared water.

'Ho, ho, ho,' went the laughing policemen. Jack tried to keep out of their way.

Eddie stopped and thumped at his head with his paws. 'I've an idea coming,' he said.

'I hope it's a good one,' said Jack. 'I'm getting my trenchcoat all dusty.'

'It's a great one,' said Eddie. 'I'll explain it to you on the way.'

'The way to where?'

'The way to where we steal the police car.'

There was a really nice police car parked near by, as it happened. It was a Mark 7 Fairlane Cruiser, pressed steel construction, hand-enamelled in black and white, with a nickel-plated grille and brass roof bell. It was all polished up and the pride and joy of a certain Special Constable named Chortle. Jack had no trouble at all picking the lock on the driver's door.

'I feel utterly confident that this will work,' said Eddie as he slid into the police car beside Jack.

'And what makes you feel so utterly confident?' Jack enquired.

'My natural optimism. Do the business, Jack.'

'Righty right,' said Jack. And he took up the little microphone that hung beneath the dashboard. He held it between his fingers and viewed it disdainfully. It was just a plastic nubbin attached to a piece of string. 'How can this work?' he asked.

'You just speak into it. You can talk to the police at the police station.'

'How?' Jack asked.

'With your mouth,' said Eddie.

Jack shrugged. 'Hello,' he said.

'Hello,' said Eddie.

'No, I'm saying hello into this silly pretend microphone on the piece of string.'

'Very professional,' said Eddie. 'Very good.'

'Hello,' said a voice.

'How did you do that without moving your mouth?' Jack asked.

'It's the police station, talk to them.'

Jack shook his head. 'Right,' he said. 'Emergency! Emergency!'

'Who's that saying emergency?' asked the voice.

'Me,' said Jack. 'Who's that asking?'

'Me,' said the voice.

'Officer down!' shouted Jack.

'That's not my name,' said the voice. 'I'm Officer Chuckles. And there's no need to shout.'

'There's every need to shout,' shouted Jack. 'I said *officer down!* An officer's down!'

'A downy officer?' said the voice. 'An officer covered in down?'

Jack put his hand over the microphone. 'Have you got any other great ideas?' he asked Eddie. 'This isn't going to work.'

'Yes it is. Explain in urgent tones that you are at the fire at the Clockwork Car Company showrooms. And that the *woman* who started the fire, the same woman who murdered Humpty, Boy Blue and Madame Goose, is attacking officers. Give a full description of her and demand lots of assistance. Do it, Jack.'

Jack did it. 'Send every officer you have,' he said. 'And quickly.'

'Ten-four,' said the voice in the affirmative.

'There,' said Eddie. 'Job done. Now all we have to do is sit here and wait for things to happen.'

'But she's not attacking any officers,' said Jack.

'Well, she sort-of-will-be.'

'How can she sort-of-will-be?'

'If she's attacking a police car, then that's almost the same as attacking a police officer.'

'I suppose so,' said Jack. 'But why should she be attacking a police car?'

'Because *we're* in it. I saw her following us through the crowd just before I had my great idea.'

'What?' said Jack.

'Here she comes,' said Eddie, pointing. 'Lock the doors, Jack.'

'Oh no.' Jack made haste with the door lockings.

The woman in the feathered headpiece, and Jack was in no doubt that she *was* a woman, strode across the street and stopped in front of the police car. She leaned forward and placed her hands upon the bonnet. And then she smiled at Eddie and Jack, who took to cowering in an undignified manner.

'Jack,' whispered Eddie, 'start the car.'

Jack fumbled in his pockets, searching for his piece of growler.

The woman raised her hands, made them into fists and brought them down with considerable force onto the bonnet of the Mark 7 Fairlane cruiser, making two nasty dents and spoiling the hand-enamelled paintwork.

'Waaah!' went Eddie. 'Hurry, Jack.'

Jack hurried. He pulled out the wire and went about the business. But it wasn't easy, what with the car now shuddering beneath the repeated blows.

'Get a move on!' shouted Eddie. 'She's smashing the bonnet to pieces.'

Jack got a swift move on. The wire clicked in the keyhole, releasing the twin-levered drop-bolt side-action tumblers in the lock, which freed the clockwork mechanism that powered the automobile. Jack put his foot down on the clutch and stuck the gearstick into reverse.

'Don't reverse,' cried Eddie. 'Run her down, Jack.'

'I can't do *that*,' Jack said, appalled. 'I can't run over a woman.'

'She's not a woman. She'll kill us, Jack.'

'I can't do it, Eddie.'

Jack put his foot down hard on the accelerator. Wheels went *spin spin spin* and *shriek* upon the road, but the police car stayed where it was.

'I can't reverse,' shouted Jack.

'That's because there's a big fire engine parked behind us. The only way is forward, Jack. Run her over.'

'I'll try and nudge her out of the way.' Jack stuck the car into first gear and put his foot down once again.

Spin spin spin and *shriek shriek shriek* went the wheels once more, but in a different direction this time.

'She's holding back the car.' Jack had a fine sweat going now. 'It's impossible.'

'For a woman, yes,' said Eddie. 'But not for whatever she is.'

'She's a robot from the future,' said Jack.

'What?' went Eddie.

'Sorry,' said Jack. 'I don't know why an idea like that should suddenly come into my head.'

'Put your foot down harder, give it more revs.'

'The cogs will fracture.'

'Do it, Jack.'

Jack did it. Well, he would. Anyone would have.

The police car edged forward.

Jack and Eddie cowered.

And members of the crowd were turning now, drawn

away from their interest in the flaming holocaust by the sounds of the shrieking police car wheels.

Lots of heads were turning. Most of the heads, in fact. Even policemen's heads.

The woman-or-whatever strained against the moving car. The visible area of her face wore a taut and terrible smile.

'What is she?' Jack pressed his foot down as far as it would go. 'What is she?'

'Robot from the future,' said Eddie. 'Definitely. Run *it* down, Jack. Run the nasty robot down.'

The wheels spun and shrieked and sparks rose and flickered; the police car inched forward. Whatever she was, or was not, she clung to the bonnet.

And then she leapt onto it.

Freed from her restraint, the police car footed and yarded it forward at the hurry-up, but not out into the open road that might have led to freedom. The offside wheel buckled from its axle; the car swerved and plunged across the street towards the gathered crowd and the blazing building.

'We're gonna die!' shouted Jack.

'We're gonna die!' shouted Eddie.

Aaah! And *Oooh!* And *Eeek!* went members of the gathered crowd, parting in haste before the on-rushing car.

'Ho ho ho,' went the laughing policemen, parting in haste with them.

'Out of the car,' shouted Eddie. 'Jump, Jack.'

'The doors are locked!'

'Unlock them!'

'Hang on to me, Eddie, I'm opening mine!'

'Waaah!'

Shrieking screaming wheels.

A smiling face against the windscreen.

Fleeing crowds.

Burning building.

On-rushing police car.

Doors now open.

Jack and Eddie jumping.

More on-rushing police car. Woman–or–not–woman clinging to the bonnet.

And into the inferno.

Mash and crash. Explode and grench. And spragger and munge and clab and plark and blander.

Jack and Eddie, bruised but alive.

The Clockwork Car Company showrooms coming down.

And then a terrible silence.

'Am I alive?' Eddie asked.

'You're alive,' said Jack. 'We're both alive. We're safe.'

And then a voice.

The voice of Chief Inspector Wellington Bellis.

'You are both under arrest,' said this voice.

16

'The secret of being a successful policeman,' said Chief Inspector Bellis, 'is in doing everything by the book. And before you ask me which book that is, I will tell you. It is the policeman's handbook. It tells you exactly how things are to be done. It covers all the aspects of gathering and cataloguing evidence. It is most precise.'

'Is there a point to this?' Jack asked.

'There is,' said Chief Inspector Bellis. 'There is.'

He, Jack and Eddie sat in the interview room of the Toy City Police Station. It was hardly a gay venue, as was, say, the Brown Hatter Nite Spot, over on the East Side.

Neither was it a Jolly Jack Tar of a place, like The Peg-legged Pirate's Pool Hall, over on the West Side.

Nor was it even an existential confabulation of spatial ambiguity, such as the currently displayed installation piece at the Toy City Arts Gallery, down on the South Bank Side.

Nor was it anything other than an interview room in any way, shape, form, or indeed, aesthetic medium.

In the way of such rooms, its walls were toned a depressing shade of puce. In shape it was long and low and loathsome. In furnishings, it was basic: chairs, a table and a filing cabinet, lit by a naked light bulb which dangled from the ceiling at the end of a piece of string. There was no aesthetic involved in this lighting. But the string was of medium length.

So it was, as interview rooms go, very much of a muchness.

Eddie quite liked it. It reminded him a bit of Bill Winkie's office.

Jack hated it.

'I've told you everything,' said Jack. 'And it's all the truth.'

Chief Inspector Bellis nodded his perished rubber head. He was accompanied by two laughing policemen. One of these was Officer Chortle. Although he was laughing, he pined for his police car.

'The truth,' said Bellis, staring hard at Jack. 'Now what would *you* know about the truth?'

'I've told it to you,' said Jack. 'All of it that I know.'

Chief Inspector Bellis shook his head, and sadly at that. 'Would it were so,' he said. 'But you see, criminals are notable for never telling the truth. You rarely if ever get the truth from a criminal. A criminal will profess his innocence to the end. Criminals do not tell the truth.'

'I wouldn't know about that,' said Jack, 'because I am not a criminal.'

'Which brings me back to doing things by the book,' said the Chief Inspector. 'Gathering evidence. Writing it all down. I write everything down. I have really neat handwriting. See this piece of paper here?' Bellis displayed the piece of paper. 'It has all manner of things written down upon it, in really neat handwriting. All manner of things about you. About how you entered Humpty Dumpty's apartment without permission from the authorities. And appeared shortly after the death of Boy Blue, disguised as a wealthy aristocrat. And later returned and broke into the premises, and later still escaped from police custody, and today stole Officer Chortle's brand new police car and drove it into a flaming building. How am I doing so far?'

'I demand to see my solicitor,' said Jack.

'Me too,' said Eddie. 'And even though I had a big breakfast, I'm quite hungry again. I demand to see a chef.'

'Anything else?' asked Chief Inspector Bellis.

'You could set us free,' said Eddie. 'After we've eaten.'

'Office Chortle, smite this bear,' said the Chief Inspector.

Officer Chortle leaned across the desk and bopped Eddie Bear on the head with his truncheon.

'Ouch!' went Eddie, in ready response. 'Don't hit me.'

'No, don't hit him.' Jack raised calming hands. 'We *have* told you the truth. That woman-or-whatever-she-was was the murderer. We're detectives; we were tracking her down. Did you find the body?'

'We found something,' said Chief Inspector Bellis. 'But we're not entirely certain what we've found.'

'Robot,' said Jack. 'From the future.'

'What was that?' Chief Inspector Bellis raised a perished eyebrow. Officer Chortle raised his truncheon once more.

'Nothing,' said Jack. 'Nothing at all.'

'Nothing at all.' The Chief Inspector sighed. 'Well, I have you two bang to rights, as we policemen say. So why not break new ground by simply confessing? It would save so much unnecessary violence being visited upon your persons. Not to mention all the paperwork.'

'We're innocent,' said Eddie. 'We were just pursuing the course of our investigations.'

'Oh yes,' said Chief Inspector Bellis, consulting his paperwork. 'On behalf of this mystery benefactor who paid the handsome advance to your employer, Bill Winkie, who has mysteriously vanished without trace.'

'He'll be back,' said Eddie. 'He'll tell you.'

'Perhaps,' said the perished policeman. 'But for now I have you and I have all my impeccable paperwork, all penned in precise terms, in a very neat hand, and all pointing towards your guilt. Go on, confess, you know you want to.'

'I certainly don't,' said Eddie.

'That's as good as a confession to me,' said Bellis. 'I'll make a note of that.'

'And make sure you spell all the words right,' said Eddie. 'Especially the word "twerp" and the manner in which it should be applied to yourself.'

Officer Chortle smote Eddie once more.

'Eddie,' said Jack, 'don't make things worse.'

'How can they be worse?' Eddie rubbed at his battered head. 'This fool won't listen to reason. He won't believe the truth. But at least the killer is dead. That's something. We'll have our day in court. He can't prove anything against us. There's no evidence linking us directly to the crimes.'

'And how do you know that?' asked Bellis.

'Because we didn't commit them,' said Eddie.

'I have circumstantial evidence.'

'That's no evidence at all. It won't hold up in court.'

'I don't know where you keep getting the "court" business from,' said Chief Inspector Bellis. 'There won't be any court involved in this.'

'What?' said Eddie.

'I was going to mention that,' said Jack. 'But I didn't have time. This is some kind of "authority from higher up" jobbie; the Chief Inspector has been given the power to simply make us disappear.'

Eddie made growly groaning sounds.

'Killing the cream of Toy City's society is a very big crime,' said the Chief Inspector. 'It calls for extreme measures. Now, you can confess all and I'll see to it that you go off to prison. Or you can continue to profess your innocence, and . . .' The Chief Inspector drew a perished rubber finger across his perished rubber throat.

'But we didn't commit these crimes.'

'I saw you drive that woman into the burning building with my own two eyes. That's enough for a murder charge on its own.'

'If it *was* a woman,' said Eddie. 'Which it wasn't. As you know.'

'There's an autopsy going on at this moment.' Chief Inspector Bellis arranged his paperwork neatly upon the desk. 'We'll soon know all about that. And you *did* steal this officer's police car.'

Officer Chortle glared at Eddie.

Eddie took to a sulking cowering silence.

'Look,' said the Chief Inspector. 'I'm a fair fellow. Firm

but fair, and I do believe in justice.' He turned to Jack. 'What say we just blame it all on the bear and let you go free?'

'Well,' said Jack.

'What?' said Eddie.

'No,' said Jack. 'Eddie is innocent. I'm innocent. Why not just wait for your autopsy report? See what that has to say.'

Chief Inspector Bellis sighed. 'I think we've said all that can be said here.' He rose from his chair and tucked his impeccable paperwork under his arm. 'I'll leave you in the company of these officers. They can beat the truth out of you. Then you'll both be disappeared.'

'No,' said Eddie. 'No more hitting. We give up, we confess.'

'We do?' said Jack.

'We do,' said Eddie. 'Just leave us alone here and we'll draft out our confessions.'

'Make sure that you do, or . . .' Chief Inspector Bellis drew his finger once more across his throat, nodded his farewells and, in the company of the two laughing policemen, left the interview room, slamming the door and locking it behind him.

'Well,' said Eddie to Jack. 'That's sorted.'

'Sorted?' Jack threw up his hands. 'We're done for. They'll disappear us. And why did you tell him we'd write out confessions?'

'To stop me getting hit again and buy us some time alone. Now, out with the wire, Jack, and pick the lock.'

'They confiscated the wire,' said Jack.

'We're done for,' said Eddie.

Time passes slowly in a police interview room when you're left all alone in it. Or even with a friend. Especially when you're waiting for something terrible to happen to you. Time should pass quickly in such circumstances. But it doesn't. It passes very slowly indeed.

'It's all so unfair,' said Eddie. 'We're heroes; we shouldn't be treated like this.'

'Eddie,' said Jack, 'what do you think this is really all about?'

'What do you mean?' Eddie fiddled at the door. 'If I had an opposable thumb,' he said, 'I'd always keep a really long nail on it, just for picking locks.'

'What I mean,' said Jack, 'is *what* is all this about? Who was the murderess? Why did she do what she did?'

'Who can fathom the workings of the criminal mind?' said Eddie.

'Detectives,' said Jack. 'That's what they do.'

'Not in this case, Jack. She's dead, we'll never know.'

'And soon we'll be dead. Disappeared. And that will be that for us. It's all been a bit pointless, really, hasn't it?'

'Don't talk like that, Jack. We did our best.'

'We were useless, Eddie. We were rubbish at being detectives. Everything we did was wrong. Bill Winkie would be ashamed of us.'

'Don't say that. All right, we made a few mistakes . . .'

'A *few* mistakes? We made nothing but mistakes.'

'We did our best.'

'And where has it got us? We're lucky to still be alive. And we won't be alive for much longer, I'm thinking. I'm going to write my confession and hope I can escape from prison.'

'Don't be so pessimistic, Jack. There has to be a way out of this mess.'

'Eddie,' said Jack, 'there is. I *could* pick the lock. You've got a new growler, haven't you?'

'Now hold on.' Eddie covered himself as best he could. 'That would really hurt. It really hurt the last time.'

'Yes, but we *could* escape. I'll just rip your stomach open.'

'No.' Eddie dropped from his chair and backed away.

'Only joking,' said Jack.

'Good,' said Eddie, still backing away.

'We'll just wait here until the policemen come back and beat you up some more and then disappear the both of us.'

'Out with my growler,' said Eddie Bear.

'No, there has to be another way.'

'I wish I knew one,' said Eddie.

'You know what,' said Jack, 'you were right. When you said that we were going about things in all the wrong way. About the hunters being hunted, and how we should do things the way Bill Winkie would have done them.'

Eddie nodded in a hopeless kind of way.

'I've read all the books,' said Jack. 'He wouldn't have ended up here.'

'That doesn't help,' said Eddie.

'No, sorry, it doesn't. But if he *had* ended up here, there would have been a twist to it.'

'There's always a twist in detective books,' said Eddie. 'That's what makes them special.'

'So there should be a twist here.'

'This isn't a Bill Winkie thriller.'

'Let's assume it is,' said Jack. 'Or an Eddie Bear thriller. Let's look at it all from a different perspective.'

'Big words,' said Eddie. 'So what's the twist?'

Jack shrugged. 'I wish I knew,' he said.

'Thanks very much,' said Eddie. 'That's all been very helpful.'

'Give it a chance, Eddie.'

'What, we simply sit here and wait for this twist to just happen?'

'That's exactly what we do. That's what would happen in the books. And when it happens here to us, it will change everything and we will go out and do the job properly. The way it should be done. The way it's done in detective thrillers.'

'I don't get it,' said Eddie.

'You will,' said Jack. 'Just trust me.'

And so they waited.

It was tense, but then, important waiting is always tense. It's filled with tension, every waiting moment of it.

The tense waiting was done at the exact moment when it ceased.

And it ceased at the sound of a key being turned in a lock and the sight of the interview room door swinging open.

Chief Inspector Bellis entered the interview room.

'Have you completed your written confessions?' he asked.

Eddie flinched.

'Not as such,' said Jack.

'So you've decided to go for the violent beating and disappearance option.'

'No,' cried Eddie. 'Have mercy.'

'Mercy?' The Chief Inspector's eyebrows were raised once again. 'You are asking me for mercy?'

'We are,' Jack agreed.

'Oh well, fair enough then, you can go.'

'What?' went Jack.

And 'What?' went Eddie too.

'You can both go free,' said Bellis. 'I'm dropping the charge.'

Jack's mouth hung open. Now this *was* a twist.

Eddie said 'What?' once again.

'You heard me, I'm dropping the charge.'

'Charge?' said Eddie. 'You're dropping *the* charge? Only the one? I don't understand.'

'Taking and driving away a police vehicle,' said Chief Inspector Bellis. 'That's the only charge against you and I'm dropping that charge.'

'Ah, excuse me, sir,' said Jack, 'but why?'

'Somethings have come up.'

'What kind of somethings are these?'

'Two somethings,' said the Chief Inspector. 'The body in the morgue. Or what's left of it. Isn't a body.'

'Then what is it?' Jack asked.

'I'm not authorised to tell you that.'

'Oh,' said Jack. 'And the other something?'

'There's been another murder,' said Chief Inspector Bellis. 'And, as you've both been here in custody, I know that you are not responsible. But it's the same killer as before; I'd stake my reputation on it.'

'Another murder?' Eddie said. 'But the body or whatever it is in the morgue . . .'

'Is obviously not the killer. I'm letting you go. Get out. Leave the building.'

'Thanks,' said Eddie. 'Come on, Jack.'

'I'm coming,' said Jack. 'But who died? Who was murdered?'

'Jack Spratt,' said Chief Inspector Bellis. 'Jack Spratt is dead.'

17

Apart from those that do, of course, celebrity marriages never last.

For although celebrities are very good at being celebrities (they would not *be* celebrities if they were not), most of them are absolute no-marks when it comes to being a caring partner in a shared relationship. They just can't do it. It isn't in them to do it.

Not that we ordinary folk blame them for being this way. We don't. After all, it is we ordinary folk who have made these people celebrities.

Which possibly makes *us* to blame.

Or possibly not.

No, not: it's not *our* fault. *We* have given these people celebrity. They owe *us*.

And as we have huddled in rain-soaked hordes to cheer them at their celebrity marriages, it is only fitting that they give us something in return: the entertainment of their celebrity divorces. Let's be honest here, who amongst us can genuinely claim that we do not thoroughly enjoy a really messy celebrity divorce? We love 'em. We do.

We love to read in the gutter press all about the mud-slinging, accusations and counter-accusations. And if there's a bit of the old domestic violence in the millionaire mansion, we revel in that too. We even love the petty squabbling about who gets custody of the penguin. And as to the sordid and startling disclosures of what the private investigator actually saw when he peeped in through the hotel bedroom window, those get our juices flowing fair to the onset of dehydration.

And while we're being absolutely honest here, let us admit that when it comes to reading about the celebrity divorce, women love it more than men.

They do, you know. They really do.

It's a woman thing.

If you ask a man, he'll probably tell you that yes, he does enjoy a celebrity divorce, but given the choice, he'd far rather watch a building burning down.

But that's men for you.

Jack Spratt was a man, of course: a rich celebrity of a man, and his divorce from his wife Nadine brought colour to the front pages of the Toy City gutter press for several weeks. It was a very entertaining divorce.

The grounds were 'irreconcilable culinary differences' but, as it turned out, there was a whole lot more to it than that.

They were a mismatched couple from the start. Jack, a man naturally destined for fame by nature of having a big face and a small body, married Nadine, a woman with a very small face and a very large body (physical characteristics which would normally have doomed anyone to oblivion). They married when Nadine was fifteen.

Jack had always had a thing about large women.

It was that little man thing which is only fully understood by little men. And these little men have no wish to confide it to big men, lest they get a taste for it too and cut the little men out of the equation.

Nadine was a very large woman, and Jack loved her for it.

That their eating habits were so diametrically opposed didn't matter at all to either of them. In fact, it worked perfectly well during the early part of their relationship, when they lived in a trailer park on Toy City's seedy South-West Side. He worked in the slaughterhouse district on the night shift, where the black meat market in offal flourished. Had they never achieved the fame that their nursery rhyme brought them,* they might still have been together today.

Sadly, the more rich and famous they became, the more clearly did the cracks in their relationship begin to show. They did not part amicably. She demanded a share in his chain of lean-cuisine gourmet restaurants. And he in turn laid claim to half of her fast-food burger bar franchises, *Nadine's Fast Food Diners*.

Neither wished to share anything with the other; these separate empires had been years in the building. So each sought to dish the dirt on the other – and when celebrity dirt starts getting dished, there always seems sufficient to build a fair-sized Ziggurat, a step pyramid, two long barrows and an earthwork.

With a little left over to heap into an existential confabulation of special ambiguity installation piece, such as the one currently on display at the Toy City Arts Gallery.

Jack's lawyer brought forth evidence that Nadine had been intimate with at least seven dwarves.

In response to this, Nadine hit Jack somewhat below the belt, dwelling far too graphically upon his sexual inadequacies. He had never satisfied her sexually, she said, because, with his refusal to eat fat, cunnilingus was denied to her.

This disclosure was met with howls of joy from the gutter-press-reading population. And much thumbing through dictionaries. Followed by even greater howls.

So much Eddie told Jack as they trudged across town to the rear of Boy Blue's where Jack had left Bill Winkie's car.

He told Jack more when, having discovered that Bill Winkie's car now stood upon bricks, its wheels having been removed by jobbing vandals, they trudged further

* A rhyme penned by the now legendary Wheatley Porterman, who, while still an impoverished rhyme writer, happened to be living in the trailer next door to Jack and Nadine.

across town to avail themselves of the whatever-she-was-that-wasn't-a-woman's car, which they had left parked at the scene of the Clockwork Car Company fire.

And if there was anything that Eddie had missed first or second time around, he revealed that to Jack when, having discovered, much to their chagrin, that the car had been removed to the police car pound for being parked in a tow-away zone, they trudged back to the police station.

If there was anything else that Eddie had forgotten to mention, it remained unmentioned when, upon learning that the car would only be surrendered to Jack and Eddie if they could prove ownership and pay the fine, they trudged, carless and footsore, across the street from the police station and into a *Nadine's Fast Food Diner.*

It was a spacious affair, with man-sized chairs and tables. These were all of pink plastic and pale pitch-pine. The walls were pleasantly painted with pastel portraits of portly personages, pigging out on prodigious portions of pie − which, considering the alliterative nature of the breakfast served by the toymaker, may or may not have been some kind of culinary running gag.

'I love these places,' said Eddie. 'High cholesterol dining.'

'What's cholesterol?' Jack asked.

'I think it's a kind of pig.'

A waitress greeted them. She was tall and voluptuous, pretty in pink and tottered upon preposterously high high-heels. She led them to a vacant table and brought Eddie a child's high-chair to sit on.

'I know it's undignified,' said Eddie. 'But it's worth it for the nose bag.'

The waitress said, 'I'll give you a moment,' and tottered away. Jack watched her tottering. She did have extremely wonderful legs.

'Something on your mind?' Eddie asked. 'Regarding the *dolly*?'

Jack shook his head fiercely. 'Certainly *not,*' he said. 'Do you have any money, Eddie?' He perused the menu. It was a wonderful menu. It included a host of toothsome treats with names such as The Big Boy Belly-Buster Breakfast, The Double-Whammy Bonanza Burger Blowout and The Four Fats Final Fantasy Fry-Up.

Jack cast his eye over the Hungry Cowboy's Coronary Hoedown: two 10 oz prime portions of beef belly flab, generously larded and cooked to perfection in a sealed fat-fryer to preserve all their natural grease, served between two loaves of high-fibre white bread and the soggiest chips you'll ever suck upon.

Jack's mouth watered. '*Have* you any money?' he asked Eddie.

Eddie shifted uncomfortably. 'I've done a bad thing,' he said. 'And I don't want you to hate me for it.'

'I won't hate you,' said Jack. 'What have you done?'

'I've stolen some money,' said Eddie.

'Really?' said Jack. 'From where?'

'From *whom*,' said Eddie. 'Remember when we were saying goodbye to Chief Inspector Bellis and he was giving us both a hug and saying how sorry he was that Officer Chortle had bashed me on the head with his truncheon?'

'Yes,' said Jack. 'And I noticed a tone of insincerity in his voice.'

'Me too. And when he was hugging us, I also noticed a big purse of coins in his rubbery pocket. And even without the aid of opposable thumbs, it was such a simple matter to ease it out. And I felt that he owed us for all the torment he'd put us through and . . .'

'Say no more, my friend,' said Jack. 'I understand entirely.'

'So you don't think I did a wicked thing?'

Jack shook his head and smiled broadly. Then he dipped into a trenchcoat pocket and brought out something black. 'By remarkable coincidence,' said Jack, 'I nicked his wallet.'

'Waitress,' called Eddie, 'two of the Mighty Muncher Mother-of-all-Mega-Meals, please.'

'With the Greasy Chin Cheesy Cream Dipping Sauce,' Jack added.

'And a double order of extra-fat fries on the side?' Eddie asked.

'And two slices of bread and butter,' Jack said. 'And butter the bread on both sides.'

The voluptuous waitress departed, leaving the now grinning pair.

'Once we've spent all the paper money, we should hand that wallet in,' said Eddie. 'There might be a reward.'

'Let's not push our luck,' said Jack. 'What are we going to do next?'

'Well, I thought that after we've dined, we might hit a bar or two.'

'What are we going to do about the case? I assume that we're still on the case? Jack Spratt's murder is another of these serial killings, is it not?'

'It seems logical. But with the weird woman-thing dead . . .'

'If she, or it, *is* dead,' said Jack. 'Perhaps she just got up off the morgue slab and walked away.'

'There's something big going on,' said Eddie. 'I think Chief Inspector Bellis needs all the help he can get. Even ours. Which is why he set us free.'

'So should we go to the crime scene and see what's what?'

'I'll bet we'll find another chocolate bunny. It's as certain as.'

'Tell me, Eddie,' said Jack. 'I didn't like to ask, but was there one in Wibbly's lower-ground-floor apartment?'

Eddie nodded grimly. 'But hey hey,' he said, 'here comes the grub.'

'Now *that* is what I call fast food.'

The waitress laid the spread before them. It covered most of the table. She returned to the kitchen, then returned to the diners with another tray-full.

'Pull that table over,' said Eddie.

Jack pulled the table over and the waitress unloaded the second tray. 'Will that be all?' she asked.

'I doubt it,' said Eddie. 'We'll give you a call when we need you again.'

The waitress, whose painted face was incapable of expression, rolled her eyes and departed.

'Nice legs,' said Eddie.

'I thought you never went inter-species.'

'One can fantasise,' said Eddie. 'Tuck in.'

And the two of them tucked in.

At considerable length they finished their gargantuan repast and took to perusing the dessert menu. The Death-by-Hog-Fat Pudding looked enticing.

'Eddie,' said Jack, 'there's something I've been meaning to ask you.'

'Ask on, my friend,' said Eddie.

'It's just that, well, you eat a lot of food, don't you?'

'As well as being noted for their sexual prowess, bears are greatly admired for their hearty eating; there is no secret to this.'

'Yes,' said Jack. 'But you haven't got a bottom, have you, Eddie?'

Eddie gawped at Jack. 'So what am I sitting on, my head?'

'No, I mean, I'm sorry if this is somewhat indelicate, but what I mean is, where does all this food you eat go?'

'Are you telling me that you don't know what bears do in the woods? When they're not picnicking, of course. Or after they've picnicked.'

'But you don't do that,' said Jack. 'I don't wish to be crude here, but you haven't taken a dump since I met you.'

Eddie scratched at his head with his paw. 'You know you're right,' he said. 'Alcohol drains slowly through me, but you're right. I *never* have taken a dump; where *does* it all go? That's as weird as.'

Jack shrugged.

'You buffoon,' said Eddie, shaking his head. 'Of course I go to the toilet.'

'But when I put my hand inside you to get your growler, there was nothing inside you but sawdust.'

'Oh I see,' said Eddie. 'You know all about digestive systems, do you? I suppose you know exactly how the human digestive system works.'

Jack nodded in a manner which implied that he did.

'Thought not,' said Eddie.

'Digestive juices,' said Jack. 'I've got them in me. You haven't.'

'How come, no matter what colour the food you eat is, it always comes out as brown poo?' Eddie asked. 'Explain that to me.'

'Er . . .' said Jack.

'Jack,' said Eddie. 'Although I greatly admire your seem- ingly unquenchable thirst for arcane knowledge, there will always be things that you'll never be able to know. Live with this. Let brown poo be an exemplar. Do you understand what I'm saying, *chap*?'

'You said *chap* again,' said Jack.

'Do you want any pudding, *chap*?'

'I think I'm full,' said Jack. 'Should we go to Jack Spratt's now?'

'You wouldn't prefer, perhaps, going for a drink first?'

'If we are going to play by the rules and do things the way that a detective should do things, then we should definitely go to a bar first. Detectives get all manner of important leads in bars.'

'Then we'll take a wander over to Tinto's. You never know, he might run down again while we're there.'

'Check please, waitress,' called Jack.

Tinto's bar was as ever it was: already crowded with members of Toy City's non-human population. And even- ing was coming on once more by the time that Jack and Eddie reached it. They were able to gain a pair of barstools without too much trouble, though, because, it had to be said, neither Jack nor Eddie smelled particularly good. They hadn't washed in a while, nor changed their clothes, and after all they'd recently been through, they were far from wholesome when it came to personal hygiene. Drinking folk edged aside for them.

Eddie had, however, visited the toilet before they left *Nadine's Fast Food Diner*. This was not to have a dump though, but to purchase some contraceptives from the machine.

Not that Eddie actually used contraceptives. But he did know this really funny thing you could do with them. Which he did on occasions in bars, and which inevitably got him thrown out.

It was a bear thing.

Eddie plonked himself down on a bar stool; Jack lowered himself uncomfortably onto the next, legs once more up around his neck.

'Evening, Tinto,' said Eddie, addressing the clockwork barkeep. 'Beer, please.'

'And for your gentleman friend?'

Jack recalled the size of the beers. 'Six beers for me,' he said. He had clearly forgotten their potency.

'Nine beers,' said Tinto, whose grasp of mathematics had never been up to much.

'So, Tinto,' said Eddie, as Tinto pulled the beers, 'how goes it for you upon this pleasant evening?'

'Don't talk to me about pleasant evenings,' said Tinto, presenting several beers and pulling several more. 'Did you hear what happened to Jack Spratt?'

'Took the ultimate diet,' said Eddie. 'Yes, we heard.'

'What a way to go,' said Tinto. 'Coated in batter and cooked in a deep fat fryer.'

'I didn't hear *that*,' said Eddie. 'Do you know where it happened?'

'At the *Nadine's Fast Food Diner* down the road. The one with the pretty waitress. Apparently Nadine wouldn't even close the restaurant. They took away the cooked corpse and she just went on serving dinners. Didn't even change the fat in the fryer.'

The colour drained from Jack's face. 'Where's the toilet?' he asked.

'I'll show you,' said Eddie. 'I need it too.'

Presently the two rather shaky-looking detectives returned to the bar. They were both somewhat lighter in the stomach regions.

'And what makes it worse,' said Tinto, continuing where he left off, pulling further beers and losing count, 'is that Jack Spratt owed me money. Him and his damned secret society. He rented my upstairs room for their meetings and now I bet I'll never get my money.'

'Secret society?' Eddie swallowed beer. 'What secret society?'

'Probably the Spring and Catch.' Jack swallowed beer.

Eddie and Tinto swivelled in Jack's direction.

'What do *you* know about the Spring and Catch?' Eddie's voice was a hoarse whisper. Which is not to be confused with a horse whisperer.

'Not much,' said Jack. 'Only that they perform strange rituals and that all the Preadolescent Poetic Personalities are members. Boy Blue was in it. And Humpty Dumpty. And Jack Spratt.'

'How do *you* know this?'

'There was a book at Boy Blue's. I saw it.' Jack took up another beer. 'Significant, eh?'

'I wonder why they'd hold their meetings here?' Eddie wondered.

'And you call yourself a detective,' said Jack.

'Excuse me?' said Eddie.

'Eddie,' said Jack, 'if this was a Bill Winkie thriller, it would now be approximately halfway through. And by this time, all the major players would have made their appearances and most of the major locations would have been established. Tinto's bar has already been established as a major location in the scenario. It's where the detectives drink. So it shouldn't surprise you to find that something pertinent to the case would have happened here.'

'You're getting pretty good at this,' said Eddie.

'It's pretty basic stuff,' said Jack, 'for we professional private eyes.'

'You're right,' said Eddie. 'So go on, Tinto, let's have it.'

'Have *what*?' Tinto asked.

'Whatever it is.' Eddie tapped at his nose. 'The all-important something that is pertinent to the case.'

'I don't know what you're talking about.'

'The Spring and Catch held their rituals in your upstairs room. I think you'll find that they left something behind. Something seemingly irrelevant to you, but of great importance to the professional private eye. That's the way it always happens in detective thrillers.' Eddie winked at Jack.

'You can't wink,' said Jack. 'Not with those button eyes.'

'See how good he's getting, Tinto,' said Eddie. 'Attention to detail and good continuity is everything.'

'Thanks,' said Jack. 'So where's the important something, Tinto?'

'Well,' said Tinto, and his head revolved, 'I can't think of anything. Except, of course – but no, that wouldn't be it.'

'It would,' said Eddie.

'It would.' Jack took up another glass and drank from it. Eddie, whose glass was empty, helped himself to one of Jack's.

'I think I have it somewhere,' said Tinto. 'Or perhaps I threw it away.'

'You didn't throw it away,' said Eddie. 'Go and look for it.'

'All right.' Tinto wheeled away along behind the bar.

'What do you think it will be?' Jack asked Eddie. 'Key to a left luggage locker? Receipt for something? Map with a big X on it? Or maybe even the Big M itself.'

'You really did read all the Bill Winkie thrillers, didn't you?'

'All of them,' said Jack.

'Then I expect you remember how fastidious he was. How he didn't like his trenchcoat getting dirty. And how much he really cared about his motor car.'

Jack dusted down the lapels of the now extremely grubby trenchcoat and wondered what the jobbing vandals might presently be helping themselves to from Bill Winkie's automobile.

'When he gets back from his holiday,' said Jack, carefully, 'I'm sure he'll be very impressed by the way *you* solved the case.'

'Ah, here comes Tinto,' said Eddie.

And here Tinto came. 'Found it,' he said, twirling something between those oh-so-dextrous fingers that Eddie oh-so-coveted. 'I hope it's what you're hoping for.' Tinto passed it over to Eddie.

Eddie placed the item before him upon the bar counter and poked at it with a paw. In terms of the looks of it, it was truly beyond description. But considering its size, or lack of it, its weight was unsurprising. 'It looks like the Big M,' he said. 'The Maguffin. What do you think, Jack?'

'Looks like it to me,' Jack agreed.

'What's a Maguffin?' Tinto asked.

'You tell him, Jack,' said Eddie. 'You've read all the Bill Winkie thrillers.'

'Certainly,' said Jack. 'In all detective thrillers, there is always a Maguffin. The Maguffin is the all-important something, the all-importantness of which will not become apparent until its important moment has come.'

'Well put,' said Eddie.

'I see,' said Tinto, who didn't. 'Then I'm glad I could be of assistance. Do you want to settle your bar bill now, Eddie?'

'No,' said Eddie. 'I don't. But Jack will tell you what I do want to do.'

Jack raised another tiny glass of beer. 'Is it, get drunk?' he asked.

'It is.' Eddie raised *his* glass. 'And when Jack and I are

drunk, we will come up with some really inspired idea for solving the case. And then, while balancing upon my head, I'll show you this really funny thing I can do with a contra-ceptive.'

'And then I'll throw you out,' said Tinto.

'Sweet as,' said Eddie. 'Whose round is it now?'

'Yours,' said Jack. 'Ten more for me.'

'Sweeter than sweet as.' Eddie grinned. 'Same again please, *chap*.'

18

They got *very* drunk.

Eddie showed Jack the really funny thing he could do with a contraceptive and Tinto threw them both out of the bar. But as it was late, and they *were* both very drunk, they didn't really care.

They wandered back to Bill Winkie's office, assuring each other, as if assurance were required, that they were 'bestest friends'.

Jack threw up in the bathroom. Eddie strung himself up on the Venetian blind. Jack collapsed onto the floor.

The night passed without further incident.

In the morning the big smiley sun arose above the roofscape of Toy City and beamed down its blessings upon each and all without due favour or prejudice.

The soundly snoring detectives awoke, Jack nursing a hangover to stagger the senses of the Gods and Eddie as fresh as the proverbial daisy that was never actually mentioned in a proverb.

'Feeling rough?' Eddie asked.

'As rough as,' said Jack.

'Perfect,' said Eddie.

'Perfect?' said Jack.

'Bill Winkie was always hungovered,' said Eddie. 'That anti-hangover lotion never worked too well.'

'What?' said Jack. 'But you . . .'

'And I had to top you up with a hypodermic full of happy juice. But all that is behind us. You keep the hangover, Jack.

It will help you to function as a proper private eye. We're professionals now.'

Jack groaned. 'Breakfast?' he suggested. 'Then we find out what this Maguffin's for.' He turned the Maguffin over on his palm. Considering the lightness of its shade, it was quite dark in colour. 'Right?'

'Wrong,' said Eddie. 'We review the situation. That is what we do. Try to gain a detached overview.'

'Right.' Jack rubbed at his throbbing forehead and returned the Maguffin to his trenchcoat pocket. 'Go on then,' he said. 'Impress me.'

Eddie climbed onto the wreckage of Bill Winkie's desk. 'Now,' said he, 'my train of thought runs in this direction. I—' But Eddie's train of thought was suddenly derailed by the sounds of frantic knocking at the office door.

Jack looked at Eddie.

And Eddie looked at Jack.

'Expecting a visitor?' Jack whispered.

Eddie shook his head. 'It might be a client,' he whispered back to Jack.

Jack made a doubtful face.

'Well, it *might*.'

'Go and answer it, then.'

Eddie made a face more doubtful than Jack's. 'Perhaps *you* should go,' he suggested.

'Did Bill leave a spare gun around anywhere?'

Eddie shook his head once more.

Jack took up a broken-off desk leg, brandished it in a truncheon-like fashion and cautiously approached the office door. 'Who is it?' he called.

'Toy City Express,' a voice called back.

Jack glanced towards Eddie. 'I think it's another train,' said he.

'Toy City Express *Deliveries*,' said Eddie. 'It's Randolph the delivery boy; put down the desk leg and open the door, Jack.'

'Fair enough.' Jack put down the desk leg and opened the door.

A golly in a dapper red uniform, with matching cap worn in the ever-popular peak-to-the-rear manner, grinned up at Jack. 'Yo Popper,' said he.

'Yo Popper?' said Jack.

'Yo, popper humbug,' said the delivery boy. 'Tootin' here a seam-rippin' hot pack for my bear Eddie, you wise?'

'What?' said Jack.

'Don't jazz me up meat-brother. Head me to the bear.'

'What?' said Jack once more.

'The popular patois of the Golly ghetto,' said Eddie, poking his head out from between Jack's knees. 'It's a delivery for me. Hey Randolph, how's it hanging?'

'Like a python wid de mumps. Yo, popper Eddie boy. Here's de pack, ink my page and it's all done yours.'

The golly passed a clipboard with a dangling pen on a string to Eddie. Eddie placed the clipboard on the floor, took the pen between both paws and signed his name. He returned the clipboard to the golly and availed himself of the package.

'Give Randolph a tip,' said Eddie to Jack.

'Fair enough,' said Jack. 'Always take care when dealing with farmers, Randolph.'

'I meant money,' said Eddie.

'Fair enough. Never spend more than you earn.'

'I meant give him some money. Tip him with money.'

'I know exactly what you meant. But I don't have any money, and anyway, it's *your* package.'

'Sorry, Randolph,' said Eddie. 'We're both broke at present. I'll buy you a beer in Tinto's some time.'

Randolph replied with phrases of popular Golly ghetto patois, which, although their specific meaning was lost upon Jack, their general gist was not. Jack closed the door upon Randolph.

'So what have you got?' Jack asked Eddie.

The package was a large envelope. Eddie passed it up to

Jack. 'You open it,' he said. 'Envelopes are tricky when you don't have opposable thumbs.'

Jack took the envelope, opened it and emptied out its contents. 'Tickets,' he said. 'Two tickets to a TV show.'

'Wibbly,' said Eddie. 'Good old Wibbly.'

'But Wibbly is . . . well . . . you know.'

'I know,' said Eddie. 'But when we were at his place, I asked him for a couple of favours. To use his contacts and get us these tickets. He obviously came through for us before he was, well, you know.'

'Why do we want tickets for a TV show?'

'It's not just any old TV show. It's Miss Muffett's TV show. *The Tuffet*. It's a talk show. Little Tommy Tucker is making a guest appearance on it today.'

'And this is relevant to the case?'

'Is there anything else there, or just the tickets?'

'There's a letter,' said Jack.

'Then read it.'

Jack read it. 'Dear Eddie,' he read, 'here are the tickets you wanted. I had to call in a lot of favours to get them, so you owe me big time. Regarding the advance money paid out to Bill that you asked me to check on, I called in a few favours there too, for which you also owe me big time. The money came, as you suspected, from a joint trust fund held by the prominent PPPs.'

'Preadolescent Poetic Personalities, before you ask,' said Eddie.

'I wasn't going to ask; might I continue?'

'Please do.'

Jack continued. 'It seems that Little Tommy Tucker drew out the cash and seeing as the guy is a recluse, then you're probably right in thinking that the only chance you'll have to question him about it is if you can corner him at the TV studios. I wish you luck. I'm having this sent to you via Toy City Express because I think I'm being followed. See you when I see you. And don't forget that when you do that, you owe me big time. Your friend, Wibbly.'

'Good old Wibbly,' said Eddie. 'A friend indeed.'

'Indeed,' said Jack. 'Well, I suppose that explains the tickets.'

'Ever been to a TV show before, Jack?'

'No,' said Jack. 'What about you?'

'No,' said Eddie. 'So I'm really excited. How about you?'

'It's no big deal.' Jack shrugged in a nonchalant fashion. 'I'm not particularly bothered.'

'You liar,' said Eddie. 'You are too.'

'You're right,' said Jack. 'I am. I'm *really* excited.'

Happily, the studios of Toy City TV were not too far distant from Bill Winkie's office. A pleasant saunter, or stroll. A pleasant saunter, or stroll, does tend to work up an appetite though, or in the case of Jack and Eddie, even *more* of an appetite. And this particular saunter, or stroll, took two famished detectives past several breakfasting places, all of which breathed tempting breakfast smells at them.

Jack gave his pulsating forehead further rubbings.

'I'm *really* hungry now,' he said.

'Me too,' said Eddie. 'But the show's being recorded at ten o'clock. So even if we had the cash, we still wouldn't have time for the breakfast.'

'Perhaps there'll be food laid on at the studios.'

'Bound to be,' said Eddie. 'And fizzy wine too, I shouldn't wonder.'

'Let's walk faster then.'

'I'm walking as fast as I can.'

'Do you want me to give you a carry?'

'In broad daylight? I may be hungry, but I still have my dignity.'

The two pressed on past further breakfasting places and finally reached the Toy City TV studios – or, at least, the queue.

'What's all this?' asked Jack, viewing the long line of chattering toys.

'It's the queue for the show,' said Eddie. 'What did you think it was?'

'I can't be having with queues,' said Jack. 'I don't like queues at all.'

'They don't bother me,' said Eddie. 'Waiting around is second nature to teddies.'

'Well I'm not having it; let's push to the front.'

'Lead on, big boy.'

Jack led on. He and Eddie reached the front of the queue. The front of the queue was at the front door of the studios. Jack looked up at the studios' front parts.

The studios' front parts were impressive. They fairly soared. Rising pilasters of frosted rainbow glass swept upwards to support glittering multi-mirrored arches. Within these, intricately tiled mosaics, of every colour and hue, arranged in elaborate geometric patterns, glimmered in the morning sunlight. The overall effect was of a jewelled palace or fantastic temple.

It was a real mind-boggler.

'Amazing,' said Jack.

'Ghastly,' said Eddie.

'Shall we go inside?'

'You have the tickets and the status; push right in.'

'Fair enough,' said Jack, and made to push right in, but his passage was barred by several large and burly fellows, sporting dark suits, mirrored sunglasses and little earpiece jobbies with mouth mic attachments.

'And where do you think you're going?' one of them asked.

'I'm Bill Winkie, Private Eye,' said Jack, flashing his tickets. 'Here on a case; stand aside if you will.'

'I won't,' said the burly fellow. 'This is a secure area; you will have to be frisked.'

'Outrageous,' said Jack.

'Please yourself,' said the burly fellow. 'Goodbye then and leave me with your tickets, I can always sell them on.'

'Frisk away then, if you must,' said Jack. 'But no funny business around my trouser regions.'

The big burly fellow commenced with the frisking of

Jack. He did a very thorough job of frisking – far too thorough, in Jack's opinion. Especially about the trouser regions. He turned all of Jack's pockets inside out, then finally said, 'All right. Go through.'

Jack went through.

The burly fellow frisked Eddie too.

Then Eddie followed Jack.

Once within the studio lobby area, Jack began frantically patting at himself.

'What are you up too?' Eddie asked.

'The Maguffin,' said Jack. 'Where's the Maguffin?'

Eddie produced the Maguffin. 'I have it here,' he said.

'But how?'

'I thought it might arouse suspicion, so I lifted it from your pocket.'

'But once again, how?'

'It's a knack. Here, stick it back in your pocket.'

Jack took the Maguffin from Eddie's paws. 'But he frisked you too,' said Jack. 'Where did you hide it?'

'You really don't want to know.'

'No,' said Jack, pocketing the Maguffin. 'I don't think I do.'

The studio's lobby was a swank affair. Its walls and ceiling and floor were all patterned with colourful mosaics. Jack wondered at the craftsmanship, and wondered what it all must have cost. It must have cost plenty, was his conclusion.

The colourful walls were further coloured by numerous painted portraits. Jack rightly assumed these to be of promi-nent Toy City TV personalities. He perused them with interest. Many were of impossibly glamorous dollies with preposterously inflated bosoms and very big hair.

So big, in fact, as to be veritable jungles.

The faces which peeped forth amidst all this big hair had the looks about them of jungle clearings, which kept the encroaching follicular foliage at bay only through the medium of extreme cosmetic cultivation. As studies in the overuse of make-up, these were nonpareil.

Jack found the faces fascinating. These were idealised images of supposed feminine beauty. Features were exaggerated, increased or diminished; the eyes and mouths were much too large, the noses all far too small.

But for the dolly portraits, no other toys were pictured. All the rest were of Jack's race: men.

These either struck noble poses or grinned winningly, according to the public image they wished to project.

Eddie looked up at Jack, then further up at the portraits, then once more at Jack. 'Your thoughts?' Eddie asked.

'Probably much the same as yours,' said Jack. 'And would I be right in assuming that there are no teddy stars on Toy City TV?'

'No,' said the bear. 'Just men and dollies. And look at those dollies, Jack. Disgusting.'

'Disgusting?' Jack asked.

'Well, you don't think that those are their *real* bosoms, do you?' Eddie beckoned Jack and Jack leaned down to Eddie.

'Fake,' Eddie whispered into Jack's ear. 'They're made of rubber.'

Jack straightened up and shook his head. He had no comment to make.

'So,' said Jack. 'What do we do now? Do you want me to bluff and bluster my way into Little Tommy Tucker's dressing room, so you can have a few words with him?'

'Let's do it after the show.'

'Why after? Why not before?'

'I was thinking that perhaps he might not be too keen to speak to us. It might even be necessary for you to rough him up a bit.'

'What?' said Jack.

'We need information,' said Eddie. 'Any information. So we might have to, you know, lean on him a little. And things might get ugly and he might call for his security men and we might get thrown out of the building. And then we'd not get to see the show.'

'Makes perfect sense,' said Jack. 'Let's push into the studio and get a seat at the front.' Jack's stomach rumbled. 'What about some food?' he asked.

'Exert a little self-control,' said Eddie. 'We're professionals, aren't we?'

'We certainly are.'

It is a fact well known to those who know it well, and indeed to anyone else who has ever been dumb enough to apply for tickets to a TV show, that the interior of TV studios, the very interior, the sanctum sanctorum, the heart of hearts, the belly of the beast, the studio proper, is a real disappointment, when you've finished queuing up and finally get to see it.

It's rubbish.

The audience seating is rubbish. It's Spartan, it's uncomfortable, it's crummy. The stage set is rubbish. It's cardboard and plywood and not well painted at all. And there're wires everywhere. And there are cameras that get in your way so you can't see properly. And there are rude crew persons who behave like pigs and herd you in and bully you about and who won't let you get up during the show, even if you desperately need the toilet. And it always smells rough in there too, as if some orgy or other has just been going on – which tends to make the disappointment you feel even worse, because you know you must have just missed it.

And the other thing is that the show is never the way you see it on TV. The show always goes wrong and there has to be take after take after take. And although for the audience this does have a certain novelty value to begin with, by the tenth retake the novelty has well and truly worn off.

There is nothing glamorous about TV studios. Absolutely nothing glamorous at all. They're rubbish. They are. Rubbish.

'Isn't this brilliant?' said Eddie.

'Certainly is,' said Jack.

As they were the first into the studio, they were 'escorted' to the very front seats by one of the 'crew'.

A crew pig in fact. All bendy rubber and portly and scowling, he had the word CREW painted in large letters across his belly. He huffed and puffed in a bad-tempered manner and jostled Jack and Eddie along.

'Sit *there*,' he ordered.

Jack and Eddie hastened to oblige. The seating was toy-sized and Jack found his knees once again up around his shoulders. But he didn't care. He was loving it all.

Jack sniffed the air. 'You can even smell the glamour,' he said.

'I can definitely smell something,' said Eddie.

More rude crew pigs were now herding the rest of the audience in.

Jack looked all around and about. Overhead hung many stage lights. To the rear of each was attached a sort of half-bicycle affair: the rear half, with pedals, chain wheel and seat. And upon each seat sat a clockwork cyclist, whose job it was to pedal away like fury to power up the light and move it this way and that when required so to.

The instructions for the requiring so to do were issued from a booth set directly above the stage: the controller's box. The controller already sat in his seat of control. Evidently purpose-built for this role, he was undoubtedly the most remarkable toy Jack had so far seen. He was big and broad and constructed from bendy rubber. His wide, flat face had six separate mouths set into a horizontal row. From his ample torso sprouted six separate arms, each hand of which held a megaphone. As Jack looked on in awe, the controller bawled separate instructions through four different megaphones. Clockwork cyclists to the right and left and the above of Jack pedalled furiously away and swung their lights here and there at the controller's directing.

The lights swept over the low stage beneath the controller's box.

The stage set resembled a woodland arbour, painted plywood trees, a blue sky daubed to the rear, with the words *Tuff it on the Tuffet* painted upon it in large and glittering golden letters. The floor of the stage was carpeted with fake grass, on which stood a number of stools fashioned to resemble tuffets and arranged in a semi-circle. To the right of the stage was a small clockwork orchestra.

'I'm really enjoying this,' said Jack, 'and it hasn't even started yet.'

Before the stage, clockwork cameramen were positioning their clockwork cameras, large and bulky affairs of colourful pressed tin which moved upon casters. The clockwork cameramen appeared to be positioning their cameras in such a way as to create the maximum obstruction of the audience's view of the stage.

Eddie was looking over his shoulder, watching the rude crew pigs herding in the audience of toys. 'Hm,' he said.

Jack pointed towards the large and glittering letters that were painted upon the pretend sky backdrop. 'What does Tuff it on the Tuffet mean?' he asked Eddie.

'Miss Muffett's show is one of those talk show jobbies,' Eddie explained, 'where toys air their embarrassing personal problems on primetime TV. I once wrote a little poem about it; would you care for me to recite it to you?'

'Is it a long poem?' Jack asked.

'No, quite short.'

'Go on then.'

Eddie made throat-clearing growlings and then he began:

'Scandalous secrets and shocking surprises,
'Secreting their persons with silly disguises,
'Or proudly parading their sexual deviation,
'With clockwork and teddy and even relation,
'Recounting their fumblings with famous Toy folk,
'Or confessing the need for the herbs that they smoke,
'All in the hope that the show will bestow,
'Media absolution.'

'Very good,' said Jack.

'Did you really think so?'

'Not really,' said Jack. 'I was being polite. But why would

anyone want to come on a TV show and air their dirty laundry in public, as it were?'

Eddie shrugged. 'That is one of life's little mysteries,' he said. 'My guess would be that either they're actors making it all up, or they're very sad individuals who crave their moment of glory on TV. But who cares; it's great television.'

'And Little Tommy Tucker is going to be "tuffing it", is he?'

'I doubt that. He's probably promoting his new hit single. He's a big recording artiste, is Tommy. He doesn't have to sing for his supper any more. Well, he does in a manner of speaking, but his singing has earned him enough for a million suppers in the City's finest eateries.'

Jack's stomach rumbled once again. But at least his hang-over was beginning to lessen. 'Famous singer, eh?' said Jack.

'Top of the charts,' said Eddie. 'Not my pot of jam though. I'm an Elvis fan, me.'

'Elvis?' said Jack. 'Who's Elvis?'

Eddie rolled his button eyes. 'He's the King.'

'Well I've never heard of him.'

'No, I suppose not. He's a bear, like me. My cousin, in fact. Tinto has an open-mic night on Fridays. Elvis sings. He's great.'

'What sort of stuff does he sing?' Jack asked.

'Tommy Tucker songs,' said Eddie, dismally. 'There aren't any others.'

'What, none?'

'Tommy sort of has the Toy City music industry in his velvet pocket. Tommy's always number one in the music charts, because the charts don't have a number two. And Tommy owns the only recording studio in Toy City, and the record company.'

'That's outrageous,' said Jack. 'So you're telling me that the only records you can buy in Toy City are Tommy Tucker records?'

'Or classical music.'

'Which is?'

'Nursery rhymes,' said Eddie. 'Sung by the Tommy Tucker choir ensemble. With the Tommy Tucker clockwork orchestra. That's them next to the stage.'

'Shut up!' shouted a rude crew pig into Eddie's ear. 'The show's about to begin. Shut up!'

'Oi,' said Jack. 'How dare you!'

'Shut up the both of you,' said the rude crew pig. 'And behave or I'll throw you out.'

Jack almost rose to take issue with the rude crew pig, but as he didn't want to miss the show, he didn't.

'It's always the same,' whispered Eddie. 'Paint a uniform on a pig and he thinks he rules the city.'

'Oh, look,' said Jack. 'Something's happening.'

And something was.

The controller shouted instructions through numerous megaphones; some lights dimmed, others shone brightly; those that shone brightly illuminated the stage.

Quite brightly.

From stage-right a figure appeared.

This figure was a clown. An all-rubber clown. An all-green, but for the red nose, rubber clown.

'Morning all,' said the all-green, but for the red nose, rubber clown.

Mumble, mumble, mumble went the audience. One or two folk managed a half-hearted 'Good morning'.

'Pathetic,' said the all-green, but for the red nose, rubber clown. 'That really won't do at all.'

'Who's this?' Jack asked.

'Warm-up clown, I think,' said Eddie.

'Shut up, you two,' said the crew pig, who had positioned himself in the aisle next to Jack and Eddie and was keeping a beady eye upon them.

'This is The Tuffet!' The all-green, but for the red nose, rubber clown made all-encompassing hand gestures. 'Biggest rating show in Toy City and you the audience must respond. You must cheer, you must applaud, you must react. Do you hear what I'm saying?'

Murmur, murmur, went the crowd.

'*Do you hear?*'

'Yes,' went much of the crowd, in an embarrassed murmur.

'And do you love Miss Muffett?'

'Yes,' went most of the crowd, quietly.

'I said, do you *love* Miss Muffett?'

'*Yes*,' went pretty much all of the crowd, pretty much louder.

'*I said, do you love Miss Muffett?*'

'*YES*,' went damn near all of the crowd.

'And you two,' the rude crew pig shook a trottered fist at Eddie and Jack.

'Oh yes indeed,' said Jack, in a tone that lacked somewhat for conviction.

'And me too,' said Eddie, in a likewise fashion.

'Let me hear you say "Yeah!"' shouted the all-green, but for the red nose, all-rubber clown.

'*Yeah!*' the audience replied.

'Not bad,' said the clown. 'But not good; let me hear you say "yeah" once again.'

'*Yeah!*' went the crowd with greater vigour.

'Yeah!' shouted the clown.

'Yeah!' shouted the audience back to him.

And yeah and yeah and yeah again.

'I don't like this clown at all,' said Jack.

'That's your last warning,' said the rude crew pig in between the yeahings.

'All right!' shouted the clown. 'Now we're rolling. Now let's have us some fun.'

And then the clown went about doing *The Terrible Thing*. *The Terrible Thing* is the terrible thing that all clowns do. It is *The Terrible Thing* that all clowns have always done, since the very dawn of clowning, *The Terrible Thing* that is ultimately what being a clown is all about.

The Terrible Thing that is . . .

Humiliating the audience.

Exactly why clowns do it is no mystery at all. They do it because they *can* do it, because they are allowed to do it, because they can get away with doing it. And they get away with doing it because they wear red noses and silly costumes which make them look ridiculous, make them look like fools, and so people let them get away with doing it – people who would otherwise beat the living life out of anyone else who dared to humiliate them – allow clowns do it.

Which serves them right, really.

But still makes it a terrible thing.

The all-green, but for the red nose, rubber clown began to move amongst the audience. He frolicked up and down the aisles. Here he mocked the leaky over-stuffed seams of a plump rag doll, and there he drew attention to a hint of rust upon the shoulder of a clockwork postman. And over there he scorned a teddy's moth-eaten ear. And right at the back he made light of a wooden soldier's woodworm holes.

The audience laughed, as an audience will, as a detached sum of its individually wounded parts. That's life. But it's not very nice.

'This is foul,' said Jack.

The crew pig glared at him.

Jack caught the green clown's attention and the green clown came over to Jack.

'Well well well,' said the green clown, grinning hugely at Jack. 'What do we have here? I love the coat, are you wearing it for a dare?'

The audience laughed. Jack curled his lip.

'And is this your little bear?' The green clown beamed at Eddie.

Jack beckoned the green clown close and whispered certain cautionary words into his green rubber ear.

The green clown stiffened. 'So, on with the show,' he said. 'Clockworks, stuffed and toy folk generally, allow me to introduce your hostess. The one, the only, Toy City's favourite Miss. Here she is. *Heeeeeeere's* Missy.'

The controller bawled instructions, overhead lights swung, focused and shone.

The clockwork orchestra struck up music.

And she made her entrance.

'The one. The only. Miss Muffett.

'Applause!' shouted the green clown.

And applause there was.

Jack turned his eyes towards the spotlit entrance of the Miss, but his view was immediately obstructed by a clock-work cameraman.

He ducked his head this way and that. And then Jack saw her: Miss Muffett.

Jack's jaw fell and his eyes became wide.

'What is *that*?' he asked.

19

If Jack had held to any religious beliefs, he might well have said that Miss Muffett was a sight to stagger the senses of the Gods.

But, as he was an atheist, he espoused no such claims. Instead he simply followed the words 'What is *that*?' with a single word.

And that single word was 'Wowser!'

'Wowser?' Eddie asked. 'What's Wowser?'

'Wowser,' Jack went once more. '*She* is Wowser. She. Well. Wowser. She is.'

Eddie gazed upon Miss Muffett. 'Wowser?' he said thoughtfully. 'That would probably do it.'

And it probably would.

From her tippy tiptoes to her tinted topknot, Miss Muffett was wonderfully wowser. She was wonderfully wowser to all points of the compass, and probably some others too.

She was remarkably wonderfully wowser, in fact.

Worryingly wowser.

As Jack viewed Miss Muffett, the wowser word came once more to his lips; Jack swallowed it back. What was so wonderfully wowser about this woman? he wondered.

Was it the hair?

Miss Muffett had the big hair of the famous.

It is a fact well known to those who know it well, and anyone in fact who ever watches TV, or goes to the movies, that although the fabulously famous may ultimately not end up always possessing big hair, they almost certainly began with it.

Big hair is a prerequisite. It is a given, as is big face and small body. It is a requirement when it comes to richness and famousness. Choose your favourite star of stage or screen; they will inevitably have had their big hair days.

Miss Muffett was currently having hers. Her hair was huge; it was blonde and it was huge. It outhuged the dollies in the lobby portraits. It went every-which-way, and every-which-way-hair is unashamedly erotic.

Curiously, bald heads on women are similarly erotic, but they're not nearly so much fun as big-haired heads. You can really get your hands into big-haired heads. And blondie big-haired heads . . .

Well . . .

Wowser!

Miss Muffett's eyes were big and blue. Her nose was tiny. Her mouth was full and wide. Slender was her neck and narrow her shoulders. Large and well-formed were her breasts, and her waist was as of the wasp. Her hips were the hips of a Goddess. Her low-necked gown, a sheath of shimmering stars. Her legs, as long as they were, and they were, were made to seem much longer by the lengthy heels upon her wowsery shoes.

And so on and so forth and such like. Da de da de da.

'She's certainly something,' said Eddie.

'I hate her,' said Jack.

'*What?*'

'That's not how it should be.' The beady eyes of the crew pig were once more upon Jack, and so Jack whispered to Eddie. 'That's not how it should be,' he said once more.

'Not *what?*' Eddie asked.

'Not how a woman should be.'

'And you, a mere stripling of a lad, know how a woman should be?'

Thoughts of Jill from Madame Goose's returned to Jack. Not that they had ever been much away. Jill was, young as she was, the way a woman *should* be; in fact, she was *everything* that a woman should be, in Jack's admittedly somewhat limited opinion. Miss Muffett's beauty was there. It was definitely there. It was amazingly, wowseringly *there*. But it was too much. It was extreme. It was wowser, yes, but it was *worryingly* wowser.

'You can't look like that,' Jack whispered. 'Not really. It's too much. Do you know what I mean, Eddie? It's too much. It makes me feel uncomfortable.'

Eddie grinned, but he said nothing.

A single spotlight illuminated Miss Muffett. ''Allo loves,' she said in a deep and husky tone. 'Welcome to The Tuffet. Today we shall be dealing with the sensitive subject of interracial relationships. Can a fuzzy felt mouse find happiness with a wooden kangaroo? Can a teddy bear truly know love in clockwork arms?'

'Not if it's me and Tinto,' sniggered Eddie.

'Shut it!' snarled the crew pig.

'Can a big fat pug-ugly rubber dancing doll with bad dress sense and a small moustache really want to marry the worm-eaten wooden chef from Nadine's Diner?'

Jack shrugged.

'Search me,' said Eddie. 'But she'd probably be grateful for anything, by the sound of her.'

'*Very* last warning,' said the crew pig.

'Let's ask them,' said Miss Muffett, ascending the stage and setting her wowseringly wonderful behind onto the central tuffet thereof.

The controller bawled the word 'Applause' through the megaphone. And applause there was.

Rude crew pigs ushered the guests onto the stage. One was a big fat pug-ugly dancing doll in a revolting sportswear suit. The other was a worm-eaten wooden chef.

'Oh,' said Jack. 'It's him.'

'Him?' whispered Eddie, cowering beneath the gaze of the rude crew pig.

'The first night I was in the city,' said Jack. 'I went into a Nadine's Diner. He was the chef. I thought he was a man in a wooden mask or something.'

'And I woke you up in the alley outside,' whispered Eddie.

The big fat pug-ugly dancing doll required two tuffets to sit down upon; rude crew pigs moved them into place. The worm-eaten wooden chef sat down beside her.

Miss Muffett introduced her guests to the audience.

Jack yawned.

'Tired?' said Eddie.

'Short attention span,' said Jack. 'We had shows like this on TV in my town. I'm bored already.'

'Jaded with the glamour of celebrity already,' said Eddie. 'The fickleness of youth, eh?'

'That's it,' said the rude crew pig. 'Out, the pair of you.'

'I've had quite enough of you,' said Jack. 'Clear off.'

'Be quiet,' said the rude crew pig. 'Keep your voice down. The show is in progress.'

'Does this show go out live?' Jack asked the rude crew pig.

'It certainly does,' the pig replied.

'Then it would be a terrible shame if it were to be interrupted wouldn't it?'

The rude crew pig made a very foul face at Jack.

'Interrupted by me throwing you onto the stage and then kicking you all around and about on it.'

Eddie flinched.

The rude crew pig stiffened.

'Then leave us alone,' said Jack. 'Or I will make a great deal of noise and cause a great deal of trouble.'

'Just keep it down.' The rude crew pig made a very worried face.

'Go away. Or else.'

The rude crew pig took a tottering step or two up the aisle.

'Away,' counselled Jack. 'Hurry up now; I suffer from a rare medical condition which manifests itself in acts of extreme violence when I find myself put under stress.'

The rude crew pig departed hurriedly.

'Well done,' said Eddie. 'Most authoritative. Most assertive.'

'Let's go and find Little Tommy Tucker,' said Jack.

'I can't believe you,' said Eddie. 'We're here in a TV studio. Watching the Miss Muffett show live. And . . .'

'It's rubbish,' said Jack. 'It's all rubbish. The rude crew pigs, the insulting clown, this patronising woman: it's excruciating.'

'That's entertainment,' said Eddie, in a singsong kind of a way.

'Well, I can't be having with it. Let's find Little Tommy Tucker.'

'He'll be on soon,' Eddie cuffed Jack on the arm. 'Behave yourself and be patient. You're a very naughty boy.'

Jack stifled a large guffaw and directed his attention once more to the stage.

'Good boy,' said Eddie.

'So tell me, Chardonnay,' said Miss Muffett to the big fat pug-ugly dancing doll, 'what it is that you see in Garth?'

Garth, the worm-eaten wooden chef, reached out a wooden hand and squeezed the podgy mitt of Chardonnay.

'He's very sensitive,' said Chardonnay.

'How nice,' said Missy.

'And he does all the cooking and he smells very nice. He has this lovely piney fragrance. Go on, give him a sniff.'

Miss Muffett leaned towards Garth and gave him a sniff. 'Piney, with a touch of cooking lard,' she said.

'And when he gets wood, he keeps it,' said Chardonnay.

'Excuse me?' said Miss Muffett.

'I'm talking about his penis,' said Chardonnay. 'When he gets an erection, it's like a forest oak. A mighty pine. A giant redwood. A great shaft of thrusting timber. A—'

'A big log-on?' asked Miss Muffett. 'What about your social life? How have your friends taken to your relationship?'

'Mine are all for it,' said Garth. 'My mates say, "Go on my son, get in there."'

'And so they should.' Miss Muffett smiled a mouthload of perfect teeth. 'But what I mean is in terms of social intercourse.'

'If you're having intercourse,' said Garth, 'who needs to socialise?'

'How true,' said Miss Muffett. 'Someone once asked me whether I liked All-In Wrestling. I replied, if it's all in, why wrestle?'

The audience erupted into laughter.

'Excruciating,' said Jack. 'I *really* hate her.'

'I think she's fun,' said Eddie. 'And dirty, of course, and I do like dirty, me.'

'Well, I don't. This show is gross. It's all gross.'

'So,' said Miss Muffett, 'do either of you have parents and if so, how have they reacted to your relationship?'

'Well, I don't have any parents,' said Garth. 'I was hewn by the toymaker. And well hewn too.'

'He certainly is,' said Chardonnay. 'Hewn like a rolling pin. The toymaker stuffed me.'

'I'm finishing where he left off,' said Garth.

'Well,' said Miss Muffett, 'it would appear that you two have the perfect relationship.'

'We do,' the pair agreed.

'But,' said Miss Muffett, 'things are not always as they appear and after the commercial break that is coming right up, I'll be introducing several other guests: a clockwork fireman who claims that for the last three years he has been having a gay relationship with Garth, and two dollies who have borne his children. And if that isn't enough, we'll be bringing on a straw dog who insists that Chardonnay is, as he puts it, his bitch. We'll be back in a moment right after this.' Miss Muffett smiled and the controller shouted 'cut', through one of his megaphones.

Chardonnay turned upon Garth and began to set about him something wicked. Garth responded by butting her fiercely in the head.

Rude crew pigs trotted forward and hustled Chardonnay and Garth from the stage.

Miss Muffett arose from her Tuffet. She straightened down parts of her frock that really didn't need straightening

down and approached Jack and Eddie upon her preposterous heels.

'You two,' she said, when she had approached suffi-
ciently. 'You two have chatted throughout my first quarter.
Are you both mad or just plain stupid?'

Jack gawped at Miss Muffett. 'We're . . .' he managed to
say.

'Yes, you gormster, *what*?'

'We're really enjoying the show,' said Jack.

'But you feel the need to talk all through it?'

'Very sorry,' said Jack.

'Just shut it,' said Miss Muffett. 'Shut your stupid ignorant
mouths. I'm a star. A big star. A famous star. You, you're
nothing. Do you understand? Less than nothing. Nobodies.
Nonsuches. Nonentities. You just do what you're told to.
Laugh in the right places. Applaud in the right places. Then
get out. Get out and go back to your meaningless little lives.
Do you hear what I'm saying?'

'All too loudly,' said Jack.

'What?'

'We hear you, yes.'

'Then shut up.' Miss Muffett's wonderfully wowser blue
eyes glared pointy daggers at Jack.

'Very sorry,' said Jack once more. 'We'll be quiet. We
were over-excited. That's all.'

'Yes, well, see that you do. Stupid trash.' Miss Muffett
turned upon her pointy heels and stalked back to the stage.

Jack looked at Eddie.

And Eddie looked at Jack.

'What a most unwowserly woman,' said Jack.

Eddie said nothing at all.

Then.

'Three, two, one,' bawled the controller, variously.

The clockwork orchestra struck up once again.

And part two of the show was on the go.

Chardonnay and Garth were back on stage, but this time
each was restrained within straitjackets. Various dubious-

looking types, a rusty clockwork fireman, a manky straw dog and some barely dressed dollies were hustled into the spotlight to tell their tales of drunkenness and debauchery, point accusing fingers and paws. They soon took to striking one another.

At length these too were hustled away, leaving Miss Muffett alone.

'Trash,' whispered Jack. 'It's all trash.'

'Ladies and gentlemen,' husked Missy, 'dollies and gollies, clockworkers, wooddeners, and all otherwises, it is now my very great pleasure to introduce you to a very dear friend of mine: a star amongst stars, making one of his rare live appearances right here on my little show. I am honoured to welcome the supper singer himself, your own, your very own, Little Tommy Tucker.'

And the clockwork orchestra struck up once again, again.

The controller did further bawlings for applause and for complicated lighting-work, but his bawlings were swallowed up by the orchestra's stirring rendition of the Little Tommy Tucker theme and the audience's obvious adulation.

The applause was such as to have Eddie's growler vibrat-ing.

'*Grrrrrrrrr*,' went Eddie. 'Pardon me.'

And then *He* walked out onto the stage.

He had the look of one who had partaken of the pleasures of the flesh in a manner that lacked for moderation or temperance. *He* had *really* partaken of them.

He was indeed Toy City's most perfectly wasted man.

Jack ducked this way and that as clockwork cameramen once more got in his way, but when he finally spied Little Tommy, Jack felt cause to whistle.

'No one can be *that* thin,' Jack said to Eddie.

But Little Tommy could.

There was very little of Little Tommy. He had the big face of the famous, but the little body was oh-so-little that it was a cause of pain to gaze upon. It was next to nothing. It was a wisp. A wistful whisper.

A willowy wistful whisper.

What little there was of it was encased in a truly spiffing triple-breasted blue silk *Oh Boy!* suit of the high fashion persuasion. He wore dapper little hyper-exclusive foolish-boy-skin shoes upon his dinky little feet. A nattily knotted pink velvet tie was threaded beneath the high collars of a pale lemon satin shirt. He had the remains of some very big hair piled high upon his head. A studio tan coloured his gauntly-featured face. His eyes were of the palest blue; his lips of the lushest red.

'Hi there,' crooned little Tommy, raising skeletal hands.

The audience cheered and those amongst them possessed of hands clapped these wildly together.

'Thank you, thank you, thank you.' Little Tommy beamed all around and about. He exchanged air kisses with Little Miss Muffett and bowed several times to the audience. He stepped up to a microphone before the clockwork orchestra. 'I'd like to sing a song that I know will be very lucky for me,' he said into it. 'Another chart topper.'

Further wild applause issued from the audience.

'Is he really *that* good?' Jack shouted into Eddie's ear.

'No, he's rubbish, and there's no need to shout. We bears are greatly admired for our aural capacities.'

'Urgh,' went Jack.

Eddie rolled his button eyes. 'Aural,' he said. 'Oh, never mind.'

'This song,' continued Little Tommy, 'is dedicated to a very dear friend of mine. I cannot speak his name aloud, but *He* knows who *He* is. The song is called "You're a God to me, buddy". It goes something like this.' Little Tommy beamed over his slender shoulder towards the clockwork orchestra. 'Gentlemen, please, if you will.'

The clockwork conductor one two three'd it with his baton; the orchestra launched into the number.

Jack's head ducked this way and that, but the cameramen obscured his view. He could however hear the song. And as Jack listened to it, his jaw dropped low once more.

It was . . .

'Awful,' whispered Jack to Eddie. 'The song's awful and he can't even sing.'

'It is my belief,' Eddie whispered back, 'that when Wheatley Porterman penned the original nursery rhyme that made Little Tommy famous, it was intended as a satire upon the poor quality of Toy City nightclub entertainers, Little Tommy in particular: that all his singing was worth was some brown bread and butter. Ironic the way things turned out, eh?'

Jack nodded thoughtfully, curled his lip, screwed up his eyes and thrust his hands over his ears. 'Tell me when he's finished,' he said to Eddie.

Eddie did not reply to this. His paws were already over his ears.

It did have to be said that even if Little Tommy wasn't much of a singer, which indeed he was not, he did put his heart and indeed his very soul into his performance. Veins stood out upon his scrawny neck and upon his ample forehead. Tears sprang into his eyes. His spindly arms crooked themselves into all manner of unlikely positions; his long fingers snatched at the air as if clawing at the very ether. Rivulets of sweat ran down his face, joining his tears to stripe his studio tan.

The song itself was of the ballad persuasion, which, given Little Tommy's rendition in the manner that made it all his own, had about it a quality which raised excruciation to an art form. Little Tommy trembled on his toes. At every high note, his lips quivered and his mouth became so wide that those in the upper seats who had particularly good eyesight were afforded a clear view right down his scrawny throat to see what he'd had for breakfast.

The deafening applause that greeted the song's conclusion was sufficient to arouse Jack and Eddie from the foetal positions they had adopted. Eddie put his paws together. 'Bravo,' he called.

'Irony?' Jack asked.

'Absolutely,' said Eddie.

'Bravo,' called Jack, clapping too. 'More. More.'

'Let's not overdo it.'

'Quite so.' Jack ceased his clapping.

'What can I say?' Little Miss Muffett rose from her central tuffet, clapping lightly and professionally. 'One of the greats. If not *the* great. Join me up here, Little Tommy, come and sit with me please.'

Little Tommy took another bow and joined Miss Muffett.

'Thank you, Missy,' he said, seating himself down upon the vacant tuffet next to Missy.

Jack's empty stomach made terrible grumbling sounds. 'I really have had enough,' he whispered to Eddie.

'We might as well stick it out to the end,' said the bear. 'You never know, it might get really interesting.'

'Yeah, right,' said Jack. 'They're just going to luvvy each other.'

And that, of course, was exactly what Miss Muffett and Little Tommy *were* going to do: luvvy each other big time.

'Little Tommy,' husked the Missy, 'beautiful song, beautiful lyrics, beautiful rendition.'

'I just love your dress,' crooned Little Tommy.

'And you're looking so well.'

'And you so young.'

'It's wonderful to have you here.'

'It's wonderful to be here on your wonderful show.'

'Wonderful,' husked Missy. 'But tell me, Little Tommy, I know you make very very few public appearances.'

'Very few,' Tommy agreed.

'But why this?'

'Well, Missy,' said Little Tommy, crossing his spindly legs, 'I just don't have the time. The way I see it, it is the duty of a superstar such as myself to maintain the appropriate lifestyle: a lifestyle to which the less fortunate amongst us, your audience for instance, can only aspire to in their most exalted, and dare I say, perverted dreams.'

'You might certainly dare,' said Missy. 'In fact you have.'

'Take it to excess,' said Little Tommy. 'Such is expected of someone like myself. It is my duty.'

'And you certainly have taken it to excess.' Miss Muffett smiled big smiles upon Little Tommy. 'Your squanderings and indulgences are of legend.'

'Well, thank you very much.'

'And you've just come out of detox, I understand.'

'Detox, rehab, it's a weekly thing with me. They say, "If you've got it, flaunt it." I say, "If you've got it, use it up, wear it out, get it flushed and start again on Monday."'

'What a thoroughly unpleasant individual,' said Jack.

'Everyone misbehaves,' said Eddie. 'That's nature. Every-one gets away with as much as they can get away with. And the more they can get away with, the more they will.'

'That's a somewhat cynical view of life.'

'You know that I'm telling the truth.'

'That doesn't mean that I want to admit it.'

Eddie grinned. 'You're a good lad, Jack,' said he.

'But *he* isn't.'

'No, *he's* an absolute stinker.'

'Drugs?' said Little Tommy, in an answer to a question from Miss Muffett that Jack and Eddie hadn't heard. 'Well, yes, all right, I must admit that I am no stranger to drugs. Not that I'm advocating them to others, don't get me wrong, I'm not. Only for me. To me, an unhealthy cocktail of alcohol and narcotics spices things up for a bit of hot groupie action.'

'There have been reports in the Toy City Press regarding the, how shall I put it, tender ages of some of your groupies.'

'If they're old enough to walk on their own,' said Little Tommy, 'then they're up for it.'

'What?' went Jack.

Miss Muffett tittered. 'You're a very naughty boy,' she said.

'I know,' said Little Tommy. 'But you can't help liking me, can you?'

'I hate him,' said Jack. 'Hate her, hate him. I'm exhibiting no preferences, you notice.'

'Very democratic,' said Eddie.

'He needs a smack,' said Jack. 'So does she.'

'Well,' said Little Miss Muffett, 'it's been an absolute pleasure to have you here on the show, Little Tommy. I think the audience would agree with me on this.' Missy smiled towards the audience. The audience gave out with further wild applause. 'So I think we should finish this interview on a high note. Would you honour us, Little Tommy, by giving us another of your marvellous high notes one more time?'

'It would be my pleasure, Missy.' Little Tommy threw back his head, opened his mouth as widely as widely could be and gave vent to a crackling high note of such appalling awfulness that Jack's hands and Eddie's paws rushed upwards once more towards their respective ears.

It was a long high note.

A prolonged high note.

An elongated high note.

And there's no telling for how protracted a period this particular long, prolonged, elongated high note might have continued for had it not been suddenly cut short.

The cause of its cut-shortedness was not viewed by Jack as a clockwork cameraman was once more obscuring his view. Eddie saw it clearly, though.

Something dropped down from above.

From above the controller's control booth.

From above the clockwork lighting-pedallers.

From the very ceiling of the studio.

Through a hole that had been drilled through this very ceiling.

Whatever this something was, and it was very soon to be apparent exactly what this something was, it dropped through this hole and fell directly down and into Little Tommy Tucker's open mouth and onward further still until it reached the area inside him where rested his breakfast.

'Gulp!' went Little Tommy, suddenly foreshortening his high note. 'What was that?'

'What was *what*?' Miss Muffett asked.

'Something.' Little Tommy clutched at his throat and then at his diminutive stomach regions. 'Something fell into my mouth.'

'Well, it wouldn't be the first time.' Miss Muffett tittered some more.

'Yes, but I didn't like this. Oooh.'

'Oooh?' questioned Miss Muffett.

'Yes, Oooh, something is going on in my guts.'

'Well, upon that high note, we have to take another commercial break. But we'll be right back after it with a love triangle which turned out to be more of a pentangle. We'll say goodbye. Please put your hands together for my very special guest, Little Tommy, and I know that you'll all be going out to purchase his latest hit. What was the name of that song again, Tommy?'

'Oooh,' went Tommy. 'Aaaargh!'

Jack looked at Eddie.

And Eddie looked at Jack.

'What's happening?' Jack asked. 'I can't see.'

'Something bad,' said Eddie. 'Something very bad.'

'Oooh!' went Little Tommy once again. And 'Aaaargh' again also. He clutched at himself and leapt from his tuffet.

And then all kinds of terrible things happened.

20

Little Tommy, arisen from his tuffet, was now clutching all over himself and howling in evident anguish.

The audience members, under the mistaken belief that this was just part of the show – albeit a somewhat bizarre part – rocked with laughter and clapped together what hands they possessed.

'What's going on?' Jack shouted to Eddie.

'Up there,' Eddie shouted back. 'Above the controller's box. Hole in the ceiling. Something dropped through it into Tommy's mouth.'

'It's the serial killer again.' Jack jumped to his feet. 'Call an ambulance,' he shouted, pushing aside a clockwork camera-man and toppling his clockwork camera.

Little Tommy lurched about the stage. Something horrible was happening inside him. He jerked upwards as if being lifted physically from his feet and then slammed down onto the floor.

Jack rushed to offer what assistance he could, although he knew little of first aid. Rude crew pigs came snorting down the aisles; the audience continued with its laughter and applause, although it was dawning upon its brighter members that something was altogether amiss.

As Jack reached the now-prone supper singer, a most horrible occurrence occurred: as if by the agency of some invisible force, Little Tommy swung upright.

He hung, suspended in the air, his tiny feet dangling twelve inches above the stage. He stared at Jack face-to-face with pleading eyes and open mouth.

'We'll get you help,' said Jack, but he could clearly see that help would be too late. Little Tommy began to vibrate and rattle about. Great tremors ran up and down his slender body. Steam began to issue from his ears.

'Oh no,' croaked Jack, taking several sharp steps backaways. 'He's going to blow. Take cover, everyone.'

Whistling sounds came from Tommy, rising and rising in volume and pitch. Buttons popped from his triple-breasted suit, strange lumps bulged from his forehead and his shoulders began to expand. The laughter and applause in the audience died away. Horror and panic refilled the momentary void.

As Jack fell back from the stage the horde of rude crew pigs fell upon Jack. 'We'll teach you some manners,' snorted the one that Jack had recently sent packing.

And oh so quickly, as it always does, chaos reigned supreme.

The audience arose from their uncomfortable seats and made the traditional mad dash for the exits. The controller bawled instructions to the lighting pedallers, but the lighting pedallers were now dismounting and abseiling down ropes, eager to make their escape. Miss Muffett was being rapidly escorted from the stage by burly men in dark suits and mirrored sunglasses who all sported tiny earphones with mouth mic attachments. And as Jack vanished beneath a maelstrom of trotters, Little Tommy Tucker exploded.

On prime time TV.

Before a large viewing audience.

Although reruns of this particular show would top the ratings charts for many months to come, the only direct eyewitness to Little Tommy's spectacular demise was one Eddie Bear, Toy City private eye.

Knowing better than to risk being flattened by the stampeding audience and being incapable of assisting Jack in his travails against the rude crew pigs, Eddie had remained where he was, cowering in his seat. He had to put his paws right over his ears, though, as Tommy's high-pressure whistlings reached an ultrasonic level, which set toy dogs in the street outside howling. But Eddie had a ringside seat to watch the explosion.

It is another fact well known to those who know it well, and those who know it well do so through personal experience, that when you are involved in something truly dreadful and life-threatening, such as a car crash, the truly dreadful and life-threatening something appears to occur in slow motion. Many explanations have been offered for this: a sudden rush of adrenalin, precipitating a rapid muscle response, affording the individual the opportunity (however small) to take evasive action; an alteration in the individual's perception of time, which is something akin to a near-death experience, in which the individual's psyche, id, conscious-ness, or soul stuff, depending upon the chosen theological viewpoint, momentarily detaches itself from the individual in question, allowing the individual to experience the event in a different timeframe. Or the far more obvious, trans-perambulation of pseudo-cosmic antimatter, precipitating a flexi-tangential spatial interflux within the symbiotic para-meters of existential functionalism.

But whether or not any of these actually apply to brains comprised entirely of sawdust is somewhat open to debate.

If asked whether he had watched the exploding of Little Tommy Tucker in what seemed to be slow motion, Eddie Bear would, however, answer, 'Yes, and it was not at all nice.'

Eddie watched the ghastly swellings, the vile expansions, the distortions of limbs and facial featurings, and then he saw the rending of flesh and shirt and blue silk *Oh Boy!* suit. And he saw the fragments of the gas-filled clockwork grenade that roared out of Tommy's shredded body. And whether it was adrenalous rush, or detached id, or pseudo-cosmic existential functionalism, Eddie managed to duck aside as metal shards and Tucker guts flew in his direction.

Not so, however, the wildly trottering rude crew pigs, who caught much shrapnel in their rubber rear ends.

As the crew pigs ran squealing and Jack, who had gone down fighting, came up prepared to do some more, Eddie raised his ducked head and saw something else.

And Eddie pointed with a paw and Jack looked up and saw it too.

Down through the hole in the ceiling it drifted, a tiny white and brown thing. The white of it was a parachute, the brown was a hollow chocolate bunny.

Now the mayhem hadn't lessened, because but a few short seconds had passed. The explosion had done nothing whatever to lessen the chaos; on the contrary, it had done everything to considerably increase it.

The fire alarm was ringing and the sprinkler system went into action. Water showered down upon the audience-turned-mob. The audience-turned-mob turned upon itself, and much of itself turned to other than itself; indeed, turned upon the rude crew pigs who were scrambling also to flee.

It was now a full-blown riot situation.

'This way.' Jack hauled Eddie after him and took off at a rush for the rear of the stage, leaping over spattered remains of the ex-supper singer. 'The killer's upstairs somewhere; we have to get after them.'

'Whoa!' went Eddie as Jack passed the painted sky backdrop and entered a backstage corridor. 'Slow down, Jack, think about this.'

'We have to get after the killer.'

'We don't have any weapons.'

'We'll improvise.'

'Have you gone completely insane?'

Jack dashed along the corridor. 'Let go of me,' cried Eddie. 'Put me down.'

Jack ceased his dashings and put Eddie down. 'The murderer may still be in the building,' he said. 'We have to find out; we have to do something.'

'No, Jack,' said Eddie. 'I can't.'

'You can't? Why?'

'Jack, I just saw a man get blown to pieces. I think I'm going to be sick.'

'Then wait here,' said Jack. 'I'll go alone.'

'No, don't do it, please.'

'But I might be able to catch them unawares.'

'Or you might walk straight into a trap. Let it go, Jack.'

'Are you sure?'

'You're very brave, but look at the state of you.'

'I'm fine,' said Jack.

'You're not, you're all beaten about.'

'Get away, they hardly laid a trotter on me.'

'Carry me back to the office, Jack.'

'Carry you? In broad daylight? What about your dignity?'

'I'll have to swallow that, I'm afraid.'

And then Eddie fainted.

Jack carried Eddie back to Bill Winkie's office. To spare his dignity, he hid the little bear beneath his trenchcoat.

In the office Jack splashed water on Eddie and slowly Eddie revived.

'That was most upsetting,' said Eddie. 'I didn't like that at all.'

'Are you feeling all right now?' Jack asked.

'Yes, I'll be fine. Thanks for looking after me.'

'No problem,' said Jack. 'As long as you're okay.'

'It was a bit of a shock.'

'But let's look on the bright side,' said Jack.

'The bright side? What bright side?'

'Little Tommy Tucker went the way he would probably have wanted: live on stage before a cheering audience. Out on a high note and in a blaze of glory.'

'Are you trying to be funny?'

'Rather desperately so, yes.'

'Then please don't.' Eddie shook his head. 'I can't believe it. The killer did it, right in front of us. Right in front of the viewing public. How audacious can you get?'

'This killer is making a very big statement.' Jack settled

down in Bill Winkie's chair. 'There's a very big ego involved here.'

'And we're always one step behind.'

'Well, we're bound to be. We don't know who this loony is going to butcher next. We don't have his hit list.'

'Hit list, a celebrity hit list,' said Eddie, thoughtfully. 'You might have something there.'

Eddie climbed onto the wreckage of Bill Winkie's desk. 'Right,' he said. 'Let's see what we have. We have Murder Most Foul: to whit, Mr Dumpty, Boy Blue, Madame Goose, Wibbly, Jack Spratt and now Tommy Tucker. I think we can exclude Madame Goose and Wibbly; they just happened to be in the wrong place at the wrong time. It's the others that matter. The old rich of Toy City. What is the common link?'

'Easy,' said Jack, swivelling about in Bill Winkie's chair, 'I know this.'

'Go on,' said Eddie.

'The common link is that they were all killed by the same murderer.'

Eddie made the kind of face that wouldn't buy you cheese. 'Was that supposed to be funny too?' he asked.

'I don't think so,' said Jack. 'But think about it, Eddie. *She*, or *it*, must have had a reason to kill them all.'

'I understand what you're saying. But *she* or *it* didn't kill Jack Spratt or Tommy Tucker. *She* or *it* was already done and dusted.'

'Oooh oooh.' Jack put up his hand. 'I've an idea.'

'Go on,' said Eddie once more.

'All right, my idea is this. There are two killers.'

Eddie groaned.

'No, I haven't finished. There are two killers, *but* they're hired killers, working for someone else. The brains behind it all.'

'What *are* you saying?' Eddie asked. 'No, wait, I know what you're saying. If the *she* or *it* was doing the killing for *her* personal motives, the killings would have stopped when she was killed.'

'Exactly,' said Jack, having another swivel on the chair. 'So if you stop this latest killer, the killings won't stop; another hired killer will take over and continue the work.'

'And our job is to find out what this *work* is. Why it's being done and who is the evil genius behind it.'

'Evil genius is a bit strong,' said Jack. 'Let's not go giving this mad person airs and graces.'

'Criminal mastermind, then,' said Eddie.

'That's more like it,' said Jack. 'So what we need to find is the common link.'

Eddie groaned once more.

'What's with all this groaning?' Jack asked. 'Are you ill or something?'

'We're going round in circles. We need to put things in order.'

'Right,' said Jack, nodding in agreement and swivelling a bit more on the chair.

'*In order,*' said Eddie, in the voice of one who has been granted a sudden revelation. 'Put things in order! As in your list. The celebrity hit list.'

Jack did shruggings which, combined with his swivellings, nearly had him off the chair.

'Why did the killer slaughter her victims in the order she did?' Eddie asked. 'Why Humpty first, then Boy Blue? I'll bet there's some reason for the order.'

'I can't see why the order matters. Why don't we go to Jack Spratt's and search for some clues there? Or back to the studios; we might find something.'

'No,' said Eddie. 'If I'm right about this, we'll be ahead of the game.'

'I don't understand,' said Jack. 'Oh damn!'

'Oh damn?'

'I've got the hem of my trenchcoat caught in the swivelling bit of the chair.' Jack yanked at the trenchcoat's hem and was rewarded with a ghastly tearing sound. 'Oh double damn,' he said.

Eddie ignored him. 'It's this way,' he said. 'I'm thinking

that the victims are being killed in a particular order. I'll just bet you that it's the order that their nursery rhymes were written. I'm pretty sure that I read somewhere that Humpty was the first nursery rhyme millionaire.'

'But how does this help?' Jack fought with the chair for possession of the trenchcoat. So far the chair was winning.

'Wake up, Jack,' said Eddie. 'If I am right and the victims are being murdered in that order, then we'll know who's going to be the next on the celebrity hit list, won't we?'

Jack ceased his struggles. 'Eddie, that's brilliant,' he said. 'Then we can beat the police to the crime scene when the next murder happens.'

Eddie threw up his paws in despair.

'Only joking,' said Jack. 'We can be there before it happens, prevent it and capture the hired killer and get Bellis's boys in blue to beat the name of the criminal mastermind out of them. Or something like that.'

'Something like that,' said Eddie. 'So, it's *The Hall of Nearly All The Records* for us.'

'The hall of *nearly all* the records?'

'The curator is a very honest man. He can't be expected to remember everything.'

'Well, obviously not,' said Jack. 'He'd look stuff up in the record books.'

'Record books?' said Eddie. 'What are record books?'

'Books with records in them.'

'A novel idea,' said Eddie. 'I'll pass that on to the curator. He has nearly all the records in his head.'

'*What?*' said Jack. 'They're not written down?'

'He does have a very large head.'

Jack shook his not-so-very-large head. 'Just one thing,' he said. 'How far away is this hall?'

'Right across the other side of the city.'

'And will we be taking a cab?'

'I don't think I have sufficient money for the fare. I was so drunk that I actually paid off my bar bill at Tinto's last night.'

'So you'll be walking?'

'*We'll* be walking,' said Eddie.

'*You'll* be walking,' said Jack. 'I did enough walking yesterday. And I'll keel over from hunger soon anyway. We should have used the Chief Inspector's money to get some new wheels for Bill's car.'

'I know what,' said Eddie. 'We'll telephone *The Hall of Nearly All The Records.*'

'Inspired,' said Jack. 'Where's the telephone?'

'Somewhere amongst all this mess; let's search for it.'

A thorough search of Bill Winkie's office turned up a number of interesting things.

It also turned up a telephone.

Jack turned up the telephone.

'Is this it?' he asked, turning it down again.

'That's the kiddie,' said Eddie.

'This toy telephone with the piece of knotted string holding the handset on?'

'Pretty smart telephone, eh? I bought it for Bill as a birthday present.'

'But it's not a *real* telephone.'

'Please don't start all that again, Jack. Just dial *The Hall of Nearly All The Records* and let's get on.'

'And the telephone number is?'

'Oh, give it to me.' Eddie snatched away the telephone. Then he looked at it in a mournful manner. And then he handed it back. 'You'll have to dial,' he said; 'no fingers.'

'I'll just dial a number at random,' said Jack. 'You never know, luck might be on our side.'

Eddie, who had tired with groaning, made a low and growly sound instead. Jack dialled out some numbers and held the wooden handset to his ear.

'*Hall of Nearly All The Records,*' said a voice.

'Wah!' went Jack, dropping the handset.

Eddie scooped it up between his paws. 'Hello,' he said.

'Hello,' said the voice. '*Hall of Nearly All The Records.*'

'Splendid,' said Eddie. 'This is Chief Inspector Bellis here. I need some information.'

'If I have it, it's yours,' said the voice.

'Splendid once more,' said Eddie, turning to Jack. 'Get a pen and paper, Jack, and write down what I tell you.'

Jack sought pen and paper. 'Go on then,' he said, when his seeking had reached a successful conclusion.

Eddie awoke with a start. 'Sorry,' he said, 'nodded off there.' And he told the curator of *The Hall of Nearly All The Records* what he wanted to know.

'Easy,' said the curator, and he reeled off the list.

'Slow down,' said Eddie, as he dictated this list to Jack.

'And . . .' said the curator.

'Yes?' said Eddie.

'Aaaaaagh!' went the curator, and the line went dead.

'Oh,' said Eddie.

'How do you spell that?' Jack asked. 'Is it a single "O"?'

'No, it's Oh! As in a surprised, if not a little shocked, Oh! The curator just went Aaaaaagh! And then the line went dead.'

'So how do you spell Aaaaaagh?'

Eddie shook his head. 'I think the curator just got murdered,' he said.

'Oh,' said Jack. 'That's bad. That's really bad. This new killer is as smart as the old one. But at least we do have the list.'

Eddie sighed. 'Read it back to me,' he said.

Jack read the list:

'Humpty Dumpty,

'er . . .

'Little Boy Blue,

'Jack Spratt,

'Little Tommy Tucker,

'Little Jack Horner,

'Little Miss Muffett,

'Georgie Porgie,

'Old Mother Hubbard.'

'Humpty Dumpty, Little Boy Blue, Jack Spratt,' said Eddie, beating the palm of his right paw with as near to a fist as he could make from the left. 'They're in the correct order. But hold on. There're only eight names. I'm sure I gave you nine. I wasn't really paying attention to which ones they were at the time, I was just trying to keep up with the curator. But I do remember how many there were. There were nine. You've left one out.'

'No I haven't,' said Jack.

'You have, Jack. I remember there were nine. Show me the list.'

'There're just eight.' Jack made to tear up the list, but Eddie knocked it from his hand and fumbled it up from the floor.

And then Eddie perused this list and then Eddie really groaned.

'I'm sorry,' said Jack.

Eddie shook his head, slowly and sadly. 'I should have known,' he said. 'I should have realised.'

'Perhaps it's not the same one,' said Jack.

'It's the same one,' said Eddie. 'There was only ever one Wee Willy Winkie. Even though he preferred to be known as Bill.'

They repaired to Tinto's Bar to take a late and liquid breakfast.

Eddie was a sad and sombre bear.

'I'm so sorry,' said Jack. 'It only really clicked when you called out his name for me to write down. Who Bill Winkie really was. But what I don't understand is, why did he become a detective? He should have been lording it up on his nursery rhyme royalties.'

'He was tricked out of his royalties by Wheatley Porterman. Signed a really bad contract. Porterman had made so much money from Humpty, he thought he'd take *all* from the next client. Wee Willy went public on the way he'd been tricked; no one ever got tricked again. But he was broke, but he *was* a natural detective, you know, all that "tapping at the windows and crying through the locks" stuff in the nursery rhyme. And checking up on whether the children were in their beds by eight o'clock. Natural detective. And now he's . . . you know.'

'We don't know he's *you know*. He's missing, that's all.'

'He's dead,' said Eddie, dismally. 'He's as dead as. This killer delights in fitting ends for his victims. Boiling the big egg man, giving the ex-shepherd the bitter end of his crook, Tommy Tucker going out on a high note, like you said. And the fellow who does all the searching goes missing. Simple as that.'

'I'm so sorry.' Jack ordered further drinks that he had no means of paying for. 'Put them on my tab,' he told Tinto. The clockwork barlord, who had been listening in to the conversation, did so without complaint.

'This time it's really really personal,' said Eddie.

'We know who's going to be next,' said Jack. 'Like you said, that puts us ahead of the game.'

'Oh dear,' said Eddie. 'We'd better hurry. Tinto, call me a cab.'

'All right,' said Tinto, 'you're a cab.'

Jack began to laugh.

'That's not funny,' said Eddie. 'That's such an old joke.'

'But I'm young; I've never heard it before.'

'I'll call a cab for you,' said Tinto, whirring away to do so.

'I thought you couldn't afford a cab?' Jack took to finishing his beers.

'We'll worry about that when we get to Little Jack Horner's.'

Eddie finished his beer, and then two of Jack's before Jack could get to them.

The cab was a fine-looking automobile. It was a Mark 9 Black Cab Kerb Crawler, with lithographed pressed steel body panels, chrome-trimmed running boards and brass radiator grille.

It came complete with comfy passenger seats in plush fur fabric and a clockwork cabbie called Colin.

'Very plush,' said Jack, comfying himself upon a comfy passenger seat.

'Where to, guvnor?' asked Colin the clockwork cabbie, his tin-plate jaw going *click click click.*

'Little Jack Horner's,' said Jack.

'He's popular today,' said the cabbie.

'Why do you say that?' Eddie asked.

'Because I've just come from his place; dropped a customer there.'

Jack and Eddie exchanged glances. 'What did this customer look like?' Jack asked.

'She was a strange one,' said the cabbie. 'Didn't speak. Just handed me a piece of paper with Jack Horner's address on it. She wore this feathered hat thing and she never stopped smiling. I could see her in the driving mirror. She fair put the wind up me, I can tell you.'

'Faster,' said Eddie. 'Drive faster.'

'Faster costs more money,' said the cabbie.

'Fast as you can then,' said Eddie, 'and you can have all the money I've got on me.'

'And all the money I have too,' said Jack.

The driver put his pressed-tin foot down. 'I'll show you fast,' he said. And he showed them fast.

'Eddie,' said Jack, as he clung for the dearness of life to whatever there was for him to cling to.

'Jack?' said Eddie, who clung on to Jack.

'Eddie, what are we going to do when we get there? We're no match for this woman-thing.'

The cab hung a left and went up on two wheels.

'Big guns,' said Eddie. 'We need big guns.'

'But where are we going to get big guns?'

'Big guns?' The cabbie glanced over his shiny shoulder. 'Did I hear you say big guns?'

'Watch the road!' shouted Jack.

'Big guns, I said,' said Eddie.

'I love big guns,' said the cabbie. 'Well, you have to in this business.' He now hung a right and the cab went up on its other two wheels.

'In the cabbie business?' Eddie was now on the floor; Jack helped him up.

'You'd be surprised,' said the cabbie. 'Folk get into my cab and ask me to drive somewhere, then tell me that they have no money.'

'Oh,' said Eddie. 'So you menace them with your big gun?'

'No,' said the cabbie. 'I shoot them. I'm mad, me.'

'Oh, perfect,' whispered Jack.

'Stay cool,' whispered Eddie. 'Mr Cabbie?'

'Yes?' said the cabbie. 'Oh hold on, there's a red light!'

'I'll wait until you've stopped then.'

'I don't stop for red lights,' said the cabbie. 'Not when there's a really big fare in it for me. I'll probably take the rest of the week off once you've paid up.'

'Ah,' said Eddie. And the cabbie ran the red light, much to the distress of the traffic that had the right of way. This traffic came to a sudden halt. Cars bashed into other cars. A swerving lorry ran into a shop front.

'Nearly there,' the cabbie called back. 'Best get your wallets out, and I'll take your wristwatches too.'

'You're a very funny fellow,' said Eddie.

'Thanks a lot,' said the cabbie, revving the engine and putting his foot down harder. 'And some people say that psychopaths don't have a sense of humour. What do they know, eh?'

'Nothing,' said Eddie. 'But about this big gun of yours . . .'

'This one?' The cabbie whipped it out of his jacket with his gear-changing hand. It was a very big gun indeed.

'Whoa!' went Jack. 'That's a 7.62 mm M134 General Clockwork Mini-gun. Max cyclic rate 6000 rounds per minute. 7.62 x 51 shells, 1.36kg recoil adapters, muzzle velocity of 869m/s.'

'You certainly know your weapons, buddy,' said the cabbie. 'And this one carries titanium-tipped ammunition. Take the head off a teddy at two hundred yards.'

'We're sawdust,' whispered Eddie.

Jack made shushing sounds. 'I used to work in the factory that manufactured those guns,' he told the cabbie. 'Do you have it serviced regularly?'

'I keep it well oiled.' The cabbie swerved onto the wrong side of the road, which made things exciting for the oncoming traffic.

'How many times have you fired it?' Jack asked.

'Dozens of times,' said the cabbie, performing further life-endangering automotive manoeuvres.

'And you've not had the chamber-spring refulgated?'

'Eh?' said the cabbie, taking a turn along the pavement.

'Surely you've read the manual?'

'Naturally,' said the cabbie. 'I'm a practising Mechanologist. But what has my religion got to do with this?'

'Nothing at all,' said Jack. 'But if you don't get that chamber-spring refulgated, that gun is likely to blow your arm off the next time you fire it.'

A grin appeared upon Eddie's face. It did not take a genius to figure out what was coming next.

'I could refulgate it for you,' said Jack.

'What do you take me for?' asked the cabbie.

The grin disappeared from Eddie's face.

'You're going to charge me for doing it, aren't you?' the cabbie said.

'No,' said Jack. 'I'll do it for free.'

Eddie's grin reappeared.

'Well.' The cabbie hesitated – although not with his driving.

'Listen,' said Jack, 'I'm only thinking of you. Imagine the unthinkable occurring.'

'I can't imagine the unthinkable,' said the cabbie. 'What would that be like?'

'It would be like us not being able to pay and you having

to shoot us, but the gun blowing your arm off instead. You'd look pretty silly then, wouldn't you?'

'I would,' the cabbie agreed.

'And you wouldn't want to look silly.'

'I certainly wouldn't.' The cabbie handed the gun over his shoulder to Jack.

Eddie looked up at his partner with a look that almost amounted to adoration. 'Wonderful,' he said.

'We'll see,' said Jack. 'Now let's get this chamber-spring refulgated. We don't want the cabbie to blow his arm off when he shoots us.'

'Eh?' said Eddie.

Jack raised an eyebrow.

'Oh I see, you're only joking again. I don't think I'll ever get the measure of your humour, Jack.'

'We're here,' said the cabbie, bringing his cab to a shuddering halt. 'How are you doing with my gun?'

Eddie and Jack ran up the sweeping drive towards Little Jack Horner's mansion. It was a worthy mansion, situated on a lower southwestern slope of Knob Hill. It was appropriately plum-coloured, and had a great many corners to it where, within, one might sit and enjoy some Christmas pie.

The plumly-hued front door stood open.

Jack cocked the 7.62 mm M134 General Clockwork Mini-gun. Its polished butt was slightly dented now, from the blow it had administered to the rear of the cabbie's head. Jack hadn't enjoyed striking down the cabbie, but desperate times called for desperate measures. Jack ducked to one side of the open doorway, Eddie ducked to the other.

'What do we do?' Jack asked. 'Rush in, big gun blazing?'

'Sneak in, I think,' said Eddie. 'Big gun at the ready. And remember, she'll be expecting us. She knows we have the list.'

'Let's sneak then.' Jack took a deep breath and then entered the mansion, Eddie close upon his heels.

As Jack did his sneaking, he also did peepings about, not just to seek out the mysterious murderess, but to generally peruse the premises.

Jack was getting a feel for grandeur. For wealth. He'd viewed the overt opulence of Humpty Dumpty's apartment, the gilded rococo chic of *Oh Boy!* and the romantic harmony of Madame Goose's establishment.

This, however, differed from those, which indeed differed from each other.

'This stuff is old, isn't it, Eddie?' Jack peeped into an elegant room, lavishly furnished with ebonised furniture trimmed with heartstone and heavy on the ormolu. 'I mean, it's *old*.'

'Antiques so often are,' said Eddie.

'Yes, but what I mean is this: the folk in nursery rhymes are the old rich of Toy City, aren't they?'

'They are.' Eddie ducked down behind a Zebrawood thuya of considerable yearage.

'So who owned this stuff before they did? Are these people the *new* old rich? Was there previously an *old* old rich that had this furniture built for them?'

'Oh, I see what you're getting at. Well, now that you come to mention it, there was something the curator said to me about the copyrights on the nursery rhymes that doesn't seem to make any sense.' Eddie rolled onto his belly and squirmed under a low mahogany side table with foliate splayed legs and rosewood inlay.

'What did he say?' Jack followed Eddie and struck his head upon the table's underside. 'Ouch,' he continued.

'What he said was . . .' And then Eddie put his paw to his nose.

'What?' Jack asked.

'Can you smell that?'

Jack did sniffings. 'No,' he said. 'What is it?'

'Jam,' said Eddie. 'Plum jam.'

Jack clipped Eddie on the ear. 'This is no time to be thinking about food,' he said. 'Naughty, bad bear.'

'Watch it,' said Eddie. 'But do I smell plum jam. Too much plum jam.'

'Can you have too much plum jam?' Jack asked. 'I'm very partial to plum jam, as it happens. And cradberry preserve.'

'Oh yes,' said Eddie, licking his mouth. 'Cradberry preserve is very nice indeed. And bongle jelly, that's particularly toothsome on hot buttered toast and . . .'

'Stop it,' said Jack. 'I'm still hungry, but I can smell it too, now. It's a very strong smell of plum jam.'

'Come on Jack, quickly,' Eddie squirmed out from under the table and jumped to his paws. 'Quickly.'

'Okay, I'm coming. Oh damn, I'm stuck under this table.'

There was a bit of a struggle, then certain damage was inflicted upon the mahogany table with the foliate splayed legs and the rosewood inlay. Jack emerged with the big gun held high.

And he followed Eddie at the hurry-up, into another kitchen.

Jack recalled all too well the horrors that he had met with in the kitchen of Madame Goose. He was not, however, prepared for those that awaited him here.

21

'Oh no,' croaked Jack, when his stomach had no more to yield. 'That is all too much.'

Eddie was slowly shaking his head. 'Much too much,' said he.

Little Jack Horner sat in the corner.

But Little Jack was not so little now.

He had been roped onto a kitchen chair, bound hand and foot. His body was bloated, the stomach distended, hugely distorted. The cause of this was the rubber tube that had been rammed into his mouth and forced down his throat. This tube led upwards to a great metal kitchen vat, suspended from a ceiling stanchion. This vat had evidently been filled with plum jam. This vat was now empty.

On the floor, about the chair, a pool of jam was spreading. It spread over around and about a hollow chocolate bunny.

'Sick,' said Eddie, giving his head further shakings. 'That is very sick.'

Jack wiped vomit from his chin and tears from his eyes. 'He might still be alive,' he said. 'Perhaps we could pump his stomach out?'

'He's dead,' said Eddie. 'As dead as, and more so besides. Not the best way to go, I suppose. But I can think of far worse. Imagine if the vat had been filled with sprout juice.'

'Eddie, stop it, please.'

'Sorry, it's nerves.' Eddie twitched his nose. 'Jack,' he said in a low and dreadful tone, 'Jack, don't move.'

'What is it, Eddie?' Jack had the big gun raised once more.

'She's still here. I can smell her perfume.'

'Stay close to me.' Jack swung the big gun around and about. 'Come out!' he called. This first 'come out' didn't come out too well; it lacked for a certain authority.

'Come out! I have a gun.' The second 'come out' came out somewhat better. 'Give yourself up!' Jack fairly shouted now. 'The mansion is surrounded. You have no means of escape.'

Eddie nudged at Jack's leg and pointed with a paw. 'Broom cupboard,' he said.

'They favour broom cupboards, don't they?'

'Shoot through the door, Jack.' Eddie mimed gunshots as best he could. 'Shoot her while we have her cornered.'

'I can't do *that*.' Jack's gaze wandered back to the bloated corpse.

'Don't start that again. Shoot her, Jack.'

'But I . . .'

But he should have done.

The broom cupboard door splintered and through it she came: slender and deadly; swift and smooth.

And then she was on them.

She swung a fist at Jack, who ducked and struck Eddie's head with his chin. And then she had Jack by the scruff of his neck. She hauled him from his feet and swung him around in a blurry arc. Jack lost his grip upon the pistol, which skidded over the flagstone floor. The struggling Jack was hefted aloft and then flung with hideous force.

He tumbled across the kitchen table, scattering crockery and disappearing over the other side.

And then she was up on the table, grinning down at the fallen Jack. And then she was stooping to take up a large meat cleaver.

Jack backed away on his bottom. 'No,' he pleaded. 'Don't kill me, please.'

The being in the figure-hugging rubber grinned on regardless. She raised the cleaver to her lips and licked its edge with a blood–red pointy tongue.

'Who are you?' Jack tried to edge away, but there was

nowhere left for him to edge to. 'Why are you doing these things?'

The being leapt down from the table and stood astride Jack, grinning evilly.

'Say something.' Jack was in absolute terror now. 'Please say something. Anything. Please.'

The being raised the cleaver. Her mouth slowly opened, as if to utter words, and then it closed again.

And then the cleaver swung down.

Jack was aware of a horrible force. Of a great pushing and pressing and cutting and tearing and . . .

An explosion of sound.

His eyes had been closed.

But now they were open.

And he saw it all happen in slow motion.

The upswing of that cleaver.

Then the down.

And then the splitting of the head.

The fracturing and shattering as the head became a thousand scattering pieces.

But it was not Jack's head.

It was that of his attacker.

The cleaver came down.

Jack ducked aside and it crashed to the stone floor beside him, dropped by a hand that was now clutching at the empty air where a head had just been. There was only neck now, with ragged sinews and tubey things spilling out dark ichor.

The hands, both hands, clutched and clawed, and then the headless body fell onto Jack.

'Wah!' went Jack. And 'Aagh!' and 'Oh,' and 'Help.'

'You're all right.' The voice belonged to Eddie. 'You're all right. I got her, Jack. Plugged her good. She's as dead as. And I'm not kidding you about.'

Jack fought to free himself from the fallen corpse. He

could see the grinning bear. The grinning bear was holding the 7.62 mm M134 General Clockwork Mini-gun.

'It's a good job it doesn't have a trigger-guard,' said Eddie, 'or I'd never have been able to fire it. The cabbie was right about it taking heads right off though, wasn't he?'

'Wah!' went Jack once more.

Then once more he was sick, which, considering that he'd had next to nothing in his stomach prior to the first vomiting, was something of an achievement.

Although not one of which he could be proud.

'She's definitely dead this time,' said Eddie. 'For all of Toy City's unfathomable mysteries, I can assure you, Jack, that nothing lives with its head completely shot off.'

Jack, who was on his knees, hauled himself to his feet. 'Thank you, Eddie,' he said. 'You saved my life.'

'That's what partners do,' said the bear. 'You save my life, I save yours.'

'Thanks.' Jack stooped and patted Eddie on the back. And then he gazed down at the headless corpse. 'So what *was* she, Eddie? What do you think?'

'Turn her over, Jack. Let's have a good look at her.'

'No way. I'm not touching that.'

'Get a grip, partner. We're fearless detectives, are we not?'

'No, *we* are *not*. Look at me, Eddie. I'm shaking all over and my trenchcoat is covered in black goo. My stomach's caving in and look at the state of my fedora.' Jack stooped to pick up his fedora. The falling cleaver had taken its crown clear off.

'The new open-topped look,' said Eddie. 'It might catch on.'

'I'm not touching her,' said Jack, and he folded his shaky arms and made a shaky-headed sulky face.

'Use your foot then.'

Jack sighed and with difficulty nudged the body over with his foot.

'Fine big bosoms,' said Eddie. 'Though rather too scrawny in all the other places for my taste.'

'Stop it, please.'

'Jack,' said Eddie.

'Eddie?' said Jack.

'Jack, those fine big bosoms . . .'

'I told you to stop that.'

'Those fine big bosoms are moving.'

'Wah!' went Jack; 'Wah!' always served him well at such times. 'She's still alive. Shoot her again, Eddie. But wait until I turn away.'

'She's not alive,' said Eddie, 'she's . . . urgh, look at *that*!'

Jack looked at *that*. 'Urgh,' he agreed. 'What *is* that?'

'It's spiders.' Eddie backed away. 'They're coming out of her, everywhere. Let's go, Jack. I don't want to look at this.'

Jack took one more look, then wished he hadn't. The corpse was now a heaving mass of spiders. They spilled from her ragged neck hole, and out of belt holes and seams and here and there and all over everywhere.

'This can't happen.' Jack gawped and gasped and backed away. 'She can't be full of spiders. What *is* this, Eddie? What's going on here?'

Eddie backed away and cocked an ear. 'Do you hear what I hear?' he asked.

Jack tried to cock an ear too, but there are certain things that bears can do and lads just can't.

And vice versa, of course.

'No,' said Jack. 'What?'

'The bells of approaching police cars,' said Eddie. 'I think the cabbie must have regained consciousness and called the police.'

'Ah,' said Jack. 'And you don't think we should just stay here and talk to the policemen? Explain things? Tell them what we know?'

'I'm not keen,' said Eddie. 'I think we should head over to Miss Muffett's at the hurry-up; she's next on the list. We don't know how many of these spider-women things there are. I can't believe that this one could move so fast as to kill Tommy Tucker, then head across town and kill the curator and still get here before us. There could be another at Miss Muffett's now.'

'You're right. Back door?'

'Back door,' agreed Eddie.

They skirted the house and slipped quietly away.

'So where does Miss Muffett live?' Jack asked as he trudged along upon wobbly legs.

'Not too far. Let's hope we can get there before our criminal mastermind dispatches another of his killers. He surely won't know yet that we just popped off this one.'

'But what do you think they are, Eddie? They're not human, and they're not toys. So what's left?'

'Only one thing I can think of and I don't want to think about that. Do you still have the Maguffin?'

Jack patted his pocket. It was a sticky pocket, all black goo'd. 'Still have it,' he said. 'And one question. Before we went into that kitchen, you mentioned something the curator said to you. Something you said made no sense.'

'I did,' said Eddie. 'Turn left here.'

Jack turned left. 'It's more fun in a car,' he said. 'But what were you going to say? It was something about the copyrights on the nursery rhymes.'

'Yes it was.' Eddie's little fat teddy bear legs were tiring. 'Walk slower,' he said.

Jack walked slower.

'The copyrights,' said Eddie. 'When I asked about the order they were registered in, the curator told me: it was the dates that didn't make sense.'

'Go on,' said Jack.

'Well, the copyright on *Humpty Dumpty sat on a wall*. That was the first one ever registered. How long ago do you reckon that was?'

Jack shrugged and the crown of his fedora fell off. Jack stooped, picked it up and replaced it on his head.

'You should throw that hat away,' said Eddie.

'No chance,' said Jack. 'You can't be a proper detective without a fedora. But I don't know about the copyright; maybe thirty or forty years ago, I suppose.'

'That would seem about right,' said Eddie. 'But it's wrong. *Humpty Dumpty: The Nursery Rhyme* was registered three hundred and fifty years ago.'

'That's ridiculous,' said Jack. 'Was it another Humpty Dumpty? This Dumpty's great-great-great-grandfather?'

'There's only ever been *one* Humpty Dumpty: the one who got boiled in his swimming pool.'

'But no one can live for three hundred and fifty years.'

'Toy Town grew into Toy City,' said Eddie. 'But I don't know *when* it did. It's always been the city to me and I've been here for a long time. I was Bill Winkie's bear. I'd never thought before about how long I'd been his bear, but it must have been a very, very long time.'

'What, you're telling me that *you* might be three hundred years old?' Jack stopped short and Eddie bumped into him.

'I don't know,' said Eddie, who, having tumbled, now struggled up. 'No one ever really keeps track of time here. Things are always the same. Nothing ever changes. We just go on and on. Until we fall to pieces. If you're a toy, that is.'

'It's all nonsense,' said Jack. 'Three hundred and fifty years old! But then, in this nightmare of a city where nothing makes any sense, who can say? Are we there yet?'

'Yes,' said Eddie. 'We are. But we're not.'

'Well, that doesn't make any sense, so I suppose it's about right.'

'No, Jack, we should be there, but we're not, because it isn't here.'

'What isn't here?'

'Miss Muffett's house. It's gone.'

'What do you mean? It's been pulled down?'

'No, I mean it's gone, just gone.'

'A house can't be just gone; where should it be?'

'There,' said Eddie. 'There.'

There was a bit of a hillside with some well-established trees and some equally well-established bushes.

'There's not been a house there in ages,' said Jack. 'If there ever was one.'

'There was,' said Eddie. 'I was here last week, on the *Tour of the Stars' Homes* bus. It's one of my favourite outings. The house was here. *Right* here.'

'You must have got it wrong. Houses do not simply vanish.'

'I never implied that there was anything simple about it. But this house has vanished.'

'You think so?'

'I know so.'

'Oh.'

22

'Listen, Eddie,' said Tinto, 'much as I like you, and don't get me wrong, I *do* like you, I can't keep giving you credit. I'm trying to run this bar at a profit. That's how business is done.'

'I know how business is done.' Eddie comfyed himself on a barstool. 'But Jack and I have just been through a very traumatic experience. We both need beer. Lots of beer. You'll get your money when we've solved the case . . .'

'Ca*ses*.' Jack uncomfyed himself on the barstool next to Eddie.

'Ca*ses*, then. You'll get your money, Tinto.'

'He might not,' said Jack. 'If we can't prevent the rest of the PPPs getting butchered, there won't be anyone left to cough up the rest of the money that was promised to Bill.'

'Stop that,' said Eddie.

'Only a thought,' said Jack.

'I saw you two on TV this morning,' said Tinto. 'I was going to mention it when you were in earlier, but it didn't seem to be the appropriate time.'

'Thanks, Tinto,' said Eddie.

'But, as it is now, I'd just like to say that neither of you are as good-looking as you look on TV. You're both shorter, too.'

'Ha ha ha,' went Eddie, in a tone that lacked for humour.

'But what happened to Little Tommy Tucker, that was terrible.' Tinto's head spun round and round.

'It was even more terrible right up close,' said Eddie. 'And please don't do that with your head; it makes me feel sick.'

'But it *was* terrible.' Tinto drummed his dextrous fingers on the bar-top, which further upset Eddie. 'Terrible, terrible, terrible.'

'As if you care,' said Eddie.

'I *do* care,' said Tinto. 'We all care really, even if we don't own up to it. Society's coming apart, Eddie. You catch this killer before everything goes down the toilet.'

'You don't use a toilet,' said Eddie.

'You know what I mean. You just won't admit that you do.'

'I admit that I *don't*,' said Eddie. 'Ten beers, please.'

'No,' said Tinto. 'Think about this, Eddie. Toy City is Toy City. It's stable. Nothing ever changes here. We may say that we don't like it, but we kind of *do* like it. We're used to it. It's all we've got. It's what we've always had. These rich and famous celebrity folk are part of the essential fabric of society.'

'Essential fabric of society?' Eddie made a face. 'What's with all this sudden articulacy on your part?'

'You know what I'm talking about. These killings. They're changing things. Things aren't the same any more.'

'You're not wrong,' said Eddie. 'Ten beers, please.'

'No,' said Tinto. 'I mean what I say. A couple of weeks ago everything was normal. As it ever was and ever would be. Then Humpty Dumpty was murdered. Then Boy Blue and Jack Spratt and—'

'All right,' said Eddie, 'I know. Don't rub it in. We're doing our best.'

'Everything's falling apart. It's as if someone is out to destroy the whole city by killing off its most famous citizens. Destabilisation. You know what I'm saying?'

Eddie looked at Jack.

And Jack looked at Eddie.

'I think I do,' said Eddie. 'Ten beers, please.'

'I'll only give you five,' said Tinto, and he whirred and wheeled away behind the bar counter.

'What do you think?' Eddie asked.

'It makes sense,' said Jack. 'This criminal mastermind of yours could be trying to bring down the entire city, starting from the top. But to what end?'

'All right,' said Eddie. 'Let's think about this. Let's *seriously* think about this,' and Eddie smote his head. '*Seriously* think,' he said, smiting again and again.

'I really hate it when you do that,' said Jack.

'It works,' said Eddie, 'don't knock it.' And he smote his head once more.

Tinto delivered nine glasses of beer.

'I see Eddie's having a good old smote,' he said. 'Although I do constantly warn him that smoting can seriously damage your health.' Tinto chuckled. Jack didn't.

'Tell me, Tinto,' said Jack, 'how long do you think Eddie's been coming into this bar? In years. How long?'

'Well.' Tinto scratched at his tin plate brow with a dextrous fingertip. 'Not *that* long, I suppose. A couple of hundred years, maybe.'

'A *couple of hundred* years?' Jack all but fell off his barstool.

'Give or take,' said Tinto. 'I suppose it's quite a long time, when you come to think about it. But then folk like Eddie and me are old-style folk. We were built to last. Craftsmanship, you see.'

'You're winding me up,' said Jack.

'*Me* winding *you* up? Is that some feeble attempt at humour?'

'I have it,' said Eddie, bouncing up and down. 'I've figured the whole thing out. You're not going to like it, but I have.'

Jack passed Eddie a glass of beer. Eddie took it between both paws and drained the beer away. 'Imagine,' said he, 'that you, Jack, are a criminal mastermind.'

'All right.' Jack tried to imagine it.

'So what would you want?'

'Whatever you've got,' said Jack. 'And everything else besides.'

'Exactly,' said Eddie. 'You'd want the lot. All of it. Everything. All of this.'

'The city,' said Jack. 'I'd want the entire city.'

'You would,' said Eddie. 'But why would you want it?'

'Because that's what criminal masterminds always want. Everything.'

'So how would you go about getting this everything?'

'Well,' said Jack, 'personally, I'd gather together a private army, dressed in really stylish black uniforms. And I'd have this secret hideout, in an extinct volcano, with all these special trains that travel along secret tunnels and a Doomsday weapon and this white cat that sat on my knee and—'

'Jack,' said Eddie.

'Eddie?' said Jack.

'Never mind,' said Eddie. 'But what would you do here, in *this* city?'

'I'd threaten it with my Doomsday weapon.'

'But if, by some chance, you didn't actually have a Doomsday weapon?'

'I *would* have one,' said Jack.

'But if you didn't!' Eddie made a fierce face at Jack. 'If you only had a very small private army, say three or four assassins at your disposal. What would you do then, in *this* city?'

'I'd have my assassins kill off all the powerful members of society. Mess things up a bit. And then when the city was in total chaos and everyone was running around like headless chickens, I'd take over. Restore law and order. Seize power. Control it and . . .'

'Right,' said Eddie.

'Oh,' said Jack. 'Yes, right. And that's what's happening, isn't it?'

'It all makes perfect sense when you piece it together.' Eddie patted his head.

'Not altogether,' said Jack, 'as nothing really makes sense here. But if I *was* this criminal mastermind, I'm not exactly sure where I'd find these superhuman killer women that turn into spiders. Do you think I'd be able to get them out of a catalogue or something?'

'Not out of a catalogue. But you'll find them mentioned in a Holy Book. Which is where I start getting to the stuff that you're really not going to like.'

'I have no idea what you are talking about.' Jack took up another glass of beer and drained it away.

'Jack, something very bad is happening here in the city. Something *different*. Something new. Something the city has never seen before and doesn't know how to deal with. Something has entered the city. Something really evil.'

'Some*one*,' said Jack. 'This criminal mastermind.'

'Some*thing*,' said Eddie. 'Some*thing* that isn't a man and isn't a toy. Something else.'

'You mentioned something about this earlier, when we were walking to Miss Muffett's. Something you didn't want to think about.'

'That's the something,' said Eddie. 'And it's a terrible something. A horrible, frightening something.'

'Do you want to tell me about it now?'

Eddie took up another glass. 'I think perhaps I should,' he said. 'Because, dreadful and unthinkable as it is, it's the only thing that seems to make any sense.'

'Go on then,' said Jack. 'Tell me.'

And so Eddie told him. 'This is what I know,' said Eddie. 'In this city there are a number of religious movements. There's The Church of Mechanology, clockwork toys who believe in a clockwork universe—'

'I believe in *that*,' said Tinto, who was listening in. 'Because it's true.'

'And there're The Daughters of the Unseeable Upness,' said Eddie, 'which is a foolish dolly cult, and there's The Midnight Growlers, a philosophical movement dedicated to high spiritual ideals and the pursuit of truth and—'

'Beer,' said Tinto.

'There's also The Spring and Catch Society.'

'Who owe me money,' said Tinto. 'As you do. What is it with you cult nutters, eh? You never pay your bills.'

'Would you go away please, Tinto?'

'Do you want more drinks on your account?'

'Yes, please.'

'I'll get to it.' Tinto whirled and wheeled away.

'The Spring and Catch Society,' said Eddie to Jack, 'as you know, is a secret organisation. All the rich folk are rumoured to be in it. It's a branch of a Jack-in-the-box cult known as Big Box Fella He Come.'

'Oh,' said Jack. 'Well, I suppose there would be Jack-in-the-boxes in Toy City, although I've never seen one.'

'And you won't; they're very reclusive. They believe that the entire universe is a construction kit, taken out of the big box and assembled by God with the aid of his little helpers. Jack-in-the-boxes live underground, which is fine by the rest of us because there are far too many Jacks in this city already. No offence meant.'

'None taken, I assure you.'

'They believe that the universe comprises a number of boxes, one inside the other. They live in their boxes, which are inside secret rooms, bigger boxes, in the city, a bigger box still, that's in a box-shaped world, which is inside a box-shaped universe.'

'Which is all rubbish,' said Jack. 'Which is why I do not hold to any religious beliefs.'

'Well,' said Eddie, 'the point of what I'm trying to tell you is this . . .'

'Oh good,' said Tinto, bearing drinks. 'I thought I was going to miss the important bit.'

'The point is this,' Eddie continued. 'Jack-in-the-boxes believe in Big Box Fella, who was one of God's little helpers. He and his twin brother were given the job of constructing Toy City, which was one small bit of the universe kit. When it was finished, it was supposed to be a wonderful place to live in. Big Box Fella and his brother would have brought joy and happiness to everyone who would later be built to live there. But his brother was evil and refused to follow the instructions, which is why the city is the way it is now: a mess. So Big Box Fella threw his evil twin out of the city, but the evil twin went off with the instructions. Some Jack-in-the-boxes believe that Big Box Fella went after him and will one day return with the instructions and make everything right. Others believe that Big Box Fella is still here in the city, trying to make things right.'

'He's not doing much of a job of it.'

'Hear me out, Jack. According to the beliefs of this cult, there exists, outside the box that is Toy City, another world, a world of men, millions of men.'

'There is,' said Jack. 'I came from it.'

'No, you didn't,' said Eddie. 'You came from a town just outside Toy City. I've heard of your town. It's not too far away.'

'You've lost me,' said Jack.

'Jack, you wandered off your little bit of the map and found yourself here. But you've always lived inside the same "box" as Tinto and me. You just never knew it before. The Jack-in-the-boxes believe that there is another world beyond, outside this box, but we can't get to it. We can't move out of one box and into another. Only Big Box Fella and his evil twin can do that.'

'Ridiculous,' said Jack. 'And I'll tell you why it's ridiculous. All your rich folk made their millions from royalties earned on their nursery rhymes, didn't they? So who paid out these millions? Not toys, but men. Men out there paid. Men out there in other cities. Out there somewhere.' Jack pointed out there generally. 'That's obvious to anyone, isn't it?'

'Yes,' said Eddie, 'it is. And somehow the money comes in. I don't know how, but it does. But you and I can't get out there, Jack. We can't leave this box.'

'Nonsense.' Jack took up another glass. 'I wish we'd had some food,' he said. 'I'm already half drunk.'

'You'll want to be more drunk by the time I've finished. Think about this, Jack. The woman-creature that attacked us: she wasn't human and she wasn't a toy. So what's left? I'll tell you what's left. She was some kind of a demon. That was the something that I didn't want to think about. I've given my head a good hammering. I'm not wrong here.'

'This is mad,' said Jack. 'A demon? Demons don't exist.'

'He's right,' said Tinto. 'Demons don't exist.'

'Thank you, Tinto,' said Jack.

'She was probably a fairy,' said Tinto. 'You know, one of those pretty little clockwork creatures that live in the woods.'

'Keep out of this, Tinto,' Eddie said. 'She was a demon. Sent by the evil brother. Who seeks to return to the city and overthrow his good twin. If you put it all together, it makes perfect sense.'

'So who is the good twin? Tinto here? Or perhaps it's you, Eddie.'

Eddie shook his head. 'No, Jack,' he said. 'I'm talking about the man who is the brains behind this city. The man who created Tinto and me. I'm talking about the toymaker.'

'What?' Jack shook his own head wildly. 'This is all insane. You've been beating yourself too hard on the head.'

'It all makes sense.'

'It's superstitious nonsense.'

'You have a better idea?'

'I'll stick to the criminal mastermind theory with no Gods involved.'

'So how do you explain the spider-woman?'

'I don't.'

'Or Miss Muffett's vanishing house?'

'So Miss Muffett's house really has vanished,' said Tinto. 'Rufus the tour bus driver told me earlier that it had, but I didn't believe him. What's going on here, Eddie?'

'It's the evil twin,' said Eddie. 'That's what's going on.'

'This is rubbish,' said Jack. 'You're jumping to wild conclusions. This is not how detectives behave. Detectives catch criminals by thinking things out logically. Detectives draw logical conclusions. They catch logical criminals. They don't get involved in mad stuff like this. Come on, Eddie, this can't be true.'

'It can,' said Eddie. 'It's the only logical explanation. A famous detective, whose name now eludes me, said that once you've eliminated the impossible, then whatever remains, no matter how improbable, must be the truth.'

'You just made that up,' said Jack. 'But what are you saying? That the toymaker is really Big Box Fella, one of God's little helpers?'

Eddie nodded. 'An original Son of God. You've been driving yourself mad trying to work out how toys can live, haven't you, Jack? So this explanation should please you: the toymaker can bring toys to life because he is a God in this world. And so is his twin brother. But he's the opposite of his good brother, Jack. The evil opposite. He's returned from outside to claim this boxed-up city world of ours for himself. His good brother doesn't know what's going on. He won't know until it's too late. When all is lost.'

'So this criminal mastermind . . .'

'He's the Devil of this world, Jack. We're not dealing with a man here. We're dealing with an evil God. We're dealing with the Devil.'

23

'Same again,' said Jack. 'And stick it on Eddie's account.'

'You don't believe me, do you?' Eddie asked.

'How can I believe you, I'm an atheist.'

'Explain the spider-woman.'

'You know I can't. But I can't explain *him*.' Jack nodded towards Tinto. 'Nor you.'

'You could if you believed that the toymaker is a Son of God, possessed of Godly powers that can bestow life.'

'That's not fair,' said Jack. 'I know that that does explain things. But not to my satisfaction. Not when I'm an atheist.'

'It explains *everything*,' said Eddie. 'How toy telephones work. How teddy bears with sawdust for brains can think. Only a God can do that kind of stuff.'

'I need another drink,' said Jack. 'Oh, I've got one. And I mean to drink it.'

'I'm sorry to mess you up.' Eddie sipped his alcohol. 'But don't get me wrong. This is messing me up too. Big Time. I've never thought too deeply about this kind of stuff. And I'm not a follower of The Big Box Fella Cult.'

'My money's on you being a Midnight Growler,' said Jack.

Tinto laughed. 'Your money would be safe then. He's the *only* Midnight Growler.'

'There's money to be made in starting your own religion,' said Eddie. 'But I couldn't persuade any teddies to join mine.'

'I'll join,' said Jack. 'But come on, Eddie, the Devil? Say it really *was* the Devil. Then what could we, devoted Midnight Growlers though we might be, do to stop the Devil?'

'Bit of a tricky one, I agree.'

'But if the toymaker *is* a God,' Jack stroked at his chin, 'he did say that there might be an opening for me some day as an apprentice.'

'We have to tell him,' said Eddie. 'Tell him what's happening. Warn him.'

'But if he is a God-of-this-world, does he really have anything to fear from his brother? How do Gods battle it out? It's thunderbolts, isn't it?'

'It's fluff,' said Tinto. 'They stick fluff in each other's clockwork.'

'Eddie,' said Jack, 'think very hard now. Bang your head about as much as you want, more so if needs be. But are you absolutely sure about this? It is a pretty way-out theory. Couldn't we just be dealing with a plain old criminal mastermind?'

'I'm sure I'm right, Jack. Plain old criminal masterminds can't vanish homes.'

'So is Miss Muffett dead?'

'Perhaps they're all dead, Jack. Perhaps this is the beginning of the end.'

'Let's not get carried away. There might still be a more logical explanation.'

'We have to go and see the toymaker.' Eddie finished the last of Jack's latest drinks. 'We have to see him now. This is all moving too fast.'

'I agree with that. So let's just slow it down a little, take a few moments to think very carefully before we go jumping into something and get ourselves into trouble again. Let's have one more round before we go.'

'Just the one then. Tinto?'

'Very generous of you,' said Tinto. 'I'll have a large oil and soda.'

'I didn't mean that. But yes, go on, have one yourself. Same again for us.'

'Eddie,' said Tinto, 'does this mean that the world is coming to an end? Is the time of the Great Stillness approaching?'

'Not if Jack and I can help it.'

'Because if it is, then I think I'll close up early today. Can I come with you to the toymaker's? He might wish to employ the services of a clockwork butler.'

'Sorry,' said Eddie. 'This is a detectives-only thing. Same again before we go, please, Tinto.'

'Same again it is then,' said the barlord.

And yes. They did become very drunk, the three of them.

And you're not supposed to be drunk when you get involved with matters such as this: *Big* Matters, *Matters of an Apocalyptic Nature*. You're supposed to be coldly sober. And you just can't be coldly sober when you're drunk.

But then, if you really did find yourself involved in *Matters of an Apocalyptic Nature*, you'd need a few stiff ones under your belt before you got going with saving the world.

'We'll have to think very carefully,' said Eddie. 'Very carefully indeed.'

'That's what *I* said.' Jack squinted at Eddie in the manner that drunken people do, in the misguided belief that it makes them appear sober.

'Why are you squinting in that drunken fashion?' Eddie asked.

'I'm not. What exactly are we going to have to think carefully about, Eddie?'

'Exactly what we say to the toymaker.'

'We tell him the truth. We warn him about what his evil twin is up to.'

'Hm,' said Eddie. 'Tricky.'

'Why is it tricky?' Jack fell off his barstool.

'Well,' said Eddie, 'it's tricky in this fashion: the toymaker has never cast himself in the role of a God. Most Toy City religions have him down as a doer of God's work, but not *actually* a God. So if he *is* a God, then he obviously wishes to remain incognito.'

'So *why* is it tricky?' Jack tried to get up, but without much success. Getting up was tricky.

'He might not take too kindly to the fact that we have uncovered his true identity.'

'But we're the good guys. We're on his side.'

'But say, in the unlikely event that I've got a wee bit of the theorising wrong—'

'The evil twin bit? The *big* bit?'

'In the unlikely event. But say I'm right about the toy-maker. He might disappear us.'

'He wouldn't do *that*, would he? He's all kindly and white-haired and loveable and everything.'

'Benign Gods generally are. But they do have the un-fortunate habit of chucking thunderbolts at folk who upset them.'

'You're right,' said Jack, floundering about. 'Best not to risk it. Let's crawl back to the office and get some sleep. We'll have one more drink before we go and then we'll, er, *go*.'

'Have you ever heard this theory about drinking yourself sober?' Eddie asked. 'It's a very popular theory. Amongst drunks, anyway.'

'How does it work?' Jack asked.

'Well, I had it explained to me once, but I was rather drunk at the time and I can't exactly remember how it works. But that's what we should do, Jack, drink ourselves sober and then go to the toymaker's house.'

'Pretext,' said Jack.

'What?' said Eddie.

'Pretext,' said Jack. 'We go to the toymaker's house upon some pretext. I'll rip your foot off and beg him to stitch you up or something.'

'You *won't*,' said Eddie.

'Some other pretext then. We'll engage him in casual conversation and subtly draw him in to a theoretical discussion. Then you could put your theory to him in a hypothetical manner, which will not imply any implicit knowledge on our part as to his potential status as a deity.'

'Say all that again,' said Eddie.

'Don't be absurd,' said Jack. 'I don't know how I managed it the first time. Somebody help me up.'

Tinto wheeled himself around the bar and assisted Jack into the vertical plane.

'Thanks, Tinto,' said Jack, clinging to the bar counter. 'Another round, please. Eddie and I are drinking ourselves sober.'

'I've always wanted to see that,' said Tinto. 'I'll join you again, if I may; I'm celebrating.'

'Oh,' said Jack. 'Why?'

'Because when Eddie pays this bar bill I'll have enough money to retire.'

'We haven't spent *that* much, have we?'

'I'm only expecting to enjoy a short retirement,' said Tinto. 'The end of the world's coming very soon. Didn't you know?'

'Same again,' said Jack. 'And as the end of the world's coming, drinks *all* round.'

Now, it is a fact well known to those who know it well that prophets of doom only attain popularity when they get the drinks in all round.

Eddie and Jack were soon richly popular.

Even though they both smelled very poor.

Several rather attractive dollies gathered about Jack.

Jack engaged a particularly tall and glamorous blondie-headed one in conversation. 'I'm a detective,' said Jack.

'Are you famous?' asked the blondie-headed doll.

'Very,' said Jack. 'This is my sidekick, Eddie; he's comedy relief.'

Eddie, now balanced on his head, made growling sounds from his barstool perch.

'It must be a very dangerous job,' said the dolly, fingering Jack's grubby trenchcoat lapel.

'Extremely,' said Jack. 'But I'm always ready for action.' He opened his trenchcoat to expose the 7.62 mm M134 General Clockwork Mini-gun that bulged from the front of his trousers.

'My, that's a big one,' said the dolly.

'Cocked and ready to shoot,' said Jack.

The dolly tittered.

'Excruciating,' said Tinto. 'I don't think he's drunk himself sober yet, Eddie.'

Jack whipped out his gun and waved it about in a most unsteady and dangerous fashion. 'This can take the head off a clockwork barman at two hundred yards.'

'You're barred,' said Tinto. 'Out of my bar.'

'He was only showing me his weapon,' said the dolly. 'No need to go all rusty-headed, Tinto.'

'Drink for the lady,' said Jack. 'And have one yourself, barlord.'

'Jack,' said Eddie, 'perhaps we should be off about our business now, even in our present condition. It's really important business, remember?'

'You're just jealous,' said Jack, trousering his weapon and putting his arm about the dolly's slender waist. 'Because I'm such a big hit with the ladies.'

'Jack, get a grip of yourself.'

'I have a grip of myself.' Jack took a grip of himself. It was a most intimate grip; not the kind of grip that you usually take of yourself in public.

'Get him out, Eddie,' said Tinto. 'Take him home.'

'I don't have a home.' Jack swayed about, supporting himself on the dolly. 'But I will have, a big home. A palace. I have come to this city to seek my fortune. And I will. I'll have a palace and I'll be a prince.'

'Prince?' Eddie performed a most remarkable, and probably once in a lifetime only, backflip, which resulted in his bum landing squarely upon the barstool.

'That was impressive,' said Tinto. And others all around and about made free with applause.

'I *said* prince,' said Eddie. 'What is *prince* all about?'

'Nothing,' said Jack in a sulky tone.

'Yes it is. Why did you say that you want to be a prince?'

'There's nothing wrong with having ambitions.'

'Not if they're feasible.'

'I don't care about her,' said Jack. 'I don't.'

'But I'm nice,' said the dolly. 'I have lovely hair; it gets longer if you turn the little key in my back.'

'No thanks,' said Jack, withdrawing his arm from the dolly's waist. 'But I wasn't talking about you. I was talking about *her*. I don't care about her.'

'Who is this *her*?' Eddie asked.

'Just someone. I don't want to talk about it.'

'It's that Jill, isn't it?' said Eddie. 'The girl at Madame Goose's. Did you do it with her, Jack?'

'None of your business.'

'You *did*. He did, Tinto. Jack did it with a girl at Madame Goose's.'

'I once did it with a clockwork mouse at Madame Goose's,' said Tinto. 'But I was young then and rather drunk. No one's going to hold that against me, are they?'

'Urgh!' went all and sundry, who evidently were.

'I was drunk!' said Tinto. 'Come on!'

'I once did it with a potted plant,' said Eddie. 'I was *really* drunk that night, I can tell you.'

'Stop it,' said Jack. 'She doesn't mean anything to me. It's not as if I'm in love with her or anything.'

'Jack's in love,' said Tinto.

'I'm *not*,' said Jack.

'He *is*,' said Eddie.

'I'm *not*!' said Jack.

'You're drunk,' said Eddie.

'I'm *not*!' said Jack.

'Are too.'

'Are not.'

'Are.'

Jack stared at Eddie. And it was a stare, rather than a

squint. 'You know what,' he said, 'I'm not drunk any more.'

'Drunk yourself sober,' said Eddie. 'Hoorah!'

'What about you?'

'It's draining down to my legs,' said Eddie. 'You'll have to carry me for a bit.'

'Do you want to come back to my house?' said the blondie-headed doll. 'I could show you my publicity pictures; I'm hoping to get a job at Toy City TV.'

'Er, no, thank you very much,' said Jack. 'Eddie and I have important business elsewhere.'

'Most important,' said Eddie. 'Are you ready for it, partner?'

'Certainly am,' said Jack.

'Then let's go,' said Eddie.

And go they did.

As almost sober as.

24

It was nearing midnight now. Toy City was still. Remarkably still, really. But then, folk were keeping off the streets after dark. There was a killer on the loose. And the fact that this killer had performed all the killings so far during the hours of daylight had nothing to do with anything. Killers always strike around midnight. Everyone knows that.

'I think I behaved rather badly back there,' said Jack. 'Sorry, Eddie, if I embarrassed you.'

'No problem,' said Eddie. 'It's as sweet as. But you're in love, Jack, aren't you? With this Jill.'

'It was my first time.' Jack put Eddie down and relieved himself in an alleyway. 'I wasn't thinking straight.'

'There's nothing wrong with young love.' Eddie seeped a bit into the gutter. 'We've all been there and done that.'

'You've been in love?'

'Don't be so surprised. Bears love too. Everything loves.'

'Who was she, Eddie?' Jack zipped himself into decency.

Eddie sighed. 'She was beautiful. An Anders Empress. Amber eyes, vertically stitched nose in black silk yarn, beige felt paw-pads, patented tilt-growler that literally purred when you leaned her backwards, and an all-over golden mohair plush.'

'Sounds very nice,' said Jack as he tucked Eddie once more under his arm and resumed his trudging. 'Especially the patented tilt-growler.'

'She came from a very respectable family. Her great-grandparents were the bears that Goldilocks shacked up with. They organised the original Teddy Bears' picnic and owned the garden that all bears go walkies round.'

Jack looked down at Eddie. 'What a load of old rubbish,' he said. 'And there was me believing you and thinking that you were going to tell me this really poignant story about love lost and everything.'

'Fair enough,' said Eddie. 'But she *was* a posh bear and she was up for it. But I lost my nerve, had a few drinks before I went round to see her. Humped that potted plant by mistake. It didn't lead to a lasting relationship.'

'Jill is very beautiful,' said Jack, in a most wistful tone.

'I could tell you all about her,' said Eddie. 'It's a sad story. But now's not the time; we're almost at the toymaker's house.'

'Are you up for it then?' Jack set Eddie down.

'I'm all but pooing myself,' said Eddie Bear. 'I greatly fear the toymaker, as you know. And now more than ever. So remember what you said you'd do. Engage him in casual conversation and subtly draw him into a theological discussion. Then put my theory to him in a hypothetical manner, which will not imply any implicit knowledge on our part as to his potential status as a deity.'

'I said *that*?'

'You did. Do you think you can do it?'

'Of course,' said Jack. 'Trust me.'

The two trudged up the gravel drive, Jack's trudge making big trudge sounds and Eddie's making lesser. When they reached the big front door, Jack reached out for the knocker.

'*You* again,' said Peter. 'This won't do. Clear off.'

'We have to see the toymaker.' Jack's hand hovered near the knocker. 'We don't have time to bandy words with you.'

'Bandy words?' Peter laughed. 'Don't come that high and mighty talk with me. The toymaker isn't home. He's gone away.'

'The lights are on,' said Eddie.

'That's to discourage burglars,' said Peter. 'If you leave your lights on, burglars think you're at home; everyone knows that.'

'Even burglars?'

'No, of course not. Burglars don't know that. How would they know that? Who'd be likely to tell them?'

'I'm sure I wouldn't,' said Eddie. 'What about you, Jack?'

'I wouldn't tell them.' Jack's hand moved closer to the knocker.

'But there's no one home,' said Peter.

'We're burglars,' said Eddie. 'How are we supposed to know that?'

'*Burglars?*' Peter's face took on that horrified look once more. 'Burglars! Help! Help! Alarm! Alarm!' And he took to knocking most loudly.

And at length the front door opened and the ancient face of the toymaker peered out into the night.

'Who is knocking so loudly?' he asked.

'It's Peter,' said Jack. 'Anxious to admit us.'

'Burglars,' said Peter. 'Call the policemen.'

'They're not burglars,' said the toymaker. 'Come in, will you? And calm yourself, Peter, please.'

'But . . .' went Peter. 'But.'

'Perhaps you should get yourself a bell,' said Jack, smiling in a most friendly manner.

'A bell?' The toymaker beckoned Jack and Eddie inside. 'A most novel idea. But as no one other than yourselves ever comes to call, a wasted expense, I think.' The toymaker closed the big front door, leaving Peter alone with his thoughts, then led Jack and Eddie along the narrow corridor and into his workshop. 'This is a most pleasant surprise,' he told them. 'Has something else happened to you, little bear?'

'He's a bit wobbly,' said Jack. 'He hasn't been walking too well. I thought you might be kind enough to take another look at him. Eddie didn't want to bother you; he holds you in such high esteem.'

'I do,' said Eddie. 'We all do. All of us.'

'That's very nice,' said the toymaker. 'But I do not wish to be held in high esteem. I'm only a humble toymaker. Sit down, sit down.'

Jack sat down in the comfy chair.

'Get your bum off me,' it said.

'Manners,' said the toymaker. The chair made grumbling sounds.

Eddie sat down on the floor.

'You're more than just a toymaker, sir,' said Jack.

'Anders,' said the toymaker. 'Call me Anders.'

'I think I'll stick with *sir*, if you don't mind, sir. Because you *are* more than just a toymaker, as you well know. You bring life to these toys.'

'Science,' said Mr Anders Anders. 'Science, not magic. I told you before: when things are not as they appear to be, it's because they're actually simpler than you think them to be. Things are never as difficult and complicated as folk believe. You'd be surprised just how straightforward and obvious things really are. The secret is in knowing how to look at them the right way.'

'Well, however it's done,' said Jack, 'it makes you very special.'

'Everyone is special,' said Anders Anders. 'It's just that most folk are unaware how special they really are, or just how special are the folk around them. If they were aware, they'd be far nicer to each other, don't you think?'

'I'm certain you're right,' said Jack, who now felt himself to be drowning in a pond of platitudes.

'Not that they aren't nice,' the toymaker continued. 'Of course they're nice. Folk are nice. It's just that they could be even nicer. Things could be perfect. I'm an idealist; forgive an old man for his ideals.'

'Yes, sir,' said Jack. 'Yes, indeed.'

'So why *are* you here?' The toymaker leaned his ancient frame against his workbench and tinkered about with a small wooden horse. 'I stuffed the little bear's legs but yesterday; they should be good for more than a while.'

'Sir,' said Jack, 'there's big trouble; you need to know about it.'

'Big trouble?' said the toymaker. 'What can that be?'

'In your city, sir.'

'My *city*?' The toymaker made a most surprised face. 'Toy Town is a town. Hardly a city.'

'It's a city, sir. A big city now.'

'I should get out more,' said the toymaker, tinkering at the horse's tail. 'Perhaps I spend too much time working. But I want to get things right, you see. It's the details that count; this horse's tail, for instance. I can't make up my mind exactly how many hairs it needs. It's all in the details. I want everything to be right. Perfect. Everything.'

'Folk are dying,' Jack said. 'Folk are being killed, here in Toy City.'

'Being *killed*?' The toymaker shook his snowy head. 'Not here in Toy Town. You must be mistaken, young man.'

'There's a murderer,' Jack said.

'Jack,' said Eddie. 'Slow down. Think.'

'He needs to know the truth,' said Jack. 'He must be told.'

'Yes, but . . .'

'Yes, but *what*?' the toymaker asked. 'What *is* this all about?'

'A murderer,' said Jack, 'in your city.'

'No,' said the toymaker shaking his snowbound head once more. 'We don't have murderers in Toy Town. Toys are naughty sometimes, but the jolly red-faced policemen give them a good telling-off when they are.'

'No,' said Jack. 'It's not like that. Those jolly red-faced policemen gave me a good kicking. Would you like to see the bruises?'

'I don't think I would.' The toymaker put down his wooden horse. 'You seem to be a very angry young man. I think perhaps you should go.'

'No, sir,' said Jack. 'You have to understand what is going on out there in your city. Bad things. Toys and people aren't nice to each other. They're not nice and now there's a murderer. Humpty Dumpty is dead. And Boy Blue and . . .'

'Stop,' said the toymaker. 'Young man, stop. You are saying terrible things. I don't wish to hear them.'

'You have to hear them. We've come to warn you.'

'Are you threatening me?'

'No, not that. Anything but that.'

'I think I must ask you to leave.'

'Eddie, tell him. Tell him your theory.'

'You have a theory, little bear?'

'No, sir,' said Eddie.

'Tell him, Eddie.'

'Shut up, Jack.'

'But this is what we came here for. It's important. It couldn't be more important.'

'The toymaker is a busy man. He doesn't have time to listen to us.'

'What?' said Jack. '*What?* What's the matter with you, Eddie? Tell him. Tell him what you think.'

'I can't,' whispered Eddie.

'Then I'll tell him.'

'No,' said Eddie.

'Yes,' said Jack. 'It's your brother, sir. Your evil twin.'

Eddie hid his face.

'He's out to take over Toy City. He's killing off all the nursery rhyme characters and—'

'Enough.' The toymaker raised his wrinkled hands. 'Enough of this awful talk. I believe you've been drinking, young man.'

'I've drunk myself sober.'

'I think not. Kindly take your leave.'

'But you have to listen. He'll kill you too.'

'Young man, I do not have a brother, let alone an evil twin, as you are suggesting. Now I suggest that you go home to bed.'

'No,' said Jack. 'You've got to listen. You've got to understand.'

'Goodnight,' said the toymaker. 'Goodnight to you.'

Jack and Eddie were ushered away from the workroom. From the corridor. From the toymaker's house.

They stood once more upon the gravel drive.

In the moonlight.

Looking at each other.

'Well,' said Eddie.

'Well what?' said Jack.

'Well, that might have gone a little better, don't you think?'

'Well,' said Jack.

'You buffoon!' Eddie threw up his paws. 'You craven gormster. You did it all wrong. You couldn't have done it wronger. That was as wrong as wrong as . . . as . . .'

'I wasn't wrong,' said Jack. 'He just wouldn't listen.'

'Unbelievable,' said Eddie. 'You are unbelievable.'

'*Me?* You just sat there saying nothing. You could have backed me up.'

'No, I couldn't,' Eddie said. 'I just couldn't, not to him.'

'All right,' said Jack. 'I understand. But what are we going to do now? He said that he didn't have a brother. You've got it all wrong, Eddie. I told you it was a silly theory.'

'Hm,' said Eddie. 'Well it's still the best theory I have and I'm sticking with it until I have a better one. But you've met the toymaker twice now, Jack. You can see that he's lost touch with what's going on in Toy City. Perhaps he's forgotten that he has a brother. It's possible.'

'Barely possible.' Jack rubbed at his arms. 'I'm cold,' he said. 'Let's go back to the office for some sleep. We'll have another think in the morning.'

'By which time more people may be dead.'

'Then what do you suggest?'

'I suggest we go back to Miss Muffett's.'

'But Miss Muffett's isn't there any more.'

Eddie tapped at his head. 'Bear with me on this one,' he

said. 'I have a theory. Something the toymaker said struck a certain chord, as it were. I'd like to test a hypothesis.'

Jack shrugged and turned up his collar. 'Let's make it quick then, it's really getting nippy.'

'We'll be as quick as,' said Eddie. 'Follow me.'

'And don't hurry back,' called Peter.

25

The lower reaches of Knob Hill, that spread around and about and somewhat below the toymaker's house, glittered in the moonlight. A little star went twinkle, twinkle. It was all very picturesque.

Eddie led Jack to the spot where, earlier that day, they had viewed the place where Miss Muffett's house should have been, but wasn't.

'There,' said Eddie. 'I'm sure I'm right. What do you see, Jack? Tell me.'

'Trees and flowers and bushes and hillside,' said Jack. 'Exactly the same as before.'

'*Exactly* the same?'

'Exactly the same.'

'Exactly,' said Eddie.

'I'm missing something, aren't I?'

Eddie nodded. 'Something very obvious.'

Jack took a second look. 'Then I don't know what,' he said.

'What about the trees, Jack, and the flowers?'

'They're exactly the same.'

'Yes,' said Eddie. 'But they shouldn't be, should they? The trees should have dark shadows under them now and the flowers should all be closed up for the night.'

'Oh,' said Jack. 'You're right.'

'Remember what the toymaker said? "When things are not as they appear to be, it's because they're actually simpler than you think them to be. The secret is in knowing how to look at them the right way." '

'I remember him saying that, but I thought he was just fobbing me off with a lot of platitudes.'

'Not the toymaker.' Eddie shook his head. 'But it set me to thinking about the vanishing house. And then it came to me: it *was* all simple; you just had to know how to look at it. This is fake, Jack. All this: the trees, the flowers, the hillside. It's a big painting, like a theatrical backdrop. It's been put up here to fool folk. To fool the murderer.'

'To hide Miss Muffett's house?'

'Exactly,' said Eddie. 'Come on, let's see if I'm right.'

They approached the trees and the flowers and the hillside and . . .

'Oh,' said Jack, as his face made contact with canvas. 'You're right. But that's absurd. How could we have been fooled by something as simple as this?'

'Because we weren't looking for it.'

'Yes, but.'

'Come on,' said Eddie, 'follow me.'

'Where are you? Oh.'

Eddie was wriggling under the canvas. Jack knelt down and followed him.

'A remarkably good painting,' said Jack when he emerged on the other side of the vast canvas. 'And that would be Miss Muffett's mansion, would it?'

Eddie dusted himself down. 'That's the kiddie,' said he. 'And it should appeal to you; it's one of the houses that Jack built.'

'Jack?' said Jack.

'As in the rhyme, *This is the house that Jack built.* He didn't build too many, because he was a pretty rubbish architect and most of them fell down. He always insisted upon there being a cow with a crumpled horn in the living room.'

Jack nodded dumbly and stared at the house and the garden that surrounded it.

Miss Muffett's mansion by moonlight was wondrous to behold. It resembled a vast wedding cake: tier upon tier of white stucco, with supporting Doric columns. Before it stood a row of white marble statues, pretty maids all. Manicured trees were hung with countless silver bells and cockleshell motifs abounded in the paving stones and low walls.

'Garden design by Mary Mary,' said Eddie. 'She has her own garden make-over show on Toy City TV.'

'I'm somewhat puzzled by *that*.' Jack pointed to a huge sculpture that dominated the very centre of the garden. It more than resembled a massive raised phallus.

'She always puts something like that in whatever garden she designs. To prove just how "contrary" she is. It's a studied eccentricity thing. Frankly, I think it's rubbish. The garden *and* the house.'

'I love them,' said Jack.

'We really must sit down sometime over a beer and discuss your tastes in architecture.'

'No, we mustn't,' said Jack. 'But when I build my palace, it will look a lot better than this. Shall we have a sneak around and see what we can see?'

'Well,' said Eddie, his words all growly whispers, 'now that we're here . . . I'm . . . er . . . I'm . . .'

'What's up with you?' Jack whispered back.

'You have a sneak around; I'll wait here.'

'Something's bothering you. You're afraid.'

'I'm afraid of no man.'

'So?'

'There's something out there, and it *ain't* no man.'

'That sounds somehow familiar, but what are you talking about?'

'It's the spider, Jack. Miss Muffett's spider. It's really big, with horrible hairy legs. It's the spider in her rhyme. They live together.'

'What, it's like, her pet?'

'Not as such. But in a way, I suppose.'

'What are you saying?'

'It's a big spider, Jack. Big as you. There's been talk, in the newspapers, about their relationship. But nothing's been proved. And I don't know how spiders actually *do it*, do you?'

'You're winding me up,' said Jack.

'I'm not, honestly. It could be on the prowl; it has terrible mandibles. And spiders sick up acid on you and you melt and they eat you up.'

'Turn it in,' said Jack, 'I'll protect you.' And Jack gave Eddie a comforting pat. 'I'm not afraid of spiders, even really big ones.'

'Thanks for the comforting pat,' said Eddie, clinging onto Jack's trenchcoat.

'Big as me, you said?' Jack did furtive glancings all around.

'Maybe bigger. Perhaps we should come back in the morning.'

'We're here now, Eddie. Let's go and see what we can see. There's a light on in a window over there.'

'After you, my friend.'

Eddie and Jack did sneakings through Miss Muffett's garden. They snuck along beside a low hedge that divided the garden from a drive lined with numerous clockwork-motor cars. Large cars all, were these, and pretty posh ones too. Leaning against these cars were many big burly men. These wore dark suits and mirrored sunglasses and had little earpiece jobbies with tiny mouth mics attached to them. Each of these big men carried a great big gun.

There was also a large military-looking truck with a canvas-covered back. A shadowed figure sat at the wheel of this.

Sneakily Jack and Eddie reached the lighted window.

Jack looked up at it. 'It's too high for me to see in,' he whispered.

'Give us a lift up then.'

'Fair enough.' Jack lifted Eddie, who clambered onto Jack's head, put his paws to the sill and peeped in through the sash window, which was, as windows so often are on such occasions, conveniently open at the bottom. Had

Eddie possessed any thumbs, he would have raised one to Jack. But as he hadn't, he didn't.

'What can you see?' Jack whispered.

Eddie put a paw to his mouth.

'In your own time, then,' said Jack.

Eddie peered in through the window gap and this was what he saw and heard:

The room was of ballroom proportions, which made it proportionally correct, given that it was indeed a ballroom. It was high-domed and gorgeously decorated, with foliate roundels and moulded tuffet embellishments. Eddie's button eyes were drawn to a great mural wrought upon the furthest wall. This pictured a number of bearded men in turbans flinging spears at gigantic fish.

Eddie nodded thoughtfully. He recalled reading about this mural. Jack who'd built the house had painted it himself, but being none too bright, had confused curds and whey with Kurds and whales.

Eddie would have laughed, but as it wasn't the least bit amusing, and contained a glaring continuity error to boot, he didn't. Instead, he gazed at the many folk milling about in the ballroom. The light of many candles fell upon the glittering company: the old rich of Toy City, extravagantly costumed.

Eddie recognised each and every one.

He'd seen their smug faces many times, grinning from the society pages of the Toy City press, and in the big glossy celebrity magazines, like *KY!* and *Howdy Doody*, pictured at gala balls and swish functions and First Nights and even the launch of the spatial ambiguity installation piece at the Toy City art gallery.

But other than Miss Muffett and Little Tommy Tucker, Eddie had never seen any of the others in the living flesh before. The living breathing flesh. He had only ever seen them, as others of his own social class had seen them, in photographs. As totems, icons even, to be revered and admired and looked up to. They were rich and they were famous. They were 'better'.

Eddie shook his furry-fabricked head and peeped in at them. He spied the 'olds': Old King Cole, Old Mother Hubbard, the Grand Old Duke of York. And the remaining 'littles': Little Polly Flinders, Little Bo Peep, and the hostess, Little Miss Muffett. And the 'double nameds': Mary Mary, Tom Tom, the piper's son, Peter Peter, pumpkin eater. And there was Simple Simon, who had famously met a pie man. And Georgie Porgie, the reformed paedophile. And Peter Piper, who'd picked a peck of pickled peppers, for reasons of his own. And there were Jack and Jill, who'd once been up a hill. And the Mary who'd had that little lamb. And the Polly who'd put the kettle on. And the Jack who'd built the house and mucked up the mural.

Eddie watched them, and Eddie slowly shook his head once more. There they were, and they were rich and famous. But when it came right down to it, *why?*

Most seemed to have achieved their fame for no good reason at all. For going up a hill to fetch water! Going *up* a hill? Or eating a pie, or putting the kettle on? What was it all about, eh?

It wasn't so much that Eddie was jealous – well, actually it was.

But it really didn't make any sense.

Eddie suddenly became aware that he was thinking all these things: thinking like Jack, in fact. Eddie gave his head a thump and watched as a wheeled rostrum affair was pushed into the ballroom by two of the burly suited types, who then helped Miss Muffett onto it. She stood, glamorously attired in another glittering gown, waving her manicured fingers about and shushing the company to silence.

'Ladies and gentlemen,' she said, 'firstly I would like to thank you for coming here tonight. We are all in great danger and if something isn't done, we will each go the way of Humpty Dumpty, Boy Blue and Bill Winkie.'

Eddie flinched.

'We all know who is doing this to us. We dare not wait for

the inevitable to occur. We have to take steps. Do something about it.'

'I don't agree,' said Mary Mary.

'Well, you wouldn't, would you dear? You being so contrary and everything.'

'We must run away,' said Mary Mary. 'That's what we must do. Run while we still can.'

'To where?' Georgie Porgie spoke up. 'To the world beyond the city's box? The world of men? We can't get there anyway, and even if we could, what chance would there be for us amongst the people of that world? How long would we last if we, like them, were doomed to a normal life-span? Toy City is our world. Here we are rich and powerful. Here we can live on and on. Or at least we could, until *he* returned to murder us all.'

Eddie nodded thoughtfully.

'We don't know for certain that it's *him*.' This voice belonged to Jack (husband of Jill). 'Perhaps it's one of us. Someone in this room.'

'Ignore my husband,' said Jill (wife of Jack). 'He's never been the same since he fell down the hill and broke his crown. Brain damage.' She twirled her finger at her temple.

'There's nothing wrong with me, woman.'

'I can think of a number of things.'

'Please.' Miss Muffett raised her hands. 'There's nothing to be gained by arguing amongst ourselves. *He's* picking us off, one by one. And I'm next on the list. I paid a fortune to have that camouflage canvas outside done. But how long will it fool *him*?'

'I doubt whether it will fool *him* at all,' said Georgie. 'We should all just flee the city. Hide out in the surrounding countryside. Perhaps if *he* can't find us, *he'll* just go away again. I'm going home to pack my bags.' Georgie made to take his leave.

'You can't go,' said Miss Muffett. 'Not until the one that I have invited here tonight has arrived and said what he has to say.'

Georgie Porgie threw up his hands. 'And what's this mystery man going to say? That he can protect us all from the inevitable?'

'That's what he told me.'

'I don't deserve any of this,' said Georgie. 'To be on some nutter's hitlist. I've served my time and now I'm entitled to enjoy my wealth.'

'If only it was just some nutter,' said Jill (wife of Jack). 'But it isn't, it's *him*. We are the founder members of The Spring and Catch Society. We know the truth about Big Box Fella and his evil twin, because we are the elite, the first folk placed here when Toy City was assembled. We helped Big Box Fella to cast his evil twin from this world, but now he has returned to wreak his vengeance upon all of us. We knew that one day this might happen and we should have taken steps earlier to prevent it. But we didn't; we just continued to indulge ourselves. We have abused our privileges and become complacent and now we are paying the price.'

Jack tugged at Eddie's leg. 'What can you see?' he asked.

Eddie ducked his head down. 'They're all in there,' he whispered. 'All the still-surviving PPPs, and they're talking about The Spring and Catch Society and the evil twin. I was right, Jack. It's all as factual as.'

'Incredible.' Jack shook his head and Eddie all but fell off it.

'Stay still,' said Eddie. 'I don't want to miss any of this.'

'We have to kill *him*,' Georgie was saying. 'Kill *him* before *he* kills us.'

'And how do you kill a God?' asked Jill. 'Get real, please.'

'I have ten thousand men,' said the Grand Old Duke of York. 'I'll deal with the blighter.'

The Grand Old Duke was ignored to a man, and a woman. He did *not* have ten thousand men. He'd *never had* ten thousand men. He and Wheatley Porterman had made the whole thing up.

'Wait until the one I invited arrives,' said Miss Muffett. 'He'll explain everything. He'll put your minds at rest.'

'He'll save us, will he?' Georgie Porgie went to throw up his hands once again, but finding them still up from the previous occasion, he threw them down again. 'Listen, when Humpty Dumpty was killed, we all knew what it meant; we clubbed together and put up the money to employ Bill Winkie. He was next on the list. He knew that. But what happened?' Georgie drew a fat finger over his throat. 'Bill Winkie couldn't stop *him*. He never had a chance. Nobody can stop *him*.'

'*I* can stop *him*.'

Heads turned at the sound of this voice, turned to its source: to the open doorway.

'You?' said Georgie Porgie.

'You?' said Jack (husband of Jill).

'You?' said Jill (wife of Jack).

'Me?' said Mary Mary (well, she would).

'You?' said the others present, but still unidentified.

'You?'

'Me,' said Tinto. 'I can save you all.'

Had Eddie's eyes been able to widen, they would have widened now. His mouth, however, *could* drop open. And so it did. Most widely.

'Tinto,' whispered Eddie. 'What is Tinto doing here?'

'What?' asked Jack, but Eddie shushed him into silence.

'Tinto,' said Miss Muffett. 'Welcome, welcome.' Tinto wheeled himself into the ballroom.

'But he's a toy!' said Georgie. 'The wind-up barman. We all know him. Is this your idea of a joke?'

'I can save you all,' said Tinto.

'Stuff that,' said Georgie. 'I'm going home to pack. Who's leaving with me?'

'No,' Miss Muffett raised her hands once more. 'Please hear him out. Hear him out, and then you may leave if you wish to.'

Georgie Porgie folded his arms and took to a sulking silence.

'The floor is yours, Tinto,' said Miss Muffett.

'Thank you,' said Tinto. 'Now, you all know me. You held your meetings above my bar. I've respected your privacy. You know that you can trust me. I am here to protect you.'

'Indeed?' Old King scratched at his crowned head with a bejewelled finger. 'Well, listen, old chap, I don't wish to cause you offence, but I feel it will take more than a tin toy to defeat our adversary.'

'I am far more than just a tin toy,' said Tinto. 'I'm all manner of things. I'm most adaptable. Would you care for a demonstration?'

Old King shrugged. 'If you like,' said he. 'As long as it doesn't take too long and provides a bit of amusement. Should I call for my fiddlers three to accompany you?'

'That really won't be necessary.' Tinto's head revolved. 'Now who, or what, first, I wonder? Ah yes, how about this?' Tinto's left arm extended, reached around behind his back and wound his key.

'Hm,' went Eddie.

And then Tinto's hand touched certain buttons upon his chest, buttons that Eddie had never seen before. There was a whirring of cogs and then all manner of interesting things began to happen. Tinto's head snapped back, his arms retracted, his chest opened and he all but turned completely inside out.

And now Tinto wasn't Tinto any more: he was instead a tall and rather imposing gentleman, decked out in a dashing top hat, white tie and tails.

'God's Big Box!' cried Old King Cole. 'It's Wheatley Porterman himself!'

'Son of a clockwork pistol,' whispered Eddie, as a gasp went up from those inside the ballroom.

'No,' said Tinto, in the voice of Wheatley Porterman, 'it is still me. Still Tinto. But you can't fault the resemblance, can you? Faultless, isn't it? Are you impressed?'

Heads nodded. The assembled company was most definitely impressed.

'Then how about this one?' said Tinto. 'You'll love this one.' There was further whirring of cogs and the gentlemanly form of Mr Wheatley Porterman vanished into Tinto's chest. Flaps appeared from beneath Tinto's armpits, his legs slid up inside himself. Bits popped out here and popped in there, further convolutions occurred and suddenly Tinto was . . .

'Me,' whispered Old King. 'You've become me.'

'And what a merry old soul am I,' said Old King Cole's all-but-perfect double. 'I can impersonate any one of you here. Rather useful to fool your adversary, don't you agree?'

'Incredible,' puffed Old King Cole. 'And not a little upsetting. But surely my belly is not so large as that.'

'Larger,' said Tinto, who had now become Tinto once more. 'I was flattering you. But allow me to explain. I am a new generation of transforming toy, created by the toymaker for your protection.'

'So the toymaker sent you.' Old King grinned. 'Built you to protect us. Damn fine chap, the toymaker.'

'Precisely,' Tinto agreed. 'Damn fine chap, the toymaker. Or Big Box Fella, as we know him best.'

Another gasp went up from the assembly. A very big gasp.

'Something wrong?' asked Tinto. 'You are shocked and appalled that a mere toy should know the toymaker's true identity?'

Heads nodded dumbly.

'Don't be,' said Tinto. 'It remains *our* secret. I was created to protect you and to destroy the toymaker's evil twin. I have just spent the entire evening with the toymaker discussing the matter. He's very upset about the whole thing. He feels that it's all his fault and he can't bear the thought of any more of his dear friends coming to harm. So he has arranged for me to escort you all to a place of safety. Isn't that nice of him?'

Eddie scratched at his special-tagged ear. Tinto was clearly not telling all of the truth.

'But pardon me,' said Old King Cole, 'although I

appreciate the quick-change routine, which is very impressive, I don't quite see how you are going to *destroy* the evil
twin.'

'That,' said Tinto, 'is because you haven't seen everything
I can do. I am capable of many other transformations, most
of a military nature. You really wouldn't want me to show
them to you here; they are all most lethal.'

'This is absurd,' cried Georgie Porgie, 'sending us a toy.
Big Box Fella has clearly gone ga ga. Time has addled his
brain.'

Another gasp went up at this. Possibly the biggest so far.

'No offence to Big Box Fella, of course,' said Georgie
Porgie, hurriedly. 'But this is ludicrous.' Georgie, whose
hands were currently in the thrown down position, made
fists out of them. 'A toy!' he shouted. 'What good is a toy?'

'I'm much more than just a toy,' said Tinto.

'So you can do a few tricks.' Georgie made a face. 'That is
hardly going to be enough. Show us what else you can do.
Show us how tough you are. In fact—' Georgie Porgie
raised his fists. It had been many years since he'd run away
from the boys who came out to play. He'd learned to fight in
prison. 'In fact,' he said, 'come and have a go, if you think
you're hard enough.'

'I think not,' said Tinto, shaking his head. 'Not here.'

'A stupid toy.' Georgie stuck his tongue out at Tinto.
'That to you,' said he. And he raised two fingers to go with
the sticky-out tongue.

What happened next happened fast. And fast can sometimes be shocking. Tinto's hand flew across the ballroom,
upon the end of an arm which extended to an all-but-
impossible length. The dextrous fingers of this hand
snatched Georgie Porgie by the throat, shook him viciously
about and then flung him down to the hard wooden floor.

A truly horrified gasp now went up from the assembly. It
surpassed all the gasps that had gone before. It was accompanied by much stepping back from the fallen body. And
much staring in blank disbelief.

'Outrage,' cried Old King Cole, finding his voice and using it. 'A toy daring to attack one of the elite. I shall have you scrapped, mashed-up, destroyed. Security guards, take this iconoclastic tin thing away and break it all to pieces.'

The security guards, however, appeared disinclined to become involved.

'I think not,' said Tinto, shaking his metal head. 'I must apologise for that display of gratuitous violence. But it was to prove a point. The killer of your friends walks amongst you. He is here in the city. He has already inflicted far worse upon your fellows. He has, no doubt, similarly hideous ends planned for each of you. The evil twin can be stopped. But only I can stop him.'

'Indeed?' said Old King. 'Then allow me to ask you one question.'

'Go on then.'

'Why have you waited so long?' Old King fairly shouted this. 'If you're capable of destroying this fiend, then why haven't you done so yet? Some of my closest friends are dead. If you could have saved them, why didn't you?'

'I have my reasons,' said Tinto. 'Good timing is everything, if you wish to succeed. If there is something that you truly want, it is often necessary to wait before you can get it.'

'Are you saying that you want something from *us*?' Old King asked. 'Is that what you're saying? I don't understand.'

'Well,' said Tinto, 'as you have seen, I am not just a mere toy. I am special, unique. And I can mobilise this city, raise an army of toys and lead them to destroy the evil twin. And it *can* be done, trust me. He may be a God, but he is a God in the form of a man. He's not immortal. He can be killed. And I can do it. But I will want something in return. I've discussed it with Big Box Fella. He has given me the go-ahead.'

Eddie did some more ear-scratchings.

'And what is it that you want?' asked Old King Cole.

'Well,' said Tinto. 'I toyed with the idea that I might become King of Toy City. As you have observed, I could carry this off most convincingly.'

'What?' cried Old King, falling back in outrage. 'But that's *my* job! I'm the king.'

Tinto laughed that laugh of his. And then a hinged jaw dropped open and the muzzle of a gun appeared from his mouth hole. Tinto cleared his throat with a pistol-cocking sort of sound. The gun muzzle swung in King Cole's direction.

'I'd be happy to abdicate, of course,' said Old King. 'If that's what you want, in exchange for saving us all. I'm sure it could be arranged without difficulty.'

'Of course *that* can be arranged. But *that* is not enough. The way I see it is this: if I kill the evil twin, kill a God in fact, then I have earned the right to more than a kingship. I have earned the right to . . .'

'Godhood,' whispered Eddie. 'Tinto wants to be worshipped as a God.'

'What did you say?' Jack asked.

'I said,' Eddie turned his head down to Jack, 'I said . . . Aaaaaagh!'

'Why did you say Aaaaagh?' Jack asked. And then a hand fell upon his shoulder.

Except it wasn't a hand.

It was more of a leg.

A big leg.

A big hairy spider's leg.

Jack turned to face the owner of this leg.

'Aaaaagh!' went Jack.

26

With a struggling lad beneath one big leg and a panic-stricken bear beneath another, Miss Muffett's spider marched upon its remaining hairy appendages into the Miss's mansion, through the front door, along a hall and into the perfectly proportioned ballroom.

Here it flung the two detectives down onto the hard wooden floor.

'Welly well well,' said Tinto. 'Isn't this a surprise.'

'Tinto,' said Eddie, struggling to his paw pads.

'Tinto?' said Jack, ramming the sections of his fallen fedora back onto his head and hoisting himself once more into the vertical plane.

'Skulking about outside,' said the spider – although to Jack, who had never heard a spider speak, these words were unintelligible.

'We were just passing by,' said Eddie. 'Didn't drink ourselves quite as sober as we thought. Got a bit lost. You know how it is.'

Tinto rocked upon his wheels. 'Of course I do,' he said.

'So we'll be on our way now; come on Jack.'

'But,' went Jack.

'Let's go,' said Eddie, turning to leave, but finding his exit blocked not only by the fearsome spider, but also by the two big burly men with the dark suits and the mirrored shades.

And the guns.

Eddie grinned foolishly towards Tinto, who shook his metal head. 'I think not,' said the clockwork chameleon. 'I think you should stay.'

'Fine by me,' said Jack. 'There was no need for that spider to be so rough with us. Any chance of some eats?'

'Plenty back at the office.' Eddie tugged at Jack's trench-coat.

'No there isn't.'

'I think you *will* stay.' Tinto clicked his hinged jaw arrangement at Eddie. 'After all, you *have* seen and heard everything that's gone on in here.'

'No.' Eddie shook his head. 'We were just passing by, honest.'

'Really? And yet I'm certain that I saw your silly furry face peeping in through the open window. I have extremely good eyesight – telescopic vision, in fact. I see all.'

'What's going on here?' Jack asked. 'And . . . oh.' He spied the prone Porgie. 'Has there been another murder?'

'Tinto,' said Eddie, 'we'd like to join up. Join your private army.'

'Join his *what*?' Jack asked.

'Tinto is raising a private army,' said Eddie. 'To fight the evil twin. Tinto is a barman of many parts. He's a real hero.'

'Is he?' Jack glanced doubtfully at Tinto.

'He *is*,' said Eddie. 'So, Tinto, where would you like me to sign?'

'No signing necessary.' Tinto's tin head went shake shake shake.

'We'll just be off then; goodbye.'

'Stay where you are,' said Tinto.

'Will someone please tell me what's going on?' Jack asked. 'Private army? What is all this?'

Tinto turned his back upon Eddie and Jack. Candlelight twinkled upon his perfect paintwork. 'Good people,' he said to the assembled company, 'great people, allow me to introduce you to Eddie and Jack. They're detectives. Eddie was Bill Winkie's bear and Jack is new to the city.'

'Hi there.' Jack waggled his fingers.

'Eddie took over the case after Bill disappeared. He and

Jack have been relentlessly, if unsuccessfully, pursuing the murderer.'

'We have,' said Jack.

'Excuse me,' said Old King Cole, 'but is this some kind of joke? A toy bear and a young gormster?'

'I'm really sick of folk calling me that,' said Jack.

'Between the two of them,' said Tinto, 'they have complicated matters no end. But their antics have given me considerable amusement, which is why I have allowed them to continue.'

'You've *what*?' said Jack.

'I'll have to explain later.' Eddie clung to Jack's leg. 'If we *have* a later.'

'Have a *what*?' said Jack.

'I'm trying to be democratic here,' said Tinto. 'I thought I'd put your fate to the vote.'

'To the *what*?' said Jack.

'This city is now under martial law,' declared Tinto.

'Under *what*?' said Jack.

'Jack,' said Tinto, wheeling close to Jack, rising high upon his wheels and opening his chest to reveal a row of wicked-looking metal barbs, 'if you say the word *what* one more time, I will be forced to kill you.'

'Forced to . . .' Jack's voice trailed off.

'Thank you,' said Tinto. 'You see, desperate times call for desperate actions. It is often necessary to sacrifice an individual or two in the cause of the many.'

'But we're on your side.' Eddie made pleading paw movements. 'We want what you want.'

'I know,' said Tinto, retracting his wicked-looking barbs, wheeling himself up and down the ballroom, and glittering beautifully as he did so. 'But the point I'm trying to make is this: would you consider yourself to be an individual, Eddie?'

'Definitely so,' said the bear.

'And what about you, Jack?'

'Is it all right for me to speak?'

Tinto nodded.

'Then yes,' said Jack. 'I am definitely an individual too.'

'And there you have it.' Tinto ceased his wheelings. 'Condemned out of your own mouths, with no need for a democratic vote. There is no room for individuals in a war, only for soldiers who follow orders without question. I can't have you two running loose any more. You'd only cause further chaos.'

Jack made a baffled face.

'But you're in charge now, Tinto,' said Eddie. 'We'll do exactly what you tell us to do.'

'That's good then.' Tinto's head went nod nod nod. 'In that case I will assign you both to my first crack squadron.'

'Absolutely,' said Eddie.

'Tinto's Tornado Force,' said Tinto.

'Right,' said Eddie. 'Great name.'

'The crack suicide squadron.'

'*What?*' said Jack.

'Gotcha,' said Tinto. 'That was your last *what*!'

'No,' said Jack, 'hold on.'

'Take them out,' Tinto told the spider. 'Take them somewhere nice and quiet and well away from here and then kill them both. And kill the big *what*-boy first. He really gets up my metallic hooter.'

'No,' begged Eddie. 'Tinto, please. We're old friends. Don't do this.'

'Desperate times,' said Tinto, turning his back once more. 'But it's all for the common good. The rest of you . . .' Tinto's arm extended and swung all around and about. 'The rest of you, prepare to leave. I have a truck outside. We will repair to a place of safety. I know somewhere sweet and secure.'

Tinto whispered certain words into the ear parts of Miss Muffett's spider. 'And sick up on their faces before you kill them,' he added loudly.

'Tinto, no, please.' Eddie waved frantic paws, but Miss Muffett's spider scooped him from his pads.

'Now just you see here.' Jack raised a fist. But then he too was similarly scooped.

'We're done for,' said Eddie. 'We're sawdust.'

He and Jack were all in the dark. All in the dark in the locked boot of a big, posh automobile: a mark 22 Hyperglide limousine with pressed steel body panels finished in whey beige enamel; alloy-trim solid wheels with lithographed brass spoke motifs and moulded tyre assemblies; full pink plush tuffet seating throughout; sunroof fitted as standard; wind-up stereo sound system optional, but installed in this particular model.

This was being driven at speed through the night-time streets of Toy City by Miss Muffett's spider.

'Don't fret, Eddie,' said Jack. 'We'll be fine.'

'Fine?' Eddie's voice was hollow in the bumpy darkness. 'We're being driven to our place of execution. We will *not* be fine.'

'Of course we will. Trust me.'

Eddie growly-groaned.

'And please tell me,' said Jack, 'what *is* going on?'

The Mark 22 Hyperglide limousine sped on. The spider tinkered with the wind-up stereo system and behind him in the darkness of the boot Eddie, having nothing better to do, filled Jack in upon all of the details.

'Well,' said Jack, when Eddie had done with the filling of him in, 'I grudgingly have to admit that it does appear that your theory is correct. There really *is* an evil twin.'

'My pleasure in the knowledge that I was right is somewhat marred by our present circumstances,' said Eddie, shuddering away.

'But at least we now know who the murderer is. And why he's doing the murdering.'

'The evil twin,' Eddie shuddered on. 'But we don't know where he is and we're as doomed as.'

'Wake up, Eddie,' said Jack. 'You're missing the obvious.'

'I'm sure I'm not,' Eddie said.

'I'm sure you are. Remember what we were saying about behaving like proper detectives? Doing things the way Bill would have done them? How they would have been in one of his books?'

Eddie made noncommittal grunting sounds.

'Well, in the books, the detectives would have encountered the murderer by now, and we just did. *That* was the murderer, Eddie.'

'Tinto? You're saying that Tinto is the murderer?'

'It's not Tinto,' said Jack.

'It's *not* Tinto?' said Eddie.

'It's *not* Tinto,' said Jack. 'Don't you understand? *Not* Tinto.'

'It *was* Tinto,' said Eddie. 'We both saw him; we both know him.'

'Wasn't Tinto,' said Jack. 'That's what I'm trying to explain. That thing back there wasn't Tinto.'

'I give up,' said Eddie.

'Looked like Tinto,' said Jack. 'And sounded like Tinto. But *wasn't* Tinto. And do you know how I know?'

'Obviously not,' said Eddie.

'Because of his back. When he turned away from us, I saw it. Tinto is called Tinto because of the name on his back: Tintoy with the "y" scratched off. You showed me; you said that he thinks it makes him special. Our friend back there, at Miss Muffett's, the "y" wasn't scratched off *his* back. His back was perfect: it glittered in the candlelight. It said *Tintoy* on his back. That wasn't Tinto, Eddie. *That* was the criminal mastermind impersonating Tinto! That was the evil twin himself!'

'You genius,' said Eddie. 'You complete and utter genius. You're as smart as.'

'I'm a detective,' said Jack. 'And that's what we detectives do. Observe. Theorise. Resolve. He lied to them, Eddie. You heard him lying that he'd been at the toymaker's house. We were there, he wasn't. And remember what Bellis said about how criminals never tell the truth? They just lie and lie. He went there and lied to them and gained their confidence, told them how he could save them all, told them that the toymaker had sent him. He was disguised as Tinto because he knew that they knew Tinto. And he was disguised because they all know what he really looks like. They were there; they helped to throw him out of the city. And now he's got them all. All his old enemies. He'll kill them for certain.'

'So how can we stop him? He's the very Devil, Jack.'

'And a formidable adversary, if he can turn himself into weapons and stuff like that. But we'll find a way. Somehow.'

'Do you think he was the spider-woman too?' Eddie asked.

Jack shrugged in the darkness.

'Was that a yes or a no?'

'It was a shrug.'

'I'm very sad about all this,' said Eddie. 'I get it right and then we get captured and sent off to our deaths.'

'It will all be okay. Somehow. Trust me, Eddie.'

'I do,' said Eddie. 'But . . .'

'But what?'

'The car's just stopped,' said Eddie. 'And I think I need the toilet.'

There was a click of a key in a lock and then the boot lid swung open. Some light fell upon Eddie and Jack. Not a lot of light, but enough: enough to illuminate the fearful face of Eddie.

'Out,' said Miss Muffett's spider.

'What did he say?' Jack asked.

'He said "Out",' said Eddie.

'Oh,' said Jack. 'Right.'

Jack lifted Eddie from the boot and set him down upon the ground. And then Jack climbed out and stood before the spider.

The creature was little less than terrifying. In fact, it was a great deal more than more so: a towering black science fiction nasty. Its glistening mandibles clicked. Its complicated mouthparts moved in and out and its multifaceted eyes stared unblinkingly at Jack.

Jack stared back. 'You're one ugly mother . . .'

But the spider struck him from his feet.

Jack rolled over on the ground and glared up at the creature. 'Ask him where we are,' Jack called out to Eddie.

Eddie cowered at the car boot.

'Ask him,' said Jack.

Eddie asked the spider.

Mouthparts moved and words were uttered.

'He says we're at the abandoned doll works on East 666,' said Eddie, in a trembly tone.

Jack climbed slowly to his feet. 'Do you know your way back to Miss Muffett's from here?' he asked Eddie.

'Yes, but . . .'

'Then get in the car; we're leaving.'

The spider spoke further words.

'It says . . .' said Eddie.

'I don't care what it says,' said Jack. 'Get in the car, Eddie.'

'But, Jack.'

The spider drew back and then suddenly rushed forward at Jack: a blur of terrible scrabbling legs and horrible horrible mouthparts.

Jack drew the 7.62 mm M134 General Clockwork Minigun from his trousers and coolly shot the spider's head right off the arachnid equivalent of its shoulders.

'Right,' said Jack, retrousering his weapon. 'Let's go.'

Eddie looked at the fallen spider and then he looked up at Jack.

'What?' said Jack.

Eddie shrugged.

'Well, what did you expect me to do, let it kill me?'

'Yes, well no, but.'

'I couldn't shoot it back at Miss Muffett's, too many big

burly men with sunglasses and guns about. I had to wait until we got here.'

'But I've been all but pooing myself. I was as terrified as.'

'But you knew I still had the gun.'

'Well, in all the excitement, I sort of forgot.'

'Sorry,' said Jack. 'So, shall we go? We have famous folk to rescue and an evil God to destroy.'

Eddie sighed. 'Right,' said he. 'But first I have to do that thing that bears do in the woods.'

When Eddie had done that thing, he returned to Jack.

'Back to Miss Muffett's?' Jack asked.

'No point,' said Eddie. 'He won't be there. He was preparing to take the famous folk away in that big truck.'

'We'll pick up some clues there, then. We'll find them, somehow.'

'No need,' said Eddie. 'I know where he'll be taking them.'

'You do?'

'Of course I do. Trust me, Jack. I'm a detective.'

The moon was ducking down now and the sun was on the up and up. Jack brought the Mark 22 Hyperglide limousine to a halt at the gates of the chocolate factory. He ran his fingers lovingly over the polished silkwood steering wheel and thought to himself just how very much he'd like to own a car like this. Along with a chauffeur to drive him about in it, of course.

'So what are we doing back here?' he asked Eddie.

'Somewhere sweet and secure,' said the bear. 'That's what the evil twin said. And what is sweeter than chocolate? And more secure than a place with such big gates and such a dedicated gatekeeper?'

'I don't see the truck.'

'We'll have a word with our man the talking head.'

They left the limousine and did so.

'You can't come in,' said the gatekeeper. 'Not without an appointment.'

'A truck went through these gates earlier, didn't it?' said Jack.

'What if it did? It's got nothing to do with you.'

'We're here on special assignment,' said Eddie. 'We're part of an elite strike force.'

'That's a coincidence,' said the head. 'So am I.'

'Really?' said Jack. 'Which elite strike force are you in?'

'Tinto's Tornadoes,' said the head. 'I've just been enlisted. I'm already a corporal.'

'Then stand to attention when you address a superior officer,' said Jack. 'I'm a major.'

'Me too,' said Eddie. 'We're both majors. Major majors. Open the gates, corporal.'

'Can't do that, sir,' said the gatekeeping head. 'More than my commission's worth to do that.'

'Major,' said Eddie to Jack.

'Major?' said Jack to Eddie.

'Major, this soldier is being insubordinate. Have him immediately court-martialled and shoot him dead.'

'Sure thing, major.' Jack pulled out his 7.62 mm M134 General Clockwork Mini-gun.

'Opening the gates, *sir*,' said the head. 'I would salute you, but you know how it is, no hands.'

The gatekeeper head-butted certain controls and the big iron gates swung open.

Jack and Eddie saluted the head and returned to the limousine. Jack drove it through the open gates, which swung slowly shut behind him. 'Tell me, Eddie,' said Jack, 'do you have any particular plan in mind?'

Eddie offered a foolish grin. 'Not as such,' he said. 'I thought we'd sort of play things by ear, as it were.'

Jack steered the limousine across the broad expanse of courtyard that lay before the factory building. The chocolate factory really was of immense size: a veritable citadel, it seemed.

'This place is huge,' said Jack. 'A veritable citadel, it seems. It's like a fortress.'

'We didn't have too much difficulty getting past the guard on this occasion.'

'That's the military mind for you.'

Jack peered up through the windscreen. 'This is an awful lot of chocolate factory,' he observed. 'Does Toy City really consume so much chocolate as to merit a factory this size?'

'Absolutely,' said Eddie. 'Everyone loves chocolate. And I do mean everyone. And you don't get better chocolate than Sredna's. But that's possibly because no one else makes it.'

'What did you say?' Jack asked.

'I said no one else makes chocolate—'

'No, Eddie. The name.'

'Sredna,' said Eddie. 'A Mr Sredna founded the chocolate company years and years and years ago. Long before my time.'

'Sredna,' said Jack. 'Then everything that man told me was true.'

'What are you talking about, Jack? What man?'

'A man I met. Back at the town where I lived. If it hadn't been for him and what happened, I wouldn't have set out on my journey to the city.'

'Do you want to tell me all about it?'

'Yes,' said Jack. 'But not now, there isn't time. Now we have to stop the evil twin and rescue the rich folk.'

'You don't have to do this, Jack,' Eddie said. 'You know that. It's going to be dangerous. You could just walk away. If you want.'

'What?' said Jack. 'But we're partners. You and me. Jack and Eddie. We're the detective dream team.'

'Right,' said Eddie. 'We're as dreamy as.'

Jack brought the limousine to a halt and looked into the driving mirror. The sun was rising higher now, above the highest heights of Knob Hill. It shone upon the rooftops of the toymaker's house. 'So what do you think?' he asked. 'Should we go and have another of our sneakabouts? See what we can see?'

'Let's do that,' said Eddie. 'Let's sneak.'

And so, once more, they snuck.

They left the limousine and snuck about the mighty edifice that was the chocolate factory. And a truly mighty edifice it was: a Gothic goliath; a gargoyled gargantuan; a towering tessellated *tour de force*. And things of that non-nominally nominative nature, generally.

'I don't see any lights on,' said Eddie. 'And frankly, my paw pads are getting tired and sore.'

'Let's just break in,' said Jack. 'Find me a lock to pick.'

A small door presented itself. Jack selected a suitable piece of wire from a pile of waste that lay conveniently to hand, picked the lock and swung the small door open.

'After you,' he said to Eddie.

'No,' said Eddie. 'You have the big gun. Very much after *you*.'

With Jack leading the way, they entered the chocolate factory. Eddie sniffed chocolate.

'Tell me about the rabbits,' said Eddie. Which rang a bell somewhere with Jack.

'The rabbits?' Jack asked.

'The hollow chocolate bunnies. What are they all about?'

Jack shrugged. 'I haven't a clue,' said he. 'But I'll bet it's something really obvious. Where do you think we are?'

'Looks like the staff kitchens.'

'Then let's go somewhere else. I have no love for kitchens.'

They passed through a doorway and into a hallway. 'You know what,' said Eddie, 'we really do need some kind of plan.'

'I think I'll just shoot him with my big gun, as soon as I see him,' said Jack.

'That's not too subtle a plan.'

'I know.' Jack edged along the hallway, his big gun held high. 'But you see, there's always too much talking when it comes to the big confrontation situation. When I used to read the Bill Winkie thrillers and it got to the point of the final confrontation with the villain, there was always too much talking. I'd be reading it and saying "don't talk to him, Bill, just shoot him". And Bill would have the gun on him and everything, but he'd talk and then suddenly the gun would get wrestled away and then the villain would talk and talk.'

'That's the way it's done,' said Eddie. 'If you want to do it by the book, that's the way it's done. Bill always triumphed in the end, though. With my help, of course, not that I ever got a mention. But he triumphed. He did it right, did Bill.' Eddie's voice trailed off.

Jack turned and looked down at Eddie.

'I'm sorry,' said Jack. 'I know how much you loved Bill.'

'Don't talk wet,' said Eddie.

'You loved him,' said Jack. 'It's nothing to be ashamed of. And when this is all sorted out, you will have sorted it out for Bill. As a tribute to him. And your memory of him. That's noble stuff, Eddie. That's doing things for love. That's okay.'

Eddie sniffed. '*You're* okay, Jack,' he said. 'You're my bestest friend, you know that.'

'Come on,' said Jack. 'Let's do it.'

Eddie grinned, and then he said, 'Stop, hold on there, Jack.'

'What is it?'

'I smell something.'

'What do you smell?'

'Something more than chocolate. Something that I've smelled before.'

Eddie now led the way and cautiously Jack followed him. They edged along the hallway.

'The smell's getting stronger,' said Eddie.

Jack sniffed. 'I can smell it now,' he said. 'What is it?'

'I know what it is, and I don't like what it is.'

Presently they reached the end of the hallway. They

passed through a narrow arch and found themselves standing upon a gantry constructed of pierced metal.

Beneath them was a vast beyond: a vast beyond of wonder.

Eddie stared.

And Jack stared too.

And, 'I don't believe *that*,' said Eddie.

27

It spread away beneath them, to dwindle into hazy perspectives: a vast subterranean factory complex.

Molten metal flowed from titanic furnaces, to be swallowed up by mighty engines fashioned from burnished brass and highly polished copper. Upon these, intricate networks of massive cogs intermeshed and glittering objects shuttled out upon clattering conveyor belts. Fountains of sparks arose above enormous lathes that tortured spinning metal. Great pistons pounded and countless funnels belched out steam.

And it went on and on and on.

And on and on some more.

'Look at it,' Eddie gasped, breathlessly. 'Look at it, Jack. It's incredible. It's as gabracious as.'

'As what?'

'You know I don't know as what.'

'I meant, what does gabracious mean?'

'How should I know?' said Eddie. 'I've never seen anything like this before. I don't have a word for it.'

Jack shook his head. 'It's very impressive,' he said.

'Assembly lines,' Eddie pointed out. 'Moving belts, but no workers. No workers at all, Jack. It's all being done by machine. It's all . . .'

'Automatic,' said Jack. 'Automated. Automation. When I was labouring away in the clockwork factory, the workers used to talk about this sort of thing: that one day factories wouldn't need workers any more. That machines would do everything.'

'But how?' asked Eddie. 'How is it done?'

Jack shrugged his narrow shoulders. 'It isn't done by clockwork, that's for certain.'

'Automation? That certainly sounds like the work of the Devil. And look there.' Eddie pointed some more. 'Look at those, on the conveyor belts there. Look what the machines are manufacturing.'

Jack did further lookings.

Robotic arms snatched up the glittering objects that shuttled along the conveyor belts, jointed them one to another, pieced them together: pieced them into all-too-recognisable forms.

'Women,' said Jack. 'The machines are making women.'

'The spider-women. Tinto's private army.' Eddie made a fearful face. 'He's building them down there, thousands of them.'

'This is very bad, Eddie; we have to stop him.'

'But the scale of all this. It makes me afraid, Jack. This must have taken years to build. Years and years and years.'

'More than a few years,' Jack said, thoughtfully. 'This has been a very long-running project. Why would he want to build thousands of these creatures? What is he really up to?'

Eddie growled hopelessly. 'And all down here, beneath Toy City. Beneath the chocolate factory. And none of us knew.'

'They do favour an underground lair, these criminal masterminds. I'm a bit disappointed that it's not inside an extinct volcano, though. But there you go.'

'Don't be flippant, Jack,' said Eddie.

'Just laughing in the face of fear, that's all.'

'Which would be why your knees are knocking, would it?' Jack made an effort to stiffen his knees. 'But look at them,' said Eddie. 'Those spider-women. Look at their hands, Jack.'

Jack squinted down. 'Their *hands*?' he said. 'What about their hands?'

'Delicate hands,' said Eddie, 'coming off the conveyor

belts, rows and rows of hands, all with four fingers, with opposable thumbs,' and there was no disguising the envy in the voice of Eddie Bear.

'This is hardly the time for that, Eddie. We're here on business. Detective business. To save the famous folk and bring the criminal mastermind, in the form of the evil twin, to justice. Or at least to this.' Jack cocked the 7.62 mm M134 General Clockwork Mini-gun. 'Forget about hands, please, will you?'

'I still have time to dream,' said Eddie, regarding his fingerless paws with contempt. 'So, shall we do some more sneaking?'

'Practice makes perfect.' Jack raised his 7.62 mm M134 General Clockwork Mini-gun. 'Follow me.'

Eddie followed Jack, who snuck down this staircase and the next, down and down, and down some more, to the factory floor below.

It was very noisy there, and very smelly too.

And even with all the furnaces, there was a terrible chill in the air.

The chill that one feels when in the presence of Evil.

'What *is* that?' Jack shivered and covered his nose.

'The smell of the spider-women. I told you I knew that smell.' Eddie looked fearfully up at the creations upon the conveyor belts. 'It's coming from them. It's the smell of whatever they're made of.'

Jack reached out and touched the leg of one of the half-completed spider-women as the conveyor belt carried it by. 'Warm,' said he. 'And it feels almost like firm flesh. Imagine an entire army of these. It doesn't bear thinking about.'

'Could we blow them all up?' Eddie asked. 'Murders, fast car-driving, drinking, underage sex, gratuitous violence and a big explosion at the end. That's a recipe for success in any detective thriller.'

'Worth a try,' Jack agreed. 'But it might be better to rescue the famous folk first, don't you think?'

'Well,' said Eddie. It was a long well. A real *weeeeeeeeell* of a well. 'Do you think anyone would really miss them?'

'Eddie, what are you saying?'

'Only joking,' said Eddie. 'Shall we sneak about some more and see if we can find them? Perhaps somewhere away from these horrible creatures.'

'After you this time,' Jack said.

Eddie led the way between clattering conveyor belts, past the titanic furnaces and the mighty engines, around one huge and scary big machine and on past many more, until at last they snuck under an arch and down a passageway, which at least was far less noisy and didn't smell so bad.

'We're lost,' said Jack.

'We're not,' said Eddie. 'Bears have a great sense of direction. They're renowned for it. How do you think we find our way back from all those picnics in the woods, breadcrumbs?'

'We *are* lost.' They had reached a parting of the passage-ways. There were several now to choose from. None seemed to be saying, 'Come this way', but then again, none didn't.

Early morning sunlight dipped in through narrow arched windows. Jack glanced up at it. 'Which way should we go?' he asked.

'That way,' Eddie pointed.

'*I'm* not so sure.'

'I don't think it matters, either way.'

'Yes it does, Eddie.'

'I didn't say that,' said Eddie. 'That wasn't me.'

'He's right, it wasn't.'

Eddie turned.

And Jack turned too.

'Ah,' said Eddie. 'It's you.'

'Surprise, surprise,' said the Tinto impersonator. 'Drop your weapon please, Jack.' Where the Tinto impersonator's left arm had been, there was now a considerable weapon: it was a 19.72 mm M666 General Clockwork Maxi-cannon.

Jack recognised it at once, and in deference to its mighty firepower, he grudgingly put down his weapon. Which it pained him considerably to do.

'Chaps,' said the Tinto impersonator, shaking his metallic head from side to side. 'Chaps, chaps, chaps. The gatekeeper called me. Sergeant gatekeeper, that is. He called me to say that you two had breached the security perimeter. You're supposed to be dead. Can't you even die properly?'

Jack chewed upon his bottom lip. 'Nice place you have here . . . er . . . *Tinto*. Can't we just talk about this?'

The clockwork chameleon shook its head once more. 'You really have no idea what you've got yourself into, have you?' he asked.

'No,' said Jack, 'we haven't. But please tell me this, who are you, really?'

'I'm Tinto,' said the Tinto impersonator.

'You're *not* Tinto,' said Jack. 'You look like Tinto. But you're not him.'

'And why do you say that?'

Jack chose his words with care. Although he and Eddie knew that the evil twin lurked behind the Tinto disguise, the evil twin didn't know that they knew. So to speak. 'I know you're not Tinto, because you're too perfect,' said Jack.

'Why, thank you very much, young man. Perfect, yes.'

'Tinto's back is all scratched up,' said Jack. 'The "Y" has worn off the word *Tintoy*. That's why he called himself Tinto; he thinks it makes him special.'

'And don't you think that I'm special too?'

'Oh yes,' said Jack. 'You're very special. Unique. You're definitely one of a kind.'

'I'm warming to you.' Several of the 19.72 mm M666 General Clockwork Maxi-cannon's barrels retracted. 'Perfection is the name of the game. And everything is a game. Everything. All fun and games.'

'So who are you, really?' Jack asked.

'He's the evil twin, of course,' said Eddie.

Jack gawped down at Eddie.

'Sorry,' said Eddie. 'It just slipped out.'

'*What?*' Gun barrels bristled from places that had previously been gun barrel-free. 'What did you say?'

'Nothing,' said Eddie. 'Nothing at all.'

'You did. You said that *I* was the evil twin. You must die this instant.'

'No, hold on please,' said Jack. 'Eddie gets lots of silly ideas into his head. It's full of sawdust; it doesn't work very well.'

'And he thinks that *I* am the toymaker's evil twin?'

'That's bears for you,' said Jack, making a helpless gesture. 'They're as stupid as.'

'He thinks that I?' The Tinto head spun round and round. '*I* am the evil twin? When here am I forging a private army to destroy the evil twin? Working unpaid around the clock, and this bear thinks that I'm the evil twin?'

'So you're not?' said Eddie. 'I mean, *no* you're not. Of course you're not.'

'Of course he's not,' said Jack. 'I told you he wasn't.'

'I don't remember you telling me anything of the sort.'

Jack gave Eddie a kick. 'Shut up!' he whispered.

'Ouch,' said Eddie. 'Oh yes, of course you did.' Eddie's knees were all a-tremble now. 'Jack did say that. He definitely said that you were *not* the evil twin.'

'That's right,' said Jack.

'Good,' said the clockwork creation.

'He said you were just a loony,' said Eddie.

'He *what?*' Weaponry appeared from the most unexpected places.

'Sorry,' said Eddie, covering his face with his paws. 'I didn't mean to say that. I'm sorry, I sort of blurt things out when I'm scared. It wasn't loony he said, it was—'

'Deity,' said Jack.

'Deity?' said the gun-bristling-whatever.

'Deity,' said Jack once again.

'Deity doesn't sound in the least like loony.'

'It does when you have tatty old ears like mine,' said Eddie, pawing at his tatty old ears. 'And a head full of sawdust. It was definitely deity. I'm sure it was.'

'It was,' said Jack. 'A deity that will soon be worshipped by all the folk of Toy City.'

'This is indeed the case.'

'So what *is* your name?' Jack asked. 'Your real name? The name that will be glorified by all of Toy City when you defeat the evil twin. When you are raised to the status of Godhood that you so justly deserve.'

'Bumlicker,' Eddie whispered to Jack.

'I'm just trying to keep us alive,' Jack whispered back. 'Please be quiet, Eddie, and let me do the talking.' Jack bowed towards the Tinto Impersonator. 'Might we be permitted to know your real name, oh Great One?'

'I don't think so, no. It's private.'

'Oh, please,' said Jack. 'You're going to kill us anyway. What harm would there be in letting us know your real name?'

'No, it's private. And anyway, you might laugh.'

'Laugh?' said Jack. 'Laugh in the face of a deity? Would even *we* be that stupid?'

'Well, seeing as you're both going to die, I suppose there's no harm. Stand back, I'm going to transform.'

Eddie and Jack stood back and viewed the transformation. It was an impressive transformation. It involved all manner of bits sliding out here and sliding in there and other bits turning around and folding down and up and so forth.

Until.

'Now I wasn't expecting *that*!' said Eddie.

'Who are *you*?' asked Jack.

A dolly now stood before them: a rather foolish-looking dolly with a big silly face, all wide eyes and rosy cheeks and little kissy mouth. The dolly had golden plaited hair with big red bows, a colourful frock and dear little court shoes of polished patent leather.

'I'm PRIMROSE,' said the dolly, in a little dolly voice.

'Primrose?' said Jack.

'Primrose?' said Eddie.

'PRIMROSE,' said PRIMROSE. 'Prototype Integrated Multi-tasking Robotics Operational System.'

'That's Primros,' said Jack. 'There's an "e" on the end of Primrose.'

The dolly's little kissy mouth became a tight-lipped scowl. 'And you wonder why I want to keep it private. My acronym is rubbish; it doesn't even work. I was designed to be a multi-purpose toy that could be enjoyed by girls as well as boys. Some stupid idea that, eh? And PRIMROSE, I ask you: what kind of name is that for a metamorphosing action figure? With the kind of weaponry that can take the head off a golly at two thousand yards. I should have been given a name like SPLAT or ZARK.'

'Or simply twat,' said Eddie.

'*What?*' went PRIMROSE, making a very evil face indeed.

'Sorry, sir, nerves again. I meant TWAT as in, er, Transforming War Action Tank,' Eddie suggested.

'Yes,' said PRIMROSE. 'Twat. I like that.'

'I'll call you Twat then,' said Eddie.

'Me too,' said Jack.

'You'll both call me Master,' said PRIMROSE. 'Or perhaps it should be Mistress. I get a bit confused myself at times. So many personality changes, I get rather disorientated.'

Eddie looked at Jack.

And Jack looked at Eddie.

'He's lying,' whispered Jack. 'He's lying again.'

Eddie looked once more at Jack and Jack looked once more at Eddie and then the two of them looked towards PRIMROSE. If there was ever going to be a better time to rush and overpower the evil twin, neither of them could imagine it.

Eddie and Jack prepared to rush.

PRIMROSE, however, was no longer PRIMROSE, she was now something more approaching ZARK.

'Whoa,' went Eddie. 'What a big, bad boy.'

The ZARK was an all-action combat mode: a martial monster, bristling with polished spikes, lean and mean, armoured and dangerous.

'So you see the problem,' it said. 'However, everything will be resolved. Perhaps I'll go with Twat. Do you wish to pray to me before I kill you? As you'll be kneeling, you might want to get a prayer or two going.'

'We'd rather just stick around, if it's all right,' Jack said. 'Then we could do a lot of praying and bowing down when you're sworn in officially.'

'I think that I'll just kill you now,' said PRIMROSE.

'No, hold on,' said Jack, 'let's not be hasty.'

'There's no haste involved, I assure you. I'm killing you at my leisure.'

'No,' said Jack. 'You really don't want to do that.'

'I do. Really I do.'

'But if you kill us, you'll never find the Maguffin.'

'The *what*?'

'The Maguffin,' said Jack. 'The all-important something that's all-importantness is not apparent until its moment has come.'

'I've no idea what you're talking about.'

'Of course you do. It's about this big.' Jack did mimings. 'And this-shaped and sort of heavyish in a lighter way than you might expect.'

'*That?*' said PRIMROSE, or whatever PRIMROSE currently called itself. 'You have *that*?'

'Got it from the real Tinto,' said Jack. 'He said that one of the famous folk had left it behind after one of their meetings above his bar. I'll bet you really want it, don't you?'

'Well, I . . .'

'Go on,' said Jack. 'Admit it. It's really important, isn't it?'

'Hand it over to me,' said PRIMROSE. 'Now!'

'I don't have it on me,' said Jack. 'Do you think I'd carry a valuable artefact like that around with me? What does it do, by the way?'

'You think I'm going to tell you *that*?'

'What harm can it do?' Jack asked. 'You're going to kill us anyway.'

'I'm getting déjà vu here,' said PRIMROSE.

'Look,' said Jack, 'I know that you think that you want to kill us because we're such a nuisance. But you don't want to *really*. You're little less than a deity. And deities are noted for granting mercy and answering prayers and stuff like that. I know we've got on your nerves a bit and any ordinary mortal would probably want to kill us for that. But you're not any ordinary mortal, are you? You're special. You're unique. You're one of a kind. Special. You can make your own rules. Do whatever you want.'

'I certainly can,' said PRIMROSE.

'So you could just send us on our way with a wave of your dextrous hand.'

'I could, if I so chose to.'

'Then go for it,' said Jack. 'Do what a God would do. Forgive and forget. That's what a *special* God would do.'

'Well,' said PRIMROSE.

'We're beneath your notice,' said Jack. 'We're nothing. Tatty old bear and young gormster. Nothing to one as special as you.'

'You're certainly that. And I'm certainly special.'

'So there you go,' said Jack. 'That's omnipotence for you. It's a done deal.'

'It is,' Eddie agreed. 'Bravo, special guy.' Eddie offered a thumbless thumbs-up to PRIMROSE.

'All right,' said PRIMROSE. 'I will be merciful. Give me the Maguffin. And you can go.'

'Certainly,' said Jack. 'Absolutely. As soon as Eddie and I and all the famous folk are set free, I will go at once and fetch it for you.'

There was a bit of a pause then.

'Famous folk *set free*?' said PRIMROSE, slowly and thoughtfully.

Eddie looked up at Jack.

And Jack looked down at Eddie.

'Oh dear, oh dear, oh dear,' said PRIMROSE.

'Poor choice of words there,' whispered Eddie. 'And you were doing so well until then.'

'Oh dear,' said PRIMROSE. 'And there was I almost believing you. But *set free*? You think that I have them captured and locked up. You're just the same as this stupid bear. You think I'm the evil twin.'

'No,' said Jack. 'Honestly I don't. And I mean what I say, I *honestly* don't.' Jack tried to make an honest face, but couldn't.

'Give me the Maguffin, and give it to me now.'

'I told you, I don't have it.'

'Then to be certain, I'll search you. Search your body, that is.' The martial monster rolled towards Jack upon grinding tank tracks. A steel claw extended from its chest regions and snatched the lad by the throat, hauling him from his feet and dragging him up the cold stone passageway wall.

'Die,' said Battle Mode PRIMROSE.

Jack fought and struggled, but the steel claw tightened about his throat. Jack's eyes started from his head and his tongue stuck from his mouth. Being choked to death really hurt. It was no fun at all. Jack struck with his fists and kicked with his feet, but it was all to no avail. The breath was going from him now. The big black darkness was closing in.

And then there was a bit of an explosion. Which lit up the big black darkness.

It came right out of the blue. Or the black. Unexpectedly. The way that most explosions do. This one was a real eardrum-splitter, coming as it did within the confines of a passageway – even a passageway that branched off into other passageways. This explosion really rocked. It was a veritable deafener.

The head of the Martial PRIMROSE turned away from Jack. The head of the Martial PRIMROSE had a dent in its left cheek.

Jack, whose popping eyes had all but dropped from his head, felt the grip around his throat loosen and fell to the passageway floor, coughing and gagging for air.

He saw the head of the Martial PRIMROSE turn somewhat more. And then he saw it take another violent hit.

The second explosion, a double deafener, had Jack covering his ears, and had him glancing with watery blinking eyes towards Eddie.

The bear had the 7.62 mm M134 General Clockwork Mini-gun raised.

'Run, Jack,' shouted Eddie, pulling the trigger once again. 'Run like a rabbit, go on.'

'No, Eddie, no.'

'No?' said the bear.

'No, I mean, keep firing.'

'But.'

'Don't but me, Eddie. Shoot him some more. Shoot him until he's dead.'

'Right,' said Eddie, 'now you're talking.' He pulled the trigger and another shell hit home.

Martial PRIMROSE rocked upon its tracks. It was armoured, it was tough; inner mechanisms clicked and clacked, shutters opened, gunnery extended. This gunnery levelled at Eddie.

Jack rolled over, snatched the gun from Eddie's paws and came up firing. 'Retreat!' he shouted.

'But you said.'

'I know what I said, Eddie. But now I'm saying retreat. Just run.'

'Like a rabbit?'

'Like a rabbit. Run!'

Jack snatched up Eddie and tucked him under his arm.

'I'll do the running,' said Jack.

And he ran.

28

Jack ran like a rabbit, with Eddie tucked under his arm, along a tiled passageway and onwards, ever onwards.

Something whistled from behind, passed near to his ducking head, and exploded some distance before him.

'Discouraging, that,' remarked Eddie. 'Somewhat superior firepower. And our gun only made a few small dents. Any thoughts on this, Jack?'

Jack huffed and puffed and had no thoughts that he wished to convey at present. His long limbs carried him and Eddie back onto the factory floor.

'I'm sure we're not really lost,' said Eddie as he jiggled about under Jack's arm. 'I'll just get my bearings. *Bear*ings, geddit?' Eddie giggled foolishly. 'Sorry,' he said, 'nerves.'

'Please be quiet.' Jack ducked this way and the next and took cover behind a big brass pumping piston. 'I don't think he'll take pot-shots at us out here.' Jack raised his head and did furtive peepings. 'He won't want to risk damaging any of his demonic machinery.'

The armoured being in full combat mode, no longer on its tank tracks, but now on sturdy steely legs, moved purposefully along between the clattering conveyor belts, a most determined expression upon its latest metal face. Its head swung to the right and left, telescopic vision focused and refocused; tiny brass ear-trumpets extending from the sides of its head picked up each and every sound, deciphered and unscrambled them within the clockwork cranial cortex, sorting the mechanical from the organic . . .

And homed in upon Jack's breathing.

The armoured being ceased its marching; hinged flaps upon its shoulders raised, tiny rocket launchers rose and fired two tiny rockets.

These struck home quite close to Jack, causing him and Eddie great distress.

'So much for your theory about not wanting to fire his guns out here,' whispered Eddie. 'Shall we run some more?'

'I think it would be for the best.' Jack ducked some more and, hauling Eddie after him, he ran. 'Which way?' Jack asked as he reached a place where many possibilities existed.

'*That* way,' said Eddie, pointing.

'Do you know it's *that* way?'

Eddie shrugged beneath Jack's arm. 'Ursine intuition?' he suggested.

'Fair enough.' Jack ran in the direction of Eddie's choice.

Presently they found themselves in a dead-end situation. To the right and left of them high conveyor belts clattered; before them was a wall of riveted steel and behind them strolled the armoured maniac.

Difficult.

'Shoot him, Jack,' urged Eddie.

'I think we already tried that.'

'He might have a weak spot. Shoot him in the goolies.'

'I don't think he has any goolies.'

'Shut up! Be silent! Cease to speak!'

Jack and Eddie shut their mouths, fell silent and ceased to speak.

'Stupid,' said the armoured one. 'Stupid, stupid, stupid. You shot at me. You tried to kill me.'

'But,' said Eddie.

'*Shut up!* You shot at *me*. The saviour of Toy City. *Me!*'

'Who's speaking?' Jack asked.

'I told you to shut up. And put that ridiculous gun down.'

Jack dropped the 7.62 mm M134 General Clockwork Mini-gun. 'We give up,' he said.

'Of course you give up.' Cogs whirly-whirled, metal plates interlocked, armoured bits and bobs shifted and jigsaw-locked. 'You're dead; of course you give up.'

'That's not what I mean,' said Jack. 'I mean that Eddie and I *really* give up. We'll tell you everything you need to know. About the Maguffin. Everything. Well, obviously we won't tell *you*. But we'll tell the real *you*, if you know what I mean.'

'What *do* you mean?' The metallic monster drew nearer to Jack. Its chest rose and fell, expanding and contracting its shining coppery links.

'I mean I'll tell everything to your leader. To the one in charge.'

'I am in charge. I am PRIMROSE.'

'No,' said Jack. 'PRIMROSE is not in charge. You weren't telling us the truth. I'll tell everything to the one in charge. The *real* you. I know who you really are. I know your real name.'

'You know his real name?' Eddie made a puzzled face.

'You're going to kill us anyway,' said Jack. 'What harm can it do?'

'Not *that* again.'

'But what harm *can* it do?'

'None. No harm at all.' The being took a step back. Steel shutters fell over the telescopically visual eye attachments. The ear trumpets slid back into the head section. The armoured chest drew back. Legs and arms twisted, inverted.

A man of less than average height, with the large face and slender body of the potentially famous, now stood before them. He had a high forehead, deeply set eyes, a narrow nose and a bitter little mouth. He wore a rather splendid three-piece green tweed suit with a golden watch chain and a red silk cravat unknotted over the winged collar of a starched white shirt. He bore more than a strong resemblance to the toymaker.

'Mr Sredna, I presume,' said Jack. 'Sredna Sredna.'

'So you really *do* know my name,' said Mr Sredna.

'I'm very pleased to meet you,' said Jack. 'At last, and face to face.'

'I would shake your hand,' said Mr Sredna, 'but it is not to my choosing. How is it that you know my name?'

'Because I work for your company: the Sredna Corporation. We have a code 15 situation in New York.'

'A code 15?' said Mr Sredna.

'*New York?*' said Eddie.

'My name is Jon Kelly,' said Jack. 'Codename Jack, deep cover operative for the Sredna Corporation, offices in New York, London and Tokyo. I could not divulge my true identity earlier, because I was not certain that I was speaking to *you*. I'm certain now. I've very pleased to meet you, sir.'

'And I you, my boy.' Mr Sredna stepped forward and warmly shook Jack by the hand. 'Jon Kelly. I know you by reputation. A corporation man, who works only for the corporation. I am very pleased to meet you too.'

'*What?*' went Eddie. 'What is going on here? Jack?'

'Jon,' said Jon. 'Jon Kelly. I'm sorry I had to deceive you, Eddie. But business is business; I'm sure you understand.'

'I'm sure I *don't*,' said Eddie.

'Well, it's neither here nor there. Is there somewhere we can talk, Mr Sredna? Away from all this noise?'

'Jack?' Eddie shook his head. 'I don't understand any of this.'

'I'll just kill this stupid bear before we talk.' Mr Sredna glared at Eddie.

'Not worth the trouble,' said Jon. 'Let him come with us. He amuses me.'

'What?' went Eddie. 'What? What? What?'

At length they were no longer in the factory. They were high above it, in an elegantly appointed office several storeys up in the East Wing of the chocolate factory building.

The sun fell through a high mullioned window. The vista beyond the windows was of Knob Hill and the toymaker's house.

Mr Sredna sat behind an expansive desk laden with many

precious things. Jon stood before the window, gazing out of it. Eddie sat upon the floor. Eddie was a very puzzled bear.

'This is a serious breach of security,' said Mr Sredna. 'It is strictly forbidden.'

'The situation merited drastic action,' said Jon Kelly, turning. 'A number of serious faults have developed in the latest presidential model.'

'Surely not,' said Mr Sredna, making a surprised face. 'I oversaw the construction of that model myself. It should run flawlessly throughout its term of office. They've not let it get in the rain, have they? The buyers were told that it's not fully waterproof.'

Eddie made an exasperated face. 'Will somebody *please* tell me what is going on?' he said. 'I'm losing my mind here.'

Jon Kelly (codename Jack) smiled down upon Eddie. 'You,' said he, 'are a very intelligent little bear. It has actually been a great pleasure working with you.'

'Thank you,' said Eddie. 'But . . .'

'We'll have to kill him, though,' said Mr Sredna.

'Of course,' said Jon Kelly. 'We can't have any loose ends dangling around. But it has been a pleasure. And as *I* will be killing him . . .'

'*You?*' said Eddie.

'It really doesn't matter if he knows the truth.' Jon Kelly smiled upon Eddie. 'My name, as I said, is Jon Kelly. I work for the Sredna Corporation, a corporation in the world beyond. Originally a toy company, it dates back two hundred years or so: Purveyors of Clockwork Automata to the Gentry. But times and tastes change. When I told you, Eddie, that there *was* another world out there, beyond the world of Toy City, I was telling all of the truth. There *is* such a world. I come from there. I grew up there. I never worked in any clockwork factory, although I do know all about clockwork.'

'But Jack, everything we've been through together—'

'It was all for a purpose, Eddie. I had to contact Mr Sredna here. He's been missing for two months. We had to know what happened to him, why he had not returned to the outer world. However, Mr Sredna is a very hard man to track down.'

'I have to be,' said Mr Sredna. 'I am known here. I've had to remain in hiding and disguise until all my plans were completed.'

'I understand that now,' said Jon Kelly.

'But soon, everyone will know my name.' There was a terrible tone to the voice, and a madness in the eyes of Mr Sredna. Neither went unnoticed by either Eddie or Jon.

'Well, what you choose to do here in Toy City is *your* business,' said Jon Kelly, 'but what goes on out there in the world beyond is a different matter. And if a presidential model fails, then the Sredna Corporation's reputation is at stake.'

'What *is* a presidential model?' Eddie asked.

'A kind of toy,' said Jon. 'Mr Sredna here employs his toy-making skills in the world beyond. And he does make exceedingly good toys. Very life-like. The Sredna Corporation supplies these toys to countries all over our world. These toys then appear to run these countries. But naturally they don't actually do that. The owners of these toys are the big business consortiums that can afford to buy them from Mr Sredna. It's all just good business. It's a businessman thing.'

'It sounds ghastly,' said Eddie. 'It sounds as corrupt as.'

'Oh it is,' said Mr Sredna. 'Totally. But then, what isn't? Who isn't?'

'I'm not,' said Eddie. 'And I didn't think that Jack was. I'm very upset.'

'Your city is quite amazing,' Jon Kelly said to Mr Sredna. 'When the corporation executives sent me here to find you, they told me that this city was inhabited by toys which actually thought for themselves; actually lived their own lives. I never really believed them. Never thought it possible. There is a magic here in Toy City, there's no doubt about that.'

'Of course there is.' Mr Sredna leaned back in his chair and interlinked his long, narrow fingers. 'If it wasn't for the fact that certain things can be done here in this world that cannot be done out there, there could be no Sredna Corporation.'

Eddie punched himself violently in the head. 'I *am* going mad,' he declared. 'Jack, you're my friend. You're my bestest friend. You and I were tracking down the evil twin. Have you forgotten about that?'

Jon glanced towards Mr Sredna. 'What about *that*?' he asked.

'Nothing you need concern yourself with,' said Mr Sredna.

'I'd like to know.'

'Then you shall.' The madness was once more in the eyes. 'Those nursery rhymers: they deserved what they got. And I gave it to them, one at a time, in the order that they became famous. I've always hated them. I didn't mean for them to become rich and famous, but they did, and they had me to thank for it. But did they thank me? No, they sided with my brother and threw me out of the city.'

'Your brother?' said Eddie. 'Tell me about your brother.'

'The toymaker,' said Mr Sredna.

'So you *are* the evil twin. There, Jack, he's confessed.'

'I'm *not* evil! How dare you!' Mr Sredna brought his fists down hard upon the table. 'Evil twin this! Evil twin that! I'm not evil. Never was evil. I am *innovative*. Imaginative. *Special!* But because I didn't play by the rules, follow the instructions, do things the way they were supposed to be done, I was cast from this world by that ungrateful scum.'

Eddie cowered on the floor.

'Let me tell *you*,' said Mr Sredna, 'who really wrote those nursery rhymes.'

'Really wrote?' said Eddie. 'Didn't Wheatley Porterman write them?'

'*I* wrote them!' Mr Sredna fairly bellowed. 'They're supposed to be hymns, not damn nursery rhymes.'

'Hymns?' said Eddie. 'But—'

'Each one of them is a parable.' Mr Sredna leaned across his desk and scowled down at Eddie. 'They're *all* parables. Take the hymn of Jack and Jill: of course you can't go *up* a hill to fetch a pail of water. What the hymn really means is that if you spend your life seeking to achieve impossible goals, rather than doing something useful, you will surely tumble to earth. It's pretty damn obvious, isn't it?'

'I suppose it is,' said Eddie. 'So they're all like that, are they? They're all, like, parables; they all have real meanings?'

'Of course they do!' Mr Sredna drummed his fists upon his expansive desk, rattling precious things. 'They all mean something. They were supposed to be instructive. They were Holy Writ.'

'What?' said Jon Kelly.

'Holy Writ!' Mr Sredna's voice rose in zeal. 'Which is another reason that I was ousted. Gods aren't supposed to write their own Holy Writ. Gods are supposed to be "hands-off". Leave the writing of Holy Writ to "inspired" mortals. And what happens to theirs? The same as happened to mine. Misinterpreted! You can't produce any kind of Holy Writ without some oaf misinterpreting it. I write deep-meaningful hymns. And the trash that I wrote those moving deep-meaningful hymns about, the examples of man's folly, they get rich and famous from the proceeds. And because I've upset them, they conspire against me and then rise up and throw me out of the city. Me, a God in my own right: they throw *me* out. What kind of insane irony is that, I ask you?'

Jon Kelly shook his head. 'I don't know,' he said.

'Enough to drive anyone mad,' said Mr Sredna. 'You think about any one of those "nursery rhymes", think about what the words actually say, actually mean. But nobody ever has. It was all wasted, all my time and effort wasted. But not any more. Away with the old and in with the new. All of this is going, all of it.'

'All?' said Eddie.

'I'm erasing the city,' said Mr Sredna. 'Starting with the rich and famous folk, then working all the way down.'

'To the toys?' said Eddie.

'All going,' said Mr Sredna, making sweeping hand motions. 'As soon as the new order comes off the assembly lines, I'll have them do away with the old. It has been all fun and games for me, wiping out the old rich one at a time, coming up with ingenious scenarios, throwing the city into chaos. This city is a mess, but I'm changing all that: a Heaven on Earth, and I shall be the God in this Heaven.'

'And your brother?' said Eddie. 'What about your brother?'

'He'll have to go too. He's an old fool. He believes in the "hands off" school of deity, that a God should simply let things happen, remain neutral. If you want someone to blame for the way this city is now, blame him. If I'd been around I'd never have let it get into this state. But I'm back now and things are going to be very different. Very, very different. So it's goodbye to the kindly loveable white-haired old toymaker. And not before time, in my opinion.'

Jon looked at Eddie.

And Eddie looked at Jon.

Neither had anything to say.

'But let's get back to business,' said Mr Sredna, smiling towards Jon. 'A problem with the presidential model, you said.'

'Its decision-making processes are not functioning as precisely as might be desired. It seems to be growing altogether too fierce. Might I say, somewhat warlike.'

'Nothing wrong with warlike,' said Mr Sredna. 'Warlike I like. You can quote me on that, if *you* like.'

'The corporation does *not* like,' said Jon. 'The Sredna Corporation's products are held in such high esteem by the companies that purchase them because they are designed to keep the peace. To uphold order and maintain the status quo.'

'Oh, *that*,' said Eddie. 'We all know about the status quo here in Toy City.'

'Shut up, bear,' said Mr Sredna.

'He has a point,' said Jon Kelly.

'Yes, and I've explained why this city is such a mess. Because I was thrown out and my stupid brother was left in charge. And what did he do? Remained neutral, let free will take its course. Free will! Free will was never a good concept. Social order is only maintained if every will is guided towards a single purpose, that of maintaining the status quo.'

'All right for some,' said Eddie, 'those at the top. Rubbish for the rest of us.'

'The rest of you will soon be no more,' said Mr Sredna. 'Those of you who will bow the knee to the new social order will survive to do so. The rest will be disappeared.'

'Jack,' said Eddie, 'say something to this loony. You're not going along with all this, are you? You don't really believe in all this? I know you, Jack. You *are* my bestest friend. I can't believe you're a part of this. Tell me it's not so.'

'Sorry,' said Jon Kelly. 'It's business. The world out there is a mess too. It needs order. It needs control. Mr Sredna's creations have given order to the world out there for the last hundred years. Apart from the occasional hiccough or two.'

'Oh, yes,' said Mr Sredna. 'You're going to mention Hitler, aren't you? Whenever there is a design problem or a mechanical fault, you people always bring up Hitler.'

'He was more than a mechanical fault.'

'A couple of cogwheels in the wrong place. I apologised.'

'So I understand,' said Jon Kelly. 'Sorry to mention him.'

'Hitler?' said Eddie. 'Who's Hitler?'

'You really don't want to know,' said Jon Kelly. 'But listen, Mr Sredna. Something has to be done about the current presidential model. You will have to come in person and rectify the faults.'

'Yes, yes, all right. But not until I've finished my business here. I have to finish off the famous folk and my brother and I want to be here when my ladies come marching off the assembly lines. I've put a lot of work into all of this, sneaking back into the city over the years – back into *my own* chocolate factory. But it's all been worth it: soon my ladies will all be up and ready to march. They're beautiful, aren't they, my ladies? An entirely new order of being. Part human, part toy and part arachnid.'

'Spiders?' said Eddie, shuddering.

'Wonderful creatures, arachnids,' said Mr Sredna. 'They don't ask any questions. They just *do*. But what I am saying is, this project is near to conclusion. You, Mr Kelly, have come here at a very bad time. But I couldn't come to your world, even if I wanted to.'

'Why not?' Jon asked.

'You know why not. I don't have the key. *You* have it though, don't you?'

'Key?' said Eddie.

'The Maguffin,' said Mr Sredna. 'That all-important something, the all-importantness of which does not become apparent until its moment has come.'

'It's a key?' said Eddie. 'To what?'

'It's *The* key,' said Mr Sredna. 'For opening the door between this world and the one beyond. There are two such keys, one mine and one belonging to my brother. When I was cast out of this world, I took with me not only the rest of the instructions for building the city, I also took both keys. Well, I didn't want my brother following me out at any time and interfering with whatever I chose to get up to out there. My brother's key remains forever on the outside. It was used, without my permission, to let Mr Kelly in here.'

'It was an emergency,' said Jon Kelly.

'I understand that. My key, however, was stolen from me and it fell into the dextrous hands of Tinto the clockwork barman.'

'I have it here,' said Jon Kelly. And from his grubby trenchcoat pocket Jon Kelly produced the Maguffin and laid it upon the expansive desk of Mr Sredna. 'Control is every-thing. Complete control; the operations out there in the world beyond need your creations to maintain that control. What you do here is of no concern to us. We only care about that.'

'Indeed,' said Mr Sredna, reaching across the desk and greedily availing himself of the Maguffin.

'Jack,' said Eddie.

'It's Jon,' said Jon.

'Jon,' said Eddie. 'You are a thorough-going piece of clockwork cat crap and I hate you.'

'Mr Sredna,' said Jon Kelly, 'do you have a hand-gun about your person?'

'I can readily convert,' said Mr Sredna. 'You've seen the might of my armoured protection system.'

'A hand-gun will be fine.'

'Then I have one here.' Mr Sredna delved into a desk drawer, drew out a clockwork pistol and tossed it over the expansive desk to Jon Kelly, who caught it.

'Eddie,' said Jon Kelly, 'you'll probably want to close your eyes while I do this.'

'They don't close,' said Eddie. 'You know that, *Jack.*'

'*Jon,*' said Jon Kelly. 'Turn your face away, then.'

'No,' said Eddie. 'I'm going to look you right in the eyes when you do this. I cared about you, Jack, and I thought that you cared about me, but it was all lies, wasn't it?'

'It's twist and turns,' said Jon Kelly. 'Just like a Bill Winkie thriller. And in a Bill Winkie thriller you never know exactly who's who until the end. And now you sort of know who's who, because this *is* the end.'

'Do it then,' said Eddie. 'If you have to do it, do it.' And a tear rose up in Eddie's brown button eye. 'But I really did care.'

Jon Kelly aimed the hand-gun and Jon Kelly squeezed the trigger.

'Sorry, Eddie,' he said.

29

A single shot rang out.

A steel bullet, powered by a clockwork action, left the barrel of the gun at approximately nine hundred feet per second, passed through a fabricated forehead and left via the cerebellum, taking a considerable quantity of sawdust with it and spreading this liberally over a wall that lay beyond.

'It is done,' said Jon Kelly.

Mr Sredna said nothing.

Eddie looked up at the young man who held the clock-work pistol.

And the young man looked down at Eddie.

'What?' said Jack.

'Jack,' Eddie said. 'You just shot Mr Sredna.'

'And why wouldn't I?' Jack shrugged. 'He was the evil twin.'

'Yes, but *you* just shot him. *You.* You're on his side. You were supposed to be shooting me.'

'I lied,' said Jack. 'You can forgive me for that, can't you?'

'*Forgive you?* I all but pooed myself!'

'I'm sorry, but I had to get a gun from him somehow.'

'Er,' Eddie smote at his head, 'I'm really confused. Really, *really* confused. I really should be able to figure this out.' Eddie smote at his head a lot more.

'You won't be able to.' Jack walked around the expansive desk and stared down at his handiwork. Mr Sredna was slumped back in his chair. There was a big hole in his forehead and a lot of sawdust beyond. 'I really hated that,' said Jack.

'*You* hated it? How do you think I feel? I thought you were going to kill me.'

'I know, and I'm truly sorry, but that's not what I meant. What I meant was, I really hated all that talking. I told you how much I hated it in the Bill Winkie books. How the hero gets disarmed and he has to listen to the villain talking and talking. Mind you, I do see the point now. Everything does have to be explained.'

'Is he dead?' Eddie asked.

'I certainly hope so,' said Jack. 'But look at that. His head was full of sawdust. He wasn't even a man at all. He was a toy all along.'

'He was a God, Jack.'

'Well, he's a dead God now.'

Eddie shook his puzzled head. It was full of sawdust too, but happily, *still* full. 'Do you think you might be up to telling me what, in the name of any God you choose to believe in, really is going on?'

'Most of what I said,' said Jack. 'All, in fact. Except I'm not Jon Kelly.'

'Brilliant,' said Eddie. 'So who *is* Jon Kelly and how do you know all this stuff and why didn't you tell me any of it?'

'One piece at a time,' said Jack, putting his fingers on the neck of the seemingly deceased Mr Sredna and feeling for a pulse. None was evident and so Jack wiped his sawdusty fingers upon Mr Sredna's jacket, took up the Maguffin from the desk and tucked it back into his trenchcoat pocket. 'I'm *not* Jon Kelly,' Jack said. 'Jon Kelly came to my town. He wanted directions to the city. He was lost. And he was a real nutter. He had a gun and he didn't seem too concerned about who he shot with it. He was looking for a Mr Sredna; he came to the factory where I worked. He thought that was the factory run by Sredna, but obviously it wasn't. He got very angry about that, pointed his gun at me, ordered me to steal one of the clockwork cars and drive him to the city. And he talked and he talked and he talked. He told me everything.'

'Why did he do that?' Eddie asked.

'Because I asked him what harm it would do, seeing as how he was going to kill me anyway.'

'Seems to work pretty well, that ploy,' said Eddie. 'But go on with this unlikely tale of yours, Jack.'

'He told me all about the world beyond, and about the Sredna Corporation and the presidential model and everything, really. But at the time I just thought he was a madman. He did tell me that there was wealth to be found here in the city, though. And I wanted to escape from the factory anyway. And we had travelled quite a distance before I . . .'

'What?' asked Eddie.

'Crashed the car,' said Jack. 'It wasn't my fault. He had a gun to my head and I'd never driven a car before. But he went right out through the windscreen. He was dead. I didn't know what to do. I didn't want to go back; I hated working in that factory. And Jon Kelly had told me all about the wealth in the city. Though he hadn't gone into any detail; he hadn't told me it was Toy City. Or about the toys. So I pressed on. I walked. I got lost. I fell into the farmer's hole. I almost got eaten. I came here and met you.'

'And now you've killed the evil twin. And saved Toy City,' said Eddie. 'Pretty good result.'

'Seems like,' said Jack. 'Although it certainly wasn't what I set out to do. I wanted to get rich. I came here to seek my fortune.'

'You've saved us all,' said Eddie. 'That's worth any fortune.'

'Perhaps it is,' said Jack. 'None of this has been exactly what I expected.'

'But why didn't you tell me?'

'Because I'm an atheist,' said Jack. 'And a sceptic and whatever. I didn't believe it all. And I thought it was better just to keep my mouth shut about it. I wasn't exactly expecting to actually meet up with this Mr Sredna that Jon Kelly was looking for. I didn't even know if there was such a person. And then you told me that this chocolate factory was founded by a Mr Sredna. And how many Mr Srednas can there be? And Sredna is, of course, Anders spelt backwards. The evil opposite of Anders, eh?'

'I suppose it makes some kind of sense,' said Eddie. 'And it's a nice twist in the tale. Is he definitely dead?'

'Seems like,' said Jack. 'And he's already starting to pong like the spider-women. There's stuff leaking out of him. How dead can you be?'

'As dead as, I hope,' said Eddie. 'I suppose we should go and find the famous folk; what do you think, Jack?'

'I think it would be for the best. I'm sorry I had to frighten you like that. But I had to get Mr Sredna out of armoured mode so that I could actually . . .'

'Kill him?' said Eddie.

'It's not nice,' said Jack. 'It's not a nice thing to do. I know that it had to be done. It was either him or you. But it's still not nice.'

'It wasn't a person,' said Eddie. 'It was a thing.'

'In the same way that you're a thing?'

'Ah yes, I see what you mean. But you did the right thing, Jack. You killed the right thing.'

'I *did* do the right thing, didn't I?' said Jack.

'No kidding,' said Eddie. 'Let's go and liberate those famous folk.'

30

Curiously, the rich and famous folk did not seem altogether glad to see Jack and Eddie. It took the detectives nearly an hour of searching before they eventually discovered them, all locked up together in a basement cell, the door of which taxed Jack's lock-picking skills to their limits.

The rich and famous folk did not smile upon their liberators.

'We were under protection down here,' said Old King Cole. 'Go away and leave us alone.'

'The danger has passed,' Jack told him.

'I don't think it has,' said Mary Mary.

'The evil twin is dead,' said Eddie. 'Jack has killed him. You can all clear off home.'

'How dare you address royalty in that insolent manner.' Old King Cole raised high his nose. 'In fact, how dare you address me at all, you tatty little bear.'

'One more remark like that,' Jack told Old King, 'and I will be forced to give you a smack.'

'Outrageous! Go away, and relock the door behind you.'

'Tempting, isn't it?' Eddie whispered.

'Very,' said Jack. 'Now all of you go home. Eddie and I have been up all night and we seriously need some breakfast.'

'And when will ours be served?' asked Old King. 'Make yourselves useful and cut along to the kitchen. I'll have double-whipped-cream-smothered muffins with—'

Jack slammed the cell door shut upon the rich and famous folk.

'I think we'll come back tomorrow,' he said to Eddie.

'Sweet as,' said the bear.

Together they plodded up the cellar steps, through this door and that, and finally out into the great courtyard.

The sun was high in the heavens now, beaming its blessings down upon Knob Hill, colouring the rooftops of the toymaker's house. All was sun-kissed and serene.

Jack took a deep breath, and then fell to coughing. 'What is that terrible pong?' he asked. 'Not the . . .'

Eddie sniffed the air. 'The wind would be in the east today,' he said. 'That would be coming from the slaughter-house district.'

'Rather spoils the ambience,' said Jack.

'Never,' said Eddie, sniffing hungrily. 'I love the smell of offal in the morning.'

'Do you know what we have to do?' Jack asked.

Eddie took another sniff. 'Eat breakfast?' he suggested. 'Definitely eat breakfast.'

'Not yet, I'm afraid. We have to go to the toymaker's house.'

'But why?' Eddie asked. 'Look at me. I may smell like dung, but I'm unscathed. Which is pretty nifty, really. Bill never came out of an adventure with less than a bruise or two. I'm not even scuffed.'

'We have to tell the toymaker,' said Jack. 'Tell him everything. Tell him about his brother.'

'Oh dear.' Eddie shook his head. 'I'm not keen, Jack. You're going to admit to him that you killed his brother.'

'I said tell him *everything*. He has to know.'

'Perhaps we'll tell him tomorrow. Or *you* could. There's no real need for me to be there.'

'We'll both tell him.' Jack made a very stern face. 'Things will have to be organised, Eddie. Someone is going to have to run this city properly from now on.'

'The toymaker?'

'I can't think of anyone else, can you?'

Eddie scratched at his head. 'Well,' he said, 'I'd be prepared to have a go at being mayor. What would the wages be like, do you think?'

Jack made sighing sounds.

'Yeah, well,' said Eddie, 'I can dream.'

Jack was for walking up the hill, the day being so sunny and all, but Eddie's little legs were tired, so Jack drove him up in the Mark 22 Hyperglide limousine.

'Probably the last opportunity I'll ever get to be driven in style,' said Eddie as Jack lifted him from the limousine and set him down upon the gravel drive.

Jack sighed once more. 'I remain optimistic,' he said. 'Remember, I came to this city to seek my fortune. Perhaps when it's under proper management, opportunities might present themselves.'

'Not to the likes of me,' said Eddie.

'Don't be so sure; when the toymaker sees the way things really are, there'll be some big changes made.'

'So I might still get a chance to be mayor.'

Jack rolled his eyes.

'I know,' said Eddie. 'Dream on, little bear.'

Jack and Eddie approached the big front door.

'Not you two *again*!' Peter scowled.

'We're really tired,' said Jack. 'We're tired and we're hungry and our tempers are very short. Knock your knocker smartly, or I will tear it right off the door and fling it down the drive.'

'Knock knock knock knock knock,' went Peter's knocker.

And presently the big front door eased open and the face of the kindly loveable white-haired old toymaker peeped out.

'Can I help you?' asked the toymaker.

Jack grinned painfully. Eddie took to trembling. 'Might we come in, sir?' Jack asked.

The toymaker wore upon his kindly loveable white-haired old head a leather cap affair, drawn down low to the bridge of his nose. Attached to this was a complicated eyeglass contraption.

The toymaker pushed the eyeglass aside. 'Pardon this,' he said. 'My eyesight is not as good as what it once was. But come in, do, I always have time for guests.'

Peter made grumbling sounds.

'You're most kind, sir,' said Jack.

The toymaker ushered them in and closed the big front door behind them. 'Into my workshop,' he said. 'Down the corridor there.'

Jack, with Eddie once more clinging to his leg, stepped down the narrow corridor and once more into the workshop.

'Sit down,' said the toymaker, indicating the comfy chair.

'I'd prefer to stand, sir,' said Jack.

'As you wish, as you wish.'

'We're very sorry to trouble you,' said Jack. 'But we have come here on a very grave matter.'

'Oh dear, I don't like the sound of this. I don't like grave matters. They are usually most horrid.'

'I think,' said Jack, 'that it might be for the best if you were to accompany us immediately to the chocolate factory. There is something you must see. Many things, in fact.'

'The chocolate factory? I haven't been there for years and years. Do they still produce those delightful little hollow chocolate bunnies?'

'Amongst other things,' said Jack.

'Wonderful,' said the toymaker. 'But not today, thank you. I'm far too busy. Perhaps in a month or so.'

'It has to be today,' said Jack. 'In fact, it has to be now.'

'No, it cannot be today.'

Jack took a step forward. 'It *has* to be today,' he said.

'I don't think I like your tone, young man.' The toymaker took a step back.

Jack took another step forward. 'I'm sorry,' he said, 'but it *has* to be today. And now. You have to know what has been going on in your city. It's very bad and you are going to be very upset, but you have to come with us now.'

'And what if I refuse?'

'I really am sorry, sir,' said Jack, squaring up before the ancient, 'but if you refuse, I will be forced to drag you.'

'Jack, no!' Eddie tugged at Jack's rotten trenchcoat.

'Sorry, Eddie, this has to be done.'

'No, Jack.' Eddie's nose began to twitch. A curious smell had suddenly reached it.

'Sir,' said Jack, 'come with us, please.'

'Jack,' whispered Eddie, 'I smell a smell.'

'Not now, Eddie. So, sir, will you come?'

'I think not,' said the toymaker.

'Then I'm truly sorry.' Jack reached forward to grasp the old man's shoulders.

'That smell,' said Eddie. 'It's getting stronger.'

Jack gripped the ancient by his narrow, bony shoulders and gently tugged at him. The old man didn't move. Jack tugged a little harder. The old man remained rooted to the spot. Jack tugged very hard this time. But the toymaker would not budge.

He simply remained right where he was. Old and frail. But unmoveable.

'Come on now,' puffed Jack, pulling with all his might.

'I think not.' The toymaker slowly reached up between Jack's dragging hands and removed the leather cap that he wore upon his kindly white-haired old head.

Jack stared and then Jack ceased his futile tuggings. And then Jack took a step or two back. Three steps in fact. And very smartly indeed.

In the very centre of the toymaker's kindly loveable old forehead there was a hole. It was a neat, round hole. The kind of hole that a bullet fired from a clockwork pistol might make.

'*You!*' said Jack. 'It's you.'

'That would be the smell,' Eddie whispered.

'Me,' said Mr Sredna.

'But I shot you dead.'

'Do I look dead to you?'

'Oh dear,' said Jack. 'Oh dear, oh dear.'

'And you call yourselves detectives.' Mr Sredna laughed. It was Tinto's laugh, the one that resembled small stones being shaken about in an empty tin can. 'But you had me going there, almost. I believed you were Jon Kelly. But I never take chances. You shot a false head.' Mr Sredna lifted this head from his shoulders and cast it down to the floor. An identical head rose up through the collar of his shirt. 'This is my real head,' he said, 'and you won't be shooting this one.'

'Oh dear,' said Jack once more.

Eddie might have had something to say, but he was far too scared to say it.

'Fun and games,' said Mr Sredna. 'It was such a delight to see you running around Toy City, always too late.' Mr Sredna glared down at Eddie, who had taken to cowering behind Jack's leg. 'I do have to say,' said he, 'that, on the whole, you're not a bad detective. Not as good as Bill Winkie though, but then he knew that I was the prime suspect. He tracked me down to the chocolate factory within twenty-four hours of receiving his advance money and being put on the case.'

'He did?' said Eddie, fearfully. 'He never told me that he did.'

'I don't think he wanted to put you in danger. He broke into Humpty Dumpty's apartment and worked out how I'd done it. The moment he saw that lens in the roof he knew it had to be me. Or perhaps it was my little chocolate calling card in the fridge.'

Eddie might have shrugged, but his shoulders were too trembly.

'And then he broke into the chocolate factory while I was asleep. Searched the place. Even found my strongroom. All that gold down there had him thinking. And so did the Maguffin. He found that along with all my maps of the outer world and my accounts books. He stole the Maguffin to trap me here in this world and must have passed it to Tinto for safekeeping. Probably, I think now, so that Tinto would pass it on to you if something happened to Bill and you continued with the case.'

'He *was* very clever.' Eddie shook fearfully.

'But not *that* clever. The next morning he went to see Chief Inspector Bellis to tell him that *I* was the murderer and lead him and all his men to the chocolate factory in the hope of capturing me. But he never got to see the real Chief Inspector Bellis; I just happened to be loafing around outside the police station, impersonating the real Inspector. He was very brave, was Bill Winkie, he never talked, even under all that torture. He wouldn't tell me what he'd done with my Maguffin.'

If Eddie had been able to make fists, he would have made very big ones now.

'And that's about all,' said Mr Sredna. 'There isn't anything else to say. I won't bother to ask you for the Maguffin, Jack. Neither you nor the bear will be leaving this room alive.'

'Now hold on,' said Jack. 'Don't be hasty.'

'There goes that déjà-vu again.'

'I'm sure that we could come to some arrangement.'

'I pride myself,' said Mr Sredna, 'upon having an all-but-limitless imagination. I can think up things that no other mortal being can think up. Apart from that one over there.' Mr Sredna gestured towards the bound and gagged and quivering toymaker, all bunched up in the corner. 'And the remaining moments of his life are numbered in seconds. But even I, with all of my imagination, cannot think of any arrangement that might be made which does not involve you dying.'

'You may well have a point there.' Jack's eyes darted all around the room in search of, perhaps, some very large and deadly weapon. Or something else that might provide a final twist in the tale and allow him and Eddie to miraculously survive.

Nothing was immediately forthcoming.

Mr Sredna snapped the fingers of his right hand. The fingers extended; the fingertips hinged; evil-looking blades sprung forth.

'You first,' said Mr Sredna, pointing at Eddie. 'Shredded teddy, I think.'

'No you don't.' Jack raised his fists.

'Don't be absurd, Jack.' Mr Sredna lunged forward, swinging his unclawed fist. It struck Jack in the side of the head, carried him from his feet, across the workbench and down the other side, where he fell to the floor next to the kindly loveable white-haired, all-tied-up-and-trembly old toymaker.

Jack floundered about amongst the sawdust bales and rolls of fabric. Jack heard a terrible scream from Eddie.

And then Jack leapt back to his feet. He saw Mr Sredna holding Eddie by his un-special-tagged ear and he saw the claws, glistening and twinkling in the glow from the firelight. And he saw the hand swing and the claws go in, piercing Eddie's chest, shredding the cinnamon-coloured mohair plush fur fabric, spraying out sawdust, tearing once, then tearing again and again.

'No,' screamed Jack, and he leapt onto the table and then onto Mr Sredna. Shredded Eddie flew in every direction: a cascade of arms and legs and belly and bits and bobs. Jack's momentum bore the evil twin over, but he was up in an instant and he flung Jack down and stood astride him, grinning hideously.

'You killed him.' There were tears in Jack's eyes. 'You evil shit. You wicked, vicious, filthy . . .'

'Shut it,' said Mr Sredna. 'It was only a toy. A toy teddy bear. A big boy like you shouldn't get weepy over a toy teddy bear.'

'He was my friend.'

'That's very sad,' said Mr Sredna. 'A big boy like you should have grown out of toys. A big boy like you should have got yourself a girlfriend.'

Jack crawled back upon his bottom, but he really had nowhere to crawl to.

'In a way I'm sorry that you have to die too.' Mr Sredna grinned as he spoke. He didn't look *that* sorry. 'Folk here are so dull, do you know what I mean? They lack any kind of spirit. But you're full of it. Independent. And tricking me into believing that you were Jon Kelly: inspired.'

'Rather obvious, I would have thought,' said Jack.

'I'm trying to pay you a compliment. Being an innovative hands-on sort of a God is a very lonely calling. You can always do with a bit of stimulating conversation. But I never seem to be able to get that. No one in my own league, you see. So I just make do with having lots of sex. They're very sexy, my women, aren't they?'

'You're quite mad.' Jack curled his lip. 'You're insane.'

'They said that about Hitler. Fancy Jon Kelly telling you about him. But Hitler wasn't actually mad. He was the way I made him: a bit of a prototype. Wait until the folk out there find out what the new president of America is going to do. They sent Jon Kelly here because they were worried about the way he was behaving. They have no idea, but it is going to be *spectacular*. He'll be employing a private army. And my private army will be unstoppable.'

'And then you'll be in charge of everything, will you? Not just here in Toy City.'

'Today Toy City! Tomorrow the World!' Mr Sredna laughed that laugh that evil geniuses laugh. The one that really gets on the hero's nerves.

'Mad.' Jack wiped tears from his eyes. 'Quite mad.'

'It's simply beyond your comprehension.' Mr Sredna reached down with his clawed hand and hauled Jack back up by the throat, lifting him once more from his feet. 'Small minds have no comprehension. I am indeed one of a kind, placed upon this planet by the Big Figure himself.'

'You'll answer to Him,' said Jack. 'You'll answer to God.'

'Oh, I don't think so. He's no longer interested in this planet. The universe really *is* a big construction kit, given to him as a birthday present by his father. But you know what kids are. Once they've done a jigsaw or completed some puzzle or other, they're no longer interested in it. God gave mankind free will, they say. God does not interfere in the affairs of man, they say. It's because he's not interested. He's done this planet. He's moved on. Perhaps one day he will put the entire kit back in its box, but probably not. You know kids, do they *ever* put anything back in its box?'

'So you'll rule here?' Jack's hopelessness was now all-consuming, and the terrible emptiness he felt, with Eddie dead, left him without much in the way of a will to live – although he would have dearly loved to have wrung the life from the toymaker's evil twin. 'You'll rule this planet and no one can stop you?'

'I don't see anyone, do you?'

Jack might have shaken his head, but with the hand so tightly fixed about his throat, he was unable to do so. 'And so can you be killed?' Jack managed to say.

Mr Sredna laughed once more. 'Of course I can be killed; I'm not immortal. I'm very much like the nursery rhyme folk in that respect; old-time craftsmanship, you see, built to last. I mean, look at me, Jack. Not bad for a man of six thousand, am I? That Adam and Eve who seeded the garden in the outer world didn't last too long. Things really are different in this world. We still have the magic. So, yes Jack. I can be killed, but not by you. You left the gun back in the chocolate factory after you shot the wrong head. There are no more twists in the tale left for you.'

And the fingers closed about Jack's throat.

And that, for all it seemed to be, was sadly that for Jack.

31

It is a fact, well known to those who know it well, that, at the moment of death, your entire life flashes right before your eyes.

In fact, this fact is known to almost everyone. Although why this should actually be is something of a mystery.

Because, let's face it, who has actually verified this fact?

Has anyone ever really come back from the dead to tell it like it is?

No, they haven't.

'Oh yes they have!' cry those who lack for a life and a girlfriend. 'Otherwise how would we know this fact?'

But, 'Oh no they haven't,' reply the knowers. 'No one has *ever* come back from the dead.'

Being dead is being dead. Being brought back from the dead means that you weren't really dead at all; you were only in a dead–like state. You just can't bring people back from the dead.

You can't. You really can't.

Now Jack might have taken issue with this, because as Mr Sredna squeezed him to death, Jack's life did flash right before his eyes. Very fast, but in very great detail.

Jack saw every bit of it: himself being born, and growing up in that small industrial town. And he saw himself indentured as an apprentice into the clockwork factory there and hating every minute of it. And he saw himself meeting with Jon Kelly. And then being involved in the terrible car crash. And then his lonely wanderings and the cannibal farmer and Toy City and Eddie.

And Jack realised that Eddie really had been the bestest friend that he'd ever had. And then things became a bit metaphysical and Jack felt himself moving towards other places, places of after-existence − perhaps to the realms where young God was still putting bits of his construction kit together, creating new worlds, worlds that, Jack hoped, would be a great deal better than this one.

All these things flashed right before Jack's eyes. In seconds.

And then Jack's eyes couldn't see anything any more − anything, that is, but the colour red, which, as those who know the facts well know, and the rest of us know too, is the colour of blood.

Jack was suddenly covered in blood.

Jack gasped and gagged and wiped his eyes and blurry vision returned.

And somebody stood over Jack.

And that somebody wasn't Mr Sredna.

Out of the redness Jack returned, at a jolt, and a hurry-up too. He felt water upon his face. He opened his eyes and he stared.

'Jill,' said Jack. 'Jill, it's you.'

'It's me,' said Jill. 'And you owe me money. I told you I charge double for virgins. And there's the other money, there's . . .'

'Eddie.' Jack struggled back to his feet. 'Is he?'

'Sorry,' said Jill.

'No, he can't be. If I'm not, he can't be.'

'Don't think about him. I saved you, Jack. I've been following you since you got arrested. I want my money.'

'You followed me for the money? You did *that*?' Jack looked down at the body of Mr Sredna. Mr Sredna was well and truly dead this time. His body lacked for a head and his chest was full of holes. Jack looked at Jill.

'Well, I had to be sure,' said Jill. 'You screwed it up when you did it.'

Jack shook his head. 'And you did this all because I owe you money?'

'Well, perhaps not entirely for the money.' Jill turned her eyes down from Jack's gaze. 'There's something about you. I don't know what it is. But it makes you special.'

'Thank you.' Jack crossed the workroom, being careful as he did so not to step upon any shreddings of Eddie. Jack stooped and untied the kindly loveable white-haired old toymaker. 'Are you all right, sir?' Jack asked as he helped the ancient into the comfy chair.

'Somewhat shaken,' said the toymaker. 'This has all been a terrible shock. I had tried my best to forget about my brother. Forget that he'd even existed. I'm a very foolish old man.'

Jack patted the toymaker on the shoulder and looked up at Jill.

'I'm sorry I didn't get here in time to save your little friend,' she said. 'When I saw what was happening, I acted as fast as I could.'

'I know,' said Jack.

'You *know*?'

'I saw you,' Jack said. 'I saw you creeping in through the window, which was why I asked him whether he could be killed. I thought the information might come in handy for you. I saw you had the gun from his office.'

'Smart boy,' said Jill.

'Yes,' said Jack in a toneless tone. 'Very smart. But too late for Eddie.'

'You really loved that bear, didn't you?'

Tears were once more in Jack's eyes. And he made no attempt to hide them. 'I'm not ashamed to say it, Jill. He really was my bestest friend.'

'Perhaps,' said the toymaker, 'I could make you another bear.'

'Thanks,' said Jack. 'But it wouldn't be the same. Eddie was one of a kind.'

'And I think I still am,' came a tiny voice from a disembodied growler. 'Will somebody help me, please?'

32

It was two whole days before Jack got around to releasing all the rich and famous folk from their place of incarceration. Well, he'd had other things to do, and actually, he'd quite forgotten about them.

They were very polite to Jack, though, when he opened the cell door. Very gracious. Very thankful. Very hungry.

Jack wasn't at all hungry. He'd just dined at the very finest restaurant in the City. It wasn't a *Nadine's Diner*.

Jack was presently dining again in that self-same restaurant. He was there with Jill, to celebrate their engagement.

True, both Jack and Jill were underage, but hey, this was Toy City; let's not let a little detail like that stand in the way of true love.

And true, Jill *had* said that she fancied marrying a prince. But then Jack was a prince now. An honorary prince, but a prince none the less. The toymaker had bestowed this honour upon him.

Eddie dined with Jack and Jill. And Eddie very much enjoyed the meal. He had double portions of everything. Especially those complicated things that need holding down with a fork and slicing with a knife.

And when, at great length, the meal had reached its conclusion, Eddie looked up at Jack. 'I don't know how to thank you enough,' Eddie said. 'There are no words to express my thanks for these.'

Eddie pulled back the cuffs of his brand new trench-coat and flexed his dextrous fingers and their opposable thumbs.

'The toymaker worked very hard putting you back together,' said Jack. 'And although he really didn't approve, I eventually managed to talk him into fitting you with those. Because, after all, there were so many spare parts in the chocolate factory just going begging, and who deserved a couple of them more than you?'

'Thanks, Jack,' said Eddie. 'Would you like to see me pick my nose again?'

'Not just now,' said Jack. 'Although, don't get me wrong, I certainly enjoyed it all the other times you've showed me.'

Eddie gazed proudly at his dextrous fingers. 'They're a lovely shade of cinnamon,' he said. 'They match my new coat.'

'You're an Anders Imperial now,' said Jack. 'Except for your head, of course. I didn't let him touch your head. Other than for putting a proper special button for your ear. And the new matching eyes, of course. They're working all right, I trust.'

'Absolutely.' Eddie blinked his bright blue glass eyes. 'They're as optically efficient as. I had no idea there were so many colours to see.'

'Glad you like them,' said Jack.

'So what do you intend to do now?' Eddie asked. 'Buy yourself a nice big house on Knob Hill with your half of the reward? It was good of the toymaker to make the rich folk cough up the money they'd promised to Bill for solving the case, wasn't it?'

'It certainly was,' said Jack. 'But Jill and I are not staying in Toy City.'

'What?' Eddie's eyes blinked and widened. 'But I hoped you'd live next door to me.'

'We're leaving,' said Jack. 'I have to go out there, to the world beyond. I have the Maguffin key and the toymaker's permission to use it. They're in a real mess out there and I can help to put things right.'

'That's none of our business,' Eddie said. 'No, Jack, don't go.'

'I'll be back,' said Jack, 'once I've made the necessary adjustments to the clockwork heads of their world leaders. And I *can* do that. I do know clockwork.'

'But you promise that you will be back?'

'Of course I promise. I wouldn't leave my bestest friend for ever, would I?'

'Certainly not,' said Eddie. 'Especially when he's a bestest friend of high standing. I've decided to take the mayor's job.'

'Oh yes?' Jack raised an eyebrow. 'And who offered you this job?'

'The toymaker, of course. I subtly broached the subject while I was removing his doorknocker and installing a new bell. It took a great deal of gentle persuasion, and Peter tried to put him off. But he came around in the end. Him being so kindly and lovable and grateful and every-thing.'

'You'll make a great mayor,' said Jack.

'There will be some sweeping social reforms,' said Eddie. 'I'm drafting out something that I like to call a constitution. It has things written into it, such as "we find it self-evident that all men and toys are created equal". And I'm working on other things too. Things of a religious nature, based on all these parables I know.'

'Sounds good,' said Jack. 'Sounds perfect.'

'Hopefully so.' Eddie grinned. 'And if I haven't thanked you enough, Jill, for saving all our lives, let me take this opportunity to thank you once again. I hope you and Jack will be very happy together. And you never know, if one day you have little Jacks and Jills of your own, and they need an old toy bear to play with, you can always bring them around to the mayoral mansion and I'll be more than happy to oblige.'

Jill smiled upon Eddie. 'I'm beginning to understand just

what you see in this bear, Jack,' she said. 'There's definitely something special about him.'

'Oh yes,' Jack raised his glass to the bear. 'He's Eddie,' Jack said. 'He's as special as.'